1891: A Novel about Stanford University

1891: A Novel about Stanford University

Jerry Franks

iUniverse, Inc.
New York Lincoln Shanghai

1891: A Novel about Stanford University

iUniverse books may be ordered through booksellers or by contacting:

iUniverse
2021 Pine Lake Road, Suite 100
Lincoln, NE 68512
www.iuniverse.com
1-800-Authors (1-800-288-4677)

ISBN: 978-0-595-43794-8 (pbk)
ISBN: 978-0-595-88124-6 (ebk)

Printed in the United States of America

CHAPTER 1

▼

"MASTER VISITING THE SERVANTS"

Monday, March 16, 1891

Ellen Elliott was broiling a thick, juicy porterhouse steak over a glowing coal fire on the kitchen range in her home in Ithaca. She turned the long-handled wire cage holding the fragrant, browning meat over and over.

Ellen had wavy blonde hair that fell to her shoulders. She was petite, a little over eighty pounds—a pretty young woman. But what she lacked in stature she made up in energy, determination, and honesty. Her father said she had the unfortunate habit of saying whatever was in her head, heedless to the opinions of those who could hear her. Sometimes that habit got her into trouble.

Leslie Elliott, her husband, walked in, using the back screen door. His given name was Orrin, but he preferred Leslie. He was breathless and had a mischievous grin on his face. He came up behind her, put his arms around her, and whispered in her ear, "How'd you like to head for California?"

Ellen Elliott thought it was part of their little joke. If he couldn't find a job, in the area, teaching economics, they would move to California. She ignored him, turned out the steak on a hot platter, and continued tending to it—peppering, salting, and buttering.

Refusing to be ignored, Leslie pulled out a yellow telegram; he was carrying in his coat pocket, and put it in front of Ellen's face, inches from her nose. "It's from Dr. David Starr Jordan, president of Indiana University. He's been named president of a university in California, founded and endowed by Leland Stanford.

Dr. Jordan requires a secretary, and he's asked me to come to Bloomington at once to take the post. In June, he wants me to accompany him to California. If it's all right with you, I'm going to accept, and we're going to California."

Ellen dropped her basting spoon. She turned around and began hugging Leslie, kissing him full on the mouth, and for a few seconds they embraced.

She whispered in his ear, "How much will you be paid?"

Leslie whispered back, "He didn't say, but I'll send him a wire and find out. If it's reasonable, I think we should go. It's a real opportunity for me to teach economics."

Ellen again whispered, "We'll go even if it's unreasonable, my darling Leslie." Her tone indicated she had made up her mind, but as she said the words, a tingle of apprehension ran down her spine. Going to California was like going to another planet.

In April and May of 1891, Ellen and her son, Louis, stayed at her parents' home in Burdett, in upper New York State, waiting to join Leslie. While there, hints about their potential new home in the far West were sent to her in Leslie's letters from Bloomington, where he was working for Dr. David Starr Jordan.

Ellen read that in California rose vines grew to more than forty feet and reached the rooftops. Senator Stanford bred racehorses, some worth hundreds of thousands of dollars, housed in immaculately clean, whitewashed stables. Millionaires' estates were near the University, and it was easy for Ellen to imagine gentle and gracious millionaire neighbors dropping by for tea and to get acquainted with the Elliott family.

Leslie wrote the University would be made up of a series of great quadrangles. One was already up and others would join it. Stone buildings, tile roofed, were surrounded by garden-like courts, and the entire campus would be beautifully landscaped with sloping, green lawns and curving roadways. Frederick Olmsted, creator of New York's Central Park, had created the site plans. And what sounded particularly inviting to Ellen's ears were that stone cottages, also tile roofed, were to be built for the faculty. And, of course, rents would be nominal.

All this news gladdened Ellen's heart. She could not wait to rejoin Leslie in Indiana, travel to California, and begin their new life.

Finally in June, filled with great hope and anticipation, Ellen, with Louis, took leave of her parents. They climbed into her father's gig, and his horse stepped off toward the nearby city of Watkins, where there was a railroad station, and their journey to the west would begin.

Before she left, Ellen's mother, with tears in her eyes, told Ellen she thought she might never see her daughter and grandson again. After all, California was on the other side of the continent.

Traveling west with the Elliotts to California from Indianapolis in mid June 1891, were eight more travelers. Dr. David Starr Jordan, president of the University, and his wife Jessie brought two of their three children: Edith who was eleven years old and Knight, three years old. The third son, Harold, who was eight, remained with relatives in Indianapolis because of an illness. Dr. George M. Richardson, who would teach chemistry at the University, brought his wife, Emily, and his mother, Mrs. Richardson. Two young people, Charlotte Rankin and Albert Fletcher, joined the group. They were going to help with the chores and might become students at the new university.

Even though they traveled Pullman class with berth accommodations, the train ride was hot, long, and confining, and soon the two youngsters became agitated and bored. Louis was relatively good, but Knight Jordan was a scamp and started throwing temper tantrums. He hurled himself to the floor, screaming, "I want to go home. I don't want to go to California." Leslie felt sorry for Dr. Jordan when he tried to calm his son and ended up with flailing fists in his face. During one of these encounters, Dr. Jordan looked over at Leslie, and Leslie was sure he was going to ask him, as his secretary, for assistance. He must have thought better of it; the moment passed.

It took eighteen hours for their train to cross Kansas. For half days at a time and sometimes overnight, their steam locomotive stopped for no apparent reason. Was it another train coming? Was it mechanical failure? Did they need another locomotive? They were never told the reasons for the delays. When questioned, the conductors merely shook their heads and muttered, "We'll soon be underway," and scurried down the aisles, quickly out of sight.

At Pueblo, Colorado, the party disembarked for six hours. Dr. Jordan arranged for a large bus-like wagon to transport them to an outlying area where the ground plan of a city-to-be had been laid out with little white stakes indicating streets, parks, lampposts, and buildings. Ellen wondered what people would want to live on the gray stark plain. She could not imagine herself being one of them.

At another stop, Dr. David Starr Jordan enthusiastically embarked upon a botanical lecture—picking up small flowers with his thumb and forefinger, holding them up for all to see, and telling the group their Latin names, how many petals each had, and how they reproduced.

Ellen looked around and saw prairie dogs sitting on their haunches, staring at the intruders. Giant cacti, eighteen to twenty feet high, appearing like unworldly figures with arms held high, surrounded the travelers. Dr. Jordan told the group their Latin names, too.

They spent a night in a mining camp, Leadville. Dr. Jordan told them ten million dollars' worth of silver was mined there each year, but Ellen was more in awe of the snowcapped mountains rimming the area and the crystal blue sky above, which became an umbrella of stars after a stunning sunset.

Traveling through the Rockies, Dr. Jordan showed them the exact spot where a drop of water split—half flowing toward the Pacific, and half toward the Atlantic.

The Royal Gorge impressed Dr. Jordan, but not Ellen. She found it lonesome, wild, barren, and tremendously useless. She could not help expressing her thoughts for others to hear, and several of her fellow travelers nodded their heads in agreement.

But compared with the Great American Desert, they were about to approach and enter; the Royal Gorge was an oasis. The desert was the worst. Gazing at its vast nothingness, Ellen made the comment, "I don't believe there is a more desolate spot on earth."

Dr. Jordan, who was within earshot, agreed with her. "There isn't," he said.

During the night, as they traveled across the desert, Ellen couldn't sleep. She lifted her berth's window shade and looked out upon a rapidly passing, pale gray desert. It stretched before her and disappeared into nothingness. For the first time, she felt pangs of remorse about leaving Ithaca's green hills. "What have we gotten ourselves into?" she said aloud. Then she looked around, wondering if Dr. Jordan had heard that remark, too.

After a ten-day trip across the country, they approached the San Francisco Bay. When they arrived at Benicia, a ferry carried their train in sections across miles of salt flats. "The salt of the Pacific," Dr. Jordan told the group. At Oakland, another ferry took them across the bay, but this time their train section sat on the upper deck, forward, allowing the passengers a grand panoramic view of the shimmering bay.

Ellen looked and cried out in joy, "I don't believe there is more beautiful body of water on earth!"

Again, Dr. Jordan heard her remark "There isn't," he said.

Ellen was beginning to wonder if he purposely stayed close to her to hear what she said. Perhaps some of her more disparaging remarks had gotten back to him. It no longer mattered. They were almost there.

She saw lovely blue water twisting around the harbor's capes and islands. Everywhere there were ships coming and going. At the wharves were steamships or the older two- and four-mast schooners. Other ferryboats, with Mill Valley or Alviso painted on their sides, churned the waters beside them. Ellen thought the scene brimmed with beauty and bustle.

On Friday, June 26, Mr. Herbert Nash, Senator Stanford's secretary, met them at the Third and Townsend Streets' Station. Leslie told Ellen that Mr. Nash had been Leland Stanford Junior's tutor. He was the young son who had died prematurely, a few years before in Europe. The Stanfords had created their university in his memory.

Nash had already met Dr. David Starr Jordan, so they quickly recognized one another. Even without that advantage, it was easy to pick out the ragtag group of men and women, dressed in heavy, hot Eastern clothes, dragging two youngsters along with them.

With great consideration, Mr. Nash quickly transferred them and their baggage to a local train that made its way south to the Menlo station. There was no station for the Palo Alto Farm—the general name given to Senator Stanford's home, stock farm, vineyards, orchards, and hay fields that were the site of the newly constructed University.

There he was, standing on the Menlo station platform, waiting to greet them: Senator Leland Stanford—senator of the sovereign state of California, former governor of that state, part owner and founder of the Central Pacific Railroads, co-founder with his wife Jane of the University, a viable candidate for the Presidency of the United States in '92, and considered by many to be the most popular man in America.

Ellen thought he looked like the many pictures and illustrations she had seen: a portly man of average height, with long arms and short legs, a prominent nose, full beard; but it was his dark piercing eyes, taking in all that was going on around him, that Ellen found to be his most prominent feature. When he first saw the new arrivals, his eyes swept from side to side and up and down each individual. It reminded Ellen of her father's perusal of horses he was considering buying. She looked over at a nearby opulent carriage, with bright red wheels, driven by a Negro in full livery. Peering out the isinglass window was another elderly gentleman, who appeared to be doing the same kind of sizing up. "Must be his friend," she almost said aloud. She brought the back of her hand instantly to her lips. She must watch what she said; otherwise she might embarrass her quiet, unassuming husband.

Dr. Jordan introduced Senator Stanford to everyone. The senator acknowledged each by shaking hands with the gentlemen and tipping his top hat to the ladies. The travelers could tell he fully appreciated the difficult journey they had made. When he saw the two little boys scampering about, he said, "So this is Knight and Louis." He touched them lightly on the tops of their heads. Both were too preoccupied to look up.

Dr. Jordan leaned over so they could hear him and insisted, "Knight, Louis, say hello to Senator Stanford."

The boys continued playing.

The senator smiled wanly and said, "Boys will be boys. A long trip is hard on the children." Even that slight smile was enough for some to recognize his heart was still broken.

Senator Stanford looked back at Dr. Jordan. "The cottage has been prepared for you. Ah Sam is the best cook in the valley, better than ours. I hope you and Mrs. Jordan and your guests find the arrangements to your liking."

Dr. Jordan drew close to the man now ruling his destiny. "I'm sure we will. And we all appreciate your coming here to greet us."

"After all your trials, it was the very least I could do. I hope you don't mind, but Mrs. Stanford and I will be coming by early this evening to say hello."

As a group, the response was, "No, no, no, it'd be a pleasure to see you both." Leslie Elliott said the words, but in his heart didn't mean them. Why tonight, he thought, give us some time to recuperate from the journey. He looked over at his wife, wondering what she might say, but she had a welcoming smile on her face like all the others. He breathed a sigh of relief.

Senator Stanford waved his broad hand, encompassing them all. "Then I bid you good-bye and will see you later."

The senator returned to his carriage. Inside, the other elderly man was already talking while the senator settled into his seat. As the carriage departed down Menlo's dusty dirt roads, Senator Stanford earnestly began to converse with the man. As Ellen watched them drive away, she guessed he was asking his friend what he thought of the new arrivals.

The group now dwindled to nine. Dr. Richardson and his wife and mother left for Cedro Cottage, another of Stanford's cottages, located about a mile and a half south.

Mr. Nash loaded the remaining travelers into a carryall with two long, lengthwise seats. He sat up front with another of Stanford's Negro drivers. He looked back at the assembly of men, women, and children now seated across from one another, and said, "I know you all want to get to your destination, but first we must pick up the mail for the University."

Leslie did not expect the detour. He had worked diligently, right up to the time he left Bloomington, to make certain all the mail for the University had been answered.

Nash saw from the looks on his charges' faces that they were not happy about the stopover. "The post office is only a few doors down," he shouted at them over the creaking of the harnesses and the sounds of horses' hooves.

Ellen Elliott had to contain a groan. Leslie returned her look of dismay with his own, which meant in any language, "Don't say a word."

The carryall maneuvered up narrow dirt roads, and since it was hot outside and noontime, past empty boardwalks and empty verandas of indiscreet hotels. Their destination was a small, one-story, white-framed building with a hand-painted, lopsided hung sign: "Menlo Post Office."

The four men—Mr. Nash, Dr. Jordan, Leslie, and young Mr. Fletcher—went in and out of the post office countless times with their arms loaded with mail. They attempted at first to stack it in tidy piles on the floor of the carryall. After the forth trip, tidiness was forgotten. The ladies, young girl, and children found their shoes disappearing under the accumulation of correspondence. It came almost up to their knees. Knight and Louis, having the time of their lives, literally swam in it. The ladies were close to hysterics.

Through it all, Leslie's face became grimmer and grimmer. Obviously, most of the mail had not been forwarded to Bloomington. From the look of it, some of it dated all the way back to the past year and had been addressed directly to the senator. Leslie asked himself why no one had bothered to go the post office and pick it up. Then he realized that in the senator's eyes it was their job to do—his and Dr. Jordan's—and no one else's. That was why they had been hired.

Now knee-deep in mail, the group made their way back onto the county road leading to their future home, which had already been named Escondite, or Hideaway Cottage, by Dr. Jordan. About a mile to the south, Leslie could see the bare outline of the university he would help administer.

As they got closer, Dr. Jordan proudly asked for the carryall to stop so he could point out his university to the newcomers.

It was far from the splendid sight Ellen Elliott expected. Across a dry, trampled hay field, she saw the bleak outline of bare, single-story buildings with a chimney, being constructed, looming behind them. In the background were rolling hills, yellowed and burnt out. There were no green lawns or gardens—none of the grandeur about which her husband had written. Of course, she thought, we are seeing the buildings from the outside; the courts and gardens must be inside. But the first impression remained in her mind, particularly with the domineering chimney. It was the site of a factory, and a bleak one at that.

As if sensing his wife's feelings, Leslie looked at the same dismal scene and mouthed the words, "I didn't know." Silently, Leslie made a vow to himself. From then on, he would be chary of Dr. David Starr Jordan's inclination to be overly rapturous in his descriptions and overly optimistic in his anticipations. Leslie would be the opposite.

After another half mile, they neared a village that Dr. Jordan told them was called Mayfield. From what they could see, it was a collection of dusty, weathered, wooden, single-story buildings. No one was disappointed when they turned right at its outskirts and headed south—back into open fields. Another half mile, and they saw the first signs of cooling shade: oak, pepper, and pine trees. In the midst of these pleasant surroundings was their destination, Escondite Cottage.

Dr. Jordan called it a cottage, but Ellen considered the long, low, white-painted house to be more like a chalet or a single-story villa. An ancient oak tree, growing from neatly graveled surroundings, shaded its front veranda. A dovecote stood secluded in the foliage, and beyond was a substantial brick building that had to be the library Dr. Jordan had mentioned. It was here that Leslie was to establish the first administrative office.

Wearily, the travelers jumped down from the bus and began the unloading process, including all the mail, which had to be taken to the brick building.

With barely enough time to wash the dust off their faces, the new arrivals were ill prepared for Senator and Mrs. Stanford's promised visit. But at exactly four o'clock they arrived and sat on the veranda with the families, gently conversing about the unseemly hot weather, and the horses the senator had been training and racing. Much of the time was taken with silently watching the two young boys constantly prancing around them. Senator Stanford appeared to enjoy watching their behavior more than joining the conversation. Even while talking to an adult, his eyes followed the children's antics.

After the Stanfords had left, in the privacy of their bed, Ellen told her husband she thought the Stanfords were kindhearted and unpretentious.

As he turned over on his side, Leslie wondered if Ellen was being totally honest. Sometimes she said untruths strictly for his benefit. He could not fault her. He had not mentioned his real feelings and concerns.

Even after three months' employment, he was not sure what Dr. Jordan really thought of him. Dr. Jordan had hired him solely on the recommendation of Dr. Andrew White, the president of Cornell. Dr. Jordan, in his capacity as one of

Cornell's trustees, had briefly seen Leslie hard at work in the Cornell administrative office, but never met him. And, apparently, Leslie was always seated.

Leslie remembered when Dr. Jordan opened the door of his residence and saw him standing there, for the first time—all five foot, two inches—disappointment like a cloud swept across his face. Leslie felt he wanted to deny entrance to the little person standing before him, even shut the door in his face. Dr. Jordan, standing six foot, two inches in his stocking feet, towered over the diminutive Leslie. And worse, Leslie, although in his early thirties, with his fine features, short dark hair, and only the beginnings of a mustache, appeared five to ten years younger.

Instantly the cloud had disappeared, replaced by a wide smile of welcome. Leslie assumed reality had set in: the little man was there and was said to be a hard worker, scrupulous with details. In a deep, melodious voice, Dr. Jordan had looked down at the man before him and said, "Welcome aboard, Dr. Elliott. Come in. Come in. We've lots of work to do."

Leslie was also not sure when he was promoted from secretary to registrar. In Bloomington, Leslie had performed all sorts of duties: secretarial and stenographic, reading and answering letters from schools and applicants across the nation, sweeping out the temporary office Dr. Jordan had created in one of the outbuildings on his property, and making certain plenty of cut newspaper was on the hook in a nearby privy.

On the way out west, out of the blue, Dr. Jordan had started referring to registrar duties Leslie would perform. He would have responsibility for all admissions, only seeking Dr. Jordan's advice in exceptional cases, and responsibility for all communications with other colleges and preparatory schools. And, gloriously, he would teach several economics classes, his special love. Dr. Jordan had mentioned there might be miscellaneous additional duties for him to perform on Dr. Jordan's behalf. Leslie could foresee those duties would include anything Dr. Jordan did not like or want to do. From that second on, Leslie was the registrar. Ellen had been pleased, but noted that no increase in salary was mentioned.

And, lastly he had not told Ellen that as far as he was concerned, the Stanfords' visit reminded him of a master and mistress visiting the hired help.

CHAPTER 2

▼

SUNSTROKE IN MAYFIELD

Saturday, June 27, 1891

The next day after their arrival at Escondite Cottage, in spite of the more than five hundred letters they had picked up the previous day, Leslie decided he should go back into Menlo and pick up any additional incoming mail arriving that day. Dr. Jordan had taken the day off and was using the provided gig and horse for a trip alone, over rough mountain roads, to Santa Cruz. Leslie understood the way was daunting and dangerous—perfect for Dr. Jordan's taste.

In spite of the hot weather, Leslie would have to hike the two miles to Menlo and back. There was no other way. Ellen wanted him to wait until Monday when a gig would be available, but Leslie insisted it must be done that day. Ellen didn't argue with him. She had learned Leslie had an unswerving allegiance to any task he began. His work and his responsibilities dominated all other considerations, even his own welfare, and at times his family's.

The unseemly hot spell continued. It was 95 degrees in the shaded cottage, and outside the thermometer read 105 degrees and upwards. Without a second thought, Leslie in his heavy Eastern gear calmly began walking to Menlo. Two miles and an hour later, when he got to the post office, he was red faced, and every bit of clothing he wore was wet through with perspiration.

Mr. Jeffers, the postmaster, was surprised when Leslie walked in. "What are you doing back here? You were here yesterday."

Finally in some shade, Leslie also wondered why he was there, foolishly doing this chore. Between breaths, he said, "I thought some more mail might come in."

"Well, you were right." Mr. Jeffers went into the back room and returned with a leather pouch filled with letters.

Leslie immediately slung it over his shoulder. His body noticeably buckled under its weight. He said good-bye and started back out the door.

As Leslie turned around to leave, Mr. Jeffers said, "Why don't you sit down and have a drink of water or something? You going right back out into that heat isn't a good idea. You should see yourself. Red face. Looks like you're about to keel right over."

Leslie hesitated, and answered, "No, thanks. The sooner I leave, the sooner I'll be home. Thanks for your concern, but I want to get back and start working." Outside, he retraced his tracks, only thinking about the welcoming shade at the cottage.

Halfway there, he could feel the heft of the pouch starting to dig into his shoulder's flesh. He paused and shifted the satchel from one side to the other. As he was changing its position, the pouch's weight pulled him off balance, and he had a hard time keeping himself from pitching forward. With great effort, he regained his footing and continued on, but he noticed his stride growing shorter and shorter, slower and slower.

So slow, in fact, a black and white dog caught up with him and sniffed his dusty pants as if he thought it were a tree trunk. He kicked the dog off, shouting, "Shoo." The dog yelped and ran off.

Thus far, the dog had been the only living creature Leslie had encountered on the county road. Apparently, he thought, only a dumb dog or me would venture out. The song "Mad Dogs and Englishmen" came into his mind. He started to hum and sing it to get his mind off his predicament.

When Leslie's eyesight started to blur, he was no longer able to deny the seriousness of his weakened condition. Objects around him were fuzzy, and he could no longer identify where he was or where he should turn onto the road leading to the cottage. He must have walked straight past the turn off. For the first time, apprehension ran through his body.

Storefronts and hitching posts loomed ahead, and he knew he was in the middle of Mayfield, the desolate little village next to the University. He needed to ask for directions, but there was not a soul to be seen. The first sign of a human presence was the sound of laughter coming from a building to his left, on the corner. With some effort, he stepped up to the wooden planked sidewalk and heard men laughing, their voices coming from behind swinging doors. It was a saloon. Leslie hesitated, but not for long. He needed help. Again he almost lost his footing, so he forced himself to go through the doors and stumbled into a cool, semi-darkened room. The smell of stale cigar smoke and cheap whiskey was in the air, but it was preferable to the scorching heat.

Seated at a bar running the length of the room, he could make out three scraggly cowboys. They were dusty and dirty—like everything else, Leslie imagined, in Mayfield. They looked around at Leslie as if he were the Grim Reaper about to claim their souls. The looks on their faces tempted Leslie to turn on his heels and go back out into the furnace-like heat. As he hesitated, a stout, bald-headed fellow with a wooden leg came from behind the bar and approached him. His face, unlike those of his companions, showed at least some compassion at Leslie's plight. He immediately took Leslie's elbow to help him stand erect.

"Young man, are you all right? I'd say you should sit down with that heavy pouch and all. My name's Fred Behn and I'm the proprietor of this saloon."

Suddenly the world around Leslie began to spin and swirl, and he had to grasp Mr. Behn's arm to keep from falling. He barely said, "My name's Leslie Elliott and I'd shake your hand, but I'd fall if I didn't hold on to your arm."

"Here, give me that pouch." Fred Behn could see from the reaction on Leslie's face he was reluctant to part with it. "It's all right I won't steal it. Here, here ..." He took the heavy mail pouch off Leslie's shoulder and pulled a chair out. "Sit down, Mr. Elliott, and take it easy for a while. Let me get you a drink of water— or beer, if you prefer."

"Water is fine, thank you." Mr. Behn was gone for a second and returned with water in a tin cup, and Leslie eagerly drank its contents in one long swig. He had never in his life tasted such cool elixir. Afterwards, he sat for a moment, decided he should be on his way, and started to get up.

Mr. Behn gently held him back and put his hand on Leslie's forehead. "Whoa there, Mr. Elliott, I think you'd better think twice before you go anywhere. I'm sure you've got a high fever. We call it sunstroke 'round here, pretty common for this time of year." Mr. Behn put his index finger to his head, as if in deep thought, and said, "For some reason, I think you're part of that eastern crowd moved into Peter Coutt's place yesterday. Am I right?"

The cowboys at the bar guffawed in unison at Mr. Behn's pretended ignorance.

Leslie had never heard of this Peter Coutt person. He answered, "I'm staying with Dr. Jordan at Escondite Cottage."

"That's it. I heard this Dr. Jordan was renaming everything around here with foreign names. So how about me getting my rig out and taking you over to that 'Iscontight' place. I can have you home in fifteen minutes, whereas you might take lots longer walking, and I'm not so sure you'd make it."

Leslie felt better, but he knew Mr. Behn was right. He was in no condition to walk anywhere. Even getting back up on his feet had made him dizzy.

Ellen was sitting with Louis on the front veranda when a strange man pulled up in his rig with Leslie at his side. The man was holding the reins in one hand and with the other supporting Leslie. Startled, Ellen jumped to her feet. Something was wrong with her husband. His face was red, his eyes glassy.

The stranger called out to her, "Mam, this here gentlemen is not feeling well, and I'm going to need some help getting him out of the rig. I'm afraid if I let him go, he'll topple right over. Nothing serious, he's got sunstroke. Give him some water and put him to bed for a while and he'll be as good as new."

Without saying a word, Ellen rushed into the house and got Mr. Fletcher, and between the two of them they were able to lower Leslie to the ground and support him so he could get to the veranda.

The stranger, in spite of his wooden leg, jumped down from his rig, holding a leather pouch. "I'm sure he'll want this." And he put it carefully on the veranda.

Because of her wifely concerns, Ellen had forgotten about the stranger. She called out to him, "Forgive my bad manners, sir. He's my husband. Thank you for getting him home. My name's Ellen Elliott. What's your name so we can thank you properly, later?"

"Fred Behn, I'm the proprietor of a saloon in Mayfield. You and your husband drop by and see me sometime. In spite of everything you hear, we Mayfield people aren't such a bad lot."

As she and Mr. Fletcher were struggling to get Leslie inside the doorway, she said, "I'm sure you're not, and I can assure you we will be seeing you."

The last thing Ellen saw of Mr. Behn was his waving good-bye to her, as if she were an old friend.

That night at about ten o'clock Dr. Jordan returned from his journey across the Santa Cruz Mountains. He was elated and immediately regaled his wife, Jessie, and Ellen with descriptions of the beautiful redwood trees he had passed through and Monterey Bay's gorgeous pounding surf. Ellen could tell he considered his feat almost on a par with his ascent of the Matterhorn, which he regularly recalled to them. He did not ask about Leslie, and Ellen did not volunteer that Leslie also had an adventure.

That night and on Sunday, Leslie recovered between cool sheets in a darkened bedroom.

By Wednesday July first, Leslie had recovered enough to begin his duties as registrar at the new university. In the morning, three candidates arrived at the cottage and took their entrance examinations on Escondite's veranda. Two passed, one failed.

In the afternoon, Leslie accompanied Dr. Jordan, who was driving his rig, and Dr. Richardson back to Menlo station to pick up late-arriving luggage, and of course more mail. On the way there, they fortuitously bumped into Frank Batchelder, the newly hired stenographer, also from Cornell, who was hiking south on the county road, headed toward the cottage. Hot and tired, Frank was more than willing to let them take his heavy valise, while he continued on to Escondite Cottage.

After leaving Frank and continuing on to Menlo, Dr. Jordan remarked, "We can temporarily put the young man up with Mr. Fletcher, but there's no room at the table for him. He'll have to find a place for board now, and a place to room later."

Leslie knew Frank and he did not consider him to be a robust young man. Others in the office at Cornell called him a mother's boy. Living and eating in Mayfield would not be to his liking. Leslie said, "That will not please him, I'm sure."

Dr. Jordan took his eyes off the road ahead and regarded Leslie. "Sorry, Leslie, but I can see that all of us will be facing pioneering times."

Leslie let the remark pass without comment.

Next day, Frank helped Leslie in the cottage's library and they held the second day of student entrance examinations. Six young people were tested. Only two passed. Leslie could only think California high schools were not doing a good job of preparing their student for college.

As soon as space was ready in the Quad, Leslie and Frank moved the administration into a classroom located in the Quad's southeast corner. They occupied Room #30, destined to be a large romantic languages classroom. Dr. Jordan, Leslie, and Frank shared the space at first. Several others—Mr. Woodruff, the librarian; Miss Stillings, another stenographer; and a part-time fellow, Bert Hoover, who had been recommended by a senior member of the faculty, Dr. Swain, later joined them. Bert's real name was Herbert, but he preferred the shorter version. Some space was provided for a desk for Irene Butler, so she might persuade parents to send their daughters to a nearby preparatory school for girls she and a friend were establishing.

The room would be crowded, but it was anticipated that within two months they would move to their permanent quarters at the entrance to the University. There, the president and registrar would have private offices.

CHAPTER 3

▼

"I No Do Beds."

Thursday, July 9, 1891

Ellen knew from the start it would not work out having two families live under the same roof at the cottage. She tried to get along with Miss Jessie—the domestic name Dr. Jordan called his wife, but it still did not work out.

Ellen could understand why Dr. Jordan idolized his wife. Miss Jessie had replaced his first wife, Susan, who died four years earlier. Even with spectacles, Miss Jessie was a striking woman, with dark eyes, olive skin, and straight black hair done in a pompadour. She appeared to have Spanish ancestry, but she was Middle Western through and through. Quick and capable by nature, she liked to be in charge. This was fine with her adoring husband, who was happy to leave domestic—and, for that matter, parenting—decisions to his wife. University decisions were enough for him.

But Miss Jessie's treatment of Edith, Dr. Jordan's older daughter from his first marriage, was particularly galling for both Ellen and Leslie. It soon became apparent Miss Jessie considered Edith to be both a domestic servant and a nanny for Knight, the youngster. Ellen wondered when Edith had any time for herself. Leslie, in the confines of their bedchamber, expressed his opinion that Harold, who was Edith's brother and Dr. Jordan's eldest son from his first marriage, was not present because Miss Jessie did not want to bother parenting a child who was not her own. The story about Harold being ill was a sham. Leslie had noticed that whenever Dr. Jordan spoke of Harold, something that did not happen often, he acted as if he were remiss as a parent—which, in Leslie's mind, he was.

Ellen felt her presence threatened Jessie in some way. At night under the covers, Leslie whispered that when Ellen and Dr. Jordan were joking about something or other, Jessie watch intently with a cold look in her eyes. All of this, of course, created tension. There were never words between the two of them, but Ellen never felt at ease in the same room with her.

Matters came to a head when Jessie asked Ah Sam, the cook, to leave. Both Leslie and Ellen were more than pleased with the bill of fare he presented at each meal and agreed with Senator Stanford he was the best cook in the area. But Jessie wanted Ah Sam to be more than a cook. There were beds to be made, sweeping and mopping to be done. Ah Sam would have none of it, and eventually Jessie told him to do what she wanted or leave.

Leslie happened to see Ah Sam as he was walking out the door for the last time, and his parting words were loud, clear, and spoken to anyone within hearing distance. "I no do beds," he said, and he was out the door, never to return. With him went any thought of good food, well prepared.

Domestic life at Escondite went steadily downhill after that. The ladies attempted to cook in the small kitchen without success. All they accomplished was to get in each other's way. The men and children sat waiting for meals that never came on time and were tasteless and cold when they did.

Whispering at night, Ellen and Leslie discussed the dilemma in which they found themselves. It was obvious they could no longer stay at the cottage. Leslie's career depended upon a good relationship with Dr. Jordan. If there was any falling out between the two ladies, it might have long-lasting repercussions. Before such a catastrophe happened, the Elliotts must leave. They had no idea where they would go, but they had no alternative. After all, in a few months they would move into the permanent accommodations they had been promised—cottages to be built south of Encina Hall, the men's dormitory.

Next day after a cold, tasteless breakfast, as they walked over to the Quad, Leslie said to Dr. Jordan, "Ellen and I talked it over last night, and we think our staying at the cottage is a burden. Jessie and you have done everything possible to make us comfortable, but it's time we moved on."

Leslie was not surprised that Dr. Jordan made no effort to change his mind and said, "Well, for the next week, I'll be traveling and lecturing in Southern California. That should give you plenty of time to find other accommodations."

Neither Dr. Jordan nor Leslie made any further comments about the matter. As simple as that, Leslie thought, we would have to find new accommodations within the week.

Of course, it was Ellen who had to begin looking for new arrangements for room and board. Leslie was reluctant to ask for any time off when there were so many things to do at the Quad. Ellen had learned from experience that taking time off from work, except for holidays or vacations, was something Leslie never did.

During the next week, Ellen found herself, along with Louis, being driven about Mayfield by young Albert Fletcher, who could use Dr. Jordan's rig while he was in San Diego.

From a distance, she had seen Mayfield and knew it was not the flowery village she had envisioned from her husband's letters. If anything, it was worse up close. She saw unkempt one-story houses—shanties or shotgun houses were the terms used to describe them in the East; a few shops for fruit and household items; a couple of hotels next to the county roads; but mostly saloons. She counted fourteen of them.

In their travels, they went past P. F. Behn's Saloon, and Ellen thought about stopping by and seeing the peg-legged fellow who had gallantly rescued her husband. She thought better of it and decided to wait until Leslie was with her.

Ellen, with Louis in her arms, accompanied by Albert, went into one of the hotels. Only men were in the lobby. They glanced at the threesome with obvious interest—the petite blonde lady with young child and the accompanying young buck. In Ellen's eyes, something about their looks suggested leers. Could they be thinking of them as a threesome? She tugged at Albert's sleeve, and they turned around and walked out.

They continued to drive along dirt roads, stopping at the homes that were the least disreputable looking. Quickly they found out it was unheard of to take in boarders. The usual response was, "Why should we take in boarders?" Doors were shut slowly and eyes peered at them through dirty windows as they got back into their rig. Albert decided it might be better if they explained that they came from the East to start up Leland Stanford Junior University. When they tried this approach at the next house, an old lady asked, "Oh, do you think Senator Stanford is really going to start his college?"

Ellen, somewhat surprised at the reaction, answered, "Yes, of course we do."

Albert was curious and asked, "Why not?"

The old lady laughed and looked at them with pity, as if they had escaped from some asylum. "Them workmen been a-buildin' over there for more years than they ought. Seems they build it up and the Stanford lady tells 'em tear it down. Build it. Tear it down." She smiled slyly, showing wide gaps between her

few dark teeth. "That's fine with us. Lots of our men folk workin' over there."
And she shut the door.

So that was what the residents thought about their university, Ellen thought, a
pipe dream.

Finally, a man at a half-empty shop said he could accommodate the family.
He would make an eight-by-ten room for them in the back.

Ellen was desperate. She told the man she'd have to consult with her husband
and let him know.

Outside, Albert told her he thought the man's proposal was impossible. "You
can't live all summer in an eight-by-ten room," he said. "What would you eat?
Saw dust and shavings?"

Albert was right. They would be sharing accommodations with a carpenter's
shop. Ellen decided to give up the idea.

That night in the privacy of their bedchamber, when Leslie heard about the
old lady's comments, he whispered, "No wonder the workers treat us as if we
were foolish to think this university will ever open its doors. Up to now it's been
a plaything to keep Mrs. Stanford occupied. Something must have happened to
give Senator Stanford a sense of urgency. I wonder what it was?"

Ellen had already fallen asleep, so there was no answer to his question. Soon
he joined her.

Luckily for the Elliotts, when Dr. Richardson heard of their plight, he agreed
to rent out his mother's bedroom at Cedro Cottage, the temporary dwelling he
and his family occupied. The only problem was that the Elliotts would have to
take their daily meals at the Oak Grove Villa Hotel, a little more than a mile's
distance from Cedro. Also, Dr. Richardson's mother, who had temporarily
returned to Massachusetts, was due back in a few weeks, so it would be a
short-term arrangement.

CHAPTER 4

▼

"A MAGNIFICENT CIRCUS"

Friday, August 7, 1891

The three men were eating their lunches from lunch pails they had brought that morning. Dr. Jordan had walked the half-mile from Escondite Cottage to the Quad. Drs. Richardson and Elliott had a longer walk from Cedro Cottage—a mile. Staying with the Richardsons was still a temporary arrangement, so Ellen had been looking for another place in Menlo to live and board, so far without success.

For the gentlemen eating lunch, it was another hot day, with a brilliant sun and no cooling breeze from the bay. What wind there was, was like heat from a hot coal fire. Every day had been hot since they arrived, six weeks earlier.

At first, the threesome ate in silence, surveying the expanse of the inner court-yard, almost 600 feet long and nearly 250 feet wide. The area was covered with black asphalt, hot to the touch, and was interspersed by eight circular plots planted with different varieties of three-to-four foot high palm trees. It reminded Leslie of a number eight domino. Around the quadrangle sat twelve, single-story buildings constructed of buff sandstone, topped with reddish tile roofs, and joined and shaded by the Romanesque arcades that, Leslie thought, were heaven sent on a hot August day such as this.

Leslie, like the other men, was dressed in dark, heavy trousers and a white cuffed and collared shirt, with a thin black tie. Because of the heat, all of the men had left their jackets in the office, but all wore hats. Drs. Elliott and Richardson had black bowlers, and Dr. Jordan a soft slouch hat of neutral shade.

At first the only sound was the men's chewing and swallowing. Leslie spoke quietly, carefully choosing his words, "Dr. Jordan, I hate to bring up a disagreeable subject during our noon repast, but we must order books for the library, if we are to have a library. Our librarian won't be arriving for a few weeks, and if we wait, we won't have books for the students starting class on October first."

David Starr Jordan did not immediately reply. He continued chewing on a chicken drumstick Miss Jessie had cooked for him. He had a white handkerchief in his left hand and a drumstick in the other. Unlike his slimmer, younger companions, he was in a slightly reclining position, with his scuffed boots spread before him. His intent, light blue eyes were concentrating on the drumstick he was about to stuff through a thin mustache into his mouth. The mustache growing under his Roman nose hid his mouth, but not his weak chin. Because of the girth of middle age—he was forty years old—it was not easy for him to bend in the middle.

After what seemed to be a lengthy period, he answered Leslie's question, "Senator Stanford—from what Charles Lathrop, his business manager, tells me—wants only a modest beginning. Mr. Lathrop says the senator doesn't want any accumulation of materials or equipment beyond what is needed."

"And whom are we talking to, the senator or Mr. Lathrop?" asked Leslie.

"We are talking to Mr. Lathrop, who says he speaks for Senator Stanford," was Dr. Jordan's reply. He slightly squirmed in place, as if the position he was in had grown uncomfortable.

Leslie recognized the signs. He was getting into dangerous territory, but he forged ahead. "And what does Mr. Lathrop say about the library on the senator's behalf?"

"He thinks a library such as a gentleman might maintain should be adequate, a library costing in the range of four to five thousand dollars."

"And what do you think?"

Dr. Jordan took the final bite of his drumstick, swallowed it, and wiped his mustache and mouth with his white cotton handkerchief. He pulled a green apple from the lunch pail and began to peel it with the large jackknife he used on such occasions, slowly and methodically. Leslie knew Jordan's perennial goal was to make one continuous peel. While attempting to accomplish this feat, he pulled himself to a sitting position and devoted most of his attention to peeling rather than replying to his registrar's question.

"I think we need a library similar to what we had at Indiana University." He paused for a tricky movement with his knife, and then resumed, "Such a library should cost two or three times what the good business manager mentioned. I think we need to begin to lay the broad foundation of an academic library that will adequately support our students' search for knowledge. That is what I think." This time he paused again and looked at Leslie. "But as you know, we must get approval for all monies expended from the business office in San Francisco. I'm sure there will be a great deal of correspondence between myself and Mr. Lathrop on this matter, but I'm also sure Senator Stanford will eventually agree with my requests." The apple was ready to eat. Dr. Jordan dropped the single peel into his pail and looked over at Leslie, with obvious satisfaction at his victory over the elements.

"And how will the senator ever learn of your requests when his brother-in-law is the go between?" Leslie was not to be dissuaded.

Dr. Jordan's wariness at the questioning showed in the tone of his voice. "Leslie, at the right time I will make the senator aware of my intentions. In the meantime, we will make purchases of books that meet my goals, not Mr. Lathrop's."

Leslie decided he had spoken enough about the library, but he had not given up. If books were not ordered, he would bring it up again at a more appropriate time, when a new member of the faculty was not present.

Evidently Dr. Richardson was not attuned to Dr. Jordan's changing moods, because he decided to follow Leslie's example. He bluntly asked, "And what about apparatus for the chemical laboratories?"

Richardson was the only member of the Chemistry Department presently on campus. He, like Leslie, was about thirty years old, but he had the makings of a full beard that made him look much older. "So far I see only enough for minimal instruction. It appears, from what Dr. Elliott has told me, that numerous students have indicated an interest in chemistry; and if we are going to have to purchase more equipment, it must be high quality. We don't want to have an explosion like the University of Pacific."

Leslie was surprised when Dr. Richardson spoke up as he did. Unlike most of the other young faculty men whom David Starr Jordan had selected and known personally, Richardson was still an unknown quantity. Because of that, Leslie knew Dr. Jordan had to be careful what he said to him.

Speaking slowly and clearly, Dr. Jordan said, "Dr. Richardson, what we need, we'll get, but first we'll need to educate Senator Stanford. And I'm sorry to say, that will not happen overnight." He abruptly stopped speaking.

There was a lengthy silence as Dr. Jordan carefully resumed his original semi-reclining position, began to eat the pared apple, and put the jackknife back into his lunch pail. He rummaged in it to see what else Miss Jessie might have prepared and looked disappointed when he found nothing.

Dr. Elliott continued to eat in silence, but in this climate of honesty, Dr. Richardson decided to bring up another tender subject he had on his mind. "I understand Coliss Huntington has referred to our university as 'Senator Stanford's circus.'"

Dr. Jordan's face showed no expression as he said, "Yes, I've heard the same phrase, and knowing Huntington and his lack of affection for his business partner, Senator Stanford, I'm sure he is correctly quoted. But gentlemen"—and here Jordan's expression became expansive as he looked theatrically beyond his companions and said, "Look at the broad expanse of our inner courtyard and the buff buildings with their red tile roofs framed by blue skies. It's like a stage setting. All we need are the players—the students and faculty."

Leslie could tell Jordan was about to make some dramatic statement. The man always appeared to be on stage. Jordan's right hand made an all encompassing gesture as he said, "And from this setting will come men and women who will be our future lawyers, doctors, scientists. We may even produce presidents, and senators, and congressmen. Gentlemen, I will tell you this: If we are to be a circus, I'm certain we will be a magnificent one."

Leslie Elliott smiled. It was an apt expression. He cocked his head slightly to one side and said, "That's well put, a good phrase, Dr. Jordan. You should write it down."

Jordan had already taken a small tablet from his vest pocket. "I am," he said.

Leslie said, "I'll try to eliminate the villains, Dr. Jordan, but I'm certain we will have our share."

Dr. Jordan smiled knowingly. "Who knows, one of them may be our president." He looked over at the young professor and decided to change the subject. "Dr. Richardson, any interest in the study of ichthyology?"

"The study of fish—being a chemistry fellow, I never really thought about it, but it might be a jolly interesting minor."

Ah-ha, the dear boy may still make it into Dr. Jordan's good graces, Leslie thought.

Frank Batchelder, who was hurrying over to where they were seated, interrupted the lunching doctors' conversation. "Dr. Jordan, your daughter brought a note. You're to call the business office. Something about needing the senator's approval for your new hires."

Jordan pulled himself up. He was instantly angry. "You know what this means. I'm going to have to walk all the way back to Escondite. Why won't they let us install telephones at the University?"

Dr. Richardson had to say it. "Too expensive, Dr. Jordan?"

With the energy it took to arise, plus his anger, Dr. Jordan's face had reddened. "And I guess my time isn't." He was also angry with Lathrop because he had discussed the topic of the call with Edith, and with Batchelder because he had read her note and announced its contents to the world. Dr. Jordan hastily gathered up the leavings from his lunch, and with a great show of haste, strode back to the office, accompanied by Batchelder, who was trying to catch up with him.

Drs. Elliott and Richardson were silent, then resumed eating the remnants of their lunches and making casual conversation about Ellen's ongoing, unsuccessful attempts to find new living accommodations in Menlo.

CHAPTER 5

▼

"NO JEWS OR NEGROES"

Monday, August 24, 1891

Swiveling in his chair, Leslie surveyed the scene before him: the temporary administrative quarters in the romantic languages classroom space. Dr. Jordan had said the move to their permanent location at the entrance to the Quad could not come too soon.

He saw Miss Stillings' back, the new stenographer. She was speaking earnestly to a bright-faced young woman, probably Sarah Bolton, about to take her entrance examinations. Frank Batchelder, whose place was next to Miss Stillings, was out of his chair, talking to Bert Hoover. Bert was a hard-working, reliable young man. He never complained to Leslie about Frank, but Leslie could see he wanted to be left alone and do his job—much like Leslie.

Both Bert and Frank got their room and board at Adelante Villa, the new preparatory school for young ladies that served as a temporary haven for students and faculty who arrived before the university began. The co-founder of the Villa was Irene Butler. She was seated at a small table, next to Bert, against the wall. She was talking to a middle-aged, well-dressed couple, accompanied by their young daughter. Irene was doing her best to get the parents to pay for their daughter's room and board at Adelante Villa and take classes—taught by herself and the other co-founder, Lucy Fletcher—to prepare their daughter for Stanford's entrance examinations. From talking to Irene, Leslie knew her perennial problem was that parents automatically thought because tuition at Stanford was free, there should be no charge at the Villa; there was. Irene and Lucy, Harvard Annex roommates, had come west at Dr. Jordan's behest and were temporarily feeding and housing boarders until, hopefully, about a dozen young ladies took the boarders' places. Directly behind Irene, to Leslie's left, in the corner, facing the back wall, was Mr. Woodruff, the new librarian. Because the fellow had arrived this past week, Leslie hardly knew him, but Ellen had spoken to him at length and said he had a quick sense of humor. Leslie thought, with all the banter going on between Charles Lathrop and Dr. Jordan about the cost of books for the library, Mr. Woodruff would need that sense.

Leslie's domain was at the back of the room, in the middle. He sat facing the wall, surrounded by four-foot filing cabinets. Seldom, if ever, did he look up from his work, except when questioned or if Dr. Jordan called him—which happened frequently. To Leslie's right, dominating most of the other corner, was Dr. Jordan's area. Unlike Leslie, Dr. Jordan always faced outward, toward the office's entrance, so he could view everything going on.

On that day, Dr. Jordan was in the city meeting with John Muir and other influential conservationists. They were creating an organization to preserve California's natural environment. Leslie took a deep breath. When Dr. Jordan was absent, tranquility reined, but when he walked through the door it was like a small cyclone had entered with him: voices became loud and strident, and minor difficulties became major problems. Leslie was not prone to cursing but it was as if all hell had broken loose.

If either Dr. Jordan or Leslie required privacy, which was often, they had to go outside and stand or sit on the foot-high curbing around the huge, inner patio. From past experience, they had found, even if they whispered, the room became so quiet every word they said could be heard and—they guessed—quoted to others, verbatim, by Frank.

Yes, Dr. Jordan was right, Leslie thought, it was time for the move to quarters where both he and Dr. Jordan would have private offices. In a few more weeks, they should be moving. That reminded him to write a cryptic note to himself: "Write registration procedures." He had been thinking about the procedures for weeks. The university's opening was less than six weeks away. It was time he put pen to paper.

Earlier that morning, he had left Ellen and Louis in a sparse bedroom in Menlo, above an unoccupied store. The Elliott family had moved there a week before from Cedro Cottage. He would not see his family again until evening, when it would already be starting to get dark. After he left each morning, he knew from Ellen's daily complaints, she and Louis fumbled down a narrow, dark stairway to the sagging porch in front of the empty store. Louis had a red wheelbarrow to keep himself occupied while Ellen sat, chin in hand, and stared at the two saloons and the livery stable across the street and watched the antics of usually inebriated Menlo residents. Yesterday their Mexican landlady had kindly lent Ellen a book to read: *Ramona*. None of the Cornell faculty families had brought books with them. It had not occurred to them that books would not be as available in California as apples had been on the trees in Ithaca.

After kissing his wife and child on their cheeks that morning, Leslie had joined the stream of fellow faculty members walking the county roads to the Quad, carrying their lunches in baskets, like schoolboys. Since no one else apparently walked in California, except tramps, locals—including the Stanford University construction workers—had taken to calling the traipsing faculty "tramp professors" or "hobo professors." Leslie didn't mind the salutation. He smiled and said his good mornings. He enjoyed the construction worker's banter.

Today, he had thought, he would borrow Dr. Jordan's horse to go back to the Menlo post office. It was his turn to get the mail. Stanford's mail pouches were now too heavy for anyone to carry over his back, and for some reason, Dr. Jordan had not delegated the task to either Frank or Bert. Leslie didn't claim to be much of a horseman, and Jordan's feisty horse was too much for him at times. Two weeks earlier, Leslie had ended right side up in a water-filled ditch, with the reins still in his hands. He had not bargained for this part of the job.

Mr. Jeffers had the university's pouches ready for him, as well as the usual complaints about how much mail the university received. Leslie, always with a smile, ignored him, slung the leather pouches onto the horse's withers, and headed south.

It was another scorching day, about 92 degrees. Somehow during the past months, Leslie had adjusted to the heat. He still wore a dark suit, tie, and shirt with its attached collars and cuffs, and a derby hat pulled down almost to his ears. It would have been unseemly to take off his coat, even though his shirt and undergarments were wringing wet.

When he arrived at the juncture with the new road they were building leading to the university—named by Dr. Jordan, unimaginatively, University Drive— Leslie considered himself lucky: the gate was not locked. Sometimes when the Stanfords were not in residence, the overzealous caretaker locked it, as if he thought the drive only led to the Palo Alto Farm. After all, the small sign at the entrance announced Palo Alto Farm *and* Leland Stanford Junior University.

Looking down the drive, Leslie saw the low outline of the Quad buildings, with the towering chimney in the background. Between him and there was absolute chaos: mounds of dirt; horses and carts crossing one another's tracks; and workers shoveling, picking, and leaning. As he passed by, they shouted in friendly voices: "So how are you today and the rest of the hobo professoors?" "When are we goin' to see some stoodents, professoor? Ain't this here a school for stoodents? Or are you fellows just walkin' and whinin'?" "Don't drink too much of the senator's wine, professoor. It'll make you feel woooozy."

As he rode over the rough roadway, Leslie smiled to himself about how involved the workers were with what was going on. "It's true," he muttered to himself, "Senator Stanford's campaign to eliminate consuming alcohol from the surrounding villages ignores the fact that he is making and selling wine and brandy."

Leslie remembered that several of the workmen had stopped him and asked him about entrance requirements. In fact, one interesting fellow, whose dull appearance turned out to be deceptive, was accepted for admission as a special student.

"Special student," Leslie said aloud as he tightly held the reins. He had no idea what the term meant. Special status was something Dr. Jordan used more than he should have when judging candidates. Dr. Jordan had no written policy regarding what it meant.

When Leslie had asked him about a questionable case—a fourteen-year-old girl—Dr. Jordan's reply was, "Let's see what happens." There was nothing wrong with this thinking, but what caused Leslie's dander to rise was that special status only applied to Anglo-Saxons.

"No Jews or Negroes." These words Leslie spoke angrily, aloud. He had hoped a new university in the West would be different from the Harvards and Yales. His ancestors had come west to Wyoming because of their abolitionist beliefs, and his father's brother was shot and killed fighting for the Union cause. Similar blood ran in Dr. Jordan's veins. But when application letters came from young people who might be Jews or Negroes, Leslie was told to hold the letters and proceed no farther. Leslie could only think that Dr. Jordan's eugenic beliefs overruled his abolitionist background and his sense of justice.

One letter had particularly bothered Leslie, and he asked Dr. Jordan, "How about the one mentioning Mrs. Stanford?"

It was from a proud father, Mr. Beverly Johnson, who lived in Sacramento. The gentleman wrote fluently and was obviously proud of his eldest son, Ernest. Mr. Johnson mentioned in his letter that Mrs. Stanford was one of his Sacramento catering customers and had recommended he get in touch with Dr. Jordan directly about his son's admission to her university. Dr. Jordan's response to Leslie was to shake his head as if to say, don't worry about it. Leslie pushed the letter down to the bottom of his *things to do* pile, eventually to be discarded.

Thinking about how Mr. Johnson had been mistreated rankled Leslie so much that a whole series of irritations poured through his mind—in particular, Mrs. Stanford's brothers, Ariel and Charles.

Ariel was the business manager at the university, and Charles was the manager of Senator Stanford's San Francisco office. "Those damn Lathrop brothers," Leslie said, loud enough anyone passing by could have heard. He was not the type to curse, but in this case, he felt it was warranted. Why in the world did the business office allow the university only one phone line, and that one line ended at Escondite Cottage? Poor Edith had to walk a mile and a half to the administrative office whenever there was a phone call. Most of the calls were from Charles Lathrop, questioning Dr. Jordan about ordering a piece of equipment, hiring a faculty member, or whether the payment of a bill was approved. Dr. Jordan had to get on his horse and ride all the way back to Escondite to return the call. Whenever he had the opportunity, Ariel expressed his dislike of the students who were, in his mind, taking money out of his sister's purse. Dr. Jordan was always patient with both of them. After all, they were Mrs. Stanford's brothers. But, Leslie could tell, both Charles and Ariel were becoming thorns in Dr. Jordan's side.

Leslie kept these irritations to himself. Only Ellen knew what was on his mind. As long as they had been living at Escondite Cottage, they never discussed the matter. Now, in the privacy of their little room in Menlo—along with the mosquitoes—it was all they talked about.

Looking around, Leslie realized he was halfway back to the office. He had done the same route so many times that he sometimes forgot where he was. In the distance, he saw the brick chimney for the steam plant. It was over sixty feet high. Underground pipes and cables running through a complex of tunnels from the plant provided heat, hot water, and electricity to the university's buildings and the faculty houses being build on Alvarado Row, one of which would house the Elliott family. The chimney could be seen from miles away—or so the local population was saying—the chimney was destined to be the university's landmark for years to come. Leslie liked to think it would, but there were warning signs the future might not be as rosy as everyone predicted.

"Dr. Jordan is so optimistic." He sighed as he said the words. Was it Leslie's nature to be the opposite? Had he trained himself to make up for Jordan's deficiencies? He had already seen signs Senator Stanford didn't have the intellect, or really the financial wherewithal, to be the sole founder and benefactor of a truly great university. From his humble beginnings as the proprietor of a hardware store in Sacramento, it was obvious the senator knew how to make money. With his Sacramento friends, he had built a railroad across the country, and from this came bounties of huge grants of property and amounts of money. Now he was raising thoroughbred horses, and selling wine and brandy. Maybe with the right bloodlines, trainers, and environment, his plans worked for horses; but for building and founding a new university, there was a whole new set of challenges and unknowns.

The building Leslie could see on his left, Encina Hall, was a good example of that. The old lady Ellen had encountered while looking for a rental knew all about the problems caused by Mrs. Stanford superintending its building. If Mrs. Stanford didn't like the look of a window or porch, it was removed and what she wanted was substituted. She said she could not judge how a thing looked until she saw it. No one cared that this kind of thinking was costly and impeded the work schedule.

Leslie had found out from documentation dating back to Frederick Olmsted's plans that early arriving faculty and their families and students were supposed to be housed at Encina. After all, it was the duplicate of a hotel in Switzerland the Stanfords admired. Those plans must have been scotched because of construction delays caused by Mrs. Stanford's meddling. Leslie hesitated to think how different the Elliotts' arrival would have been if they had moved right into the hall.

He also heard Encina's construction costs were almost as high as the entire Quad's. It appeared Senator Stanford's concerns were neither financial nor for the welfare of early arrivals, but to keep his wife happily occupied.

Encina Hall, according to the construction reports Leslie had read, would be almost ready for the male students arriving during the next few weeks. The ladies would not be so lucky. Because of an unforeseen increase in the number of women admitted, or perhaps because of financial reasons, the senator and Dr. Jordan had decided to stop construction on a stone structure similar to Encina Hall. Instead, Roble Hall, a smaller, less expensive dormitory using reinforced concrete, was being built. But it was four weeks behind schedule.

October first was still the planned date for classes to begin. The ladies would be arriving soon. They would have to put up with no electricity and no hot water for an indefinite period, just as the Elliotts would do when they moved to their new cottage. Roble's kitchen facilities were not close to completion. Leslie said aloud, "They'll have to take their meals at Encina." He smiled when he said that and thought; the ladies will soon learn to be pioneers like all the rest of us, the Elliott family included.

Leslie had reached the end of the oval that was taking form at the entrance on the north side of the Quad. On his right, was the location of the permanent administrative office. There in the distance Dr. Jordan was striding toward him, back from his meeting.

As he got closer, he could hear Dr. Jordan calling him, "Leslie, Leslie. I need you."

"I'll be right there, Dr. Jordan," he shouted back. "It must be another crisis," he said to himself.

CHAPTER 6

▼

"CUPID UNSHEATHES HIS ARROWS"

Tuesday, September 8, 1891

Dr. Jordan had asked Leslie to go outside with him to discuss a private matter. Leslie could tell it was to be a brief discussion; Dr. Jordan turned to his right and headed for a space under the eastern archway. He turned around, and the two men stood about three or four feet from one another. For longer discussions, Dr. Jordan sat on the curb.

Dr. Jordan put his hands on his hips as he began to speak. "I'm going to have a visitor this morning and I want you to meet him."

Leslie remained silent.

"He's Fletcher Martin, a West Point graduate and formerly a United States army officer, fought in the Indian Wars."

Leslie remembered the fellow's entrance papers. He volunteered, "Yes, yes. Graduate student in ancient languages. Even though he graduated ten years ago, his West Point professors remembered him favorably and wrote glowing recommendations. His grades were middling for his class."

"That's the chap. He's staying at Irene's Adelante Villa and he'll be moving to Encina in a few weeks. As you know, Senator Stanford wants some sort of military training, and I thought he'd be the right type to help Captain Harkins, the Civil War veteran who volunteered to organize our training."

Leslie waited for the shoe to drop. How did all this involve him? "Yes, yes," he said, hoping his words did not reveal his slight exasperation. Sometimes Dr. Jordan forgot how much work he had to do. Last night he had worked until nine o'clock.

Dr. Jordan stretched his arms over his chest. "I'd like you to watch over the matter. Training for the military is not my cup of tea. I'm not sure you knew that my older brother died after joining the army. He got malaria. One day his body was delivered to us in a pine casket. I shall never forget my feelings when I got home from school and my parents were waiting for me, hysterical with grief."

Leslie said, "I never knew. You never told me." Dr. Jordan's shoulders drooped, his chin fell, and his eyes turned down and gazed at the patterns on the cement walkway. Leslie continued, "Of course, I understand. Do you want me to speak to Mr. Martin?"

Dr. Jordan looked up at Leslie and said, "No, I'll merely introduce you two, then out of courtesy to Irene, I'll speak to him. She must like the fellow. She's twice mentioned he'd be here this morning. As if I might forget. I've begun the matter and I'll talk to Mr. Martin and then to Captain Harkins, and give him my thoughts, but I'd like you to oversee the progress of the program and keep me informed. I'll tell both gentlemen you'll be my surrogate. So I want to introduce you to Mr. Martin this morning."

Leslie nodded, and Dr. Jordan dropped his arms to his side. Their conversation was over. Both men turned around and returned to the administrative office.

About an hour later, Leslie was deeply engrossed in some statistical tables he was developing regarding the backgrounds of the undergraduate, graduate, and special students entering the university. Working as he did, facing the wall, he had developed a sixth sense that told him when someone was behind him, waiting to speak to him. In addition, this time he heard Dr. Jordan say in a subdued voice, "Dr. Elliott, I'd like you to meet Fletcher Martin."

Leslie turned in his chair and got out of it at the same time, with his right hand extended. It was an automatic gesture; he had done it several times before. But the sight before him was surprising. He was not expecting Mr. Martin to be two or three inches taller than Dr. Jordan, and looking enough like President Lincoln to be his younger brother. There were differences, one startling. On the left side of Mr. Martin's face was a six-inch jagged scar. Leslie had never seen a scar quite like it. It looked like something had just missed taking out Mr. Martin's eye. Because of the scar, Leslie at first glance thought the man was grotesque looking. And there were other, subtle differences: he was slightly bearded, and his features were not coarse like Mr. Lincoln's, but were more refined. However, the general appearance of a weathered oak tree was the same.

Mr. Martin's long, thin fingers shook Leslie's small hand firmly but with great restraint, as if Leslie's fingers might be sensitive. Unlike the academic hands Leslie usually shook, Mr. Martin's hand was rough like a workman's.

"Pleased to meet you, Dr. Elliott. I'm Fletcher Martin." There was a slight pause, and he added, "The scar's from a tomahawk."

Leslie's face had showed his feelings. He wasn't sure he should apologize.

Mr. Martin must have sensed his unease because he hastened to add, "It's all right. I'm used to it."

Dr. Jordan was anxious to move on. He put his hand on Mr. Martin's shoulder and began to guide him back toward the entrance. "Now, gentlemen, if you don't mind, Mr. Martin, for privacy we'll have to go outside to continue our conversation. In a few weeks, all that will change when we have private offices."

As Dr. Jordan spoke, Leslie noticed, Mr. Martin's eyes glanced over at Irene, still busy speaking to prospective parents. Without stopping, she glanced back and her left hand slightly fluttered, as if waving. The brief exchange took only a second or two, and Leslie doubted Dr. Jordan had even noticed it.

Mr. Martin let Dr. Jordan continue to guide him, but turned back to Leslie and gave him a warm parting smile and said, "Good to meet you, Dr. Elliott. I'll be looking forward to seeing you again."

Leslie said a similar good-bye and returned to organizing his analytical tables. He couldn't help thinking how he had instantly taken a liking to the tall fellow. It was peculiar how his scarred face quickly faded from memory.

Thirty minutes later, Dr. Jordan returned to his desk without making any further comment to Leslie. Leslie reasoned it must have been a quick exchange. Dr. Jordan asked, and Mr. Martin agreed.

Shortly afterward, Leslie heard a murmur—a collective muddling of voices that could only have been provoked by an unexpected event viewed by the entire office staff, with the exception of him. He looked around and saw Fletcher Martin standing in the middle of the room and looking over at Irene, who by now was alone working at her study table. Miss Stillings started to get up to see if she could be of assistance, but it was obvious Mr. Martin knew exactly whom he wanted to see. He took manful strides toward Irene. Bert and Frank looked up at him as he passed them, as if they wanted to say hello, but he ignored them. Everyone in the room, including Dr. Jordan, was watching—even Leslie now, out of the corner of his eye.

Mr. Martin, looking neither to his left nor right, strode up to Irene's table and carefully took a folded piece of paper out of his inner coat pocket and held it out for Irene to take. Leslie, who was ten to fifteen feet away, could see his hand was shaking like a leaf. For a second, Leslie almost chuckled at the ridiculous scene of such a huge man acting as nervous as a schoolboy. He restrained himself because of the serious expression on Mr. Martin's face.

Irene quickly took the note, glanced at it, and nodded. Leslie guessed she had agreed to whatever Mr. Martin's note had asked. But there was more. Irene whispered some words, perhaps a question. Mr. Martin whispered something back, an answer. The note must have asked, "Can we ... something?" Irene had responded, "Yes, but where or when?" Mr. Martin had sealed the arrangement with a time and place.

Everyone in the room held their breaths as Mr. Martin wheeled about, as if dismissed by his commanding officer, and post haste retreated out the doorway.

Quickly the administrative staff resumed their normal duties, as Irene looked around, embarrassed that her personal life had been publicly displayed. Leslie avoided her eyes by grabbing a letter and pretending to read it. But Dr. Jordan did the opposite. He stood up and made broad gestures of full approval with his hands and arms. Irene couldn't help herself; she smiled.

Later Dr. Jordan drifted by Leslie's desk and commented in low undertones, "Methinks Cupid has unsheathed his arrows. Early love's such a beautiful sight."

That night after Louis had been tucked into his small cot beside their bed, when the Elliotts were under covers, Leslie whispered to Ellen what had happened during the day. She was not surprised in the least. She said, "I haven't met Mr. Martin, but Irene has told me about him. She's a handsome woman, and I can understand why he'd take to her. I much prefer her to the other one, Lucy, who's the ravishing beauty and plays the violin and all, but looks as if a slight breeze could blow her away. Irene's the sturdy one, the backbone of that couple. She's the one who picked up the broom and mop and started cleaning up that gloomy overgrown mansion Dr. Jordan had them rent from Senator Stanford."

Leslie wondered at all this new information about Irene, which he had not heard before. "How do you know all this? I didn't know you even knew her."

Sometimes Ellen could not believe the naiveté of her loving husband. His work was the only thing of which he was aware. Did he not know, she wondered, that the ladies of the campus knew one another? Before too long, she would know more about the workings of the university than he did. He was right, though. She had not told him about Irene. She explained, "A lady in Menlo does the Villa's laundry, and Irene picks it up every other day. If she sees me, she'll stop and play with Louis, and we chitchat for a bit. Louis thinks the world of her, and I consider her along with Harriet Marx as a good friend. She told me after she graduated from Harvard Annex she was engaged to a young mining engineer, but on his way home from China to marry her, he was lost at sea during a storm off Australia. All of her plans to be a wife and mother went and sank with him. She was at wit's end to know what to do, until Dr. Jordan approached Lucy and her to establish a preparatory school for the university."

Ellen could hear the steady breathing of her loved one. It didn't take much to put him to sleep, and his interest must have waned. He worked so hard all day long. Even though no one heard her, she said, "Good for Irene. Perhaps her dreams will still come true."

CHAPTER 7

▼

"ALL THE MAKINGS OF A MASSACRE"

Friday, September 11, 1891

Three days later, Dr. Jordan again asked Leslie to join him outside on the patio. This time Dr. Jordan sat on the curbing, with Leslie beside him. Dr. Jordan said, "Fletcher Martin will be here in an hour and I want you to talk to him."

Leslie thought, it must be bad news; Dr. Jordan does not want to do it. Leslie was never the bearer of good news. "And what shall I say to him?" he asked.

"That is precisely why we're sitting here, Leslie. I'm not sure what you will say to him. Yesterday, midday, I dropped by to see Captain Harkins, and he gave me some unfortunate news about our Mr. Martin. After ten years of service, he was given a general discharge. Captain Harkins told me this type of discharge means he did not honorably serve his country."

Leslie asked, "And what pray does that mean—'did not honorably serve his country?'"

Dr. Jordan's hands went out in front of him, palms up. "I don't know, Leslie, and I don't think Captain Harkins does, either, but whatever it is, he no longer wants Mr. Martin to assist him. He absolutely won't have anything to do with the fellow."

Leslie was not satisfied. "Was he a deserter? Did he flummox his commanding officer? Desecrate the flag? How can the poor man be accused when we don't know what the charges are?"

Dr. Jordan said, "That's what you and I think. It's not Captain Harkins' opinion. As far as he is concerned, if Fletcher Martin has a general discharge, he is less than honorable and should not be part of his military training program."

"So he will be here within the hour and I am supposed to tell him that?"

Dr. Jordan said, "Fletcher must have some idea why I asked him to come here. I assume he'll be expecting we're setting up a meeting with Captain Harkins. You'll have to tell him what the Captain uncovered, and that his assistance will not be needed. But I want to make certain he understands whatever he did will in no way jeopardizes his career with us. I have high hopes for the gentleman and expect he might become a member of our faculty. There's no need to tell him about my brother. Suggest instead that, no matter what happened, we will be most understanding. I don't want to rile Irene, either. She's a real peach."

Leslie wanted to put his superior's mind at ease. "Mr. Martin made a favorable impression on me, too. I will be very sensitive in my dealings with him."

A look of relief crossed Dr. Jordan's face. Leslie would do the right thing.

A large oak tree grew about one hundred feet from the Quad's northwest corner. If Senator Stanford had not ordered otherwise, the tree would have been cut down because it was directly in the way of a cement walkway running from Encina Hall, past the Quad, and ending at Roble Hall. Instead, the walkway split in two and rejoined after passing the oak's trunk. To commemorate the tree's survival, workmen had voluntarily built a wooden bench around its trunk. It was the only bench in the immediate area.

About an hour later, Leslie and Fletcher made their way to this bench. Leslie never felt comfortable sitting on the Quad's cold cement. The conversation between the two men as they walked from the Quad was forced at first, but became warm and friendly after Fletcher said, "I arrived in Mayfield at four o'clock on a Saturday morning."

Leslie laughed as he said, "I can imagine what that was like."

"You're right. All I could see were drunken bodies sleeping off all the drink they had the night before. I tried the hotel, but the door was bolted, so I decided to sleep out in the back of a saloon, under a bush."

Leslie said, "I did that a few times when I was growing up in Wyoming."

"Well, I've done it so often it's almost second nature. When I finally got to sleep, I had a dream; I seem to have often, of being struck by an Indian tomahawk. It was so real; I felt blood dripping off my face." Fletcher chuckled. "But it turned out to be a dang dog peeing on my face."

Leslie had no idea how to respond.

"I toweled off my face as well as I could and walked around to the front of the saloon, and this peg-legged gentleman says howdy to me, real friendly like."

Leslie could not believe his ears. It had to be the same fellow who had rescued him when he had sunstroke. He blurted out, "Fred Behn."

Fletcher eyes lit up. "Yes, yes. That's the fellow. How did you know? I didn't think you Stanford people were that friendly with your Mayfield neighbors."

"Mr. Behn saved my life." Leslie was very serious.

"Saved your life. My goodness. What happened?"

Leslie hesitated. It was not a story of which he was proud. "Like a fool, I decided to pick up the mail the day after we arrived, and walked from Escondite Cottage and back in the scorching heat. I got sunstroke so badly I must have become delirious and lost my way and ended up in Mr. Behn's saloon. He recognized my plight and brought me back to Escondite. If it weren't for him, who knows where I might have ended up."

Fletcher said, "My story is not as dramatic. Fred gave me a hot breakfast and hot water and soap so I could get rid of the dog piss smell. And when I told him I needed a place for room and board, he took me out to Adelante Villa so I could get settled there and ..."—here Fletcher's voice changed ever so slightly—"and meet Miss Irene Butler."

Leslie said, "Well, I think both you and I owe Mr. Behn a visit one of these days."

"Yes, we do. I'll see if I can borrow the girl's rig and we'll go and see him. I know he'd like that. I've seen him a few times since. I get my hair cut by a barber across the street from his place. Fred always talks about how he'd like to get friendly with the university people, and I'm sure he'd like to talk to you."

There was a brief pause in the conversation, and it dawned on Leslie that with all this talk about Mr. Behn, he had almost forgotten the purpose of getting together with Fletcher.

It was as if Fletcher could read his thoughts. He said, "Dr. Elliott, if it's about the military training, I understand. I'm not the right one to help Captain Harkins. He must have found out about my general discharge and doesn't think I cut the mustard."

Leslie didn't know what to say, so he kept quiet.

Fletcher continued, "I don't know what I was thinking when I told Dr. Jordan I'd help Captain Harkins. I love my country and I'd do anything to protect it, but I'm not the one to tell young men the U. S. Army is good because sometimes it is, but mostly it isn't."

Leslie said, "Dr. Jordan wanted me to tell you that we think whatever you did must have been honorable, no matter what the Army or Captain Harkins think."

Fletcher thought and said, "That's kind of both of you. Would you like to know what happened?"

"If you want to tell me. But I want to make certain you know I'll pass on to Dr. Jordan what you say, but no one else."

Fletcher said, "I'm not ashamed of what I did. Irene knows and she said she'd have done the same thing, if she had been in my shoes. Yes, I'd like to tell you. And it's fine with me if you want to pass on what I say to Dr. Jordan. It'll take a little time. I don't want to leave out anything."

"Take as much time as you need." Leslie settled back on the bench.

The story Fletcher Martin told him went like this: "It was back about a year ago, December twenty-ninth, 1890, to be exact. The night before, at a briefing of officers of the Seventh Calvary, I'd been told by my commanding officer, Colonel Forsythe, that the next day's operation was a routine disarming and relocation of Chief Big Foot's Sioux tribe. The Indian Braves would peacefully turn over their weapons, and we'd accompany them to the Pine Ridge Indian Agency so they could be relocated to more distant parts of the Dakota Territories.

"I'd served in the Seventh Calvary since my graduation from West Point in 1880 and missed by four years being under the command of General George A. Custer. From what I'd heard, I wouldn't have enjoyed it. Custer's troops killed too many Indian women and children for my liking.

"That December morning was bitter cold, and snow from a previous storm was still on the ground. All of my men were dressed in their winter overcoats. Our breaths hung in the wintry air. We stood next to four fresh-from-the-factory Hotchkiss machine guns, capable of shooting two-pound explosive shells at the rate of fifty rounds per minute. The guns were trained on an Indian village about a hundred yards south of Chief Big Foot's tent.

"The Indians pitched their teepees in the open plain next to Wounded Knee Creek. In the center of their village was a tall pole flying a white flag. Colonel Forsythe and his staff were gathered in front of Big Foot's tent. Inside, the chief was sick with pneumonia. The braves were still in their village, inside teepees with their families. Indian scouts were stationed south of the village. Army sentinels were posted around the entire area, backed up by another troop of mounted cavalry. More than five hundred soldiers surrounded a gathering of two hundred and fifty Indian men, women, and children.

"Shortly after eight o'clock, I heard Colonel Forsyth's adjutant, Major Whiteside, shouting to the warriors to come out of their teepees. About a hundred braves appeared and slowly lowered themselves to sit on the ground in front of their chief's tent. To keep warm, they covered themselves with blankets, but I thought the way they placed the blankets over their laps looked mighty suspicious.

"No weapons were visible, so Major Whiteside ordered the Indians back to their teepees to get them. About twenty braves disappeared, and after what seemed to be hours but were more like twenty or thirty minutes, they came back with two ancient rifles. They didn't trust us any more than we trusted them.

"All this made Major Whiteside lose his patience. He ordered his sergeant to take forty men and find the weapons that had to be inside the teepees. He ordered the remaining troops to draw their weapons and approach the seated braves. Slowly the surrounding troops closed in on the squatting Indians, until they were only ten yards away. The braves sat like clay ducks in a shooting gallery.

"Captain Bourke, my commander, whispered that my men and I should be ready with the Hotchkiss machine guns.

"'Yes, sir,' was my reluctant answer.

"I started hearing strange, shrill noises. The commotion was being made by the Sioux medicine man blowing on his eagle-bone whistle and making all kinds of taunting motions with his arms, which made the braves even more tense and uneasy.

"In the village, I saw soldiers entering teepees and driving out women with children in their arms, followed by old squaws and their men. Some of the old people could barely move. The women emerged screaming and shouting for help from their braves.

"As the soldiers returned with the guns they had found, one of them couldn't resist the temptation to raise a warrior's blanket to see what was underneath. Instantaneously, the medicine man kneeled, grabbed a handful of dirt, and threw it up into the air, and at the same time gave a blood-curdling scream that caused my heart to skip a beat.

"The braves drew their hidden weapons and fired at the surrounding troops. The standing soldiers, with their rifles already cocked and loaded, replied with a volley fired directly at the warriors crowded together, some still seated. I watched as the medicine man's face became a mass of bloodied and exposed bone, veins, and tissue. The soldiers were so close their first volley instantly killed almost half of the braves. Survivors sprang to their feet and tried to overcome the soldiers, hand-to-hand, but the Indians were outnumbered and hacked to pieces by bullets, knives, or axes. Within minutes, none of the Indians appeared to be alive. I had never seen a massacre before, but this had all the makings of one, and I wanted no part of it.

"My captain ordered me to commence firing the machine guns aimed at the village. I refused. He shouted at me, and I refused again. He called me a coward; I didn't say a word. He drew his pistol and aimed it at my heart. I'm sure he'd have shot me right then and there if Sergeant Miller hadn't interfered and told him they had to reposition the guns, otherwise the remaining Indians might escape. My captain put his pistol away and turned around, and I was put under arrest.

"They sent me to the prison at Fort Collins, and I waited to be court-martialed. I could have been shot for disobeying an order, but because of the presence of reporters from the Eastern press at the Fort, and because of the public's reaction to the massacre, a panel of officers was quickly convened. They offered me a general discharge and an immediate release from prison. Without hesitation, I accepted and was freed.

"That's my story, Dr. Elliott."

Leslie knew he should say something. Fletcher's bravery was awe-inspiring. "I'd like to think I might have done the same as you, but I'm not sure. You're a brave man; most of us are not."

There was nothing more to be said. Fletcher was deep in thought, as if in his mind's eye, he were seeing the mayhem again.

Leslie got up from the bench. "I have to get back to work. Thank you, Fletcher, for telling me your story. I'll tell Dr. Jordan what you said."

Fletcher looked startled for a second as he faced the reality that he was sitting under an oak tree and Leslie was standing in front of him. He said, "Thank you, Dr. Elliott, for listening."

When Leslie turned toward the Quad, he looked back. Fletcher was still sitting there, with his long legs stretched out, staring at the open field.

CHAPTER 8

▼

"NO MANSIONS ON NOB HILL"

Tuesday, September 15, 1891

There they stood, the bright sun of a mid-September day pouring down on them: ten new, bare cottages built for members of the faculty and their families. The cottages were behind Encina Hall, on Alvarado Row.

The homes were almost completed, and Ellen Elliott had selected the tenth cottage, the one farthest from the campus. And, of course, Harriet Marx, her bosom friend, selected the one next to hers. The women thought they might have something to say about the tints of the cottages' inner walls, so they asked Professor David Marx, Harriet's husband, to drive them over in his rig to see if they could persuade the tinter to do their bidding. Dr. Marx, like others, preferred his middle name to his given name, Charles.

When she first saw the cottages being built, Ellen described them in letters to her Cornell friends as "a ragged little string of skeletons." Her honest words moved like lightning from Ithaca back to Stanford, and must have been quoted to the Stanfords because Dr. Jordan told Leslie they did not appreciate her honesty. He suggested that, in the future, Leslie might ask Ellen to keep some of her inner thoughts to herself.

Leslie shook his head. "There is no way in the world I would say that to her," was his reply. From the look on Dr. Jordan's face, Leslie could tell he was not happy with this response.

Still, compared with living in a small bedroom at Cedro Cottage along with Professor Richardson and his family, and then moving to a room above an unoccupied store in Menlo where the mosquitoes literally ate them up, all the time taking their meals at a sordid hotel, the accommodations at Alvarado Row were glorious

On that sunny day, Harriet Marx was wearing a colorful green cotton wrapper, and Ellen a yellow one that was cool in the summer heat. They both wore perky hats with assorted artificial flowers and carried matching parasols for protection from the midday sun. Compared with the dull colors of the workmen's coveralls and Dr. Marx's dark suit and bowler, they sparkled in their Indian summer attire.

Under her arm, Ellen carried a yellow tablet with each room sketched out, and their different and harmonizing tints. The interior walls were tinted plaster, not papered, as they had been in Ithaca. Ellen and Harriet thought their schemes would give their homes some sense of individuality.

Inside Number 10, Ellen found the tinter about to begin his chores. He was dressed in coveralls, splashed with paint obliterating their original white duck cloth. Judging by his overalls, terra cotta appeared to be the prevalent tint.

As the tinter strode toward his workstation, Ellen stepped in front of him and raised her hand, as if stopping an oncoming steam engine.

"Sir"—as she said the word, her tone raised an octave—"if you don't mind, please hold for a minute so we can discuss the tint you are about to apply to my home's walls."

The tinter did not stop. He acted as if he had a pestering fly circling him. If he ignored the fly, it might go away. Without a word, he circled around the strange little woman, who seemed to him nothing more than an encumbrance, and continued, on his original path.

But if Ellen Elliott was a fly, she was a persistent one. She circled back and placed her four-and-a-half foot figure before him so close he could not budge.

"Sir, sir, I believe you did not hear me." She held her yellow tablet within inches of his nose. "Here is the tint scheme I'd like you to follow and I do believe Mrs. Marx has her own instructions to give to you, as well."

The tinter looked over the hat, festooned with bits of artificial fruit and flowers, and said in a thick, hardly recognizable voice, "Terra cotta, all walls tinted terra cotta." The words were spoken without emotion and without bothering to look down at the woman before him.

Ellen was not to be denied. "What! Can't I have one room different?" she cried out.

"Now these h'ain't no mansions on Nob Hill that we're puttin' up," he retorted. A dam had finally been breached and his face reddened with the beginnings of anger.

Dr. David Marx, who had quietly walked into the house, quickly stepped between the tinter and Ellen. He said, "See here, you! I'll have you understand these are ladies you are talking to." But while he said these courageous words, he was already beginning to shepherd Ellen and his wife out of the cottage and back to his rig. Disconsolate in defeat, they drove back to their temporary dwellings in Menlo.

During the following days, Ellen and Harriet busied themselves with preparations for the grand day when they'd move into their new abodes.

Except for some shipped furniture held in storage in one of Senator Stanford's barns and a few family heirlooms, everything both families had in their previous homes had been sold or left to family members or friends back in Ithaca. Ellen and Harriet had to buy hundreds of articles. The Mayfield and Menlo shops could not help them. Flour and clothespins were all they offered. Leslie was forced to take time off from work so that Ellen might join other faculty wives taking early trains to San Francisco on buying outings. Since time in the city was precious, Ellen compiled detailed lists of her needs—from rugs and ranges to brooms and mop pails.

She found the frugality inherited from Eastern dealings was not compatible to Western ways. A bit, twelve cents, rather than a penny or a dime, was the common denomination of exchange. Clerks only dealt in bits. When she asked for ten cents' worth of oilcloth, an impolite clerk told her she might as well take a bit's worth because that was what she'd be paying.

On Saturday, the twenty-sixth of September, the Elliotts moved into Number 10. The first night they slept on bare parlor floors and looked up at the stars in the heavens because the windows had no curtains. The Marx family moved in the same day. Ellen and Harriet knew, by feminine intuition, the families would need one another. It turned out that while the Elliotts had no blankets but did have mattresses, the Marxes had the reverse. By sharing, both families slept well the first night.

Ellen could look through the bare windows, across the expanse of dead hay separating the two homes, and see the Marxes were blowing out their candles at about the same time as the Elliotts. It was a warm and comforting feeling.

CHAPTER 9

▼

"CHILE? CHILE? WHAT ABOUT CHILE?"

Saturday, September 26, 1891

On that same night, Rubin Weinberg dragged himself and his heavy valise toward the enormous building that loomed in front of him. There it was, "ENCINA HALL" carved in stone above the entrance. As Rubin climbed the ten steps to the porch that encircled the front of the building, he felt as if his short legs were about to give out. His wire eyeglasses fell off the end of his long, thin nose and clattered on top of a concrete step. He grabbed them, and with one hand forced them back on his face. Mounting the porch, for him, was a minor triumph.

He tried the front door and found it locked. Pounding on the door, he shouted, "Is anyone there?" Silence. He did it again. He knew there was someone inside. Silence.

The hall's windows were pitch black. There were no sounds, except Rubin's deep breathing. He could feel his heart beating from the exhaustion of carrying or dragging the heavy valise all the way from Menlo. He decided to sit on the top step and catch his breath. He took off his derby hat and ran his fingers through a mop of thick black hair. He thought how tough a day it had been after the strenuous two thousand mile railway trip from Omaha.

He knew someone was inside because a workman whom he had seen on his way from the Menlo station had asked him where he was going and volunteered that someone was already staying at Encina Hall. Again, Rubin pounded on the door and shouted. Still no reply. He looked back down the steps he had climbed and at the darkness beyond. He did not relish the thought of sleeping on the ground in that darkness, but it was better than sleeping on the porch's cold concrete.

After pounding on Encina's door several more times, Rubin gave up. He picked up his valise and started walking back down the steps. As if someone were watching him, the oak door slowly swung open.

A large, rawboned man with a scruffy red beard, his derby, pulled back on his head, stood there with a small lit candle that looked out of place in his big hands. "Whoa, boy. Where do you think you're going? If you're looking for Encina Hall, this is it. Sorry, I was sleeping and might not have heard you." He opened the door wide, and Rubin hustled back up the stairs and inside, dragging his valise with him. In the candlelight, he could barely made out the outline of a large reception hall.

The men introduced themselves and shook with their free hands.

He was William Greer, a transfer student from Boston and MIT. "I arrived the day before and spent last night here. I must tell you, it's weird when you're alone. I do appreciate your company. All through the night, I kept hearing timbers creaking and sounds like footsteps. The workmen told me four men were killed here when a scaffold fell. I kept thinking it might be their ghosts."

That news did not hearten Rubin. Suddenly shadows became sinister, and he made sure to stay close to his new friend. They continued down a darkened hallway, with William Greer leading the way.

As they walked, William said, "I found this Encina place not nearly ready for occupancy, but there was no other place to stay. A friendly worker let me in. I don't think he was supposed to. There's no bedding and the kitchen's not half finished. I hear the generator that's supposed to provide the whole campus with light is still in a boxcar, waiting to be unloaded."

Rubin asked, "But you stayed here last night?"

William responded, "Yes, I did, but barely. But I guess if I did, you can, too."

William guided Rubin to a room next to what must have been his. In the candlelight, Rubin could see metal cots with rolled up mattresses, some chairs, a table, and a commode.

William looked into the room and said, "I do have an advantage over you. There's no bedding or blankets, but I brought a bedroll with me, so with that on top of the mattress, it makes a fairly decent bed."

Rubin looked bedraggled. It had been a long, hard day, and he needed to sleep. Sleeping on a bare mattress was not what he was looking forward to, but it was better than sleeping outside under a bush. .

William could see Rubin was at the end of his tether. "Here, tell you what you might do," he said, and went out of the room, leaving Rubin alone in the pitch-black darkness. He came back with a trunk rope in his hands. He gave his candle to Rubin, took the mattress from the other bed in the room, and flung it on the nearest cot.

"We can tie these two mattresses together, and you can crawl in between. I learned to do this when my roommate hid my blankets."

William encircled both mattresses with the rope and made a tight knot. Rubin could see he had at least some elements of a place to sleep.

After he'd finished his task, William said, "You keep the candle. I'm used to the dark." He pointed to his left. "Down the hall there's a lavatory with running water. Not hot, but at least you can take a piss, or whatever you want to do. Tomorrow morning, we'll go into Mayfield for eats. I'll say good night to you, Rubin, sleep well." He gave Rubin a hefty pat on the back, tipped his derby with his index finger, and walked out the door into the hallway. Rubin could hear the door to the room next to his open and close.

Candle in hand, Rubin made his way down the wide corridor to the swinging double doors behind which he knew would find the urinals. Inside he could see gleaming, white floor tiles and eight porcelain urinals on the wall to his left and eight porcelain washbasins to his right. At the back were narrow closed stalls, which he knew must contain the water closets. Since he had hardly eaten anything, he was not concerned with that. He could wait until the next morning. He unbuttoned his pants, pulled out his penis, and made a vigorous stream onto the white porcelain surface. Above the sound of rushing water, he said, "I'm the first Jew that's pissed here. May I not be the last!" His words resonated from the surrounding tiles.

Next morning at about eight o'clock, Rubin Weinberg and William Greer emerged from Encina's lobby to find two young men anxiously waiting for the front door to open.

Sleeping between two tied-together mattresses, Rubin had been warm enough but not comfortable, and the constant chorus of dogs howling somewhere in the distance had not helped matters. When he complained to William about the howling, William explained it wasn't dogs, but packs of coyotes descending from the foothills. Rubin could only think how different California was from Omaha.

The two young men waiting introduced themselves as Bert Hoover and Fred Williams. Fred did most of the talking, while the other fellow—the tall, gangling one—was pushing their luggage toward the open door.

William asked them, "Where're you from?" That question always seemed to be at the beginning of every conversation, Rubin thought.

Fred answered, "We're from Oregon. We got here about two months ago. Bert and me passed the examinations, but Dr. Swain said we needed to brush up on our English and mathematics. We've been boarding at Adelante Villa, up in the hills, that'a way." And he vaguely pointed in a westerly direction.

William turned and spoke to Bert, the other young man. "Hold on there, Bert. I'm afraid I can't let you in until Mr. Fesler and Mr. Lathrop arrive. Rubin and I weren't supposed to be here last night, and I can imagine what they would think if they found out I'd let you two in. All hell would break loose. They should be here soon, and if you want to join us for eats in Mayfield, we'll be back in an hour or so."

Bert reluctantly pulled their luggage back to the porch and shook his head. "No thanks. Fred and me ate at the Villa before we left. Miss Butler gave us a big going away breakfast."

Fred's face wrinkled up as if he were going to cry. Bert said, "It's all right, Fred. We won't have to wait too long." Rubin could see from the expression on Bert's face he was getting tired of consoling his friend.

Fred, between semi-suppressed sobs, whined, "I told you there was no hurry to get over here, but you insisted we be first in line. As if that matters."

As he was going down the steps, William looked back and said, "Well, suit yourselves." He motioned for Rubin to follow him.

Fifteen minutes later, William and Rubin were on their way, walking the mile and a half to Mayfield. William decided this was a good time to get to know his companion. He forgot Rubin would have a difficult time keeping up with him because William's legs were longer.

William said, "I'm from Massachusetts. Went to MIT for two years and hated every minute of it. My father's a civil engineer and he wanted me to be one, too, since I am the only son. Join his firm and all that. But I love to write and I want to be a poet or writer, one or the other. I'm not sure which. I wanted to change my major at MIT, but they don't grant degrees in English. My father was upset, but he went along with my idea. We worked it out for me to drop out of MIT, come West, and go to Leland Stanford Junior University."

The two continued to walk in silence. Rubin knew he was expected to respond with similar information about himself, but he was breathless from trying to keep up.

When William realized Rubin wasn't about to trade information, he blurted out, "I hope you don't mind me asking this …"

Rubin already knew what was coming. Many others had said the same thing.

"You're a Jew, aren't you? Excuse me for being so forward, but I've never really talked to a Jew and I'm really surprised to see you here."

Rubin appreciated William's honesty. Between breaths, he managed, "Yes, I'm a Jew—and as for being here, I'm as surprised as you are."

William said,. "You know, I never saw Jews at MIT, and from what I hear, I don't think there are any at Harvard or Yale or Princeton or any college I know of."

Rubin was getting his second wind and was able to say, "There probably are, but you couldn't tell because they didn't have Jewish-sounding surnames or look Jewish, like I do. They've passed."

William stroked his stubby red beard. "I know you're right. But you certainly couldn't pass, could you? So what makes you so different?"

Yes, Rubin thought, you are forward, William. But he said, "Well, I guess it helps if your uncle is very rich and he contributes lots of money to Senator Stanford's campaign to become president."

"President? I didn't know Senator Stanford was even thinking about it. I thought President Harrison was a shoo-in for another term or possibly Blaine, but never Stanford."

Rubin explained, "President Harrison is not liked by some influential Republicans, including my uncle. They think he dithers too much. They preferred Blaine, but now with the aggressive way Blaine is handling Chile and his health problems, they're not so sure. Everyone seems to like Stanford, and establishing this no-tuition university certainly helped raise his stature."

"Chile? What about Chile?" William asked.

Rubin looked over at him, slightly incredulous, as if he thought William were a hermit sleeping in a cave. "Don't your read the Boston papers? I'm sure they're full of it."

William shook his head. "No."

Rubin tried again. "*The Atlantic Monthly?*"

Another shake. "No."

Rubin decided to be blunt, as well. "I can see there's much in this world you're not aware of. There's been a problem with American sailors in Valparaiso, and

Chile sees no reason it should bow down to American dominion, particularly with Germany's support. But all this takes some explaining, and I should tell you back in Omaha I have a terrible reputation for being a progressive or worse—an anarchist or some other type of renegade—so my point of view is far from conservative."

William looked over at Rubin with a new look of admiration in his eyes. "That's all right with me, Rubin. I like seeing things shaken up every now and then. Thunder, you're right. I've had my nose in those blasted engineering books so long I don't know what's going on in the world."

He stopped talking, and his brow furrowed. Rubin thought it looked as if he were doing some deep thinking, so he kept quiet. Finally William said, "I was hoping to find someone like you—someone who knew what was going on and could bring me up to date. How can I be a writer if I'm so stupid about such matters? I know you don't know me very well, but I think you and I can get along. You don't have to say right now, if you don't want to, but how about you and I being roommates?"

Rubin was surprised. It was almost as if William were proposing to him. He had thought it would be difficult to make new friends at Stanford, and here he already had someone who wanted to be his roommate. William was not brilliant, but he was a likeable enough chap, and certainly it didn't hurt to have a roommate who was a bit of a brute and rough around the edges. Life was indeed strange. Rubin smiled as he said; "I don't see anyone waiting in line for the privilege of sharing a room with me. In fact, I can think of a few who would absolutely refuse to be near me. I'd be happy to be your roommate."

William abruptly stopped walking, causing Rubin to pull up at his side. He turned, stuck out his right hand, and with a serious expression on his face said, "So let's shake on it."

They shook hands—as far as Rubin was concerned, for far too long. His hand began to ache from the pressure on his fingers.

As they shook, William said, "We're roomies."

Rubin thought William was making a little too much out of all this. He had never liked the term "roomies," but he still repeated it and said, "Yes, we're roomies," and put a grin on his face.

Later, William said, "I was a Sigma Chi at MIT, but I know you won't be in a fraternity. You'll be a barbarian."

Rubin had never heard the term. "A barbarian. What a terrible word. I assume it means someone who does not join a fraternity, but what a thing to say about a person."

William looked like he agreed with him. "I have no idea who made up the word, but that is what they call people like you."

Rubin had nothing more to say, so the two of them continued in silence as they continued walking on the county road, turning east toward Mayfield.

They found the village to be deserted. They looked on both sides of the road for some kind of sign that food was being served. There were plenty of saloons, but only one appeared to be open at that hour on a Saturday morning.

A gentleman with a peg leg was standing on the boardwalk. He shouted to them, "Hey, you young men, looking for a place to eat? We've got hot coffee, fresh eggs, and fresh-baked bread. How does that sound to you?"

William spoke for both of them. "Sounds good. How much?"

"Two bits a piece should do it."

William and Rubin walked up the steps and followed the pegged leg fellow through swinging doors into a saloon. It was the first time Rubin had ever been in such a disreputable place, but the food turned out to be good and hot, even though he found two maggots in the marmalade. The pegged leg fellow laughed when Rubin showed them to him. He said he wouldn't charge them extra for the meat. William laughed, but Rubin didn't think it was funny.

A half hour later and Rubin and William were back at Encina Hall. Bert and Fred were no longer on the porch, and the scene in front of the hall had vastly changed from what it was two hours before. At least a dozen carts, wagons, and gigs—filled with all kinds of furniture, lamps, and pictures—were tied up to hitching posts. From what Rubin could see, some fellows were planning to make their rooms comfortable, very comfortable indeed. He saw framed pictures, plush chairs, and footstools; a mounted moose head, complete with widespread antlers, was tied to the top of one load of furniture.

Without hesitating, William strode right up the stairs and tried to push his way through into the lobby. "After all," he insisted, "we were here earlier."

But the fellows by the door would have none of it and playfully but purposely pushed him back. Rubin waited at the bottom of the stairs. He saw William was about to lose his temper. But seeing he was outnumbered, William wisely retreated to the end of the line, joining Rubin.

Another gig drove up, and after hitching up their horse; three more young men joined the line. From what they said Rubin deduced they were members of a fraternity at the College of Pacific in San Jose and were transferring to LSJU. Two of them called each other nicknames fittingly derived from their appearance: Freck for the freckled one; every inch of his exposed flesh was dotted with multitudes of freckles. Pudge was for the fat fellow; his round, full face sat on top of a ballooned body that appeared as if it might take off in a stiff breeze. The third one, Winko, looked and acted as if he were in charge. Rubin reasoned Winko must be the president of the frat. While they were waiting, William struck up a conversation with them.

In answer to his question about why they were transferring, Freck responded, "We had a big explosion in the Chemistry Department."

Pudge added, "And one poor chap was blown to smithereens."

Winko put that right. "Well, not to little pieces, but pretty well put out of commission. I think he lost a leg and an arm. Unfortunately, COP is not doing well—running out of endowment money and that sort of thing. I guess they skimped on equipment for the chem fellows. Hell of an explosion: damage, attorneys, lawsuits. Most of our fraternity decided to transfer to LSJU, along with a good portion of the faculty and the rest of the students. I think COP will close its doors because of this."

"We're going to transfer the fraternity here. Aren't we, Winko?" Pudge asked.

Rubin noticed all of the conversation was between the three of them and William. Rubin stayed in the background and did not join in, and none of the three new arrivals attempted to have him participate. For them, he was invisible.

Winko answered Pudge's question. "It looks like it. Jordan is a frat man himself. And he's all for the rite of passage thing." Looking at William, he said, "You look like a stalwart sort of chap—our sort of person. Any interest in becoming an Alpha Phi?"

William said, "No thanks. I'm Sigma Chi. Joined at MIT and I'm thinking of starting a new chapter here once I get permission from chapter headquarters." He looked over at Rubin, and was about to say something else, when he saw Rubin slightly shake his head. Whatever words William was about to say, he swallowed.

Winko continued talking to William. "Well, good luck with Sigma Chi. Wonderful song, that sweetheart thing. Wish it were ours."

Once William declared himself a Sigma Chi, Rubin noticed the College of Pacific fellows lost interest in continuing their conversation with him. A sizeable gap in the queue developed between them and William and Rubin as the line slowly moved ahead, up the stairs, and into the lobby. When new arrivals joined them, Rubin could hear the three fraternity men retelling their College of Pacific explosion story, and the new additions were questioned about their interest in joining a fraternity. One fellow was sincerely interested and acted as if he were pleased with the opportunity. Rubin knew he would not be approached.

Finally, after at least an hour waiting, Rubin and William ascended to the porch and reentered Encina's lobby. Rubin had only glanced at the lobby when he passed through that morning. Daylight gave him an opportunity to see it was about forty feet wide and forty feet deep, with massive, brick fireplaces at both ends and four large columns supporting the expansive roof. It reminded Rubin of the Broadview Hotel's lobby in Omaha, which he had visited a few times with his uncle's family for religious gatherings. The furnishings weren't all that plush—wooden chairs and tables looked out of place with such elegant surroundings. It looked to Rubin as if someone had run out of money before buying the furnishings. The room was paneled in dark wood and the ceiling must have been at least fifteen feet high, with six gilded chandeliers supporting electric light bulbs, as well as porcelain candleholders—in case the electricity didn't work, Rubin guessed. The oak floors were bright and shiny from coats of lacquer. A single red carpet ran up the middle of the room to a half step and a short landing, and then more steps to another landing and double doors to what must be the dining room. On both sides of the entrance were oak staircases to the next floors.

Once inside the doorway, the line of waiting took a wandering path, diagonally across the lobby, to the right corner where there was an enclosed office with sliding glass windows. Inside the office, Rubin could see, two gentlemen. The younger man was at the counter, taking money and giving instructions. He was probably Mr. Fesler, master of Encina Hall. William had told Rubin he knew Fesler slightly from back East. Behind him, seated at a small desk, was an older fellow, with his back to the entrance. He must be Mr. Ariel Lathrop, Mrs. Stanford's brother and LSJU's business manager. Rubin couldn't see much of the older man except the back of his thick, hairy neck and large head, topped with black, thinning hair.

When Rubin and William got to the counter, Mr. Fesler asked for their names. As he did this, Mr. Fesler took a long look at William as if he recognized him. Immediately after Mr. Lathrop heard the two young men say "Rubin Weinberg and William Greer," he slowly turned around and faced them. Rubin's first thought was that time and drink had not been kind to Mr. Lathrop. His skin was mottled and lined with blue veins, particularly in the area of his bulbous red nose, which looked as if it were pulsating like a red beacon. Wild eyebrows grew above eyes like burnt coals. His mouth sneered as he repeated the names he had just heard—this time with obvious distaste, as if the names themselves tasted bad. But what grabbed Rubin's attention was a painfully inflamed carbuncle in the middle of Mr. Lathrop's forehead. It hurt Rubin just to look at it.

Mr. Lathrop said, "So you're the two scalawags who wormed their way into the hall last night against my sister's wishes because kerosene lamps could burn down her million dollar hotel for you roustabouts in minutes." Getting angrier by the minute, he looked directly at Rubin. "What are you looking at?"

"Nothing, sir," was Rubin's meek reply. With difficulty, he averted his eyes from the carbuncle to the floor.

Mr. Fesler's greeting was decidedly less threatening. "Good morning, Will. Good to see you again. Best wishes to your lovely mother and sister."

William's eyes lit up. "And you, too, Bertie. I thought you might be Mr. Fesler, but I wasn't sure."

Mr. Lathrop was chagrined. "So you two know each other?"

Mr. Fesler turned to him. "Yes, from Boston. We both attended the same prep school."

Mr. Lathrop turned back to face William. "So, you're lucky, Mr. Greer, very lucky. I was thinking of giving you both marching orders straight out of this hall and out of our university. Now, since you two have grown so fond of one another, we'll make you roommates. What do you think of that, Mr. Greer?"

William feigned the distaste on his face he knew Mr. Lathrop wanted to see.

Knowing his superior's changeability, Mr. Fesler rushed to get the two of them out of Mr. Lathrop's sight. "We'll need the eighteen dollars from each of you, and I'll get the keys and bedding. You can have the room you slept in last night."

They had the money ready, and the transaction went quickly. Before they left, Mr. Lathrop turned around again and gave them another volley of snide remarks, "Either Mr. Lathrop or I will be here at the end of each month, and if you don't have the money, you'll be out on your ear that very day. *Particular you two.*" The last three words were shouted so loudly that the two boys next in line jerked to attention.

But Mr. Lathrop had more to say. "And, Mr. Greer, no matter how much you complain about your new roommate's slovenly habits, you're stuck with him. There will be no switching of roommates. Understand?"

Both William and Rubin nodded their heads in silence and complete obedience.

As fast as they could, they scurried out of the curmudgeon's sight. The minute they were behind the swinging doors leading to the corridor where their room was located, they cuffed each other like playful puppies and chuckled heartily at how they had hoodwinked their newfound nemesis.

CHAPTER 10

▼

"THEY'RE ALMOST HERE."

Sunday, September 27, 1891

William Greer had heard they were taking on student janitors to tidy up the rooms, and when he approached Mr. Fesler for the job, he was quickly taken on. The pay was four dollars for twenty hours of work per week. When William nodded toward his roommate as another possibility, Mr. Fesler shook his head, emphatically. The cursed discrimination Rubin had feared was very much alive and thriving.

Over the next two days, before the university formally opened its doors, Rubin felt more and more threatened by the influx of young men moving into and roaming Encina's halls. When William was present there was no worry, but he was now busy most of the day with his janitorial duties. Without his protection in the stairwell or the darkened portions of the halls, Rubin was pushed, pestered, punched, or bumped from all sides by unknown, uncivilized youth who had discovered there was a Jew amongst them.

Rubin was heartened that his cousin, Delores Payson, who would also be attending LSJU, would not get the same treatment. Her Jewish father was Rubin's uncle, but her mother was Spanish and California born, so Delores had been raised on a huge hacienda on the outskirts of Los Angeles and educated in Catholic schools. Because of her background and beautiful, dark Spanish features, she hobnobbed with California's upper society. Rubin's mother had told him to acknowledge Delores only as a friend of the family and never as a blood relative. He was told Delores had high hopes of becoming a member of a sorority, and any careless word from him might spoil her chances. Rubin understood

Delores' concerns and agreed to go along with the subterfuge. If he'd had the same opportunities, he would have done the same. His Jewishness was like a target on his back; there was nothing he could do about it.

Monday, September twenty-eighth, was the first day Encina's dining room would be open. Rubin had hopes of seeing his cousin because William had told him the young ladies from Roble Hall had to walk over each day for their meals. Delores should be one of them. Rubin had no idea what her reaction might be when she saw him. Of all his cousins, Delores was his favorite, but for all he knew she might pretend not to know him.

Monday morning arrived, and William had to be up at six o'clock so he could assemble with all the other student janitors in the middle of the Quad at seven. Mr. Lathrop wanted them to start cleaning up and preparing for the multitudes of visitors expected to be attending the opening ceremonies on Thursday morning. Rubin slept soundly and did not hear William get up and get dressed. Eventually he was awakened by all the commotion outside his room in the hallways. He jumped out of bed. It was almost six thirty. Quickly he dressed and did his ablutions.

Not until he tried to squeeze his way down the stairway to get to the landing overlooking the dining room did he realize he was not the only one anxious to see the Roble ladies on their maiden visit.

Over one hundred young men—some with beards and mustaches; others with innocent, beardless faces; most of them wearing derbies—were crowded on both sides of the entrance to the dining room. It was as if they were waiting for a circus parade to pass by.

Someone shouted, "We can see them. They're almost here." Top floor sentinels must have sighted the procession of young ladies, about to make their appearance.

By now, Rubin was up front, standing against the landing's railing and balusters on the right side, overlooking the dining hall entrance. The landing was about ten feet above ground level. Looking around at his fellow viewers, Rubin saw Freck, the deeply freckled fellow from the College of Pacific fraternity. He was busy talking to a tall, curly haired young man Rubin had not seen before. Freck must have been making some kind remark that his companion did not like because he appeared to be embarrassed by whatever Freck had said.

For no apparent reason, everyone in the lobby became deathly quiet, as if some silent signal had alerted them. What they were waiting for was about to happen. The entrance's double doors were flung open, and the initial reaction was one not of excitement, but of being let down. In waltzed a matronly woman dressed in what had to be her finest costume, complete with feathered hat. The woman was probably Roble's mistress, Rubin thought. She strode through the mass of males without batting an eyelash—piercing eyes straight ahead, thin arms beating a steady cadence at her side as if she were pounding a drum. Closely following her were the hoped-for young ladies, coupled, holding hands as if they were bridesmaids. Rubin was not impressed. They were all too blonde or too bookish looking for him. Delores, his cousin, was nowhere to be seen.

As the ladies entered, Rubin felt young bodies pressing against his back for a better view. He could smell their sweat and breaths. Turning his head to see who was directly behind him, he saw the face of Freck's friend. The fellow said, "I'm sorry, there's nothing I can do about this." He held his hands straight up in the air to show how powerless he was to stop the forward surge. Rubin tried to push back, but he did not have the strength to do any good. He was forced to press up against the railing and he could hear the oak wood creaking with the stress.

Worse, he was not alone. Beside him was another young gentlemen who was trying to keep from being pushed, and he looked as if he were starting to get frightened. Rubin understood why when he glanced down at the fellow's legs: both of them were wooden. My God, Rubin thought, he's got wooden legs. The side of the young man's head was inches from Rubin's. Rubin turned and whispered to him. "I'll try to keep them from pushing you."

His whisper caused the wooden-legged fellow to turn toward him. He was a handsome fellow, very young, clean-cut. He said, "I don't know what to do." Looking down at the floor ten feet below, he said, "If I fall, it'll be disastrous."

The curly headed fellow must have picked up on the conversation because he said to Rubin, "I'm David. Let's see if you and I can keep the pressure off our wooden friend." Suddenly Rubin found his new found acquaintance beside him with his arm thrown over Rubin's shoulder as if they were rugby players in a scrum, now facing away from the railing toward the oncoming surge. David assumed a crouching position and Rubin followed suit. With arms locked, heads down, and shoulders solidly placed against the ones who were shoving, David called out, "One, two, three, push. One, two, three, push."

It was nip and tuck for a while; a sort of reverse tug of war was taking place. Others at the railing, also in jeopardy, joined Rubin and David, shoulder to shoulder, in a crouching position. Slowly the mob behind them was pushed back and some breathing space was created.

Rubin realized that members of Freck's fraternity were their adversaries. Freck, Pudge, and Winko, and the likes of them—including a muscular fellow with close-cut, blond hair—seemed to be urging them on. At first Rubin thought he might be imagining the conspiracy, but out of the corner of his eye he could see the blond fellow looking directly at him, as if he were the main target they wanted to shove off the edge, and the other chaps happened to be in the way.

While all this pushing and shoving was going on, most of the young ladies made their way into the dining room. Someone—it sounded like Winko—shouted, "Enough, enough, Sam, we're going to miss all the ladies. I hear there's a real beauty coming up."

As quickly as the surge began, it slacked off. Both sides of the skirmish forgot about the contest and together gawked at the passing parade.

It was as if nothing had ever happened, Rubin thought. But he caught the blond fellow still watching him. Could this be Sam? Yes, there was no doubt about it: there was malevolence in his eyes. Rubin was right, and not paranoid. All of this activity was directed at him. Someone, probably Sam, had decided to force him off the platform and do him bodily harm. Without William's protection, he was in danger.

Rubin's thoughts about his personal plight were interrupted when Delores, his cousin, glided through the front door into the lobby. Another young lady Rubin recognized, Betsy, Delores' friend from Southern California, preceded her. Delores looked as beautiful as ever. Her dark hair fell in waves below her shoulders and her Spanish features were in sharp contrast with those of the other Anglo-Saxon ladies. Rubin looked down on his cousin as she made her way across the lobby. He was tempted to shout out her name, but knew this was exactly what he had been told not to do. All he could do was hope she might glance up at him and at least acknowledge his presence. No such luck. Her head was down and she was concentrating on every step she took, trying to blank out all the smiles, grins, and sheepish looks of her watching audience.

When it was her turn to go up the steps to the dining room, Rubin could see she was trembling, but she grabbed her skirts with both hands and started to make her way toward the dining room doors. Unfortunately, she was not prepared for an immediate, single pesky step that led up to a short landing, and five more steps to the main landing and the doors. She caught her heel on the pesky step and fell mightily to her knees. For just a moment, she was on all fours. A sound of concerned "oh's and ah's," and a few evil laughs emanated from the viewing throng, as she righted herself with one hand, arose in as ladylike a fashion as she could, and without glancing to either side, continued toward the opened doors, her face flushed. Once she was safely inside, a cheer went up. Rubin was one of the cheerers. He could imagine how embarrassed his cousin must be.

But the parade was not over. The next young lady quickly made everyone, including Rubin, forget Delores' mishap. She had straight white-blonde hair to her shoulders, and was wearing a simple blue gingham dress. As if she were entering a library, she carefully closed the door behind her. She must be the last one in the procession, Rubin thought.

Instead of ignoring the viewers, she not only acknowledged them, she encouraged them with both hands, waving to the crowd and flashing winning smiles to every side of the room. She was pretty, not beautiful. Her blonde hair fell back, showing pert little ears. She was taller than the others, with broader shoulders and hips, but the narrowest of waists, which served to accentuate her most observable attributes: prominent breasts that protruded seductively, even in the modest blue dress she was wearing.

At first, the throng of young men was struck dumfounded by what they were seeing. As the realization slowly sank in that this was a woman, a real woman— not like anyone they had ever seen before or were likely to see again—a spontaneous roar arose, like a tidal wave. The sound became deafening as the young lady made her way gracefully past the pesky step and up the stairs, as if she were savoring the moment as much as her viewers. But it did not end there. As she went through the doors, she turned around and gave one final all-encompassing wave of both hands, and a beautiful smile everyone in the lobby felt surely was only for him.

When she disappeared into the dining room, pandemonium ensued: heavy boots stomping on the new wooden floors, shouting, screaming, and general mayhem as if it were an assembly of wild men from Borneo. Mr. Fesler, who was in his office at the time, came out, with arms and hands waving, to quiet the unruly mob.

Rubin and his new friends were still in jeopardy. The landing where they were standing had windows facing into the dining area, where the ladies could be seen seated at four narrow dining room tables, eating their cold porridge. Most of the young gentlemen in the lobby decided they wanted another view of "Dollie," as they had already dubbed her, and were scrambling up the stairs, vying to be the ones pressing their noses at the windowpane. Rubin thought they looked and acted like animals in a zoo.

When he saw this happening, Rubin shouted out, "We've got to get out of here." And without further comment, he and David got on either side of the young man with wooden legs and pulled him up by his elbows. Like three drunken sailors, they teetered up the stairwell to the next floor and safety.

It was like a different world. The floor was deserted, except for them. At last the fellow with wooden legs had an opportunity to introduce himself. "My name is George Gardiner," he said. "And I'm from San Diego, and I'm sure you're wondering how I got like this." He looked down at the wooden legs supporting him. "I had to have my legs amputated when I was seven years old because of diabetes. So by now I've learned how to deal with my handicap. My room is in the corner on the bottom floor. And I'd like to invite you to come there now with me, while we wait for the young ladies to clear out."

The tall, curly haired fellow was David Cooper, and Rubin introduced himself.

Rubin and David cheerfully accepted George's invitation to go to his room and walked with him across the second floor to the staircase on the west side of the hall, and from there, down to George's room. George's supported gait with his two canes was just right for someone, such as Rubin, with short legs. David, who was much taller, appeared to be slowed down a bit, but he didn't appear to mind tarrying for the others. Rubin immediately decided he must be an easy going fellow.

On the way, Rubin and David decided to go together with George to breakfast and then to the temporary chapel in the Quad's southwest corner, where Dr. Jordan would be giving a short sermon at eight fifteen. A posted notice had announced that everyone was required to attend.

Rubin looked at his pocket watch: it was seven fifteen. The Roble girls would have to vacate in fifteen minutes, which would leave the men only forty-five minutes to eat breakfast and get to the chapel. He could see that college life was going to be very hectic.

George's room was nicely furnished, with a stuffed chair and ottoman in the corner and individual photos of his mother and father prominently displayed. Rubin quickly glanced at them and noticed George definitely favored his mother. Compared with William and Rubin's room, the place was exceptionally tidy.

Once they were settled—George in the stuffed chair with his two canes at his side, and David and Rubin sitting at the study desk—George said, pointing at the photos, "They came up with me, day before yesterday, on the train. It was hard for Mother to leave me. I've never been on my own. And to be honest, I am sort of frightened about the whole thing. Last night, I heard boys being daunted in the hallway. I don't know what I'd do if they did that to me."

Since Rubin had his own bad experiences, it was difficult for him to be reassuring. He said, "I feel the same way. If it weren't for my roommate, William Greer, who's twice as big as I am, I wouldn't feel safe, either."

David said, "I don't have the same problem. My problem is my roommate, Jarvis Hall; you might know him as Freck. He's part of that Alpha Phi gang. Someone shouts, 'Rush,' and everyone jumps on one another and starts punching whomever they land on. They don't care what they break—bones or china."

A light went off in Rubin's head, "You must be in one of the rooms William cleans. He's a floor janitor. He told me there are gangs of students who jump on one another and like to break whatever is near by and don't bother to clean it up."

"Does William have a red beard?" David asked.

"That's him," Rubin answered.

"You're right, he cleans our room. He introduced himself to us when we first moved in. Nice fellow. Tell him I try to keep the room tidy, but it's impossible. They asked me to pledge their fraternity, but I don't want to. After that, they lost interest in me."

George wanted to know more about his new friends. He asked, "But how about you fellows? Where are you from, and all that?"

Rubin looked over at David to see if he wanted to go first. David moved his head as if to say "You first."

Rubin said, "I'll try to make this short and sweet, but I notice when I start talking about myself, I never seem to stop."

They all laughed.

George said, "It's a common disease."

Rubin continued, "I'm from Omaha, Nebraska. We say it's the city you can tell when you're in it by the smell of the stockyards, but it's a good city. I've lived there all my life. My last name is Weinberg, and if you lived in Omaha, you'd know Weinberg's is the biggest department store in town. My uncle owns it and my cousins work in the store, but my father, who's dead now, never had anything to do with the store. He was an artist, painted pictures no one wanted. We have them everywhere: under the beds, in closets, even in the barn. My brothers—I have three of them; I'm the oldest—have told my mom to get rid of them, but she won't do it. She insists they'll be worth lots of money one of these days, but I doubt it. The reason I'm here is the tuition is free and Senator Stanford owed my uncle a political favor. To get here, I had to promise to work in the store after I graduated. I've always been interested in politics, but it looks like those dreams have gone up in smoke." He scratched his head. "Well, that will give you some idea."

George said, "I have to ask you ..."

Rubin didn't let him finish. "Yes, George, I'm a Jew, and except for the political favor, I have no idea why I was admitted. When I graduated from high school, I didn't expect to go on to college." Rubin could see George's feelings were hurt by what he said.

George said, "I'm sorry. I shouldn't have said anything."

"No, no, please don't apologize. You and I have much in common. It's something we both have to deal with."

David was shaking his head. "You fellows are going to have to forgive me if I ask some dumb questions. Freck and his friends are already calling me Bump for being a country bumpkin. I was born and raised in Riverside, a little town south of here, toward Los Angeles. We have about two thousand residents, just big enough to have a high school. I never met anyone like either of you two. We had a few war veterans who lost a leg or two who used to march in the parades, but the only Jew I knew ran the five and ten on Main Street. His children didn't mix with us and never played with us. I have no idea where they went to school. We had mobs of Mexicans come through town when it was orange-picking time, but they stayed near the groves in little tents or shacks. So you can see, I have lots to learn. My dad had orange groves and I helped him plant; prune; and irrigate; and when it got cold, put out the smudge pots early in the morning. In school, I played sports, mostly football and baseball. That and getting good grades so I could go to college was what I did most. Both mom and dad are alive. Thank the Lord. I have a sister, Polly, a year younger than me, who's thinking about coming here. So you can understand why I don't like Freck making bad remarks about ladies and doing bad things to them. It could be my sister he's talking about."

Rubin had to say it. "Not all ladies think it is bad, David. Some like it almost as much as men."

David made a face indicating his displeasure. "Sorry, Rubin, that's not the way I was taught or what our preacher says in church."

Rubin thought he shouldn't question David further and decided to drop the subject. David had firm ideas about what was right and what was wrong.

George quickly added, "Well, you already know about me. Raised in San Diego." He looked over at David. "My dad wanted me to be a football player, but with these"—he moved his wooden legs—"no such luck. So, I was very smart in high school, got top grades, and could have gone to Harvard or Yale, but I wanted to stay in the West. I met some people from Massachusetts and didn't like them."

They heard the clamor of young men shouting. The young ladies must have finished, and now everyone else was rushing to eat breakfast.

George pulled himself up using his two canes. "You two better get going or there won't be anything left to eat."

Rubin and David got up, too, and Rubin said, "No, George, we'll go with you."

He waved them on. "No, I insist. There's no reason you should be held up by me."

"Shut up, George, we're all going together," David said.

A smile lit up George's face as they made their way out the door, toward the dining room.

CHAPTER 11

▼

HIRED UNDER FALSE PRETENCES

Monday, September 28, 1891

Leslie Elliott was sitting at his desk in his new office to the right of the entrance to the university. He was looking at the "Schedule of Lectures and Recitations—First Semester, 1891–1892," delivered by their San Francisco printer that day.

Dr. Pease, Dr. Jenkins, Bolton Brown, and Dr. Woods had recently arrived, so all of the instructional staff was now on hand. Leslie glanced at his own name in the schedule. He would be teaching two economics classes: "Principles of Political Economics" on Monday, Wednesday, and Friday at nine thirty to ten thirty; and "Tariff Controversy" at the same time on Tuesdays. He was particularly proud of the last class because Dr. Jordan had allowed him to teach such a current, controversial subject. Tariffs—whether to have more of them or do away with the ones already initiated—was the principal controversy that set apart the two national political parties. The Republicans, led by President Harrison, with Leland Stanford supporting him, were for tariffs. Ex-President Grover Cleveland and the Democrats were against. Leslie's heart was with the Democrats, but he planned to be completely objective in his class presentations. He wasn't sure whether Dr. Jordan had discussed his class with Senator Stanford. He doubted it. To Leslie's knowledge, the Stanfords had no hand in creating or modifying the curriculum.

Looking over the schedule, it was easy to see that his friend, Dr. David Marx, had the heaviest teaching load: nine civil engineering classes every day except

Tuesday. David appreciated Leslie recommending his brother-in-law, Bolton Brown, for the mechanical drafting instructor position. Otherwise, David would have had to teach it himself.

Leslie's problem was he had never liked Bolton, but he knew it pleased his wife to have her brother gainfully employed and living close by. Undoubtedly, Ellen had also mentioned Bolton to Harriet Marx, her best friend and David's wife. Even though Ellen never said anything, she missed her mother and father, but with two of their four children in the Bay Area, there was good chance they, too, would move to California.

At first Leslie thought the reason for his disliking Bolton was that, unlike his sister, Bolton had taken after his father and was of average height, which meant he usually peered down at Leslie with a disdainful look on his face. But soon Leslie realized it was more than his being short. Bolton acted as if his beautiful, petite sister had married far beneath her. Bolton considered Leslie to be an uncouth Westerner from Wyoming, whose only attribute was that he had a doctorate degree. Otherwise, he was unschooled in the finer things in life: art, music, and the theater. And it was true; Leslie's interests were more parochial and of the common sort: vaudeville, boxing, baseball, and horse racing. Because of this, when he was alone with his brother-in-law, they had absolutely nothing to say to one another. There was no subject they had had in common. The two struggled for any kind of conversation beyond the usual salutations. At first, it bothered Leslie. Now he was quite used to having his own thoughts instead of making small talk. Bolton never said anything, so Leslie guessed he was also just as happy.

Now that Bolton was here, it was clear he did not have an ounce of loyalty or any kind of appreciation for the opportunity David Marx had given him. Leslie heard Bolton telling Ellen how he was planning to establish a famous art school at Stanford, rivaling the schools of Paris but more up-to-date. As far as he was concerned, the mechanical drawing, instructor job was only a stepping stone to his real goals. Leslie heard and seethed. He could imagine how David would have reacted if he had heard what his new instructor was keeping to himself.

At least one problem had been averted. When Bolton first arrived the previous week, Leslie was afraid he might be living with them on Alvarado Row, but Ellen talked Bolton into living at Encina Hall, so he could get to know his students better and make a good impression on Dr. Marx and Dr. Jordan. Leslie had breathed a sigh of relief.

Another new arrival, the opposite of Bolton, was Dr. Thomas Denison Wood. Unlike the other members of the faculty, he was truly a doctor, having got both his A.B. and AM from Oberlin and received his M.D. from the College of Physicians and Surgeons in New York City. Dr. Wood and his wife would be moving into a cottage only two doors from the Elliotts.

Leslie could always tell Dr. Jordan's inner feelings about a new member of the faculty by how that individual was greeted on his first day on campus. Because of Leslie's relationship to Bolton, Dr. Jordan took some time out of his schedule to shake his hand and welcome him on board. Without the tie to Leslie, and particularly Ellen, it was doubtful whether Dr. Jordan would have bothered to greet an instructor.

Because Dr. Wood was a full professor and quite tall—which was another way Dr. Jordan judged staff members—Leslie had been surprised when Dr. Jordan said he had an appointment in the city and asked Leslie to speak to him when he arrived.

Later, that day, Leslie met Dr. Wood at the long wooden counter, facing the entrance doors of the newly occupied administrative offices at the Quad's northern entrance. It was always interesting for Leslie to see people's reactions to his shortness: sometimes their eyes blinked with surprise, or their eyebrows arched like inverted parentheses, or their mouths slightly grimaced. Dr. Wood—God bless him—who stood well over a foot above Leslie, merely smiled and shook his hand and cheerfully told him that his wife was staying in the city and they would soon be moving into their new cottage.

Leslie motioned to Dr. Wood to follow him around the counter to the hallway leading to his office, first on the left. Dr. Jordan's office was at the end of the hall and twice as big as Leslie's. Ellen thought her husband's office was too small. Leslie said it suited his needs.

As soon as Dr. Wood was settled in a side chair, the expression on his face turned serious, and Leslie knew he was about to learn the reason for his being asked to greet the new arrival.

Dr. Wood said, "I am a little surprised that Dr. Jordan was not here to discuss the matter I questioned in a letter I wrote two weeks ago."

Leslie replied, "I'm sorry he was called away. I'm certain, after the excitement of the opening ceremonies has died down, he will be getting together with you."

Dr. Wood looked at Leslie intently. Whatever was on his mind was too important to wait for a later meeting, and he must have realized Leslie was close to Dr. Jordan and whatever was said he would pass on. Dr. Wood said, "Well, I think I can again express the concerns in my letter, and you will be good enough to bring them, again, to Dr. Jordan's attention."

"Be assured of that," was all Leslie said, and he thought Dr. Wood was not happy, not happy at all.

Dr. Wood began, "Prior to coming here, I did a little research and found there were no medical facilities, no hospitals or clinics—or for that matter, physicians—within a fifteen mile radius of this institution."

"I'm sure that is true. San Jose and San Francisco are probably the closest." Leslie had a good idea where the conversation was leading.

"Dr. Elliott, I am a physician, licensed by the sovereign state of New York, and it is my sworn duty to care for the sick and needy. Dr. Jordan hired me to be in charge of the men's physical training program and teach hygiene. There was no mention of me providing medical care for an institution with over four hundred people or the outlying areas with hundreds, perhaps thousands, more."

Leslie nodded in agreement and said, "Dr. Wood, may I give you some information that may help you understand Dr. Jordan's situation?"

"Yes, sir, please do so."

"As you know, Senator and Mrs. Stanford founded this university in honor of their young son, who died when he was a young man. I have been told many times by several people that they blamed the doctors who cared for him in Europe for his death."

Dr. Wood started to say something, but Leslie held up his hand and said, "But there is more. I have also been told that within the past four years, Senator Stanford suffered a series of maladies and received medical advice from a number of very distinguished doctors. His health continued to fail to the point where there was some thought he would die. A local physician in the city diagnosed his case as blood poisoning brought on by the prescribed medications he was taking—medications such as arsenic, magnesium, lead, morphine, and others. As a result, the only thing he does now for his health is to go to health spas in Europe."

"So the Stanfords are not happy with the state of medical care. Well, I can tell you I am not, either. That is one reason I wish to teach hygiene. I do realize that, as a profession, we have much to learn. And as with all the professions, there will be some charlatans among us."

Leslie appreciated this comment. Perhaps Dr. Wood did understand the situation. "You are right. They are not happy; in fact, they have a preconceived notion that anything associated with medicine or doctors or hospitals is unhealthy to the point that they may be life threatening. And they are also fearful the parents of our students might go through the same kind of despair they did. Dr. Jordan knows this type of thinking is not right and having a doctor on staff will, of course, be beneficial. So you were hired for physical training and hygiene …"

"So I was hired under false pretenses."

"Not entirely. You will have those duties, but I am sure there will be others, as well."

"Such as caring for the sick and needy."

"Yes. Unfortunately, at first you will be alone, but I am certain with time other doctors will locate to this area, and clinics and hospitals will be built."

"But not for the foreseeable future."

Leslie could only be honest when he said, "No, not for the foreseeable future."

Dr. Wood sat back in his chair, looking as if he were about to laugh out loud. "So if I am to take this position, after traveling three thousand miles to get here with my wife and our furniture on its way, I will have to accept the rather bleak prospect you have outlined of working my fool tail off, probably night and day." After saying this, he sat there with a foolish grin on his face, as if to say, "Do you think I am a fool?"

Leslie did not acknowledge that look. In his mind, it was important for the university to have a medical doctor. They had enough of the other kind. "Dr. Wood, may I say this? From our brief conversation, I am convinced you'll make a considerable contribution to the success of this university—whether it is physical training and hygiene or applying your medical knowledge. Whichever it is, it will be caring for the health of members of our institution."

"And neighbors," Dr. Wood interjected.

"Yes, and neighbors. That will be up to you, and I am sure you will be recompensed for such care. I do sincerely hope you will accept this challenge and stay and be one of us. I am certain Dr. Jordan feels the same way."

Dr. Wood sat quietly, turning over in his mind what had been said to him. Leslie was thinking he might get out of his chair, wave good-bye, and bolt for the door, but Dr. Wood took a deep breath, exhaled, and said, "I understand you and your family will be our neighbors."

Leslie jumped out his chair, came around to their new doctor, shook his hand again with both of his, and said, "Yes, we will."

CHAPTER 12

▼

"YOU KNOW GOOD, OLD FRED."

Thursday, October 1, 1891

When Rubin walked over to the Quad after breakfast to see the opening ceremonies, he saw David Cooper headed in the same direction. David was by himself. "Hey, David, do you want to go with me? Will's working," Rubin shouted to him. William Greer, Rubin's roommate, had decided to shorten his name to Will.

David stopped in his tracks, looked pleased, and trotted over to Rubin. "Thanks for inviting me. Hated to go by myself. Everyone's going. Freck wanted me to go with his bunch, but I said no. I guess, for sure, they'll give up on me now."

The two of them mixed in with the crowd moving en masse toward the buff-colored buildings. Both boys wore the usual derby hats and dark, heavy suits. Church-going clothes were what they were wearing. Most of the other male students were similarly attired.

It was nine o'clock, and visitors were arriving from all directions and in all types of conveyances. With some difficulty, the drivers of gigs and carriages found posts or scraggly trees for hitching their horses. Some of the Mayfield boys were offering to hold a horse's reins for a nickel while the ceremonies took place. There were only a few takers. Rubin thought the boys did not look one bit trustworthy.

When Rubin and David got to the Quad, they found the student janitors had placed chairs from the classrooms so they were facing the Spanish Arcade at the east end of the Quad. They could see, from the early occupants, that the chairs at the front were for the faculty, and those behind were for the students. They weren't officially students yet, but that afternoon they would be, after they registered. The boys sat toward the back of the student section.

Once settled, Rubin had a chance to look around. He saw visitors had to stand in the back or sit on the curbing. Both places didn't appear to be good for hearing or seeing. Some young boys ran to the ovals, where trees had just been planted that were perfect for them to climb to get a better view. Several of the trees were not strong enough to bear their weight and toppled over. Surviving the slight fall, the young climbers moved on to another young tree. Photographers had erected wooden stands in the ovals for themselves and their cameras. More daring photographers stole or borrowed ladders and climbed to the top of the Quad's tile roofs. Other adventuresome guests, including some young boys, joined the photographers on the roofs. They were casually sitting on the edge and dangling their feet as if they were fishing at a creek's edge. Rubin had never done such a thing. He hated heights.

Looking straight ahead, Rubin saw the platform for speakers and distinguished guests. A lonely rostrum sat squarely in its middle. Up front and to the right were Dr. Jordan and his wife. His head was down, scrutinizing notes in his lap. Undoubtedly, the speech he was about to give, Rubin thought. His wife busied herself with greeting new arrivals on the platform or waving to less privileged friends in the audience. Her face was glowing. Rubin guessed she was in her glory.

Behind the Jordans, was a large portrait of Leland Stanford Junior. Somehow the painting was suspended so it was midway up the long black velvet curtain used to fill in the other side of the arcade. The son appeared to be deep in thought, his index finger to his cheek, with Greek or Roman ionic columns as a background. Even from the painting, young Stanford appeared to have been a pampered, young man, Rubin thought. Too bad he had died at such an early age. But if he hadn't, Rubin and all the rest would not be here.

To the right of the platform, a marching band, complete with tasseled uniforms and German-like headgear, was assembling. To the left, members of different choirs, with varied colored robes, were getting organized.

When Rubin saw his cousin Delores walking in with her friend Betsy, he vigorously waved to her and shouted, "Delores, Delores, it's Rubin. Over here."

Alerted by the shouting, Delores turned and faced in Rubin's direction. When she recognized who it was, she slightly nudged her friend's ribs with her elbow and made a movement with her hand toward Rubin. There was more conversation between the two. No doubt about it, Rubin thought, Delores was considering whether to ignore or to acknowledge her cousin's salutation. Her eyes lit up with recognition when she spied David at Rubin's side. She had more words with Betsy before she finally gave an answering shout. "Rubin, good to see you. We'll be right over."

Rubin breathed a sigh of relief. It was good to have family in this strange place—no matter that the family was reluctant. Now he could prove to his cousin she had nothing to worry about. But, he realized, it was David's presence that must have swayed her.

As the girls approached, the two boys moved over two seats so there would be room for them. Rubin, looking over at David, saw for the first time that his mouth was agape in surprise. Obviously there was something about which Rubin was not aware. Did David know Delores? Or more likely, did David want to know Delores?

The answer soon came from David whispering in Rubin's ear. "I cannot believe my good fortune. I have secretly admired the dark one from the staircase each morning, and you know her." He gave Rubin a resounding punch in the chest that sent him reeling back.

Rubin was about to say, "She's my cousin," but held his tongue. "Hi, Delores," is what he did say, as she and Betsy came closer.

"Nice to see you, Rubin," replied Delores, in a voice that was pleasant but somewhat cool, as if not to intimate any close relationship. She immediately took the initiative for the introductions. "Betsy Marshall, this is my good friend Rubin Weinberg. His parents know mine."

Rubin took his cue from his cousin. "And Delores Payson and Betsy Marshall, this is my new friend David Cooper."

David, Delores, and Betsy nodded and said "Hello" and "Glad to meet you" to one another. There was an awkward silence.

Rubin quickly added, "David is from Riverside. Isn't that near where you live, Delores?" This kind of information usually bridged early strangeness, Rubin thought.

He was right. Delores immediately chimed in with, "Not too far. Betsy, didn't you know someone from Riverside?"

Betsy thought, finger to temple. "Yes, I remember now. His name was Fred Farr. I think he went to high school there."

Rubin looked at Betsy. She was not a raving beauty, but her oval face, with its small, rosebud mouth, topped with tousled, curly blonde hair, was not unattractive. From past experience, he knew blonde ladies rarely appreciated his dark Jewish features.

If David only barely knew Fred Farr, he certainly didn't show it. His face immediately brightened with recognition. "Fred Farr. You know good, old Fred. He was in my class. Tremendous fellow. We played baseball together."

Betsy was impressed, and so was Delores. Betsy said, "You played baseball. I just love the game, the way you boys bat the ball around."

Rubin was also impressed. He thought David might be shy with strange young ladies. He was wrong.

David, Delores, and Betsy were soon engaged in idle conversation about others they knew and what classes they'd be taking and how awful the meals were at Encina. Rubin remained happily silent. He hoped his cousin no longer feared being with him.

CHAPTER 13

▼

"FRITZ KRISLER IN NEW YORK CITY"

That Same Day

Leslie Elliott was sitting in the faculty area, directly in front of the platform. He was next to Bolton, who was seated next to Ellen, who was taking care of her own son, Louis, and Dr. Jordan's children, Edith and Knight. There were vacant seats next to Leslie, so when Irene, Lucy, and Fletcher came down the aisle looking for somewhere to sit, Leslie and Ellen waved, and the threesome decided to join them. Lucy ended up sitting next to Leslie, and Leslie introduced Bolton, his brother-in-law, to the three new arrivals.

After the introductions, Bolton whispered into Leslie's ear, "What a beauty."

Leslie guessed he was speaking of Lucy. Of the two young women, Leslie preferred Irene. But if Irene was gold; Lucy was diamonds. Her cool English beauty, with wavy dark hair and blue eyes, was set off by skin that was translucent. Leslie had heard Ellen say Lucy was the most beautiful woman in the area, if not the state. Obviously, since his brother-in-law was an artist, he appreciated such beauty. Looking at Bolton deep in thought, Leslie imagined he was trying to determine some way he could engage Lucy in conversation while the little man whom his sister had married was seated between them.

For her part, Leslie noticed, Lucy hardly gave Bolton a second look. With his wide-set hound dog eyes and droopy beard, he did not have half his sister's zest. Leslie thought that in this pioneer area, where there were few females and no lacking of male suitors, Bolton must appear to Lucy as just another man with a thick beard and new bowler hat.

Bolton was having some kind of whispered conversation with his sister, who was probably giving him background information about Lucy, such as that she was a Harvard Annex graduate and an accomplished violinist and the founder of a new preparatory school for girls. Because, above all, Bolton considered himself an artist not a mechanical drafting instructor, being a violinist added to Lucy's luster.

At exactly nine thirty, Mayfield's University Band started to play. Leslie had read about it in the *Mayfield Gazette*, the weekly newspaper he read to find out about local goings on. Mayfield reminded him of Wyoming, not California. The band was made up of eighteen of Mayfield's most prominent residents, businessmen, and professionals. They were dressed in bright yellow and red uniforms, complete with tousled headgear that Senator and Mrs. Stanford had bought for them. Apparently, the band members, unlike many other Mayfield's residents, realized the importance of a close relationship with the University—hence, the name. To put the crowd into a good mood, they struck up a rollicking tune by John Phillip Souza.

Soon Leslie found himself being talked over and around by the two young people seated on either side of him. Because the band was playing, shouted over was more like it.

Bolton began it all by looking up at the blue sky with a few clouds drifting by, and saying, "Lovely day."

Lucy did not realize Bolton was talking to her, not to Leslie. She did not respond.

Bolton said it, again, "Lovely day." He even looked up at the sky again.

Leslie, in the middle of Bolton's thwarted attempts at small talk, had to touch Lucy's shoulder and say, "I think he's talking to you."

That got her attention, but she still had not heard what Bolton said. She glanced in Bolton's direction and asked, "Sorry, what was that?"

For the third time, Bolton repeated his passing remark, complete with the skyward look. Leslie had to suppress a snicker.

"Yes, it is," was Lucy's cool response.

But Bolton had an immediate follow up. "What do you think of the band music?"

"Pardon, what was that?"

In a louder voice, Bolton repeated, "I said, what do you think of the band music?" Leslie thought Bolton said the words just a little too loudly, almost as if he was irritated. Certainly, not the way to make a good impression.

Lucy said, "Loud, quite loud."

Leaning around Leslie, Bolton said, "Yes, I agree. I'm not much for band music. Prefer classical."

After a moment of silence, during which Bolton let his classical music remark sink in, Leslie had enough. He said to Bolton, "If you don't mind, please change seats with me so I can sit by Ellen."

Bolton smiled, understanding Leslie's intent. "Certainly," he said. The two men got up and quickly the exchange was accomplished. Ellen looked at the newly arrived Leslie, smiled sweetly, and reached over to hold his hand. It was so nice to have such a sensitive man as a husband, she thought.

Leslie hoped Bolton's classical music remark would be successful; the talk about weather and band was going nowhere.

It was as if Bolton had heard Leslie's thoughts because his next words, spoken in a deep, mellow voice because he no longer had to shout, were, "I understand you play the violin."

Lucy's face brightened. "Yes, I do. So, your sister told you. How sweet of her."

"I had the opportunity to see Fritz Krisler in New York City last time I was there."

"You did. How wonderful! Tell me about it."

Bolton proceeded to, in great detail. Within a few minutes, Lucy was bending her head down, closer to Bolton, so she could hear every word he said.

Leslie didn't at all mind being completely ignored. The crowd, the music, and everything that was happening at once fascinated him. Dr. Jordan and his wife, Jessie, caught his attention. Leslie could see that Jessie was just able to get around, being with child. But he knew it would have taken wild horses to keep her from this celebration. Dr. Jordan was hunched over, still tinkering with his speech. To his left was President Kellogg from the California State University, along with Judge Shafter and other appointed University trustees, including Timothy Hopkins—a man Leslie hardly knew except by sight, but who was well liked by the Stanfords. The two benefactors, Leland and Jane Stanford, had not yet arrived, but two chairs—in front and on the end nearest the rostrum—were vacant, saved for them.

Leslie, thinking Bolton was preoccupied with his lovely Lucy, was surprised when he felt Bolton pulling at his coat sleeve "That fellow, Fletcher Martin, has something he wants to say to you."

Leslie leaned forward and looked down the row of seats, and saw Fletcher's face grinning back at him. Leslie felt the warmth of true friendship, as if he had known Fletcher from Wyoming days. Fletcher cupped his hands and shouted, "It's Fred Behn. He's ten rows back. He wants to say hello."

Leslie stood up and turned around, and there, about ten yards away, was the hatless, grinning face of the man who had been such a Good Samaritan when they first arrived. Leslie felt badly he had not visited him since. He waved and said, "Good to see you, Mr. Behn."

Fred's voice came booming back. "Good to see you, Dr. Elliott. I told Fletcher to bring you 'round one of these days."

"I will, I will. I promise you."

Both of the men gave a final wave and sat back down.

One of the photographers' camera lights exploded with a loud bang. Fletcher jumped out of his seat as if he had been shot. Lucy, Bolton, Ellen, and even Lewis, Edith, and Knight stared at him, questioning looks on their faces, but not Irene or Leslie. Irene gently pulled Fletcher back down to his seat. Her look told Leslie she cared a great deal for this man. What happened at that Indian massacre must have left indelible scars, Leslie thought—scars that would always be there, even more powerfully so than the scar on his face.

Leslie looked back over his shoulder at the bright faces of more than four hundred students—the girls with their brightly colored hats and parasols and the men with their derbies and sombreros, and some wearing straw hats with colorful headbands. From their faces, he did not know them. But by their names, Leslie knew where they were from, the personal information from their applications for admittance, and particularly the scores on their entrance examinations. Some of those who were there had not passed, but were special students. I will soon get to know them all by face, he thought.

At first, the students were uncommonly quiet and subdued, but as they started to share acquaintanceships and places they knew in common, the hum of conversation steadily increased in volume to a continuous roar, not unlike the sound passengers made at a great railway station.

Over the din, a student shouted out, "There are our University of California friends." And as a group, everyone's head turned toward the east end of the Quad as students from the Berkeley-based university, another three hundred strong, strolled in, accompanied by their faculty. As a body, they had made the arduous trip down the East side of the Bay and through San Jose.

Leslie could see the Quad was filled from one end to the other. All these days it had been empty. From now on, it would be different.

As if controlled by a common mind, many of the men, including Leslie, were taking out their watches and glancing at them. It was ten o' clock, time for Leland and Jane Stanford to appear, and time to get this ceremony started.

Except for the occasional child crying or shouting, the crowd became quiet, so the sounds of horses' hooves and the creaking of a carriage drawing up behind the western archway could be heard. Leslie waited and watched, breathlessly. He was aware of the fact he was seeing a historical event unfold. He could tell from their concentrated silence that the other viewers felt the same way.

Hand in hand, the two founders emerged from the shadows of the alcove and into the bright sunlight, and stood for a tender moment under the portrait of their beloved son. Senator Stanford was unsteady on his feet and needed his pearl-handled cane and Mrs. Stanford's shoulder for support.

When the couple came into view, the young Stanford men sprang to their feet and gave them a lusty, impromptu greeting. "Wah hoo! Wah hoo! L-S-J-U! Stan—ford!" Leslie thought it was the first cheer, and a chill ran down his spine.

Dr. Jordan, with Timothy Hopkins at his side, jumped up to help the senator into his chair; both of the Lathrop Brothers—Charles and Ariel—tended to their sister.

Smiles lit up both of the Stanfords' faces when they heard the boys cheer. Once seated, Senator Stanford looked directly out into the audience and tipped his hat, and Mrs. Stanford raised her bejeweled arm and hand in a courtly wave. It was like a king and queen acknowledging the common folk, Leslie thought. It was impressive.

For a moment there was an awkward silence. Then the Presbyterian Chorus burst into song with a boisterous, "Glory be to God on High."

When the singing was finished, there was a pause while Reverend Robert Mackenzie, pastor of the Congregational Church of Oakland, made his way to the rostrum at the front of the platform.

At the other end of the Quad, Leslie could hear raucous voices and the laughter of those who could neither see nor hear what was transpiring. They had quieted for the drama of the Stanfords' arrival, but the hymns and a clergyman were not that interesting. For them, the day was a holiday, an event that should be celebrated with food, drink, and laughter.

Leslie thought about the irony of the event. Here at one end of the Quad were people celebrating a solemn, almost religious happening. At the other end, citizens of the area were drinking in excess, at mid morning, the senator's wine and brandy.

Reverend Mackenzie looked down at the Bible before him, and in a dour voice that could put even the wide-awake to sleep, said, "Let us pray."

The crowd in unison began the Lord's Prayer. "Our Father, who art in Heaven …"

When the prayer was over, a new minister, Reverend Stowe, took Mackenzie's place at the rostrum and in a loud, dramatic voice gave a reading from Proverbs: "Get Wisdom, get understanding. Take fast hold on instruction, let her not go." Finally he proudly introduced the senator, saying, "The ex-governor of the sovereign state of California and the current senator from our great state and the founder, with his wife, of Leland Stanford Junior University"—the pastor paused for dramatic effect—"Senator Leland Stanford."

A lusty cheer rose from crowd gathered at the Quad's western end, drowning out any of the extraneous hoots from the other end.

CHAPTER 14

▼

"CIRCLES OF PALMS WILL HAVE THEIR PART."

That Same Day

Leslie watched as Leland Stanford, appearing much older than his fifty-six years, slowly rose from his seat and faced the crowd. Everyone around him looked up at him, including Mrs. Stanford, their faces beaming with admiration. As he approached the rostrum, he supported himself with one hand, holding onto the backs of chairs and shoulders as he passed. One time he teetered from side to side, and the audience held their collective breaths until he righted himself and continued his journey. When he reached the rostrum, Leslie heard audible sighs of relief from both those in the audience and on the rostrum. He had made the passage without incident.

Senator Stanford solemnly looked at the crowd, as if he were speaking to another person across the room, and began to speak in a voice that was somewhat gruff but earnest. He did not have the qualities of a man speaking down to his listeners, nor did he lower his eyes to see his notes. Leslie thought it was a speech he did not need to memorize because it came from his heart.

The sun, now at its midday zenith, was shining into his eyes, so he probably could not see the faces of the people sitting in front of him. Leslie guessed the senator thought about raising his arm to shade his eyes, but decided not to because it was an unseemly way to appear before the gathering. Leslie thought of grabbing Ellen's parasol and jumping onto the platform, but decided it would not be proper.

The senator began, "For Mrs. Stanford and myself, this ceremony marks an epoch in our lives, for we see in part the realization of the hopes and efforts of years. We do not believe there can be superfluous education ..."

Leslie looked around. Everyone he saw was intent on watching and remembering the scene taking place before his or her eyes. Except, to his left, within the oval garden, directly in front of the rostrum, the young trees were moving as if induced by a northern breeze, but no breeze was blowing. Leslie guessed it was some child swaying on a tender bough.

"The knowledge man has acquired through education," the senator continued, "will be not only of practical assistance to him, but a factor in his personal happiness and joy forever."

Leslie noticed Mrs. Stanford was aware her husband was having a problem with the bright sun shining in his eyes. She got up from her seat and quickly stood by his side, protecting him with her lavender parasol. Leslie was impressed with her wifely concerns, and so apparently was the senator. He glanced at her with deep appreciation and continued his speech without interruption.

After Mrs. Stanford took her place at her husband's side, Leslie heard a perceptible exclamation, as if someone were vexed. The sound once again came from the oval of young trees and palms facing the rostrum, but it was impossible to see its source because of the foliage and spectators. No other sound ensued, so attention immediately returned to the senator.

"You students are the most important factor in the university. It is for your benefit that it has been established. To you our hearts go out especially, and in each individual student we feel a parental interest."

Leslie usually did not enjoy speeches: this one was an exception. He felt that Senator Stanford deeply felt what he was saying.

"Remember that life is, above all, practical; that you are here to fit yourselves for a useful career; also, that learning should not only make you wise in the arts and sciences, but should fully develop your moral and religious natures."

Senator Stanford was finished. Leslie thought the speech had ended abruptly. The senator must have tired; his breathing appeared to be painful. With Mrs. Stanford still at his side, he slowly retired to his chair. Once seated, he immediately slumped down into his chair, shut his eyes, and appeared to fall asleep. This must be his napping time, Leslie thought.

The next person on the program was Dr. Kellogg, president of the University of California, who conveyed his words of greetings and good wishes. "Today we see the birth of a university that unites the memory of the departed with the vigilant supervision of the living. To the living, we offer our congratulations; for the lamented dead, we are sure there is raised a worthy and enduring monument."

When Dr. Kellogg returned to his chair, a rousing cheer arose from the assembled visiting students and faculty at the rear of the Quad.

"UC rah! UC rah! California, rah, rah, rah. Cal-i-forn-ia rah!"

Kellogg raised his hand as a sign of appreciation, and in light of the serious words he had just spoken, contained his inclination to smile. Leslie concluded it was difficult to say which of the two college cheers had been the loudest. It was the first contest between the two universities, and it ended in a draw.

Now it was Dr. David Starr Jordan's turn to speak, and Leslie watched as he bounded to the rostrum and took a firm hold of both of its sides with his long, slender hands, as if it might fly away. His voice was higher and more resonant than Dr. Kellogg's, and he spoke with an arresting exuberance that should have awakened dozing listeners. He said, "It is the personal contact of young men and women with scholars and investigators that constitutes the life of the University. Ours is the youngest of universities, but it is heir to the wisdom of all the ages. It is ours at the beginning to give to the University its form, its tendencies, its customs."

No matter how excellent a speaker Dr. Jordan was, Leslie's eyes strayed over the scene before him: the mass of male hats with their dull colors, except for an occasional white straw or light brown sombrero, and the multitude of gaily festooned female hats with every sort of feathers, bits of fruit, and flowers. The fruit and flowers were not real, but the feathers were. He wondered how many birds had been sacrificed for appearance's sake. A glint caught his eyes, again from that same oval from where the sigh had come. What was it? A mirror, or what? Probably a reflection from part of a photographer's gear, he thought. It was strange, more like a piece of shiny metal. The glint disappeared into the shadows, as did Leslie's interest.

Dr. Jordan continued, "The student has no need for luxury. Plain living has ever gone with high thinking." Leslie thought those students and faculty suffering through the initial hardships of life on the campus—no housing, no accommodation or board, rotten water—knew these words were directed to them.

"But grace and fitness have an educative power too often forgotten in this utilitarian age. These long corridors with their stately pillars"—and here he used his arms and hands to point to what he was describing—"these circles of waving palms, will have their part in the students' training as surely as the chemical laboratory or the seminary room."

Dr. Jordan's voice ascended with emotion as he said, "The golden age of California begins when its gold is used for purposes like this. From such deeds must rise the new California of the coming century, no longer the California of the gold seeker and adventurer, but the abode of high-minded men and women, trained in the wisdom of the ages and imbued with the love of nature, the love of man, and the love of God. And bright indeed will be the future of our State if, in the usefulness of the University, every hope and prayer of the founders shall be realized."

Dr. Jordan had concluded his speech. He returned to his seat beside Jessie, whose face was glowing with pride. Those who could hear, including Leslie, cheered. As the cheers subsided, Mayfield's University Brass Band briefly struck up another catchy tune and faded to silence as Reverend Mackenzie reassumed the rostrum. He asked everyone to rise, and gave a reasonably short benediction, completing the ceremony.

Most of the crowd did not realize the opening ceremonies had ended until some of the notables on the rostrum got to their feet. Leslie felt the reaction was as if the air had been let out of a rugby ball. The ceremony had not produced the drama for which they were hoping. By that time, those in the back did not care either way. Drink had served its purpose.

The band started playing a patriotic tune, "American," by John Gilmore. No one on the platform moved until the Senator and Mrs. Stanford and their honored guests, including Timothy Hopkins, had filed off the rostrum and made their way to several carriages, which were waiting for them on the dirt road that ran next to the west side of the Quadrangle. They would be going to a luncheon at the Stanford's mansion. Ellen, Louis, and Bolton were also going, but not Leslie. There was too much work for him to do. Registration began at one o'clock.

As the Senator and Mrs. Stanford left, waves of plaudits, hands clapping, and cheers accompanied them. Leslie felt the people of California sincerely appreciated what had been done for them and their children. Judging by Mrs. Stanford's beaming face and the senator's smile, they had found it extremely gratifying.

Irene, Lucy, and Fletcher said their good-byes. As Fletcher shook Leslie's hand, he said, "Don't forget. You and I are going to visit Fred Behn soon."

"I'll get a message to you," responded Leslie. Until the press of registering and getting students to their proper classes was over, he could think of nothing else. He heard Bolton making overtures to see Lucy again. From the smile on Bolton's face, Leslie assumed he was successful. He turned to his wife and gave her a husbandly hug. "Have a good time," he said.

"We'll miss you," was Ellen's reply. By now she was used to her husband's dedication to his work.

Bolton gave him a brief departing wave. He would not miss his brother-in-law's presence. The feeling was mutual, Leslie thought. He turned his back on his departing family members who were joining Dr. Jordan and Jessie for the walk over to the luncheon. Knight and Louis were happily running together, free at last from the confines of sitting still.

Making his way toward his office, Leslie found himself in the midst of the visitors. Many of them had brought picnic lunches. They commandeered the wooden chairs left vacant by departing students and faculty, and arranged them into more hospitable groupings under whatever shade was available. Others improvised by using the curbs as a place to spread their tablecloths and put their hampers. As desert, they took the senator's grapes, which had been used as decorations on the rostrum and columns surrounding the Quad. Leslie took one and popped it into his mouth. It was ripe and extremely sweet to the taste, too sweet for Leslie.

He saw student janitors, including Bert Hoover, taking chairs from the visitors so they could be returned to the classrooms. The chairs would be needed for the classes convening tomorrow. The visitors were sullen about their loss, but not combative. Leslie assumed it was due to deference for the senator. They retreated to the curbs.

On a whim, Leslie decided to look for his state university counterpart, Dr. Holland Rollins, among the students and faculty at the other end of the Quad. He had met the man on one occasion and hoped he could remember what he looked like.

It was interesting walking among the University of California group. None of them had a kind word for their new neighbors.

"Did you hear what they considered to be a cheer?" one said.

"What God-awful buildings. All the same and all drab looking."

"With all their money, you'd think they put out some food. To spend four hours to get here, for this, wasn't worth it."

"At least our campus looks like a university. This looks like a Catholic mission for the local natives."

After looking at many faces very similar to those about to register, Leslie gave up and doubled back toward the administrative office. The strenuous task of registering more than four hundred students would begin shortly. Leslie was looking forward to it.

CHAPTER 15

▼

"A SMALL REVOLVER"

That Same Day

"Delores, Betsy, hello. May I walk back with you?" It was the blonde girl who had caused such a ruckus at Encina. She shouted out to her friends after the ceremonies.

Delores hesitated, then motioned with her hand for Dollie to come over to where the foursome was standing. Rubin knew Dollie wasn't her real name, but that was the nickname boys at Encina were calling her.

When Dollie got there, the girls briefly embraced, and Delores introduced Rubin and David to her. "Rubin and David this is Sally, our new friend from Anaheim."

Rubin noticed Sally's grip was surprisingly firm. Both boys were shy and stammered, "Glad to meet you."

When Sally was shaking hands with Rubin, she looked startled by his appearance. Probably she had never touched a Jew before, he thought. If anything, he was troubled by meeting the girl about whom everyone was talking. Someone from Encina was bound to see him and David talking to her, and he was sure they would be jealous. Put this together with hatred of Jews, and Rubin could be in for trouble.

The five of them were standing close to one another, and Rubin couldn't help himself. He wanted to voice an opinion and could not keep his mouth shut. He whispered to the group in lowered tones so they all had to draw closer to hear what he was saying. "I haven't seen the man before, except in illustrations. He didn't appear to be the villain I always thought him to be."

David did not understand what Rubin was talking about, and said so, loudly enough that anyone nearby could hear. "Villain, villain, who are you talking about?"

Rubin looked at him, and a worried expression crossed his face. He had slipped and forgotten where he was and to whom he was talking. "Oh, right, forget it, David. I didn't know what I was saying."

Delores looked as though she knew exactly to whom her cousin was referring. She had heard about his socialistic tendencies from other cousins. She quickly turned the conversation to other matters. "So, does everyone know which classes they want?" she asked.

Rubin realized his mistake. Like many people, David was completely unaware of how the railway barons, including Senator Stanford, had accumulated their wealth. How they had made millions of dollars, illegally, bribed officials, and taken advantage of the lower classes. This was not the place or time to educate him.

Rubin noticed a smile cross Sally's face, as if she not only knew about whom he was talking, but also agreed with him. He could feel her dark blue eyes looking at him with renewed interest. Her feelings were verified as the group walked back to the north side of the Quad, where they would take their separate ways to their dormitories. Sally purposely fell behind the other girls to walk beside Rubin.

"So where are you from, Rubin?" she asked.

Rubin was taken aback by her friendliness. Why would the most beautiful girl at the university, the most beautiful he had ever seen, want to talk to him? He was usually not speechless, but this time the words barely came out. He stammered, "I'm from Omaha. How about you?"

With all the noise, and because of his Midwestern drawl, Sally's brow furrowed. She could not understand a word he said. "I am sorry, what did you say?"

Rubin turned around to repeat what he had said and inadvertently knocked a small black velvet purse out of Sally's fingers. The purse fell to the ground. Sally looked startled and started to reach down to pick it up, but Rubin, always the gentleman, beat her to it and retrieved it. He could not be fully certain—it was only a second—but through the purse's fabric, he could feel the outline of a small revolver. Before he could say anything, Sally snatched the purse from him, her eyes filled with apprehension.

Rubin realized what he had surmised was correct. It was a gun and Sally did not want anyone to know. He calmly said, "I'm sure nothing was broken."

Sally regained a normal, calm attitude. She appeared to understand Rubin knew her secret, but would not say anything about it. Instead she said, "Thank you, Rubin, for being such a gentleman. I deeply appreciate it."

The rest of the group looked and waited while this apparently inconsequential moment took place and then resumed walking.

Trying this time not to stammer, Rubin returned to Sally's original question. He tried to speak more clearly, this time. "I'm from Omaha. Where are you from?"

Sally paused, the lines of anxiety in her face relaxed, and she said, "I'm another Californian, like all the rest—from Anaheim, to be exact. I wager you've never heard of our little village?" Before he could respond, she had another question. "I'm lucky. Tomorrow, my first class isn't until nine thirty. How about you?"

"Me, too," he blurted out. Why was his tongue so thick?

Obviously Sally was used to having this effect on young men. As they walked, Rubin could smell the soap she must have used that morning when she bathed. It was totally different from the fragrance young men emitted.

Sally said, "My class is French 1, from Dr. Todd."

"Mine is, too". Rubin couldn't believe his good luck.

"Well, we'll have to sit together." She said it as if the matter were settled.

They continued to walk side by side, but now Rubin's face was brightened with a smile. The contents of Sally's purse were momentarily forgotten.

The group arrived at the beginning of the oval driveway, which was still being constructed to the north of the Quad. Here the boys went right, the girls left.

"See you tomorrow at class, Rubin," Sally said and waved good-bye to David, as everyone said their good-byes.

After the two groups parted, when they were out of earshot, David could not help but congratulate his newfound friend on his success with Sally. "I cannot believe your good fortune. Every man and boy in Encina was dying to know Dollie's name, and now you're beyond that. You two might even sit next to one another in class."

Rubin felt a sudden surge of happiness at his luck, "I cannot believe it myself. Why she was so friendly is beyond me." He was pleased with himself. He thought he'd be friendless at Stanford, and he not only had Will Greer as a friend, but also David and perhaps Sally.

As they walked, David asked again, "Who was the villain you were talking about?"

Rubin said, "David, please forget I said the words. I don't know what I was talking about."

Rubin could tell by the look on David's face that the matter was forgotten. He wished he were like David and could put things out of his mind, but the small revolver still bothered him, and he had second thoughts about Sally's interest. Would her attention cause him more pain?

CHAPTER 16

▼

"LEARNING FRENCH SHOULD BE FUN."

Friday, October 2, 1891

Next day, Friday, was the first day of class. Bad weather and rain were still in abeyance. But, unlike the day before, fall was definitely astir. In the morning, a bank of low fog blanked out the sun until almost ten o'clock.

Students attending chapel at eight fifteen heard a brief lecture from Dr. Jordan on the subject of the orderly use of time. He said students who found out how to use their time to best advantage would be successful. Those who did not would not be. Time was the most precious commodity they possessed. "Spend it wisely," he counseled. At the end of the lecture, the chapel quickly emptied. Students had five minutes to get to their classes.

Leslie Elliott had suggested an iron triangle, previously used to sound dinnertime at Escondite Cottage, be suspended in the archway in front of the administrative office. Members of the staff, Dr. Jordan and Dr. Elliott included, would take turns clanging the dinner bell to signal the beginning and ending of classes. At eight thirty sharp, the first "clang, clang, clang" of the triangle could be heard as far away as Mayfield and Menlo, where residents could only guess what the sound signified. Some thought a fire might be in progress on the campus.

From eight thirty to nine thirty, the Friday sessions of Latin 2, German 1, Philosophy 1, History 2, Mathematics 1 and 2, Civil Engineering 4, and Mechanical Engineering 1 and 2 met.

While classes were in session, the Quad was ominously vacant, except for lone students crisscrossing the expansive patio because they had found themselves in the wrong classes; and silent, except for an occasional authoritative professorial voice heard drifting through an open window or students' forced laughter at a faculty member's lame joke.

Students soon found themselves the recipients of assignments to be done over the weekend, due on Monday; warnings of snap quizzes to be given at any time; and ten-to-twenty page papers to be written during the next months. Like a cat pouncing on a mouse, academic stress had caught up with them.

When the triangle was rung at nine thirty signaling the end of the eight thirty classes and the beginning of the nine thirty classes, students who had been unlucky enough to have scheduled two consecutive classes had virtually no time between classes. They were expected to get to their next classes as quickly as possible. Some ran, including female students with long skirts and petticoats who picked them up and ran for their lives. Tardy students learned from professors' sarcastic remarks that their reputations had already been sullied.

Lucky students had schedules beginning at nine thirty or a second class that started at ten thirty, and they had an hour off.

During these breaks, females wishing to use the lavatories rushed back to Roble Hall. There were no water closets for them on the Quad. Men's facilities were discretely concealed in underground, cellar-like structures hidden by bushes, behind and between classrooms. Unfortunate female students who felt the urge but had no time to get back to Roble were forced to be creative in how and where they relieved themselves.

Activities at the nine thirty "clang" were varied. For about five minutes, the air was filled with sounds of students talking and shouting to one another.

Rubin's heart was in his throat when he saw Sally approaching. His feelings were ambivalent. He was looking forward to seeing her and appreciated the interest she had in him, but he knew everyone was watching every move she made. Why was she interested? Did she know about his knowledge of the small revolver? Was her show of friendship real or was it because she thought it would keep him silent? He could not help but be pleased when she walked up to him.

"Rubin, Rubin, good morning. I looked for you this morning," she said in a bright and cheery voice.

That morning at breakfast, Rubin had purposely stayed in the background when Sally made her usual grand entrance. Sally's wave or smile personally directed at him might have had serious consequences.

"I was late for breakfast. I overslept," he lied.

"Let's go in now and get seats up front. I want to hear every word. Learning French should be fun."

Rubin would have preferred seats in the back, but he could not deny what she wanted. Were these the early pangs of a self-denying love? He wondered. Such thoughts had never crossed his mind before.

He graciously let Sally walk ahead of him by three or four steps. As the two of them were walking by some boys waiting to go in, Rubin recognized the blond fellow with close-cropped hair. He was the one they called Sam, and the one who had led his tormenters outside the dining room three days earlier. He was standing next to Winko, the president of the Alpha Phis. Seeing the threatening look on Sam's face, Rubin sensed trouble, so he moved quickly. When he was safely past Sam, he relaxed. Then he realized Winko, with an innocent look on his face, had stuck out his leg to trip him. From the rear, Rubin felt an overpowering shove. It had to be Sam. Rubin pitched forward, landing on hands and knees. Both knees were bruised, possibly bleeding, and his trousers were torn by the fall. As Rubin was picking himself up, he heard Sam snarl, "Stay away from Dollie, Jew boy. Stay away from her, or else." Other students, waiting to get into the classroom watched the encounter without saying a word or offering assistance.

Face flushed, hands trembling, Rubin went into the classroom and saw Sally seated in the front row. With a bright smile, she waved at him and pointed to the seat next to her that she was saving for him. He was still wobbly from his accident, but he managed to sit down beside her.

From the miserable look on his face and quick breathing, Sally knew something was wrong. "What happened back there," she asked.

"Nothing," was his reply.

"Rubin, I want to know. Tell me." She was whispering, but Rubin could tell she was upset.

"Please, not now. Later I'll tell you." He looked at her with pleading eyes.

Everyone in the class was watching. Out of the corner of his eye, he could see Sam and Winko had come in and were sitting in the back row. Sam was mouthing the words, "Stay away from her."

Sally leaned back in her seat and said, "All right, not now." She added, "Rubin, do as I do: ignore them. Ignore them."

Professor Todd strode to the podium. He was about to call role. Rubin thought, easy enough for you to say. You don't have to live with them.

CHAPTER 17

▼

THE FLATCAR PRANK

Tuesday, October 6, 1891

A railroad flatcar was parked on a siding north of Encina Hall, about a mile from where the spur went into the main Southern Pacific railway line, which ran from San Jose to Mayfield, north to San Francisco. The forty-foot railway car had been used to transport construction materials: lumber, piping, and nails, but mostly uncut limestone from an Almaden quarry. Now that most of the University's buildings were completed, the flatcar was seldom used. It sat waiting for its iron wheels to roll again.

On Tuesday, at about four o'clock in the afternoon, during the first full week of class, George Gardiner had several guests casually sitting around his room, reading and studying: David Cooper, the footballer from Riverside; Rubin Weinberg; and a new fellow, Milton Grosh, another footballer, but from Pomona, who was David's new roommate.

Freck, David's old roommate, had left the campus, or as the phrase coined by the students put it, he had jumped off the edge of the earth. Freck had thrown a heavy wooden chair down the stairwell to see what would happen. Unfortunately, Dr. Swain was coming up those stairs and was almost killed. Next day, Freck was not to be seen.

The group of four young men had taken to eating dinner together. They would gather in George's corner, ground floor room and go as a group to the dining hall. The Alpha Phis and other fraternities were already beginning to commandeer some of the tables.

George was about to help David with some homework for English 1 when they heard the sound of boys shouting and screaming at the top of their lungs: "Wah-hoo, Wah-hoo, Stanford, follow us! Wah-hoo, Wah-hoo, Stanford, follow us! Follow us!" Then they heard the clump, clump of many heavy boots on the wooden stairs. A large number of male students were making a quick exit from Encina Hall.

But why and where were they going? Rubin, George, David, Milton looked at each other, wondering what was happening. Milton was the first one to get to his feet. David followed his example and said, "What the devil is happening?"

George didn't lock his room when his friends were there, and suddenly the door burst open. Several fellows passed through and proceeded to climb out the window. Because all the exits were jammed, they were using George's room as a short cut to get outside. One of them turned and said to George as he passed, "Woody, come on, follow us. I've no idea where we're going or what we're doing, but it should be fun." And he was out the window like the rest.

Rubin looked at George. "Woody?" he asked.

George said, "That's what they call me, and I like it."

"Well, then, Woody it is," David said.

Boys were swarming by in the hallways. Some followed the others through the room and out the window. All of them shouted excitedly, "Wah-hoo, Wah-hoo, Stanford, follow us! Follow us!"

Woody looked at the others and pointed with his index finger. "Go, go. I'll follow you as best I can." No one moved. Woody pulled himself to his feet with his canes, and made menacing gestures with one of them toward his friends, as if to hit them. But with a broad smile on his face, he said, "Go, damn you, before I start breaking some heads."

That was all it took. The three boys joined the others in a mad dash out the building, down the steps, and across the hayfields. Like a stream of ants converging on edible goods, they moved toward a derelict flatcar standing knee-deep in weeds on a seldom-used siding.

As he got closer, Rubin could see the only ones up on the bed of the car were two of the dreaded Alpha Phis—in particular, the blond, shorthaired one, Sam, and Winko, their president. Everyone else was gathered around the car, wondering what they were supposed to do. Sam and Winko were bent over, trying to turn the wheel brake. Lights went on in Rubin's head: all this commotion was about taking a joy ride on the flatcar, but the spur led to the main line and from there, Mayfield or Menlo. It was a dangerous undertaking.

Without being asked, David Cooper and Milt Grosh jumped on board and joined Sam and Winko in their attempts to turn the brake wheel. It still didn't budge. Rubin heard David shouting, "Try the other way."

Hands now moved in the opposite direction, and the shrill sound of steel grating on steel was the first indication David was right. The car was moving. Six iron wheels were turning, moving inch by inch, but they were going the wrong way—back toward the Quad, not Mayfield. What would be the fun in a trip to the Quad? The brake wheel was turned as far as it would go. Now, Rubin reasoned, sheer momentum would take them back to the campus unless other forces were applied.

Sam quickly took charge. In a commanding voice, he looked at David and Milton and said, "Everyone off."

They did not budge.

Sam made a move as if to force them off, but Winko held his arm and said, "Let's get this thing going, Sam. We can use the footballers' help."

Sam turned his attention to everyone still on the ground. He motioned with both arms towards the end of the car moving slowly toward the Quad. The group was bright enough to know they would have to get in front of the car, stop it, and start pushing it the other way.

Rubin was thinking there was no way he would stand in front of a moving railroad car and try to stop it. He couldn't believe his ears when a new battle cry thundered from the mob: "Toward Mayfield, toward Mayfield," uttered by more than a hundred male voices. "Toward Mayfield!"

Except for Sam, Winko, David, and Milton, everyone ran in front of the car and started pushing against it. At least twenty-five stalwarts were up front with their hands on the bed. Behind them were another fifty or so with their hands on whatever they could touch—pushing and shoving. Everyone else stood back and watched, including Rubin. It was dangerous work. If anyone slipped and fell, who knew what would happen. The flatcar was moving, slowly, but it was moving. Those who were pushing were not laggards, either. Their faces showed they were straining to stop the car and then move it in the other direction. Rubin heard moans of exertion. It was like a huge rugby scrum, but the other team—the flatcar—was winning.

David and Milton jumped down to the ground and worked their way up to the forefront of the pushers. It could not be helped—some of the boys tripped on the hard rocky ground. When they fell, others came crushing down on them. The fallen ones were pulled to safety or jumped to their feet, with torn and bloodied shirts and pants partially hiding bruised and scabby elbows and knees.

Rubin saw hats and caps bouncing to the ground, unattended. It seemed their loss and the pain of scraped flesh was forgotten in the exhilaration of the moment. He couldn't help himself. He joined in with the rest and noticed all the other sideliners had joined in, too.

David realized the pushing had to be synchronized, so he started yelling out, "All right now, *push*! All right now, *push*! All right now, *push*!"

Slowly, very slowly, the flatcar stopped moving toward the Quad. It lingered in one location and then started to move back the other way. More grating, screeching sounds. Rubin thought, we've pushed it over a slight rise; it should be clear sailing now.

Simultaneously, everyone realized what had happened and joined in thunderous cheers. "Wa-hoo,wa-hoo, wa-hoo!"

The car, heading now toward Mayfield, started to gain speed. It was going about five to six miles per hour. David and Milton saw what was happening and jumped back on board. David shouted down to Rubin, "Jump on. Jump on. If you want to ride, jump on."

As many as could, did. It was not easy. The ones already on board helped the others, but as the car sped down the track it became difficult and dangerous. Rubin made one attempt to climb on board, but wasn't able to pull himself up until he felt David and Milton pulling him aboard. Sam came over and looked as if he were going to push Rubin back off the car, but David intervened. Rubin could not hear his exact words, but it was something like, "Don't touch him or both of us will push you off with him."

Milton was standing side by side with David, and Sam must have decided he had better things to do. Rubin got to his feet and gained a position beside David and Milton., It was exhilarating to hear the shouts and screams and sounds of the railway wheels and to see the brush and weeds whipping by.

The flatcar approached and then exceeded ten miles per hour. Students who were not already on board gave up and ran along side. Some of them found it difficult to do that, so they dropped out along the railroad track and walked behind. Everyone was shouting and screaming Stanford cheers, but the voices were feebler: "Wah-hoo, Wah-hoo."

Rubin looked at the horizon ahead of them. The county road was getting closer, and he could make out the outline of several carts and a carriage. Where the spur crossed the road there was only a white RR crossing sign. Another quarter of a mile and the spur swung into the railway's main north-south line, with its passenger and freight traffic.

The cheering died down. Others, like Rubin, must have begun to think it was time to stop. Rubin pulled on David's arm and pointed ahead to the traffic on the county road. David took one look and moved toward the brake wheel and motioned for others to help him to turn it. Rubin could tell everyone felt it was time to end the joy ride before any serious accident took place. After all, it was just a prank.

But Sam did not agree with David. Rubin watched with dread as Sam reached out, as if to put his hand on David's shoulder to restrain him, forcefully. Sam looked as if he had enough of David's interference and was ready for a show-down. Sam's face had contorted into a weird, almost crazy look.

But, again, Winko came between them and shouted something in Sam's ear. With all the noise, it was impossible to hear anything. Rubin guessed he said, "It's over, Sam. We're stopping."

Quickly, a sly smile worked its way over Sam's face. Rubin could not tell what was going through his mind, but it had to be dastardly. Sam returned to his leadership role and hollered out, "Watch out, everyone. We're going to stop."

Rubin assumed David had not felt Sam's hand and was not aware of his intentions or Winko's intervention. With the help of other hands, David was still trying to turn the brake wheel and stop the car. With more grunting and groaning, they were successful.

It was a slow process of squealing steel against steel; screeching; and ear splitting sounds, like those drills make when they hit hard metal. Even after the car's wheels were locked, it skidded another fifteen yards. By the time the flatcar came to a complete stop, it was only twenty yards from the main county road. Rubin watched a liveried carriage go by, its passengers unaware of the catastrophic event almost befalling them.

The happy mob of bruised and battered LSJU students scrambled off the flatcar and joined their mates running along side. Together, they ran back to Encina Hall, retrieving lost headgear along the way.

Halfway back, the group met Woody, limping after them. In the midst of the excitement, David and Milt raised Woody to their shoulders, Rubin grabbed his canes, and they all ran back together, shouting and cheering. They couldn't wait to tell everyone what they had missed. With the running and carrying, David's breath was coming in big gulps. Woody was getting heavy, but David could feel his heart beating with pride as he thought, is this the beginning of the Stanford spirit Dr. Jordan talked about?"

They were a bedraggled-looking crowd. No broken bones, but the next thing to it. Several were limping from sprained ankles; others had banged-up toes that had collided with oversized rocks. All had torn, dusty pants and jackets and dirty, smiling faces. Several were bareheaded, or with the wrong size hats on their heads. They were laughing and shouting to one another about falling off the car and rolling on the hard ground.

Once Encina Hall was in view, the crowd became subdued, and smiling faces became quite solemn. The realization of the enormity of what they had just done, and the potential consequences, began to creep in. As a result, no one ventured up the front steps and through the front lobby. No one wanted to go near Burt Fesler's office. As the master of Encina Hall, he would be the one who would discipline them. They all used side or rear entrances, or went in through windows on the ground floor, such as Woody's. If a word were spoken, it was whispered. The going and the returning of this assembly were in stark contrast.

Woody asked David and Mitch to lower him to the ground. His canes were returned to him, and he began his arduous return trek. Milton, David, and Rubin stayed with him. The four boys were the last to reenter the hall.

They slowly went up the back stairway, down the hallway, and into Woody's room. When the door was closed, Woody plunked himself down in his stuffed chair. All of the excitement had completely tuckered him out. David, Rubin, and Milton remained standing, looking down on him.

"Sit down, please sit down. Wherever you can. Sorry the room is in such a mess," Woody said, still catching his breath.

David looked around. Compared with his and Milton's room, this room was immaculate.

They sat on the bed and in the wooden chairs. No one said a word.

Woody broke the silence. "What will they do to us?"

David was surprised at how Woody had taken on the burden of the group. Really, he had only been an onlooker. He said, "I have no idea, but you should be—"

Woody interrupted him. "No, I was a participant, and if there is any punishment, I should be punished along with all of you."

Rubin decided to break up the seriousness. "Well, no one knows what will happen next, but I think it was the most exciting thing I've ever done in my short life, and it was certainly fun. Luckily, we didn't kill ourselves, and I have a hunch that when we're old and gray, we'll be telling our grandchildren about what just happened."

Everyone nodded in agreement, and broad smiles returned to their faces. It had truly been an adventure.

David said, "Let's get to dinner before all the meat is eaten up."

CHAPTER 18

▼

"I HID IN A CLOSET."

Wednesday, October 7, 1891

Early next morning, a note was personally delivered for David Starr Jordan by Ariel Lathrop—even before the president of the University had arrived.

Leslie took the note from Ariel's hand. From the smirk on Ariel's face, Leslie knew the note's contents bode badly for both Dr. Jordan and, as Ariel felt, the ungrateful rascals attending the University and taking advantage of his sister's generosity. Leslie put the note in his coat's breast pocket. From the rigid, masculine handwriting on the envelope, slightly slanted to the right, he knew it was from Senator Stanford.

Shortly afterwards, Dr. Jordan arrived. He was always out of breath when he first walked into the office. Leslie followed him. His wife was too pregnant to get out of bed, Dr. Jordan complained, and since Edith was rooming at the Adelante Villa, he had to prepare breakfast for young Knight and himself. Nothing had gone right. Leslie fingered the note in his pocket but hesitated to add to Dr. Jordan's misery.

Dr. Jordan was about to start the routine he always attended to first thing in the morning—getting a cup of coffee and using the men's room directly outside—when he realized Leslie was still standing there. Usually he greeted him and left.

"Yes, Leslie, what is it?" he asked.

"A matter, sir, probably most urgent from the fact that it is note from the senator, personally delivered by Ariel."

Dr. Jordan's face dropped. This day was not going to go well. "Well, what is it, this time?" he asked as he tore the small envelope open. As he read, his chin noticeably drooped an inch or two.

The note read:

> *My dear David,*
>
> *Your presence at our home is urgently requested today at two o'clock. Our purpose is to mete out punishment to the perpetrators of the scandalous removal of railway property that might have caused innocent victims loss of life or limb.*
>
> *Senator and Mrs. Stanford*

When he finished reading, Dr. Jordan supported himself by putting his fingertips on the top of his desk and then moving around the desk until he could sit down in his chair. Leslie watched, wondering what he should do. Whatever was in the note was not good. Dr. Jordan finally realized Leslie was still there, watching him.

He read the note in his hand to Leslie and, afterwards, said, "I have no idea what this is all about—our students removing railway property that might have caused loss of life or limb. Leslie, do you know what is going on?"

"No idea at all, sir."

"Could you please ask Bert and Frank to come in here. Maybe they know what happened."

Leslie went in the rear entrance of the main office. Frank and Bert were standing there, looking at the doorway as if expecting him to come and get them. "Dr. Jordan would like to see you two."

Frank glanced at Bert with an "I told you so" look. Bert looked straight ahead, but Leslie could tell he knew what had happened. Both of them followed Leslie straight away, back to Dr. Jordan's office.

Dr. Jordan had pulled up two side chairs so they faced him. He motioned to the boys to sit down. Frank was nonchalant, but Bert was just the opposite—worried looking even frightened. Leslie thought Bert couldn't be guilty of participating in whatever had riled the Stanfords. He wasn't that kind of fellow. And he doubted whether Frank was, either.

Leslie had never seen Dr. Jordan in the role of inquisitor, but as he spoke to the two students his eyes narrowed and it was obvious he was serious about getting to the bottom of whatever happened. He waved the note he had just read before them and said, "I have here a note from Senator Stanford. He's asked me to come to their mansion at two o'clock today to discuss students being punished for removal of railway property that might have caused serious damages. Do you either of you know anything about this?"

Bert jumped to his feet and said with deep conviction, "I had nothing to do with it, Dr. Jordan. I was at the Villa yesterday late afternoon taking care of Jim. I didn't do it, Dr. Jordan. Please don't send me off the edge of the earth." He sat back down, making a great effort to hold back his tears.

Dr. Jordan tried to lessen Bert's fears. "No one is accusing you or Frank of anything, Bert. I want to find out what happened. Right now I am completely in the dark." He looked at Frank, who was watching Bert and wondering why he was so upset.

Frank said, "I was in Mayfield yesterday afternoon talking to Reverend Thoburn about the student meeting we had Wednesday night. When I got back to Encina, the place was humming with the news that most of the students—perhaps as many as one or two hundred—took a flatcar for a joy ride to Mayfield yesterday afternoon."

When Dr. Jordan heard what the hubbub was about, he looked as if he had to suppress a smile. Trying valiantly to remain dead serious, he said, "Took a flatcar to Mayfield, did they? It couldn't have been easy. Those cars weigh tons. No one was hurt?"

Frank was matter of fact as he said, "Only a few nicks and bruises. No broken bones that I know of."

"Good, and that's it. They took a flatcar for a joyride."

"Well ..." Bert held back what he was about to say.

"What, Bert? I have to know so I'll be prepared to talk to the senator."

"There was talk ... I heard talk some of the boys wanted to go all the way to Mayfield and didn't want to stop before crossing the county road."

"Yes, that could have been dangerous, very dangerous. But cooler heads prevailed. Am I right, Bert? Cooler heads prevailed?"

"Yes, sir. Cooler heads prevailed," Bert said.

Leslie noticed Bert's hands were wringing wet from nervousness.

"Anything else you want to tell me, boys? You wouldn't know who the ringleaders were, would you?"

They both emphatically said, "No, sir," at the same time.

Frank added, "Both of us weren't there, and no one I talked to mentioned anything about a ringleader. Perhaps there was none. Perhaps it was, as they say, spontaneous, sir."

"That I doubt very much, Frank. But that's all I need you for, gentlemen. If I need more information, I'll let you know."

Both boys got up and returned to the main office. Leslie remained. He had been standing behind the boys, watching the proceedings.

Dr. Jordan appeared relieved as he said, "Well, it could have been worse. No one was injured and no property damage, other than the car being moved from one point to another."

Leslie was not as optimistic. He said, "The senator and his wife must be extremely upset because they used words such as 'scandalous' and 'loss of life or limb.' One thing we both must remember, Dr. Jordan, is that neither the senator nor his wife had the collegiate experience. They married at an early age and the senator worked hard, exceptionally hard, I understand, all of his life, while his wife stayed dutifully at home. I doubt if either of them has ever done, or even thought of doing, anything as outlandish as a prank. So you will find no sympathy there."

Even though it was a serious situation, Dr. Jordan had to smile. "I know I have done such a thing, but I'm not so sure about you, Leslie. Did you ever join a group of daredevils?"

"I never helped move a flatcar, I must say, but believe it or not, as an undergrad at Cornell, I pushed over my share of outhouses. And one time we cut the boughs from the campus trees along the main entrance to use as decorations for a dance, and then stole a university cart and horse to haul the boughs to our fraternity. When they found the cart and horse had disappeared, there was hell to pay. I could have been expelled for that. I wasn't the ringleader, but I was certainly a willing follower. I'll never forget how two burly campus gendarmes chased us into our frat house. I hid in a closet, with my heart pounding."

"They never caught you?"

"I would not be here if they had."

Both men shared a chuckle at the thought of Leslie in the closet, and he and his mates in their cart and horse careening through Cornell's campus with their purloined boughs.

"That must have been a sight, Leslie. Bully for you. I would have never thought you had it in you. As you can guess, I was always the ringleader. I think you have already heard about several of the escapades I instigated, but this exchange of prank stories doesn't help me with what I must say to the Stanfords to prevent a mass expulsion."

Dr. Elliott said, "If I were you, I would appeal to Mrs. Stanford. She appears to be the more understanding of the two. In their hearts, neither of them wants this university to fail. I don't think they will do anything to jeopardize their son's heritage."

"You're right. Now, I must get back to work. There is much to do. Leslie, I'll speak to you before I leave."

The morning went quickly for Leslie. During his visits to the front office, he did happen to see Sam Cutter being escorted back to Dr. Jordan's office. He had never liked the young man. He always had a smirk of superiority on his face. And he bumped into Dr. Anderson, the head of the English Department, arm in arm with Dr. Jordan as they adjourned to Dr. Jordan's sanctuary. Leslie felt Dr. Anderson considered him an underling—Dr. Jordan's assistant. As they passed in the hallway, Dr. Anderson acknowledged him with a slight nod.

Shortly afterward, Dr. Jordan came into Leslie's office and slumped into his side chair. Already Leslie knew Dr. Anderson had not been the bearer of good news.

"I've just heard the senator wants to expel all the students who participated in yesterday's prank."

Leslie's face turned ashen. "That has to be a rumor."

"No, Mrs. Stanford's private secretary told Dr. Anderson, and he told me. Knowing the source, I'm sure it is true."

"That could be two hundred students." Dr. Elliott, who was usually not demonstrative, held his head in his two hands and moaned, "My God, that's almost half of our enrollment. That would decimate us."

Dr. Jordan found himself consoling his registrar. "Leslie, as you've surmised, my heart is with the students. In fact, I am sure this will be a bonding experience for them. What bothered me was Sam Cutter came forth with the name of the ringleader. That I do not like, but I must admit, may be helpful."

"Yes, I saw young Cutter come in this morning to gain your ear. What did he have to say?"

Jordan looked with admiration at Leslie and said, "Is there anything that misses your eye? It's as if you are always on my shoulder. Cutter named Timothy Lambert Wilkins, known as Pudge, as the leader. I know that the traitor did it to ingratiate himself with me. I did verify what he said with two other students whom I have befriended. When I confronted them with Wilkins' nickname, "Pudge," they nodded reluctantly in agreement. So all the fingers point at Pudge,

I'm afraid. I will expel him today, right after my meeting with the senator. Hopefully, that will mollify him and his wife."

Leslie stood up and grasped Dr. Jordan's hand in a firm, farewell handshake. "Don't forget my words about the wife. She's the one to appeal to."

"Yes, I haven't, and I absolutely agree with you. I'm not sure what I'll say, but something will suggest itself. Now, I must be on my way. I still have to walk home and saddle up Winter. Wouldn't do for the president to walk to a meeting with the founders about expelling half of his university's students."

CHAPTER 19

▼

"OUR FIRST CRISIS"

That Same Day

"Tell me every word. Don't leave out a syllable."

Leslie hadn't been able to do a stitch of work this past hour because he knew Dr. Jordan was fighting for the life of the University. Upon his return, the good doctor had smiled bleakly and said, "I did it," and sat down at his desk without giving details. He sat there, breathing deeply and rapidly, as if he had run back from Stanford's mansion instead of riding his horse. Between breaths, he said, "Of course, you'd want to know every word."

Like an echo, Leslie repeated his words, "Of course I do, every word."

Heightening the suspense, Dr. Jordan spoke slowly at first. "The man is not well. He barely made it into his study, where we met."

"Where was Mrs. Stanford?"

"He said she would be down later. She always makes a late appearance. Where was I? Oh, yes, barely making it, he supported himself, as usual, with his pearl-handled cane. He stationed himself in front of his favorite brown leather chair and plunked himself into it. As it was, I had cooled my heels for over thirty minutes—tapping my fingers, twisting my moustache. I, of course, was there precisely at two o'clock. Finally, I heard him coming down the main stairs, clump, clump, clumping with his cane.

"Even though I had seen him a few days earlier, his complexion was grayer, dark eyes not as sharply focused. I stood before him, and it was as if he didn't know I was there. His eyes were misted over and concentrating on some distant, unseen object above and to the right of my head. He was in a different world. I was completely discombobulated. I didn't know what I should do to attract his attention.

"'Ah, hem,' I gently muttered.

"'Yes, yes,' he said. His eyes refocused and recognized me. He said he was sorry, but his mind had wandered back to the grocery store in Sacramento. He smiled as he said how those were good, simple days, and recalled how when he arrived in town, he didn't have a penny in his pocket. Leslie, you have to admire the man. Back East, some fire destroyed everything he possessed, and Mrs. Stanford returned to her parents' home and lived with them while he forged a new life with his brothers in the West. But, I digress. He did say how it was just plain hard work and long hours that made him successful, and what drove him was the thought he could bring his dear wife out West so they could be together. The senator's eyes misted over as he said again how those were the good days, and how he could remember exactly how his first store looked—as if he were standing at its entrance, preparing to greet customers."

Enough, enough about greeting customers, Leslie thought but did not say. Get on with it. What about the boys? The University? What punishment?

Dr. Jordan realized from the look on Leslie's face that his companion was anxious. "Before my very eyes, the wistful look on the senator's face disappeared and a stern look of judge and jury replaced it. With his left hand shaking, he motioned for me to sit beside him.

"He mentioned, again, how Mrs. Stanford would be down shortly. As he spoke, he did not look at me, and I felt he wanted to put me at ease in preparation for the dire decision he was about to reveal. He asked about Miss Jessie and said it appeared, from what he had seen at the ceremonies, our new addition was imminent. I attempted conviviality, going along with the charade, and said something like, 'Doing comfortably, thank you. You're right it should be soon. We think it's going to be a girl, comparing Jessie's discomfort with all the activity she had just before Knight was born.'

"A slight smile crossed the senator's face, and he said he thought Knight was quite a boy. And he recalled, when we were last there, he saw Knight climbing over all the furnishings and putting his fingers on everything within sight. He couldn't sit still and was into everything. 'A real boy,' he said.

"I said, 'Yes, he can be a handful.'

"His quick response was, 'You wouldn't want him to be any other way.'

"I told him I was proud of all the members of my family, and they were all different in their ways."

Leslie couldn't help himself. He must have rolled his eyes, wondering when Dr. Jordan would get to the decisions that had been made.

Dr. Jordan reacted. "Sorry, Leslie. You did say every syllable, and it's the best way for me to recall the chain of events. We did have one more digression. He turned his head toward me and asked if I were still riding my feisty black bronco. I replied yes. I could feel myself being drawn in by the warmth of his tone and conversation, and I started to breathe normally, but my hands were still wet with perspiration.

"I told him how fond I am of riding Winter. 'Yes,' I said, 'he's feisty, but he's taken me all over these properties, even to San Jose and Monterey.'

"For the first time, I felt as if I were talking with a friend when he told me he'd seen us, and there were days when he would have been out there with me—but not now. He put his finger to his temple and spoke as if he were thinking aloud. 'Yes, we do have to get you a better mount, though,' he said. 'Yes, Floodmore, a fine bay thoroughbred, would be good for you.'

"Can you believe it, Leslie, a thoroughbred filly for me, worth thousands of dollars? And he said he would talk it over tomorrow morning with his head trainer, Mr. Tompkins, and after a little more preparation, she'll be mine."

Dr Jordan's face had become red with the excitement of being given a thoroughbred filly. All thought of his university losing its male students was forgotten. Leslie could only sit there and wonder. The senator certainly knew how to maneuver people; after all, he was a politician.

The same thought must have struck Dr. Jordan because he looked embarrassed at his lack of respect for the seriousness of the situation. He sat back in his chair as he described how Senator Stanford put his two hands together, prayer like, in a moment of deep concentration.

Dr. Jordan continued, "Neither of us spoke. I knew the gavel was about to fall.

"The senator, in an emotional voice, said, 'How could they do this deed? How could they? If they had met a moving train, surely all of them would have been killed. Can you imagine the grieving parents on our doorstep? I am sure my Jane would not have survived such an ordeal. Even the retelling of the tale takes me aback.'

"I could see his beloved railway and the boys were secondary. The primary consideration was Senator Stanford's thought that the grieving parents would revive their own personal loss. I could think of no other way to act, but in a straightforward manner. I said, 'We have the name of the ringleader, and after this meeting I plan to expel him.'

"'Good, the sooner, the better,' he said. 'But Mrs. Stanford and I have considered going beyond the ringleader and expelling the whole lot of them—anyone who was even close to the scene of this potential calamity. We have reasoned that if the followers were left unpunished, later they might contaminate the few who knew better, or even repeat a similar act.'

"I said, 'That could be almost two hundred male students, Senator.'

"'We understand that.'

"This final verdict shocked me into silence. I thought of all our work—the recruiting of faculty members, the testing of students. Suddenly, all of our dreams for the future were about to be dashed. A thought struck me: logic might not prevail, but sentiment might. Which student's expulsion would touch the senator's heart? George Gardner, the wooden-legged one, I thought.

"I got up and stood before him like an attorney before a judge. If all we had done was about to be destroyed, I wanted, at the very least, to have his full attention. I stood as if pleading for clemency for my client—which I was—and said, 'If that is the case, one of the students we would have to expel is George Gardner. George is a boy who suffers from diabetes, and unfortunately had to have both legs surgically removed. He has two wooden legs and gets around the campus with the aid of his canes as well as he can. You may have seen him struggling along his ways, but I predict, because of his strong will, he will graduate in spite of his infirmities.

"I could see the signs of the senator's distress. He said, 'I did not know. I've seen the poor chap from my carriage—dragging himself along, step by step. What a brave boy, I thought, and how lucky we are to have him amongst us. But a boy with two wooden legs, how could he be one of the culprits?"

"'He merely followed, Senator. Tried to keep up. But afterwards, I was told, when the boys returned to the hall, they hoisted him on their shoulders.' In the telling of the story, I became animated. It was as if I were describing something I had seen. In spite of myself, tears came to my eyes, and I noticed the senator's eyes were beginning to mist over. 'And they ran back to the hall with him so that he could be one of them, as I am sure with all his heart he was. And there were others who were merely following. Except for the ringleader, it will be impossible for us to determine who followed and who led."

"'Yes, yes, not an easy decision. I have to wonder if young Leland would have been one of them. He was mostly in the company of adults and had few young friends. But I am sure he would have befriended Mr. Gardner and he may have followed the gang, just to protect him.'

"Tears did come to the senator's eyes, and he said, 'I probably have already told you how he befriended a poor crippled boy whose name was Wilsie. He saw Wilsie on the streets near where we lived in San Francisco and brought him back to our home and made sure he was fed; and the boy regularly came back to visit us, even up to the time when dear Leland went to Europe and never came back alive. We have not seen Wilsie since, but we've made certain he will be cared for. With little Leland gone, we did not have the heart to bring him back into the house.'

"At that moment, Mrs. Stanford strode briskly into the room in a business-like manner, and sat beside her husband. Her face was set and determined. She spoke my name and nodded to acknowledge my presence. I could tell, in her mind, the jury had met and made its decision.

"'I'm sorry to keep you waiting, Dr. Jordan,' she said in an unemotional voice. I had never seen her in such a frame of mind and I surmised she thought I had been told all the culprits must go. For the first time, I realized that we were wrong. Mrs. Stanford was the tougher of the two.

"She looked directly at me with cold, penetrating eyes and said, 'My husband told you of our decision?'

"I said nothing in response, so her gaze turned to Senator Stanford and saw the distressed look on his face. 'What's wrong, my darling?' she asked and put her ring-encrusted fingers on his arm.

"'Nothing, nothing, Jane. As always, I was thinking about little Leland.' He grasped her hand tenderly. 'Jane, please forgive an old man. I've changed my mind. I'll explain why later, and I know you will agree with what I am going to do. Dr. Jordan has the name of the ringleader and he will go henceforth and expel him. The rest of the boys will be severely reprimanded and told if there is even the rumor of a similar occasion, they will be instantly expelled.'

"I was dumbstruck. Before my eyes, the man had changed courses. But I knew enough to leave before there was any further discussion.

"'Yes, sir, I will go immediately.' I was still on my feet and quickly said my good-byes. I had learned long ago when the winning cards come up, leave.

"But Senator Stanford raised his hand to halt my departure. 'And, Doctor, one more thing.' Mid-step, I hesitated. Had he changed his mind? 'Would you be so kind as to say that it was only because of Mrs. Stanford's generosity of spirit that such a decision was made, and that I was dead set against it?'

"I nodded in the affirmative, and just in case, glanced over at Mrs. Stanford to make sure she was in agreement.

"Throughout the disclosure of the altered plans, her face remained passive—unchanged and unemotional. To me, it appeared she had learned to hide her feelings when situations were not going as she wished. For my benefit, she allowed her face to break into a puzzled smile. 'As long as you are satisfied, dearest Leland, that is all that matters.' She took his hand in hers.

"I took that as affirming what I had been told. As I left the room, the two of them were still holding one another's hands."

Dr. Jordan took another deep breath and exhaled slowly. His story was finished.

Leslie got up from his seat and came over to Dr. Jordan, leaned over him, put his arms around the doctor's shoulders, and gave him what would be considered to be a manly hug. No words were exchanged. Dr. Jordan put his two hands on Leslie's arm. It was an emotional experience for both of them. For a second or two, they shared it.

Composure was regained when Leslie returned to his seat and Dr. Jordan sat straight up in his chair. Now he was ready to take control of the situation.

"I didn't have time to ride Winter home. He is hitched up, out back. I'd like one of the boys in the office—Bert perhaps—to ride him back to Escondite. And on the way, drop off a note to Mr. Fesler, informing him to tell Pudge that he is immediately expelled. And Fesler should convene all of the boys in front of the hall for a meeting just before supper with the president of the University. I plan to give it to them with both barrels, and tell them if it were not for the grace of Mrs. Stanford, they would have all joined Pudge. Sorry, Leslie, I have no idea what his real name is."

Leslie was on his feet, heading for the door as he asked, "Do you want me to write the note?"

Dr. Jordan was already busy at his desk. He hardly looked up when he said, "Would you, please?"

When Leslie was at the doorway, Dr. Jordan had one more thought. "Thank God, George Gardner followed the group. I never knew the story about Leland, Junior and the crippled boy. So his name was Wilsie. And thank God that turncoat Sam Cutter snitched Pudge's name to me. Without that, we would have been in a dilemma.

"Now, on your way, Leslie. There is much to do, but our first crisis is assuredly assuaged. With Miss Jessie about to have a baby, I have enough on my mind."

CHAPTER 20

▼

"I THINK HE'S FROM CHICAGO."

That Same Evening

Fletcher Martin was alone in his room at Encina Hall. He had just returned from the dining room, where he had heard from numerous conversations buzzing around him that one of the boys, Pudge, was expelled for instigating the flatcar prank. Some of the boys were laughing about how Pudge was the one expelled, when it was some other fellow called Sam Cutter who was the real leader. The boys at Fletcher's table were talking about how Dr. Jordan had shown his feathers as he chastised them before dinner for even considering moving railway equipment. He warned them Senator Stanford wanted to send the bunch of them off the edge of the world. Mrs. Stanford's intervention on their behalf was the reason the senator changed his mind. If it happened again, Dr. Jordan assured them, they were gone. An impromptu cheer had gone up for Mrs. Stanford. "Hip, hip, hurrah, Mrs. Stanford! Hip, hip, hurrah, Mrs. Stanford!"

Fletcher had listened to the chattering, but made no comment. Because he was older, thirty-three years old, and a graduate student, his status at the hall was unique. Being a grizzled veteran with ten years service in the Indian Wars, he found himself to be neither fish nor foul—too old to hobnob with younger fellows and still a student in the eyes of the faculty. This position of betwixt and between didn't bother him in the least. He was happy being out of it.

And he didn't mind some of the boys referring to him as "Abe Junior" when they passed him in the halls. The occasional "Hatchet Face" was aggravating, and he thought about chasing the brat down and giving him a "what for." But "why bother" overruled the display of displeasure. He was used to the Lincoln comparison, though for the life of him, except for his height and color of hair, he did not see the similarity.

Fletcher's reaction to all the exuberance going on at Encina was similar to his observations of old male wolves. Midst the playful antics of younger pups, the old males focused on hunting and breeding, and weren't bothered by the playful snipping and yipping of the younger members of the pack. At times, the old ones appeared to be encouraging it as part of some primitive learning process. So, too, Fletcher managed to ignore all the craziness that prevailed at Encina, reasoning that from this play the strong would survive. It was a fact of life that, even though he tried, he couldn't ignore. That fellow, Darwin, had verified its relevance.

Another fact of life at Encina was that the electric lights still didn't work. Supposedly, transformers had been unpacked and were being installed at the powerhouse, but were not yet operational. Only the Quad was lit. Rumor had it, electric lights would finally be on at Encina over the weekend, but there was no word about Roble Hall, where the young ladies resided, or the professors' homes on Alvarado Row. That might be a while, Fletcher had heard.

With the flickering light from two tallow candles, he was attempting to read the miniscule type of a paper Frederick Jackson Turner was about to publish in the University of Wisconsin's *Journal of Education*. Dr. Jordan had given him an advanced copy he had received from one of his colleagues at UW. Dr. Jordan thought Fletcher should be aware of Turner's observations.

Fletcher sat back in his chair and looked around at his surroundings, shrouded in shadows. Dr. Whitman, his roommate, was still at the Quad. With electric lights on there, he had stayed in his office to review and correct student papers.

Alone in the semi-darkness, his thoughts reverted, as they often did, to his beloved Irene. He loved Irene so very much. She had opened the doorway to a whole new realm of feelings and sensitivities and tenderness. She had been his teacher in the ways of love. He was so naïve in so many ways, but now it was natural to touch and feel her, and to have her touch and feel him. Even the thought of their closeness was enough to arouse him.

Except for a few times with young women he met while attending West Point, he had not had sexual activity with the opposite sex. And those times were always under the duress of time, limited space, or being observed. In the army, although Indian women and prostitutes were available, he never thought it right to use their services. Paying money for love, or having the threat of chastisement hanging over an Indian woman's head, was not right as far as Fletcher was concerned.

These feelings must have originated from his relationship with his younger, mentally handicapped sister. He had found some of his young schoolboy chums about to disrobe her. If they had not scattered to the winds, he would have killed all of them. Now, with Irene, everything was different. Ovid's lines from Ars Amatoria came to his mind:

> *If she summons you*
> *Love detests laggards. You've no transport? Walk.*
> *Don't be put off by bad weather,*
> *Or a heat wave,*
> *Or snowdrifts blocking your road.*

Fletcher suddenly felt the warmth of happiness and love.

But he turned his eyes back to Turner's writings and read, "Artistic and critical faculty find expression in Herodutus, father of Greek history, and in Thucydides, the ideal Greek historian. Both write from the standpoint ..." At that point, the door to Fletcher's room was flung open and a breathless Bert Hoover ran into his room.

"Mr. Martin, Mr. Martin, you have to come with me. They've got Rubin Weinberg, the Jew, and they're doing bad things to him." He pulled Fletcher out of his chair into the darkness of the hall. Bert had a candle in his hand, and Fletcher followed him without questioning, as he ran up the stairs to the next floor.

When they opened the door, Fletcher could not believe his eyes. The room was dark, except for Bert's candle and another lone candle held by a boy standing near a cleared study desk, upon which a diminutive, naked boy—undoubtedly the Jew—was attempting to perform the gyrations of a slow Negro dance. Fletcher couldn't help but notice the fellow sported a splendid penis that would have looked more properly placed on a much larger man.

Around the Jew were gathered about six or eight students Fletcher did not know. A medium height, blonde, shorthaired fellow was leading the group in taunting the Jew and attempting to get him to be more Negro-like in his dancing. The boys were concentrating on the dancer, and it took them a few seconds to realize Fletcher and Bert had entered the room. When they did, the room became silent and all eyes, including the Jew's, focused on Fletcher. The look on the curly haired one's face turned disdainful. Fletcher felt his presence was not wanted.

In spite of his desire to remain cool and aloof, Fletcher could not help himself. He felt his heart rate quicken as he instinctively shouted out, "What's going on, here?" He pushed his way through the group without regard for who stood in his way and helped the naked boy jump down from the table. Fletcher looked around at the now-sheepish faces surrounding him and demanded, "Where are this man's clothes?"

One of the boys wearing a UOP sweater leaned down and gathered Rubin's clothes, which were scattered on the floor, and politely gave them to the Jew.

Fletcher watched him put his clothes back on. He could feel his heart rate returning to normal. He had liked it when one of the boys had helped find the clothes. Out of the darkness, the curly haired boy came up close to Fletcher, faced him—his cleft chin only inches from Fletcher's face.

"And who do you think you are? We're doing a scientific study of Jews doing nigger dancing to see if they have any rhythm, and you—you scarred, old fool—are interrupting us," he said with a broad smirk on his face.

The rest of the boys couldn't help themselves; they had to chuckle at their leader's audacity.

Fletcher did not like being called a fool, and particularly an old and scarred one. He told the smirking face, "Out of my way, scum," and enforced his words with a single sweep of his long arm. The Jew was pulling on his trousers. To the rest of the group, Fletcher ordered in a voice more suited to the parade grounds, "I want all of you out of here."

His commanding voice sounded throughout the hall, acting like a magnet to attract everyone on the floor to drop what they were doing and come running into the room to see whatever was going on—a fight, hopefully.

With this kind of audience, the blond fellow was not to be faced down. "Now, hold on, old boy," he said to Fletcher and cheekily grabbed him by the shoulder.

"I'm not your old boy, and take your hand off my shoulder," Fletcher said in a voice warning of impeding disaster.

The blond fellow answered the warning by tightening his grip on Fletcher's shoulder and attempting to throw him off balance. Fletcher's left hand brusquely removed the hand from his shoulder. The removed hand was made into a fist and tried to hit Fletcher full in the face. Fletcher glided out of the way of the blow, and brought his right fist up under both of his opponent's hands, and hit him in the solar plexus, full force.

In seconds, the encounter was over. Those boys present heard wind whistling out of lungs as the blond fellow slumped to the floor. And to add to his ignominy, Fletcher pulled him out of the room by his shoulders into the darkened

hallway and left him there. The onlookers sheepishly followed the two combat-
ants out of the room and attempted to help their fallen hero get up from his inert,
supine position on the floor.

Fletcher walked back into the room, closed the door, and locked it. His heart
was beating wildly and he could feel the animal tension of man's basic instincts of
survival. He did not like those feelings and he wished Bert had never sought him
out, but what could he do?

By now, Rubin was fully dressed, and Bert was helping him get his room back
into order.

Rubin could see Mr. Martin was not happy with himself or what he'd done.
His dark hair was disheveled and his eyes had the look of a trapped beast. He was
perspiring profusely and his clothes were awry from the scuffle. He was breathing
heavily, his chest rising and falling like water in a pump.

Bert introduced the two. "Mr. Martin, this is Sosh—that's the new name for
Rubin Weinberg because he's a socialist."

The two shook hands, "I'm not really a socialist, or an anarchist, for that matter. It's just what the boys want to call me after they've heard what I think," Sosh,
formerly Rubin, said, looking up at Fletcher, who towered over him. He spoke
calmly, as if he had just finished a game of hearts.

Between gasps of breath, Fletcher managed to say, "Sosh, sorry about all this.
You shouldn't have to endure any of this." He was trying to regain his composure, but he could feel his heart still beating like a drum. At least his voice,
between deep gulps of air, was beginning to sound normal.

As if it were a boring subject, Sosh responded, "What Sam did was far from
original. They really wanted to see my penis. They hoped it would be small, but
it isn't. I went through the same comparisons when I first went to high school.
For some reason, Anglo-Saxons always like to see a Jew's penis. They think
because I'm circumcised, it is a forgone conclusion it will be short and they can
tease me. But when they see it is not, the game is no longer fun. You certainly
gave him a pasting, Mr. Martin, I'm sure he won't forget."

Fletcher couldn't get over how Sosh was taking all of this so calmly. It was as if
nothing had happened to him. He must be used to it. How terrible!

Bert Hoover was excited. "Yes, Mr. Martin, I couldn't get over how hard you
hit him, right in the belly. I walked in, trying to get some more laundry business,
and what should I see but poor Sosh up there on the table, dancing naked. And
the only person I could think of to save him was you …"

Fletcher interrupted Bert. He had heard enough. He wanted to get back to his room. "All right, Bert. I understand." Looking back at Sosh, he asked, "Are you all right? Who was that fellow anyway, taunting you?"

"Sam Cutter. He's a bad person. His gang, the Alpha Phis, just follow him. They're not such a bad lot. In fact, Mitch, the one who helped find my clothes, is really nice. But there is no limit to what Sam might get up to. I'd be watching over my shoulder, if I were you, Mr. Martin."

"What's his name, again?" asked Fletcher.

"Sam Cutter." Both Bert and Sosh said the name at the same time. Bert added, "I think he's from Chicago."

CHAPTER 21

▼

"Cardinal Is Associated with Social Change."

Friday, October 9, 1891

At around seven o'clock, the Stanford males converged on Roble Hall. They had been invited to the first social event on the campus. Most of them started their strolls from Encina in groups of twos and threes, heading east past the Quad and past the old oak that stood squarely in the way. As they approached their destination, these groups mingled, so that by the time they were ascending the steps to Roble's entrance, they were twenty and thirty strong. In keeping with Mrs. Stanford's proclamation about the danger of a fire, a kerosene lantern was suspended on a pole outside the hall to illuminate the steps, but inside the doorway it was strictly candlelight.

Mrs. Leach, Roble Hall's mistress, greeted the arrivals at the door. She directed the boys to one of the card tables just inside the entrance. Behind the table were seated several young ladies who were filling out blue name cards, with attached safety pins, to be pinned to the young men's jackets. All the young ladies were identified with pink cards.

The boys wandered to dim corners, where they spent several minutes pinning their cards on their jackets and repining because the cards were slightly askew or were overlapped by a lapel.

With the pinning job done, they had a chance to look around and see what Roble's reception hall looked like and compare it with their own. It was about one-third the size of Encina's, and its walls, instead of having dark wood paneling, were stucco and rough textured, painted in delicate shades of blue and ecru. At each end of the reception area was a mantel over a brightly burning grated coal fire; in front of the fireplace, pink and blue stuffed chairs with ribbons, also of ecru, had been placed. Mrs. Stanford had participated in the selection of the colors and fabrics. Ecru was one of her favorite colors.

Numerous lit candles had been placed around the room, their soft light enhancing the gentle, ladylike atmosphere. Almost all of the seventy Roble women were present; only a few had been too timid to put in an appearance. Most of them were dressed simply, as Mrs. Stanford had suggested, in calico and gingham wrappers, in soft shades of yellow, green, primrose, lavender, and blue. A few were wearing their Sunday dresses of black satin, but the austerity of their dresses appeared to be out of place on such a casual occasion.

The girls were talking nineteen to the dozen to one another, in small groups along the wall facing the entrance, and some were in the hallways, which went left and right, as they did at Encina.

While the boys whispered and shyly watched their hostesses, the girls gaily spoke about all manner of things. Their voices mingled, creating a high-pitched murmur, like at a fashionable restaurant in the city.

"Don't you love that new song, 'Sweet Marie'"?

"We plan to go to San Francisco and have lunch at the Women's Exchange. It's the only decent place to eat in the city."

"I'm taking German, French, Latin, and English. I have to remember which class I'm in."

"Wasn't Professor Anderson cute when he gave the lecture about Matheny Arnold?"

"Dr. Wood came by and saw me and prescribed cherry phosphate. I think the man is adorable."

"I love Dr. Jordan at the morning chapel. He has such a droll wit."

"Have you read the new book by Thomas Nelson Page?"

"Last night, Room 12 had a dainty spread of chicken wafers and pickles. Everyone was there."

By eight o'clock most of the male students had gathered near tables filled with china plates, upon which had been placed dainty sandwiches; soda crackers with chicken salad spreads; and cups of tea, cider, and sarsaparilla. By now, space near the food was at a premium. Standing off to the side were Rubin, who was now called Sosh because of his interest in socialism, and Will Greer, who had recently shortened his name from William.

Out of the corner of his eye, Sosh saw Sally approaching. She was with Delores, his cousin, and Delores' friend, Betsy.

Sosh turned his back to the girls, hoping Sally would pass by and not see him. He would have liked talking with his cousin, but he still had mixed feelings about Sally. Being with her was like putting a noose around his neck.

Will, looking out at the crowd, saw this lovely blonde girl—the one who had been the object of everyone's attention—walk toward them, come up behind Sosh, and stand there, waiting for him to turn around. Her friends had followed her. Will whispered, "Sosh, I think someone wants to talk to you. She's right behind you."

Sally had her hands on her hips, as if she did not appreciate looking at Sosh's back. When he turned around and said, "Hi, Sally, Delores, Betsy," her expression turned into a smile. She was happy to see him.

"And who is your friend?" she asked, looking at Will.

"Oh, I'm sorry." Sosh shouted introductions over the babble of conversations, "Delores, Sally, Betsy, this is my good chum and roomie, Will Greer."

The girls shook his hand. Sally took charge. "Come on, boys and girls, let's get some food and move out of this clutter so we can talk."

The group of five made their way past a table with cups and plates, took what they needed, and went back to the buffet to fill their plates with crackers and sandwiches. Sally, like a mother hen, guided them to a quieter area to the extreme left, near the hallways leading to the rooms. Sosh thought his cousin followed them reluctantly. It was as if she were hoping to see someone else and preferred to stay in full view.

Betsy grabbed two vacant chairs and pushed one toward Delores. The two girls sat and ate and listened, while Sally, Rubin, and Will conversed.

Sosh said enthusiastically, "Remember, Will, I told you about Sally. We met at the opening ceremony and we have the same French class."

"Well, I would say you are a very lucky person, Sosh, to have made such an acquaintance. I think you mentioned she had similarly dangerous thoughts as you, with all your radical ideas."

Sally, in her usual direct manner, said, "Mr. Greer, did Rubin—sorry, Sosh—use the term 'dangerous' to describe my thoughts?"

"Those were his exact words, Miss."

"Well, he is a good judge of people. I am exceedingly dangerous." A smile of sweet innocence crossed Sally's face. Sosh wondered if the smile were for his benefit, knowing he was aware of the small revolver she had hidden in her purse at the opening ceremonies.

Between mouthfuls, he said to Sally, "I am so lucky to have Will as a room-mate. I may have told you this already, but he's from Boston and now he regularly gets the Boston papers and magazines. So, even if we are two weeks behind times, I at least know what's going on in the country."

Sally agreed. "You are lucky. My only source of information is what I read in the *Chronicle*. Is there anything new about those miners in Tennessee? I remember reading they were being replaced by convict labor."

Will Greer responded, "Nothing violent that we know of yet, but at this point, it's bound to happen—too many hotheads down there. I'm expecting the Army will be called out to quell any riot. President Harrison, our founder's bosom friend, is always on the side of the corporations. But have you heard what happened in New Orleans?"

"I've no idea of what's happening anywhere," Sally said.

Sosh answered for Will. "A mob lynched eleven Italian citizens because they thought they were going to take their jobs. The Italian government is all over President Harrison to do something to protect their citizens, but I would bet he won't do a thing."

Will added, "Thank goodness he has James Blaine as Secretary of State. He'll be able to quell the Italians. Harrison is completely incompetent. I've heard the Republican Party wants to ditch him and nominate Blaine for President, but Blaine doesn't want it because of his health. So there are rumors flying that groups are being organized around the country to nominate Leland Stanford, our illustrious benefactor, instead of Harrison, for president in '92."

Sosh commented, "I don't think Stanford would accept. Too friendly with Harrison to do that, plus from what I hear—and what I saw at the opening ceremony—I don't think the man has long to live."

When Sosh said those words, he noticed, Sally slightly winced. Soon she recovered and looked at Sosh with obvious admiration that they were allowing her to hear comments about the political situation in the United States, even though, as a woman, she could not vote. As he spoke, Sosh was aware of Sally looking at him as if she were seeing another person, someone she admired a great deal. Again, he was both flattered and flustered at the same time.

He looked over at his cousin and could tell she was bored and listening with only half an ear. She and Betsy were chatting about different matters. They, like most young ladies, had been taught by their mothers to leave politics to the men.

Without any forewarning, Sam Cutter sauntered up to the group with other members of Alpha Phi in tow, including Winko, Freck, Mitch, and three others. He walked directly up to Sosh, disregarding Sally and Will. He stood face-to-face about a foot away from Sosh, and with a beaming smile, said, "Hi, Sosh, how are you?"

Sosh was at first surprised, then resolutely looked Sam straight in the eye. "Fine, no thanks to you, Cutter."

With what appeared to be sincerity, Sam said, "Now, Sosh, no grudges. It was supposed to be fun, until your Army friend showed up. As it was, I'm the one who was punched and thrown to the floor. He almost killed me. You know I was knocked unconscious. Come on, no grudges. What's past is past." He put out his hand and smiled broadly.

Will Greer was watching what was going on between Sam and Sosh. Will made a move, as if he were about to impress upon Sam the urgency of keeping away from Sosh, but Sosh's hand held him back. Sally looked as if she had no idea what was going on.

Sosh took a deep breath and exhaled. He preferred not to have enemies. He shook Sam's outstretched hand, but noticed Sam tightened his fingers hard enough that Sosh almost pulled his hand away. Instead, he acknowledged Sam with a slight smile, indicating the matter was over and done with.

Sam released Sosh's hand and gazed longingly at the young ladies, expecting to be introduced. "And who may these lovely ladies be?" His eyes took in Delores and Betsy, but remained fixed on Sally, who appeared to be looking through him.

Sosh now realized Sam's motivation for the apology was to meet the young ladies, particularly Sally. Sally looked as if she had no desire to make Sam's acquaintanceship. She did not appreciate him interrupting her conversation with Sosh and Will.

Sosh introduced the girls and Will to Sam, who in turn introduced his fraternity brethren. When Will was shaking Sam's hand, he drew him close and whispered something in his ear. From the look on Sam's face, Sosh assumed it was a firm warning to stay away from his roomie.

After the formalities, there was silence until Winko, the president of the Alpha Phis, took up the conversation. He looked curiously at Sosh and said, "So you're the one they call Sosh? I hope you didn't bring any dynamite with you."

"That's me. Apparently, my slight socialistic tendencies have been noticed. Be assured words are my weapon, not dynamite."

Winko continued, "I noticed this afternoon at the Student Association meeting, your words put you in good stead. You were heavily involved, and your freshmen friends supported you."

"Yes, there are quite a few of us. I was there and saw you with all your fraternity brothers. As I remember, you were appointed to be on the bylaws committee."

"Yes, but not half as important as your chairmanship of the Constitution group. You appear to be quite the political whizzo, Sosh. We're all supposed to report back by October twentieth with our conclusions, right?

"Right." Sosh could see that the rest of the group wasn't interested in student politics. He, Winko, and Will moved to the side and continued talking about the decisions that would have to be made during the next few weeks: school colors, what the official cheer would be, and the organization of the student publication. Sosh wanted cardinal as the school color because cardinal was associated with social change.

Sally was left alone with Sam at her side. Sosh kept an eye on her. She gave him a quick look of exasperation for leaving her. Sosh could see Sam was trying to engage her in conversation, but she hardly glanced at him. She didn't try to hide her feelings: she didn't like him. Sosh felt a wave of happiness sweep through his body. Her eyes moved toward the entranceway and brightened. Sosh heard Sally say to his cousin, "Look, Delores"—pointing toward the entrance—"there's David with three others. They just walked in. I think he's with the cripple boy I was telling you about, and the Chinese boy."

Sally turned away from Sam, as if he weren't there, and shouted out so almost everyone in the room could hear, "David, David, over here, over here."

CHAPTER 22

▼

"BIT BY A TARANTULA"

Saturday, October 10, 1891

The following day, Fletcher Martin had recovered from the previous evening encounter and decided to go into Mayfield to get his haircut and drop by Fred Behn's saloon for breakfast.

He got to the barbershop about ten o'clock, just about the time when the town started to come to life after a night of hard drinking. There was no one in Frank's Barbershop, not even Frank, so Fletcher made himself comfortable and sat in one of the wooden chairs underneath the long mirror that ran the length of the room. He waited for Frank to appear. Because the front door had been left open, Fletcher assumed Frank was across the street getting a cup of coffee at Fred's saloon.

Fletcher grabbed some of the old *Police Gazettes* lying on the chairs and thought to himself this was the one of the few times he wasn't reading something in Latin or Greek. The magazines were in shreds, with covers off and pages missing, from so many hands turning or purloining their pages. Some dated all the way back to the 1880s.

Fletcher chuckled at the pictures and articles as he leafed through the magazine. Most of the women pictured were dressed in tight-fitting corsets or tights, with black hose covering legs about twice the size of Fletcher's. Fletcher could not help but compare Irene's small, wiry figure with those humongous women. He preferred Irene's dimensions, but he knew most men preferred what he was seeing.

The magazine's articles were about extremely odd animals and people. A three-headed cow and a three-headed sheep were pictured, belonging to a West Pennsylvanian farmer. And there was a long story about a strange tribe of women living in a remote section of East Africa who ate their husbands after mating with them. This article's title was "African Spider Women." Lurid illustrations pictured the gory details.

Frank Schmidt, the errant barber, walked in with a tin cup brimming with steaming coffee. He was a scrawny fellow, with thinning black hair plastered across his baldhead and squinty little eyes looking as if they knew some Mayfield gossip you didn't—which in Fletcher's case was true. Frank walked in with a quick, jerky gait, as if he was trying to catch a train, but his feet were stuck in mud.

"Well, aren't you the early bird. Ouch! Now, that is hot coffee. I like it that way. Let me put it down; it's scalding my fingers." From a cupboard, he whipped out a white apron and tied it behind his back. It made him look like a doctor, which he was at times, if it were called for. Fletcher noticed there were pink blotches on the apron, probably patches of washed-out blood. Fletcher had heard from Fred that before there was a real doctor in the area, Frank had amputated an arm or two and even a leg that had become gangrenous. Fred did not know what had happened to the patient.

There were two shiny chromium barber chairs in the shop. Sometimes, if Frank were busy, his son, Andrew, who was fourteen, helped out.

"Need a cup, Fletcher?"

"No, no thanks. I'm going over to see Fred after this."

Fletcher stepped up to the gleaming barber chair and made himself comfortable. With one motion, Frank threw a light green cover cloth over Fletcher, pinned it around his neck with a safety pin, and poked a bit of tissue between the neck's skin and the cloth to make sure no errant hairs came through. Fletcher could feel the tightness, but it soon became comfortable.

"So, what can I do for you, today?"

Fletcher replied, "The usual."

Frank took another sip and said, "Looks like you could use a shave, too."

Fletcher nodded.

Frank cranked back the chair, putting Fletcher in a reclining position, and using a horsehide strop hanging on a nearby hook, sharpened his prized Swedish-made razor. When he was done, he picked up a white enameled mug filled with shaving soap, wetted his lather brush with hot water from a porcelain pitcher, and vigorously churned his brush in the cup to created a mug of hot lather, which he proceeded to douse on the lower portion of Fletcher's cheeks and chin.

Like an artist surveying a painting he was about to begin, Frank stepped back from his subject, razor held like a brush in a raised, poised right hand, and with his left index finger cleared the lather from the thick, hairless scar tissue running from Fletcher's chin up to his left eye.

Fletcher appreciated what Frank was doing. Because no hair grew on the scar tissue, and it was thin, sensitive skin, a razor's nick would create a flow of blood that would take considerable time to stanch.

Fletcher enjoyed the sensation of the hot lather on his face, even though Frank managed to get some of it in his mouth and up his nostrils. That came with the territory. With other barbers, he usually declined the shaving part, but Fletcher knew Frank was extra careful with his memento from the Indian Wars. He was quietly efficient when he shaved people.

With a keenly honed razor in his hand, a gabby barber who got caught up in whatever he was saying could do immense damage. In the Territories, Fletcher had gotten a shave that left his face, particularly his scar, bleeding in several places. The offending barber put little pieces of tissue over the cuts to absorb the blood. When he walked out of the shop into the street, Fletcher could see people chuckling when they passed him; he must have been a sight.

After several minutes of shaving, Frank wiped Fletcher's face clean with a hot white towel he kept near a coal-burning pot stove in the center of the shop. Fletcher glanced at the towel and didn't see any blood. Usually, Frank did a good job, but even he could be distracted, and the razor was sharp.

Frank stepped back and looked over his handiwork to make sure he hadn't missed anything or cut anything he shouldn't have. What he saw must have to his liking because he cranked Fletcher back up to a sitting position, took up his shears and comb, and started cutting Fletcher's hair. It had been a while—six weeks or so—since the last cutting, so lots of straight black hair dropped to the floor to be swept up later.

Fletcher thought, now it will begin. If anyone wanted to know the latest goings on in Mayfield, they came to Frank's Barbershop and in ten minutes they knew anything and everything worth knowing, plus. After the shaving, it was Frank's time to palaver like a rush of cold water through a spigot.

"You knew Mr. Mathews, the County Health Officer, made his annual official visit to our fair city last Wednesday?" All Frank required from his clientele was a grunt that could signify either yes or no. It didn't matter which because they were going to find out all about the subject in question whether they liked it or not.

"Well, as you can guess, the results of his survey were pretty negative. Thirteen notices were served to abate nuisances, and I'm thinking if he had looked closer he could have served thirteen more." Clip, clip, clip.

My Lord, thought Fletcher, who had perhaps eaten in some of those places, but he merely grunted. He knew an exchange of words was not called for.

Frank continued, "You and I know our town contains about as many back-yard cow, pig, duck, and goose hatcheries, as well as butcheries, as any in the valley—no, the state. And we've all the filth, stench, and water poisoning that go with it. If we didn't have that stiff breeze from the bay, it would get downright unbearable around here. I'm hoping Mr. Mathews doesn't wait another year before he comes back." Clip, clip, clip.

"And as you can guess, after paying their dollar fine, the questionable establishments went right back to doing whatever they were doing."

Frank continued his snipping and combing—a snip there, a comb here. "I guess you heard Mrs. West was bit by a tarantula last Wednesday morning."

Fletcher grunted. Both he and Irene had encountered their share of tarantulas. When they did, they had given the little beasts a wide berth. They were pesky creatures, and if you came upon one, difficult to ignore.

Frank had definitely caught Fletcher's attention. He continued, "Mrs. West was sweeping down the ceiling of her house when a tarantula that was up in one of the cracks ran down her broom handle and right onto her face. Can you believe it? Well, Mrs. West let out a scream that would have awakened the dead. I heard it here, three blocks away. Everyone rushed out into the street, thinking someone was being killed. And in a way, they were. While she was screaming, Mrs. West used her broom handle to smash the creature, and she struck it and herself such a blow, she knocked herself out. Killed the tarantula, though. But not before it had bit the poor woman right there on her cheek." Clip, clip, clip.

"Well, we all rushed to her house and found her unconscious, flat on the floor. Right away, we sent one of the boys for Dr. Wood, out at your university. But before he got here—which took him almost an hour—the deadly poison almost done Mrs. West in. She's a Catholic, you know, and her folks sent for Reverend O'Reardon to do those final rites Catholics do. But Dr. Wood got there first and drained the poison. Although Mrs. West is still feeling the effects, she's out of danger." Clip, clip, clip.

"In fact, I saw her yesterday buying groceries at La Piere's, with a big bandage covering half her face. Everyone was stopping her to see how she was doing, and she was retelling how the whole thing happened—seemed to enjoy herself in the retelling, waving her hands in the air and pretending to hit herself with the broom handle. Now she's getting to be celebrated around here.

"Can't ever tell when one of those dang things will jump down on you." Frank stopped his cutting and looked up at the ceiling to check if all were clear overhead. Fletcher looked up there with him. What they saw were plenty of cobwebs and plenty of long squiggly, deep cracks in the plaster, but no tarantulas grinning down on them. Frank sighed, as if he were thinking, no immediate sightings, but what will be, will be. Then he returned to his snipping. Fletcher thought he'd better retell Fred's story to Irene, if she hadn't heard it already, so she'd be more careful sweeping the ceilings.

As a sure sign the end of barbering was nigh, Fred started using the chrome clippers to catch the hairs on the back of Fletcher's neck. He lathered the area around Fletcher's ears, stropped his razor one more time, and did the delicate job of cleaning up the hairs' edges over the ears and the back of the neck.

He stepped in front of Fletcher to make certain he had his full attention. This must be the highlight of the story telling, Fletcher thought.

"Well, Constable Coulter is beginning to show signs he's got some spunk in him. Monday afternoon, he brought into the jail three Chinese damsels of questionable repute from Quong Wo's Laundry on Main Street and charged them with being inmates of a whore house. They're supposed to go before Judge Quinn next Tuesday, but my hunch is we won't see hide or hair of them again. I would bet all the gold in China they're in the city plying their wares. Some of our city fathers and your Stanford friends are going to be mighty unhappy when they go looking for their yellow playmates. But there'll be plenty of others to take their places, I'm sure."

The front door swung open, and Fred Behn stuck his head inside the doorway, using his wooden leg to hold the door back. "Hey, Frank, how long are you going to keep my friend in the chair? We got some bacon and eggs on the griddle, ready to serve."

"He's all yours, Fred. Just let me dust him off a bit and get a few of those hairs off his coat."

Frank swooshed the cover cloth off Fletcher and used a stout brush on Fletcher's jacket, just in case there was some cut hair there. Fletcher pulled out four bits and gave them to him—as much for his work as for all the local news he had provided.

Feeling like a new man, Fletcher walked out the barbershop's doorway and followed Fred. Now, for a good breakfast, he thought.

Traffic was heavy on Mayfield's Main Street. It was Saturday morning, and people were shopping or going some place to drink and jaw.

Fred, in spite of his wooden leg, scampered across the street and disappeared through his saloon's swinging doors. Fletcher couldn't figure how he did it. All he could see between him and the saloon was a dusty, rutted dirt road filled with horses pulling carts, wagons, and rigs—all of them going every which way. A man could get killed or permanently maimed if he didn't move quickly and have his wits about him.

Fletcher left the safety of the boardwalk and weaved his way in and out; he gave way for a wagon on his left, ran in front of a gig to his right, putting him about half way there. He thought he had clear sailing to the other side, but a black stallion thundered up on his left when he wasn't looking. He almost managed to get by the horse, but felt horsehide from its flanks brush by his back. The jolt was strong enough to throw him off balance, and he ended up flat on his belly—not damaged except for dirt and dust on the front of his clothes.

Not being hurt, he immediately picked himself up and took a look at the black horse's flanks. The horse had stopped, and its rider was hitching him to a nearby post. The rider was tall, dressed in black, complete with a black sombrero, and—Fletcher could tell from the authoritative way he walked—well to do. Fletcher had seen him before, but couldn't remember where or what his name was. He grabbed Fletcher around his waist and graciously helped him get to the safety of the boardwalk.

The man was apologetic. "Sorry, sir. It was entirely my fault. My mind was on another matter." He took an embroidered kerchief from his breast pocket. "Here, use this to brush yourself off." Fletcher took it and brushed off what dirt he could see on his trousers and coat. He started to give the kerchief back, but the man refused. "No, no, you keep it. You may need it later." He looked at Fletcher's still mussed-up clothing. "Sorry about the damage." He took out his purse and pulled out a ten-dollar eagle and held it out for Fletcher to take. "This should buy your replacements."

Fletcher was not inclined to take the money. "That amount would buy ten replacements. There's no need for that."

"I insist." The man took the gold coin and dropped it into Fletcher's breast pocket and said, "It was my fault. You deserve it. My name is Timothy Hopkins." He held out his hand. "I've seen you around the Quad, but I've never made your acquaintance."

Fletcher took it Mr. Hopkins was used to having his way, so he didn't bother about the coin in his pocket. At first, Fletcher was ready to give the careless rider a real talking to, but now the fellow had been so nice, Fletcher didn't know what to say. He shook Mr. Hopkins' hand and let it go at that. "My name is Fletcher Martin and I accept your apologies," was what he said.

A few minutes later, Fletcher was walking into Fred's saloon. A cloud of dust appeared when he used Mr. Hopkins kerchief to dust himself off a little better. He made his way to the back, where Fred was sitting with his younger brother, Jorgen, having breakfast.

As usual, the two Behn brothers were arguing in Danish about something or other. Jorgen was just like his brother, except larger and younger. The brothers quieted down when Fletcher sat at the table.

Fred, looking over at Fletcher's appearance, said, "What happened to you? I thought you were right behind me. What took you so long? You look like death just crossed your tracks."

"Well, not death, but Mr. Hopkins' horse darn near did me in. His black stallion sent me sprawling as I was crossing behind you." By then Fred's Chinaman was pouring some coffee for Fletcher. It was so hot, Fletcher had to blow on it to cool it down, and the brothers waited patiently while he was blowing and taking little sips. "He was nice enough about it. Gave me this fine kerchief to dust myself off with and forced me to take an eagle for my troubles. So I guess I have no real complaints."

Fred looked thoughtful. "You're sure it was Hopkins?"

"Positive," answered Fletcher. "He introduced himself. Dressed all in black like some villain in a dime novel. I've seen him around the Quad, but never knew exactly who he was."

"Well, I swear, strange he should be hereabouts on a Saturday morning," Fred said, while holding his cup of coffee to his lips and taking a swig.

Jorgen said, "I bet the man was carrying a revolver or at least a stout whip if he was riding in this town. Mayfield folks are not too happy with him. I guess you heard how he fandangoed poor Alex Gordon. The man was planning to use the name of Palo Alto as part of a Mayfield development.

Between sips, Fletcher managed to say, "Yes, your brother told me." It really didn't make any difference. He would still hear Jorgen's version. He could smell eggs and smoked ham and bacon being cooked in the kitchen.

"Sir Timothy goes to Alex and tells him how upset the senator is that he has appropriated the name of his farm, and if he will give it up, the senator promises to point his university's front entrance toward Mayfield. Front entrance, he tells him."

Fletcher remembered the mounds of earth being moved to create Frederick Olmsted's oval, and he wondered how anyone could have believed a front entrance to Mayfield would be possible.

"So poor, gullible Gordon gives up the name and renames his area College Terrace. Tim Hopkins and his University Park crew pick up Palo Alto for their own array of vacant lots."

Fred added his comments. "And I would bet on my mother's sacred honor"—he crossed himself and looked to heaven—"they will hold that name in a death grip for as long as we see the light of day, and the entrance will be to the north and not east."

The Chinaman quickly served the men breakfast along with newly baked bread and freshly churned butter. More coffee was poured from a tin pitcher.

Between bites, Jorgen said, with a slight smile on his lips, "You know, the man is a complete sham."

"You're talking about Timothy Hopkins?" asked Fred.

"Of course I'm talking about Sir Timothy."

"Well, I've known lots of shams. It seems the West draws lots of them," said Fred.

Fletcher kept quiet. He was used to the brothers bickering.

Jorgen acted as if he'd never heard what his brother said and continued telling his story. "From what I hear, Mark Hopkins and his new wife took young Timothy in as a young punk. Why they did this no one seems to know, but I've heard more than one story, and who knows which one is true. One story was that Tim's father worked for the Hopkins and died from an accident while working at the Hopkins' Sacramento home. Another story—and this was a good one—was his father was drowned when he tried to swim out to the boat carrying his wife and little son from Massachusetts to California, and the Hopkins took in the bereft wife and boy. In this story, Tim's mother married a local rancher and went off to Montana to start a new family, and was never heard from again. Whatever the story, the mother always leaves the boy; just plain disappears, and is never heard from again. Mighty strange, I would say. Particularly with him gallivanting around the countryside, acting like he owns the place."

"Well, he darn near does, dear brother, with five hundred acres of choice land, and the huge mansion Mrs. Hopkins gave him and her niece as a wedding gift. He's almost as big a landowner as the senator," Fred said, sitting back in his chair and taking a breather from eating.

He looked over at Fletcher and said, "Now, take what my brother is telling you with a wee grain of salt, Fletcher. There's lots of tales about Tim Hopkins, and none of us know which is true and which isn't." He paused for a minute. "I still wonder what he was doing in town this morning."

The men concentrated on dipping their fresh bread into the remnants of eggs and bacon and ham, and savoring the concoction as they plunked it into their mouths.

Fred asked, looking at Fletcher, "Do you ever run into Dr. Elliott?"

Fletcher knew it was a thorn in Fred's side that Leslie Elliott had never followed up on his promise to visit him. "Not often. He mostly stays in his office. Seems like it's night and day. He's the busiest man on campus. Like today, even on a Saturday, he'll be there most of the day."

"I understand from lots of folk he's the real doer over there. Dr. Jordan is the president, but Dr. Elliott is the one who makes things happen."

"Honestly, Fred, I don't know about such things. During the week, I'm mostly doing research or helping Dr. Whitmore with his classes."

Jorgen ears perked up. "Research? What kind of research are you up to?"

This was not a subject about which Fletcher enjoyed talking. He preferred hearing news from the Behn brothers about Mayfield and its concerns. He said, "I'm in the early stages of writing my master's thesis. I think it'll be about the futility of wars, particularly the last one."

"Well, I swear. You're going to write that all those men died for nothing— after all they did to keep these United States together and free all those slaves."

Fletcher could see Jorgen was sparring with him, just as he did with his brother. Fred came to his rescue. "Now, Jorgen, if Fletcher has a mind that the Civil War was futile, that's his concern and none of your own."

As Jorgen thought over his brother's defense, Fletcher brought up a new subject. "Irene and Lucy will be looking to buy ground for a new school. The villa is just too broken down and far out for their purposes."

Fred said, "Well, I hope you'll put in a good word about talking to Alex Gordon about building in College Terrace. A girl's school would be a real asset for this town."

"I'll try, but you know what the problem is, Fred."

"Yes, I know. I told you how, when the senator first came to us and asked that we close the saloons, I was all for it. Even though it's the only way of making a living I know, I figured there would be lots of opportunities if we got the University heading in our direction. Now, with all the students drinking up a storm, it will get worse. More saloons are opening up, and I hear whores are coming in from the city and using Mayfield, with its student clientele, as a vacation spot in which to rest up for the more rigorous city life."

"You hear; I know they are," added an eager Jorgen, grinning from ear to ear. "Some real corkers, they are." He saw his brother's scornful look. "Now, Fred, you've got your Widow Malgren with her eight children to sleep with every night." He looked at Fletcher as if to gain his approval. "There's nothing wrong with ladies of the night. They perform a useful service for old men like me without a wife to bed, and for young sprouts like your Stanford friends who need some education not offered at your university."

Fred responded, "For old geezers like you, I have no problem. You should be able to take care of yourselves. When you talk of young students, I don't think so. Exposing them to the wages of sex and sin at such an early age could be terrible if syphilis and gonorrhea go along with the lessons."

"Luck of the draw," said Jorgen, looking up to the ceiling.

"Let's say I wish the cards were being dealt at another town, not Mayfield," said a dead serious Fred.

CHAPTER 23

▼

THE '95 WATER TANK

Wednesday, October 28, 1891

Two dogs were barking, and a single kerosene light went on in Dr. Elliott's cottage, the one nearest the water tank. Sosh's heart was racing. He could hardly hold the brush in his hand. All he wanted to do was run away. He still managed to get down the ladder's steps once more, dipped the brush in the paint, went back up the steps, and firmly handed the brush to David, who handed it up to Milton, who was doing the actual painting as he stood on a narrow catwalk running around the base of the water tank.

By now, another light had come on, and Sosh could see a candle flickering through the windows, making its way toward the back door.

Milton made more swooshes and a rather crude "5" was completed. He had already painted an apostrophe and "9." Sosh, on the ground, was loudly whispering, "Let's get going. Milt, Dr. Elliott's coming out. Let's get going. Woe is me, it's over the edge of the world for all us if we don't get out of here. Let's go." Each word was more frantic.

A voice rang out from the back of the cottage. "Who's out there?" It was Dr. Elliott. He had a lantern and he was looking toward the tank.

There was no time for ladders. Milton and David, remembering all the times they had either fallen or been pushed out of tall trees, jumped down from the tank and fell to the ground. Both of them luckily landed on their feet, though David felt a slight twinge in his ankle, as if he might have sprained it. Ladder, pail of paint, and brushes were left on the ground. Sosh was already running across the field to the safety of Encina Hall. With racing hearts, Milton followed, with David limping behind.

Leslie Elliott saw the three boys running toward Encina. He was not at all angry or in the least disturbed. At first, he didn't know why they were in the neighborhood, but then he saw the '95 on the side of the water tank, and the ladder, paint, and brushes strewn on the ground. His dogs were still barking, and he was sure that everyone on Alvarado Row would be asking him next morning what had happened. All he'd have to do would be to point up at the white '95 painted on the water tank.

The diminutive figure leading the painters had to be the Jew, the one they called Sosh, he thought. Leslie would tell Dr. Jordan about all this tomorrow morning. His theories about eugenics and the superior race were being put to the test. From what Leslie had heard, Sosh was becoming a leader of the Class of '95. What would he get up to next?

CHAPTER 24

▼

"Someone Tried to Assassinate the Senator"

Tuesday, November 10, 1891

The autumn days of 1891 followed one another without anything perceptibly changing. As November 1891 began, more clouds appeared and sunsets, once dreary and gray, became brilliantly radiant, with sharp colors ranging from coal-like blacks and muted grays to oranges and yellows shimmering like tempered steel. There was moisture in the air. Some called it heavy dew; others called it light showers, mist, or heavy fog. It was not yet wet enough for black or yellow slickers, but wet enough to evoke the dog-like smell of wet wool. Old timers cautioned newcomers that winter's rain was up there, somewhere in the heavens, waiting to come down in sheets and torrents.

For two days, Dr. Jordan had been absent from his duties. He was caring for his Miss Jessie. On November 10, she gave birth to a daughter, Barbara. Leslie kept in touch with Dr. Wood, who daily visited the Jordan's Escondite Cottage.

"Lady and baby are doing as well as can be expected," Dr. Wood reported to Leslie. "It's Knight, the son, who's the problem. Poor Dr. Jordan is completely befuddled by his conniption fits. Has no idea how to handle him. If he were my son, I'd take the back of my hand to his bare bottom. That would hush him in a hurry."

Leslie, who had no such problems with his docile son, Louis, said, "From what I've seen, I doubt Mrs. Jordan would allow that."

On Wednesday, when Dr. Jordan returned to the office, he briefly acknowledged his staff's words of congratulations, all the while looking at Leslie and mouthing the words, "I must see you."

Leslie followed him into his office.

Even though he was absent for only two days, Dr. Jordan's desk, usually fastidiously clear, was cluttered with things to do. Not noticing all the work awaiting his attention, Dr. Jordan forcefully shut the door behind Leslie, and without bothering to return to his desk, said, "Yesterday, someone—we've no idea who—tried to assassinate the senator."

Leslie was overwhelmed at the news. He immediately dropped into a side chair and held onto its arms as if he might slide onto the floor. "No, no, I don't believe it," he said, and brought his hands to his face in disbelief.

Dr. Jordan continued, "He was on one of his usual inspection tours, driving toward home on University Drive, when George, his driver, heard a single shot. Luckily, the senator had drowsed off because he was and is still not aware of what happened. George returned later to the site and found this on the ground behind the bushes the perpetrator used for cover." Dr. Jordan reached into his trouser pocket and produced a single casing for a spent revolver bullet. "It's small caliber—small, but lethal enough to kill."

Leslie was still reacting to the news. "Why, why would anyone do this?"

Dr. Jordan answered stoically. "I've no idea, but it was done, and Mrs. Stanford is absolutely crazy with anxiety. I've not seen her, but Timothy Hopkins came twice to our cottage to convey her feelings. Because of this, the Stanfords' plans to return to Washington were rescheduled for this week, not next. Thank goodness the senator has no idea what happened. But we do: the driver; Mrs. Stanford; Timothy Hopkins; and I am certain, her brothers; myself; and now you. Mrs. Stanford, through Timothy Hopkins, has ordered me to make certain of the senator's safety and to find the guilty party."

"Did you notify the local constable or the San Francisco police?"

"Neither. Mrs. Stanford doesn't want the public to be aware such an act could even be contemplated. Once we know who did it, we'll hand the villain's name over to the authorities and try to keep the matter out of the hands of the press."

Leslie knew such a plan was not feasible, but was not about to argue the point. He did ask, "So, how will we find out who did it? We're not detectives."

Dr. Jordan returned to his desk, sat down, and pushed aside the papers and folders waiting for his perusal. "I remember you mentioned some detective from the city dropped by—perhaps he or someone else. Check on his credentials, and if he's trustworthy enough to keep our matter confidential, have him come in and set him to work. Above all, we do not want the San Francisco's yellow sheets to get hold of this. They'd have a field day at the senator's expense. In the meantime, both you and I will be working behind the scenes to uncover possible suspects. Can you think of anyone with anarchist or socialist tendencies who might do such a dastardly deed?"

Leslie was reluctant to say the name, but felt it was his duty. "The only one I can think of is the Jew, Sosh Weinberg. He makes no bone of his leanings, but from what I hear, his bark is worse than his bite, and he's become quite a political force among his classmates."

"Have him come in and see you, supposedly on another matter, and feel him out. Perhaps if it's not he, he'll give us the name of another suspect."

To Leslie, it was as if he were in a scene from one of Sherlock Holmes' recent novels, all of which he had relished reading. "I assumed not a word of the real reason for our tête-à-tête."

"Miss Jessie has no knowledge of what happened and Ellen should not be told, either."

"My lips are sealed." Leslie was tempted to physically use his fingers to seal his lips, but thought better of it. Too dramatic.

"Now to another happening." It was as if Dr. Jordan had turned a page—a slight smile replaced his worried expression. "With all this happening, you may have forgotten our faculty team plays baseball against the seniors on Saturday."

Leslie was surprised baseball should be brought up at such a serious time, but such were the vagaries of working with this man.

"The game," as Dr. Jordan referred to it, was the athletic high point of his now-diminished career in sports. At one time, Leslie was told, Dr. Jordan considered playing semi-professional baseball, but the call of academia and an early marriage thwarted those plans. As president of Indiana University, he had instituted an annual baseball game, which he played in, between the faculty and senior class. As Leslie was constantly reminded, "the game" did wonders to forge a spirit of comradeship between Indiana faculty members and students. As expected at LSJU, in mid-November posters were placed on bulletin boards throughout the campus announcing such a game would be played on Saturday, the fourteenth. Seniors had begun practicing on a makeshift diamond south of Encina Hall. Only one practice, this Friday, had been scheduled for the faculty.

"Leslie, we need an umpire." Dr. Jordan gave him a long, hopeful look.

Leslie knew, considering Dr. Jordan's love of playing, there was no thought of his doing the job. "You're asking me to be the umpire?" he asked incredulously.

"Yes, I know you have no love of physical sports, but I would deeply appreciate it, especially with all these worries of a new daughter and an attempted assassination besetting me."

From what Dr. Jordan had told him, the game was a joke, a charade, with grown men wearing costumes and acting like fools, or worse, clowns. Dr. Jordan had forgotten he told Leslie the umpire would be the butt of many of the jokes.

This was not a role Leslie wished to portray. "I'd rather not," is what he said.

"You'd rather not," Dr. Jordan was visibly disappointed as he repeated the words.

"Yes. I'd rather not." It was the first time he had refused anything Dr. Jordan wanted. But even as he said the words, he knew if Dr. Jordan insisted he would do it.

Dr. Jordan sat back in his chair, seemingly accepting Leslie's decision as final, but with one caveat, "If you won't do it, you must find someone between now and Saturday who will."

Leslie perked up his ears. "I must find an umpire." It was not a question, but a statement. He rummaged through his brain for possibilities, but came up empty handed. "No one comes to mind. Do you have any candidates?" He could not help but find his two assigned chores grossly different: first, find the assassin, next, a baseball umpire. He wished he could tell Ellen about this when he got home, but knew he could not.

Dr. Jordan scratched his nose and said, "The only one I can think of is that fellow, Reverend Wilson Wllbur Thoburn, Mayfield's Methodist minister. He's made some overtures about becoming a member of our faculty, so he should be willing to do this slight favor for the University. He had taught biology at the University of the Pacific, but lost his job after the explosion."

"Perhaps you should be—"

"No, I want you to do it." From his uncommon interruption, Leslie knew Dr. Jordan was adamant.

"All right, I'll see what he has to say."

"And talk to the Jew and any other contacts about individuals who might bear a deadly grudge against our illustrious founder, and also check out the detective's availability. Get back to me with what you find out." Dr. Jordan's eyes took in the piles of paper before him. "Now I have catching up to do. Thank you, Leslie."

Why was it, Leslie could not help but think, Dr. Jordan considered the baseball game more important than the attempted assassination? He took his cue, got up, and walked out of the office. He had lots of work to do, but it would have to wait for his two assignments.

As it turned out, it was a simple matter to induce Reverend Thoburn to be the umpire on Saturday. All Leslie had to do was send a short note, delivered that afternoon by Frank Batchelder. Frank was one of the few Stanford males to regularly attend Mayfield's Methodist church. Frank returned that same afternoon with a carefully penned reply:

> *Dr. Elliott, I will happily perform the umpiring duties. Since I know nothing about the game of baseball, would you be so kind as to have Frank deliver some sort of rulebook I could use in my deliberations, and the place and exact time of the encounter. Sincerely, Reverend Wilbur Thoburn*

Leslie smiled. From the sounds of it, the reverend would be the perfect foil. From Dr. Jordan, he secured a small, much used book, similar to a pocket Bible, with "Rules for the Game of Baseball," printed on its cover. That, with a note giving the place, time, and a friendly "See you there," was sent via Frank to the minister, fulfilling his requests. The problem of the umpire was solved; now on to interviewing the Jew.

CHAPTER 25

▼

"UNDOING THE YOKE OF CAPITALISM"

Thursday, November 12, 1891

Sosh felt queasy. Why would Dr. Elliott want to talk to him? The first thing he thought of was Dr. Elliott had recognized him on the night they painted the water tower. But that had happened two weeks ago. Why would he wait this long to bring him to task?

Mr. Fesler had called out to him in the lobby and given him a small envelope. Immediately he knew it was from the registrar, Dr. Elliott. While Dr. Jordan spoke at the daily chapel meetings and was seen regularly around the campus, the registrar was seldom seen and known. Instead, this type of envelope was used to inform students their presence was no longer required; in other words, tossing them off the edge of the world. Even holding the envelope was enough to cause hearts to beat faster and beads of sweat to form above brows.

Sosh waited until he was in his room to open and read its contents, which turned out to be innocuous enough: *Mr. Weinberg, please meet me tomorrow at 10:30 A.M. Dr. Orrin L. Elliott, Registrar.* Still, without a stated reason for the meeting, Sosh continued to be concerned.

The meeting began innocently enough with small talk about Sosh's political activities. Dr. Elliott asked a few questions about a minor rebellion Sosh had fomented among his '95 classmates at the meeting held on November third to adopt the constitution of the student association and to elect officers. Winko, president of the Alpha Phis and head of the Bi-Laws Committee, had attempted to get a rule passed forbidding freshmen students, who were in the majority, from holding any association office. On the spot, Sosh talked his fellows into walking out of the deliberations. It was only through Dr. Swain's intervention that the rule was dropped from consideration and the first-year enclave returned. As it turned out, only one '95 member was elected to a minor office. Nevertheless, as a result of the maneuver, Sosh over night became a class hero and someone of importance.

Dr. Elliott congratulated him on his accomplishment.

Sosh demurred with a shrug of his narrow shoulders and a hardly audible, "It wasn't anything," while thinking this surely could not be the only reason for the meeting.

Leslie was friendly when he said, "I hear they call you Sosh. May I call you that?"

Sosh nodded.

Leslie continued, "I understand the name comes from your socialistic tendencies."

Could this be the reason? Sosh thought, but said, "Yes, it does." And quickly added, "But I'm no anarchist or radical. Violence in any form is abhorrent to me. I still remember hearing about the explosion in the Haymarket Square when I was thirteen years old. And I thought at the time it was a senseless act."

Leslie looked pleased with Sosh's words. He said, "You must admit most people with your predilections do not feel the same. They think violence is the only way to undo what they call the yoke of capitalism."

"That's not my way. Senseless violence only serves to tighten the yoke," Sosh said. His words conveyed the strength of sincerity. It was something he felt with all his heart. "It's the people in the middle who must be aroused if anything is to be accomplished—not the radicals on the fringes. Look, if the police had shot the workers instead of the radicals killing the police with their dynamite, it would have been an entirely different matter." Sosh hesitated. Perhaps he had said too much. He had no idea where Dr. Elliott stood.

As Leslie watched Sosh's expressive hands flailing in midair and his voice rising and falling with his sincere convictions, he could understand how Sosh's classmates had been motivated. In those few seconds, Sosh convinced Leslie he was no assassin.

Leslie said, "Sosh, I may not agree with everything you stand for, and you know most of my fellow faculty members and members of the administration do not agree with your politics, but I will always stand up for your right to express your thoughts. If in the future, I can be of assistance, please call upon me."

Sosh could not believe it. Was Dr. Elliott on his side? Was this all there was to it? He almost said something, and then thought better of it. He stood up, shook Leslie's extended hand, and moved toward the door.

As he turned to leave, Dr. Elliott said, "Since you abhor violence as I do, would you do something for me?"

Sosh hesitated. Now he would find out. Leslie continued, "There is a good possibility others among our students may have more radical ideas than you do and may consider using tools of violence. If you become aware of such thoughts, would you please let me know? I would like to talk to them before they act, and see if we can work out another remedy. You will have to trust me. There is no thought of disciplining. Would you do this for me?"

Sosh hardly knew the man who stood before him and who was about the same height as he was. Dr. Elliott was asking him to be an informer. But he was right. Sosh was against violence. What else could he say but, "Yes, I will."

Outside, on the way back to Encina Hall, Sosh thought about how Dr. Elliott had used the term "tools of violence." The only person he could think of that might interest Dr. Elliott was Sally. She was obviously interested in Sosh because of what he had said about Senator Stanford being a villain. And there was the small revolver he felt in her purse. Was she trying to shoot Senator Stanford? Had Dr. Elliott uncovered some kind of plot? Should he tell Dr. Elliott about Sally? Before he could say anything, he decided he should confront her with his questions. But how? It was all very confusing and mysterious.

CHAPTER 26

▼

"A SHELL LIKE A TORTOISE"

That Same Night

Leslie worked late and did not arrive home until after seven o'clock. Unusually, Ellen was waiting for him as he stepped through the back door and began his ritual of taking off his dusty shoes to put on comfortable slippers. That evening, she was waiting for him with hands on her hips—a bad sign. During the day, something had happened to disturb her.

When he attempted to kiss her on her cheek, which was his usual evening greeting, she turned her face from him and said, "And I thought you trusted me."

Of course, he trusted her, but his heart told him there was something he had not told her. She continued, "Jessie assumed you had told me about the senator being shot at. Out of deference to you, I told her I knew nothing about it. I could see by the satisfied look on her face what she thought. She asked me not to tell you she knew. But I'm not the same as you. You're my husband. At least on my side, there are no secrets between us, and I told her that, which I'm sure she did not appreciate."

If Leslie had a shell like a tortoise, he would have shriveled up inside it. She was absolutely right. There was nothing he could say in his own defense. He should have known Dr. Jordan would tell his Miss Jessie everything. He also knew he would not confront the good doctor, nor would Dr. Jordan apologize for what he had done. In many ways, Leslie was glad Ellen knew. He needed her common sense and insight to guide him. He knew their relationship was too strong to let his lack of judgment cause a major upheaval. Next time he would know better.

By the time they were in bed that night, Leslie felt he could discuss his meeting with Sosh. After Ellen had heard the crux of their conversation, she said, "You did the right thing. The only way you'll learn anything is from the students. It has to be one of them. An outsider wouldn't know the senator's inspection schedule and would stand out like a sore thumb."

"Do you think Sosh knows who it is?"

"I'm not sure. To find out, you must gain his trust. After all, it was your first meeting, and he has nothing to base his trust on except what you said. Try to talk to him about other matters. Perhaps at that game you'll attend on Saturday."

"What about the detective?"

"Awful, a simply awful thing to consider. Has Dr. Jordan lost his senses? You're no better, standing by and letting him even consider such a possibility. You and your Sherlock Holmes novels. Someone, particularly of the bogus type you described to me, plying his stupid questions on campus would cause even more of a stir. I'd tell Dr. Jordan to rely on you keeping your ears to the ground and hearing what your faculty members and students say. Forget the San Francisco detective. He'll only cause more grief."

"But none of the students or faculty know about what happened."

Ellen held back laughing out loud. Her husband's naiveté tickled her funny bone. "Poor Leslie, I doubt very much if that is true."

She was right. By the next afternoon, three faculty members had come up to Leslie and whispered questions about the shooting. When Leslie asked how they knew, there were some vague remarks about how Knight, Dr. Jordan's young son, asked a playmate if he knew about someone trying to shoot the senator. The playmate asked his mother, and so the chain of inquiry began. Leslie reasoned Dr. Jordan and Jessie must have talked about the shooting in front of Knight, not realizing his little ears would perk up when words such as "shoot" and "senator" were uttered. At this rate, the whole campus would be astir with news of the attempted crime. Only its supposed victim, hopefully, would be oblivious to what had happened.

CHAPTER 27

▼

"IT HAD BEEN A SHAM"

Saturday, November 14, 1891

On the day of the game, Leslie was among the first to arrive. He was always early for an appointment, event, or anything with a stated starting time. His wife did not have the same proclivity. He had learned to wait.

One advantage of leaving early was he didn't have to go with Bolton. Ellen told Leslie that Bolton was going later, with Fletcher. Bolton was not an early riser.

As Leslie approached the makeshift diamond from the West, he wondered about the tall ladies he could see from some distance, out in the field, wearing plump skirts and outrageous hats. As he got closer, he realized the ladies were male seniors costumed as women with long skirts—and in some cases, numerous petticoats—and wearing grotesque headgear clad with feathers that would more fittingly adorn vultures. One player had charcoal all over his face and was dressed as a minstrel, with a red kerchief tied around his head. Another wore black tights; a pink garter adorned his left leg and a blonde wig was askew on top of his head. Another wore a suit of red underwear, under which was, hopefully, more under-wear.

They were playing catch, and one was hitting a long ball to several others out in the field. Leslie watched as several balls went through outstretched gloved and bare hands. He felt relieved: there was no worry the seniors would be more profi-cient at the game than their older opponents were. In fact, only two of the players appeared to be semi-professional: the tall, thin fellow who was practicing pitch-ing, and his squatting catcher. They had good form. Like their teammates, they were dressed as women. Leslie wondered at this tendency for cross-dressing. Sexuality was so complex; he had no idea what it all meant. It seemed the manliest had no fear of appearing to be a Nancy boy? Or was it just the opposite? The thought was quickly forgotten.

The senior players were friendly and said hello to him as he passed by. "Morning, Dr. Elliott, should be a good game."

Unfortunately, Leslie did not know their names, so he could only briefly acknowledge them with a "Morning," or smile knowingly. He did know their records, and assumed the pitcher and squatting catcher were two young men with outstanding athletic records from their former colleges: Jack Whittemore and Charley Chadsey. The pitcher had to be Jack Whittemore because of his height. He had played all kinds of sports at William and Mary College, including Walter Camp's new version of football being played at Harvard, Yale, and Columbia. The catcher, Charles Chadsey, was known for his athletic prowess at Indiana University, particularly in baseball.

So far, Leslie saw no sign of the faculty members. While he was waiting, he decided to inspect the newly created diamond, south of Encina. Home base lined up with the hall's western edge, and devil-may-care students were already beginning to sit precariously, three and four stories up, on stone windowsills and narrow ledges overlooking the playing field, waiting for the game to begin. Ah, the optimism of youth, Leslie thought: they think they are immortal. Leslie knew otherwise. He could imagine the potential injuries, even fatalities, resulting from such bravado.

The diamond and viewing area had been cleared of hayfields and transformed into parched, hard gray dirt. Home plate was a simple wooden board, sawed to proper dimensions and held in place by four long stakes driven into the dry soil. Burlap gunnysacks filled with gravel from the dry creek bed served as bases. Sheer weight would keep them in place. Heavy boots shagging baseballs had tamped down the outer fields—left, center, right—which still bore traces of hay. That hay remained in clusters on the field, places where baseballs might disappear. Beyond the designated playing field, in the outer reaches near where the Elliott's cottage stood on Alvarado Row, no baseballs were supposed to be hit. Those hay fields were still mauve with so much sun and no moisture. There, baseballs would be lost forever. To Leslie's eyes, which were used to the manicured greens of Ithaca and Cornell, the site of today's game was primitive.

Walking full circle, Leslie saw Dr. Jordan approaching from the east. A retinue of fellow faculty players followed him. They must have gathered at Escondite Cottage and decided to descend as a formidable group upon their rivals. If anything, they were dressed more outlandishly than the seniors. It was like a parade of circus clowns. Dr Jordan was completely in character——attired in knickers several sizes too small for his hefty figure, held up by garish red suspenders. His denim shirt and rakish slouch hat must have been worn at previous games, judging by their frayed, dusty appearance. Knickers and shirt were ripped at the elbow and knees, revealing the doctor's usually protected fair skin. Leslie concluded it was meant to be the apparel of one who played the game with manly vigor.

As expected, their arrival was greeted with titters and jeers from the students—who had cowered before them during the week—and applause and murmur-like cheers from their nonplaying cohorts, friends, and families.

At about fifteen minutes before game time, Leslie could tell Dr. Jordan was on edge, worried. The full faculty team was now on the field. Baseballs were flying fast and furious, but no umpire was in view.

Spectators were alerted to potential danger when errant fly balls or throws landed close by. Several carriages had to be moved from proximity to the diamond when a hard ball spooked the horses. It became obvious to Leslie that not even the simplest throw or catch by either team could be taken for granted. The players were amateurs in the truest sense of the word.

By now, about five hundred students; members of the faculty; their families; and visitors from Menlo and Mayfield, curious about what their neighbors were up to, were in attendance. Eighteen to twenty carriages, rigs, and buses were parked next to the diamond. Among them was Jasper Paulsen's long bus, which had brought a group of Menlo people and remained in case the victors—most likely the seniors—needed a conveyance for celebrating afterwards.

Student maintenance workers had delivered five wooden chairs to the site, set up almost directly behind home plate. These seats were reserved by name for nonplaying notables. A seat was reserved for Leslie between Timothy Hopkins and Ariel Lathrop, who was seated next to Charles, his brother, and finally Burt Fesler. The rest of the faculty either stood or stayed in their rigs with their families. Leslie looked for Bolton and Fletcher, but did not see them.

Here in the casual environment of the game, women were dressed in colorful skirts and blouses. They had brought jackets and sweaters to put on as the coolness of evening approached. Men wore sweaters as well as jackets, and corduroy or heavy cotton pants. The ladies for the most part were bareheaded, with a few wearing bonnets, but all the men wore hats. Some wore dark derbies, but Leslie saw linen and navy blue yacht caps, as well, and several Stetsons. Newly acquired safety bicycles were lying on the ground. Their riders wore golf caps or bike hats. Leslie picked out Sam Cutter, wearing a cream-colored top hat. If headgear were any indicator of personality, Stanford students certainly prized their individuality.

Until Reverend Thoburn stepped out onto the diamond, Leslie Elliott had never seen him before. In the office, Leslie had heard Frank Batchelder, who regularly attended Thoburn's church, singing his praises. Leslie was not a religious man. He had gone to chapel at the Quad when well-known clergyman visited, but had not felt a Mayfield Methodist minister warranted walking to the little village. Leslie's first impression of the fellow was that he looked like a second-rate poet with long, oily hair hanging to his shoulders and a fringe of ill-kept bangs almost covering his eyes. Those bangs won't help his vision, thought Leslie. But as a matter of habit, Thoburn kept brushing his locks back with both hands, like a young lady. The habit did not add to his masculinity. His eyes were bigger and darker than most, and his sallow complexion contributed to his unmanly exterior. All of this added to Leslie's contention that Thoburn was perfect for his role as the comedic umpire.

Leslie watched as Dr. Jordan, who must have been looking out for the reverend, hurried up to him and shook his hand heartily. Leslie could see the surprised look on the latter's face when he saw how Dr. Jordan was attired. Apparently no one had warned him of the upcoming shenanigans, poor soul.

By now, it was almost two o'clock and the crowd was growing impatient for the game to begin.

A young man attired in red pajamas led the upper and lower classes in a yell: "Rah, rah, rah! LSJU '92! Rah, rah, rah!"

In the midst of the approaching affray, Reverend Thoburn stood quite alone, and Leslie couldn't help but feel a bit sorry for him. He was reminded of the young steers he had seen in Wyoming, standing in the corral, waiting to be slaughtered.

Suddenly the reverend's expression changed to that of slaughterer. He bellowed, "All right, let's get this game started!"

The students were both surprised and delighted. They cheered, egging on his exuberance. This was what they had come for.

He shouted out a question, more like a demand, looking directly at Dr. Jordan and Jack Whittemore. "Where are your lineups?" is what he asked.

Dr. Jordan looked back at Thoburn as if to say, "Who do you think you're talking to?" But he thought better of it. He had his list of players in his pocket, and Jack Whittemore, captain and pitcher for the seniors and president of the student body, had his. Both of them stepped forward and obediently gave their respective lineups to Umpire Thoburn.

Umpire Thoburn read them, aloud. Here is what he said, "For the faculty we have: George Bryant, shortstop; Joe Swain, second base; David Starr Jordan, captain, first base; Graden Howard, pitcher; George Richardson, catcher; David Marx, third base; Jack Miller, right field; Amos Griswold, left field; and Albert Warner, center field.

"For the seniors we have: Ed Richardson, first base; Joe Wallingford, third base; Charley Chadsey, catcher; Jack Whittemore, captain and pitcher; Frank Dennis, second base; Jason Trebgloan, right field; Paul Cooley, left field; Jeb Stephens, shortstop; and Steve Brown, center field."

Thoburn put the two lists in his pocket, took a two-bit piece out, and said, "Dr. Jordan, please call heads or tails while the coin is in the air to determine which side will choose whether to bat or take the field."

Dr. Jordan obediently called out, "Heads."

They all looked down at the coin, which was now lying in the dry dirt. "Tails, it is," Thoburn said, and he turned to Whittemore. "What say you, captain of the seniors, bat or field?"

Whittemore had no doubt about the outcome. The faculty was old and out of shape. His seniors would prevail. "Bat," he said.

Thoburn shouted for all to hear—even the fellows sitting precariously on Encina's windowsills, with their feet dangling over the edge, could hear him, "Faculty, take the field. Let"—and here he paused for sheer dramatic effect—"the game begin, and may the best team win!"

Everyone cheered.

Leslie decided it had been a sham. He, like the others, had been completely misled. Frank Batchelder, or someone like him, must have told his beloved reverend what to expect, and so he was fully prepared. Leslie had new respect for the fellow. The joke was rally on Dr. Jordan—that in itself made it more fun for Leslie to watch the game unfold.

CHAPTER 28

▼

"PUPPIES CAN BITE"

That Same Day

Leslie did not enjoy sitting between Timothy Hopkins and Ariel Lathrop. Ariel hardly spoke to him, and if he did have any comments, made them to his brother, Charles, or to Burt Fesler, who sat next to his brother. Leslie heard Ariel, upon seeing the plethora of red and blue Stanford blankets spread on the dirt, tell Burt he should put out a note that LSJU blankets were not to be taken out of the dormitories. Burt responded by pulling out a little notebook he carried in his breast pocked and making a note. Timothy Hopkins obviously considered Leslie to be an underling, a mere lackey who did Dr. Jordan's bidding. When Hopkins did speak to him, it was in a condescending tone, as if he were talking to his valet or one of his foremen. This was fine with Leslie. For reasons he could not put his finger on, he had never liked Mr. Hopkins.

Leslie was so deep in his thoughts about his companions he missed the first plays. The faculty's pitcher, Dr. Howard, had already managed to strike out Ed Richardson. Joe Wallingford hit a fly ball to Dr. Jordan, who cleanly caught it and fired it over to Dr. Swain, at second base. Dr. Swain appeared surprised to find a ball in his thin mitt. Belatedly, he tossed it underarm to third baseman Dr. Marx for a little "pepper" in the infield, which drew a ripple of appreciative sighs from the Roble ladies.

Hopkins punched Leslie in the ribs with his elbow and said, "Aha, our stalwarts are showing those young pups a thing or two."

Leslie silently wondered if Hopkins had ever thrown a baseball in his sheltered life.

Charlie Chadsey was up next; Leslie knew from his scholastic records that he was admirable in all sports. Dr. Howard was pitching and Reverend Thoburn was behind Dr. Richardson, the catcher, calling strikes and balls. The count had gotten to three balls and two strikes, when Howard threw a ball right over the plate, which Chadsey hit squarely. The ball ended up in front of Dr. Miller in right field. He picked it up as if it were a hot coal and threw it to Dr. Jordan, at first. Chadsey was already safe at second base. With a man on second, Umpire Thoburn moved into the middle of the diamond, behind Howard. So far, Leslie was impressed with the job he was doing.

A spontaneous cheer went up from the students rooting for the seniors. Jack Whittemore, the campus hero, was the next batter. Leslie knew and liked Jack. Everyone did. He was quiet and unassuming, with a handsome, square-cut, beardless athletic face, without the usual handle bar moustache some of the other athletic types flaunted like a badge. But Leslie knew, again from his records, that underneath Whittemore's clean-shaven exterior he was very, very competitive. He was the U.S. record holder in the one-mile swim. Howard, the pitcher, must have known this, too, because his first pitch to him was a fastball, which Jack just managed to hit. Unfortunately, it was another high fly. Dr. Griswold playing left field juggled it, but finally cradled it safely in his mitt. Jack was out. Leslie could almost hear the wind going out of the students' sails. The top of the first inning had ended, and it was the faculty's turn at bat.

Jack Whittemore assumed the pitching chores, and using a combination of fast and curve balls, quickly retired the faculty side: one, two, three. Dr. Bryant, who looked as if he knew how to play the game, still struck out. Dr. Swain, who appeared to be unable to even see the ball, made three vain swipes, without coming close. Finally, Dr. Jordan, with his tight pants just barely staying up under his ample belly, was no better. He was so far off from making contact; students were holding back their laughter. Someone tittered, and Leslie heard an audible, "Shhh."

The first inning ended zero to zero, and Leslie thought perhaps the faculty might just barely have a chance at making it a good game. He knew that if Dr. Jordan lost the game by too many scores, he would be a bear on Monday morning.

An improvised scoreboard had been erected in foul territory, just behind first base. Two boards were nailed together, painted black and marked off in chalk to represent the upper and lower halves of the nine innings. The scoreboards had been bound with bailing rope to two high ladders, borrowed from the maintenance department. Two elongated goose eggs were up on the scoreboard for all to see.

In the top of the second inning, Frank Dennis, second base, hit a single to left field. Jason Trebgloan followed him with another single into center field, so two seniors were on base when lanky Paul Cooley, the left fielder, approached the plate.

Cooley looked uncomfortable swinging the bat, and Leslie guessed he was going to strike out after Thoburn called two straight strikes. Leslie saw pitcher Howard's face light up with anticipation. Perhaps it was this anticipation that caused him to send a fastball right over the center of the plate, slightly below Cooley's waist. Cooley sighted the ball and swung his bat mightily, causing it to soar into space over the head of center fielder, Dr. Warner.

For reasons know only to Dr. Warner, he ran toward the ball, not realizing he should have been running in the opposite direction. What might have been a two-base hit quickly turned into a home run because, after the ball sailed over Dr. Warner's head, he also had problems finding it in the underbrush, and more problems picking it up. At last, he threw it to Dr. Swain as a relay, but it was too late. All the runners had circled the bases and were home. Cooley had hit a home run. The seniors led three to zero.

Again, Timothy Hopkins' elbow hit Leslie in his ribs, causing him to jump, as Hopkins made the comment, "The puppies can bite."

That was enough. Leslie decided, as soon as he could, he would move away from him, out of range of the sharp elbows. Already Leslie was beginning to get bored with the game. It was not unusual. Grown men playing with a bat and ball did not mesmerize him the way an interesting essay about the economy did, or a funny vaudevillian at the theater. Leslie could feel his eyelids growing heavy, as if they needed an afternoon nap.

Dr. Howard, the pitcher, somehow pulled himself together and managed to strike out Jeb Stephens; then got Steven Brown to fly to Dr. Marx at third base. Marx looked very professional when he caught the ball and threw it to Jordan just for good measure. The final out came when Ed Richardson, on a curious play, tripped on a slight rise in the dirt on his way to first base, after hitting what looked like a safe single. He briefly fell to the ground, getting both of his knees quite dirty. Shortstop Bryant was slow at getting the ball to Jordan, but with Richardson getting up and dusting off his pants before continuing his run, the ball arrived at first before he did, and Reverend Thoburn called him out. The seniors were retired. Now it was the faculty's turn.

Leslie looked on as Dr. Jordan gathered his team around him for a quick pep talk. He didn't hear all the words because Dr. Jordan spoke in a low, confidential voice, as if he had a secret plan to win the game. From what Leslie could hear, he said, "Now, gentlemen, if we let these young scalawags get too far ahead of us, we'll never catch up. It's now or never. Let's get some runs up on the board."

He led them in an improvised cheer: "Rah, rah, rah, faculty! Rah, rah, rah!" A few faculty members and their families joined in, but the cheer was barely audible over the rumble of the students' conversations. Leslie was not the only one getting bored.

Graden Howard, the faculty pitcher—and other than George Bryant, the best athlete on the faculty team—looked as if he could hardly wait to get his hands on a bat and hit the ball. He wasn't given an opportunity because suddenly Whittemore lost control, and for the life of him, could not throw a strike over the plate. Thoburn called four balls in a row, and Howard walked to first base.

It progressively got worse for Whittemore. When Dr. Richardson was up, he threw a ball that floated over the head of his catcher and landed very close to Dr. Griffin's carriage, with his wife still in it. The ball not only frightened Mrs. Griffin, it frightened Griffin's sorrel mare, who reared up on her hind legs and looked as if she might bolt. All of this commotion stirred Leslie to consciousness. He had been falling asleep, with his head teetering toward Timothy Hopkins' shoulder. He jerked himself upright and awake, and watched as Dr. Griffin grabbed the horse's reins and quietly calmed his wife and horse.

While this was going on, Howard ran to second base standing up. With the horse rearing and the ball going close to Mrs. Griffin, Whittemore became unhinged and proceeded to walk Dr. Richardson. He had not thrown a strike in the last eight pitches.

Chadsey asked Thoburn for a time out. He motioned Whittemore to meet him halfway between the plate and the mound. As the two conspired in low whispers, Leslie watched as a smile crept onto Whittemore's face and he looked as if he might laugh out loud. Whatever Chadsey said must have relaxed him because he proceeded to strike out the next two batters: Marx and Miller. Only Dr. Griswold remained at the plate to be vanquished, and the faculty would be retired without scoring a run.

Dr. Griswold appeared impervious to what was happening around him. He stood at the plate, with his bat balanced on his shoulder, watching Whittemore wind up and deliver a ball that zinged by him, unseen and untouched. "Strike one," Thoburn shouted. A second pitch followed, also a strike, also untouched. Griswold's bat had not even trembled in its resting place on his shoulder. He had one more chance, and raised his bat ever so slightly to acknowledge this fact. For the first time, he saw the ball leave Whittemore's right hand. He even saw the stitching that held the ball together and the name of the ball's manufacturer. He soundly whacked what he saw, resulting in a crisp pop. Griswold was surprised, just as everyone else was, that the ball flew like a released homing pigeon over center fielder Steve Brown's head, into no man's land. There was no doubt about it: he had hit a homer. As Dr. Griswold rounded third base, Dr. Jordan rushed out and clapped him soundly on the back. The faculty had a new hero. The team was up and cheering, with Griswold grinning from ear to ear. As he crossed home plate, Howard and Richardson, who had preceded him across the plate, immediately surrounded him and gave him manly pats and hugs. Leslie had never seen faculty men so familiar with one another. It was a tie ball game, and the faculty still had one more out.

Even Leslie and Tim Hopkins were on their feet. The Lathrop brothers looked out of place with silly smiles on their usually sour faces. Hopkins embraced Leslie around his shoulders like a long, lost brother; he even patted his back. Leslie had no idea how he should react, and ended up giving Hopkins a brisk cuff on his left shoulder. Hopkins responded with a surprised look on his face.

After the faculty supporters calmed down, Whittemore quickly dashed any hopes of a faculty lead with three called strikes on Albert Warner. At the end of the second inning, it was a tie game: three to three.

Innings three and four went by uneventfully. Leslie managed to keep awake and alert by viewing what was going off the field, rather than on. The only excitement was a foul ball Dr. Marx hit into the crowd. The sharply hit hardball came dangerously close to a lady visitor whom Leslie knew only slightly. She was the wife of Captain Harkins, the ex-Civil War officer who had turned down Fletcher Martin's services because of his general discharge. The Harkins family had befriended Ellen, but not Leslie. Captain Harkins thought he and his wife had a safe seat in their carriage next to the field. He was wrong. Dr. Marx immediately left his batting position at home plate and approached the poor, frightened woman and apologized for his actions.

The lady tried to be a good sport, but she immediately had her husband move the carriage about twenty yards further from the playing field. This took some time because they had to wait while their horse relieved itself. Because Captain Harkins could no longer see what was going on, he left his wife sitting by herself and returned to watch the game, standing with the other men on the side lines. Without the ladies present, most of them were smoking cigars or cheroots. Some were even betting on the outcome. The betting odds were more lopsided than the score. The seniors were favored four to one.

Leslie saw Fletcher in the crowd, on the other side of the field, behind first base, but not with Bolton. Bolton must have begged off to stay at home with Lucy and help her with the weekend chores. Fred Behn, the saloonkeeper with the wooden stump, was at Fletcher's side. Leslie waved both hands and caught their eyes.

Fletcher waved and made a motion for him to join them.

Leslie responded with the mouthed word, "Later."

Leslie's eyes wandered to the left side of the field, behind third base, where most of the students were lounging on their LSJU blankets, watching what was going on. Most of them, like Leslie, appeared to be bored with the game. They were busy chatting, eating, or looking around at the other spectators. Leslie picked out Sosh, who was with his usual group of colleagues: George Gardiner, now called Woody; the two footballers; and the only Chinese student in the freshmen class, whose name was Walter Ngon Fong. Leslie knew from his records that his father was a wealthy merchant in San Francisco, a business associate of Senator Stanford. Sosh was engrossed in a conversation with Sally Forrest, the young lady who had caught everyone's eye. Leslie had heard even some of the faculty men were smitten by her charms. Her well-rounded figure reminded Leslie of the buxom, beguiling ladies he had seen on vaudeville stages, who cavorted around magicians, making theatrical gestures. Leslie had to agree: the lady was something. She and Sosh looked as if they were carrying on a conversation much more engrossing than the game they were supposed to be watching.

CHAPTER 29

▼

"KISSED HIM HARD AND SOUNDLY"

That Same Day

Earlier, Sosh and his four friends had found a good spot right behind third base. Everyone was there: Bump, who had decided to change his name from David, Milt; Woody; and their new chum, Walt. The only exception was Will Greer, who was busy with his Sigma Chi fraternity brothers. Will had tried several times to get Sosh into Sigma Chi without success.

Bump saw Delores Payson, Sosh's cousin, walking toward the field with Sally and Betsy, and shouted out their names. He was openly interested in getting to know Delores better.

When Sally saw Sosh beside Bump, she immediately steered the other two girls to a spot right next to him and ended up spreading her blanket next to his. Sosh couldn't get over how blatant she was. She made no bones about it: she wanted to be near him. With his new accumulation of friends in the class of '95, due to his political acumen, Sosh was much more comfortable with her attention. He knew many eyes would be watching. Let them. He was one of the class leaders now.

After the girls had settled, Sosh wanted to talk to Sally, but was too shy to commence a conversation. He continued watching the game, but his thoughts were about Sally. He had no idea what he was looking at.

To get his attention, Sally finally had to pound his back with her fists. Like a spoilt child, she said, "Sosh, Sosh, I want to talk to you. I want to talk to you."

"Oh, sorry." Sosh looked back at her; surprised her slender hand had such force. He enjoyed her attention, even the pounding. No female had ever been like this to him before. He was mystified why anyone as beautiful as she would associate with someone as short and ugly as he was. He moved closer to her, supposedly so she could hear him better, but actually so he could smell her fragrance. It reminded him of the most delicious smells he had experienced in his short life: spring flowers, babies fresh from their bathe. He breathed it in the way a trapped miner breathes fresh air. And he moved a little bit closer so that perhaps his elbow or shoulder or hand might touch hers. He wished his dead father, who had been an artist and truly appreciated beauty, could be there to see her.

Sally said, "I want to continue our conversation about the Tennessee coalminers. There's been nothing in the *Chronicle* about them, and I must know what happened."

Everyone else around them was watching and cheering as pitches flew by and batters struck out. Sosh and Sally were oblivious to all this as they drew closer so they could hear what they said to one another.

Sosh said, "Will's *New York Times* is three weeks old by the time we read it. Remember how I told you how the miners were replaced by convict labor and were evicted from their homes when they wouldn't sign a contract reducing their pay? We talked about it at the reception."

"Yes, of course I remember," she said, as if Sosh should know better. "And that horrid Sam Cutter interrupted our conversation. He is such an ignoramus." Even the mention of Sam's name sent a chill down Sosh's spine. "I was hoping the miners would run the militia out of town," she added.

Their two young heads were a foot or so apart. Sosh could tell Sally was examining his face closely. Her scrutiny made him nervous, and his steel-rim spectacles slid down the ridge of his nose. He pushed them back up with his index finger. Even his voice started to quiver as he continued speaking. "Well, they did that and more. On Halloween Night, more than a thousand armed miners marched to where the state militia had imprisoned the convicts in stockades. When the militia saw the miners approaching, they fled. The miners not only set the convicts free, they burned the stockades holding them to the ground."

Sally said with sincere empathy, "Good for them. I wish I could have been there to help."

Sosh thought that although he was also on the miner's side, he was not sure he would have physically helped them. Cheered them on, perhaps. Sally was much more courageous than he was. In some ways he admired her, but something in the pit of his stomach made him wary. First there was the revolver in her purse.

And now the rumors he had heard that someone had attempted to shoot the senator. Was that what Dr. Elliott was asking him about at their meeting—whether he knew of anyone? Sosh couldn't get it out of his mind: it could be Sally. Should he tell Dr. Elliott? These thoughts kept running through his mind, but he kept them to himself.

He said to Sally, "The *Times* article said it was quite a sight to see former Union and Confederate soldiers, white and black, standing side by side, fighting for their rights. Some of the convicts instead of skedaddling joined the miners. The company finally had to give in. They gave the miners' homes back to them and restored their wages."

Sally asked, "What about the prisoners? Did they all get away?"

Sosh had not considered their plight. He said, "I don't know. There was no further mention of them, so I presume they got away. I'm not sure about the ones who stayed to fight with the miners. I really don't know."

Sosh saw a frown cross Sally's face; then she brightened up and said, "Still, it's good news."

A homerun must have been hit, or something happened causing everyone to rise to their feet and cheer loud and long. But not Sally and Sosh. They were still seated, surrounded by students, with their faces almost touching. Without warning, Sally grabbed Sosh's face with her two hands and kissed him hard and soundly on his lips. Sosh was so surprised his glasses were knocked off and fell to the blanket.

Delores happened to glance down at the couple and saw what had happened. She pretended to be looking elsewhere. No one else was aware of the intimacy taking place.

Sosh was breathing hard, as if he had been running the bases, not sitting and being kissed. And he could feel his nose was running. Or was it blood from the collision of their faces? He pulled a well-used handkerchief from his pants pocket and blew into it. No, not blood. He fumbled to find his glasses and carefully put them back on—upside down, so they fell off again. He was completely and totally confused.

Sally at first leaned back and smiled at her flustered companion. She came close to him and whispered, "I hope I didn't frighten you, but I'm not sorry I kissed you. I've wanted to do that since I first met you."

Within his heart, Sosh was elated, but he also knew their relationship had taken a new direction, one he might not be able to control, and this troubled him. He decided to keep quiet until he had his breath back. He took in several gulps of air. He could hear his heart beating. Sally looked around at the people surrounding them to give him time to compose himself.

Finally, he was able to speak. He rolled over on his stomach and held his head up with his hand. With the other hand, he motioned for Sally to do the same. He wanted to say something to her, but he wanted to make certain it would be for her ears only. Everyone around them seemed to be engrossed in the game. Sally mimicked his position. Their noses were almost touching. Sosh had to fight off the urge for another kiss. Not now.

He whispered, "Sally, on the opening day ..." He paused. It was not easy, but he managed to say, "Why did you have a revolver in your purse?"

Sally's demeanor did not change perceptibly. If something stirred within her, it did not show on her face. She whispered back, "So you did notice. I thought so. I want to tell you why, but not now. I'll find some place where we can meet and I'll give you a note in class on Monday morning. Trust me, Sosh. When I tell you what happened, I think you'll understand." Without waiting for a response, she immediately got to her feet, dusted herself off, and began talking excitedly to Delores about what must have just happened in the baseball game—as if nothing had happened between her and Sosh.

Sosh could not believe how quickly her demeanor had changed. He felt foolish being left alone on the ground. Had he imagined what had happened just seconds before? No, Sally had kissed him. He could still feel a slight bruise on his lips from her exuberance. He slowly got up and stood there, as if in some kind trance.

Bump said something to him, and he nodded his head, but he did not hear what was said. He had no idea what was going on, except that he and Sally had been submerged in a world of their own making, and he had just returned to reality.

For some unknown reason, Sosh suspected he was being watched. He looked around at the crowd surrounding the diamond. He saw Dr. Elliott, who was seated with the bigwigs behind home plate, glancing over several times. When their eyes met, Dr. Elliott looked as if he were asking, "What you are you two up to?"

On the other side of the field, he saw Sam Cutter watching him, and from the expression on Cutter's face, it was apparent he did not like what he was seeing.

Dr. Elliott's interest bothered Sosh more than did Sam's. Did Dr. Elliott suspect Sally could be the assassin? What had he gotten himself into? Sally said he would understand, but was that possible when a revolver and trying to kill the senator were involved? He doubted it very much. He could still taste Sally's kiss on his lips.

CHAPTER 30

▼

"STAUNCHING THE BLOOD"

That Same Day

Trying to act like his hero Sherlock Holmes, Leslie sat in the notables' seats directly behind home base and attempted to decipher what was going on between Sosh and his lady friend. When everyone else was on their feet, they were not in view. Something was happening between those two, but what? Were they merely queening—the campus word for being romantic—or what? All of this became more interesting when Leslie noticed that across the field, behind first base, accompanied by all his fraternity friends, Sam Cutter, his top hat slightly askew, was also watching. Leslie could not quite make out the expression on his face, but it was not a happy one. Was he watching the beginnings of a romantic triangle? If so, he would not want to be in Sosh's shoes.

Leslie saw that, by the end of the fifth inning, Sosh and the girl were standing with their companions. Both of them were more interested in their friends than each other. Something must have happened. But what? Only four more innings and they could all go home, Leslie thought.

Ed Richardson led off for the seniors in the top of the sixth. By now, the seniors had batted twice, so this was Richardson's third time at bat. He could tell that Pitcher Howard was tiring. The first ball pitched was slower and lower than any other ball Richardson had seen on his previous trips to the plate, and he hit it with a resounding swack. The ball flew over the diamond, out into no man's land. It was a homer, and Richardson rounded the bases with a slow, calculated gait. The seniors led four to three. The crowd's flagging attention returned to the game and they gave a belated cheer as they realized what was happening.

Leslie and everyone who knew anything about the game could tell Howard's right arm was hurting. It hung loosely at his side, and he spent a great deal of time between pitches rubbing or resting it. Dr. Jordan was watching him carefully.

Miraculously, Howard managed to pull himself together, and after pitching two balls to Wallingford, got three strikes over the plate and struck him out. Charles Chadsey quickly came to the plate, perhaps too quickly because his aggressiveness may have unnerved Howard, and instead of giving his arm a rest, he immediately threw another slow, low ball to Chadsey, right over the plate. Chadsey took advantage of it, and again the sound of hard wood against a baseball rang out over the field. Only this time, the ball did not travel quite as far as Richardson. It went over the head of center fielder Albert Warner, and landed just beyond him, but it was still in sight and playable.

Chadsey, being the excellent athlete he was, had immediately taken off for first base and was rounding second by the time Warner was able to pick up the ball. Warner hesitated, wondering what he should do. He knew his arm was not strong enough to get the ball to third base, so he threw it to the relay man, Dr. Swain. By now, Chadsey was rounding third and starting his run for home plate. Swain threw the relayed ball with all his strength toward Dr. Richardson, the faculty's catcher, who was standing directly in front of home plate, guarding it.

Those in the crowd who were watching the game, rather than being lost in conversation, grew tense. What they had been waiting for was about to happen: a confrontation between student and teacher. Chadsey was running with a full head of steam directly toward Dr. Richardson, who was standing like a brick wall between him and home plate.

Leslie, Hopkins, the Lathrops, and Fesler slowly and simultaneously arose from their seats to observe the collision.

Reverend Thoburn placed himself about five feet from home plate He realized the importance of getting a good view of what was about to take place. Swain's relay arrived in Richardson's mitt, but on the side toward the pitcher's mound, where Thoburn stood. Chadsey saw this, so he dived on the other side of Richardson, away from the ball. Richardson, while moving his right hand across his body to tag Chadsey, dropped his head, which was partially protected by a leather and metal catcher's mask, and part of his mask grazed Chadsey's cheek as he careened by him. By the time Richardson tagged him with the ball, Chadsey had already touched home plate with his left foot. Thoburn shouted out, "Safe." But as congratulating teammates surrounded him, Chadsey was far from safe; blood was oozing robustly from the gash created by Richardson's mask.

It was not just the Roble ladies who were concerned and uttered words of sympathy and pity; Leslie Elliott was on his feet and silently condemning what he had just seen. Dr. Woods was there, but he had turned away from the action to discuss something with his wife. Leslie immediately went over to him and touched his shoulder so he could see Chadsey needed his services. Woods ran to his rig, got the first aid box he always carried with him, and strode over to the seniors bench, where Chadsey was sitting amidst his concerned team members. He was manfully staunching the blood on the side of his face with a dirty shirt he had been given by a team member.

Everyone was silent as all eyes watched Dr. Woods methodically clean the wound. It was a fairly deep gash, but did not require sutures. The doctor put a tight bandage on it to keep it from getting infected. Chadsey stood up, with a broad grin on his face, and turned around, facing the crowd, so everyone could see he was all right, ready to continue the game. The students cheered their stricken hero.

Dr. Richardson, after gathering himself together, went over to Chadsey to see how he was doing. Everyone on the faculty team left the field to mingle with the seniors around Chadsey. Swain, Marx, and Jordan stood close by Chadsey, who was still on the bench, and eventually, everyone on the faculty team ended up touching him or saying encouraging words to him. Dr. Richardson was particularly concerned and sat down beside him and whispered something into his ear that made Chadsey smile.

After a few minutes of this comradeship, Thoburn felt he had been derelict in his duties and shouted, "Play ball."

The faculty team slowly returned to their positions on the playing field, but Leslie could sense the game would be played differently after that. The air of competitiveness and desire to win had vanished like a gust of ill wind. Perhaps now we will have circus time, Leslie thought, and was relieved.

The score was five to three, with the seniors leading, and with Howard still trying to pitch with an arm that appeared to have taken on a will of its own. Howard was tired. As far as he was concerned, the faculty team had been defeated, and he wanted to go home, but no one else on the faculty team could pitch. And Jack Whittemore was up at bat.

Howard feebly tried to get his next pitch over the base, but failed miserably. Whittemore purposely moved out of the batter's box to hit an errant ball into left field. Dr. Griswold tried to catch it, but it went straight through his outstretched glove onto the ground. Whittemore looked back as he was dashing to first base, and saw what had happened. Instead of rounding first base, he slowed his gait and stopped at first, surprising everyone, including Dr. Jordan, who was poised to catch the ball Dr. Griswold never threw. Whittemore made a deep bow to Dr. Jordan, and muttered words Leslie could not hear, but deciphered as a request for a dance. Jordan picked up on the premise immediately. He curtsied like a young belle and shyly held his mitt to his face, while putting out his right hand for Whittemore to grasp. The twosome made lavish, sweeping waltz steps toward second base, passed it, and continued toward third—all the while making long, twirling strides to the one, two, three of a silent waltz beat. Someone in the crowd start to hum the Blue Danube Waltz, and instantaneously the whole crowd picked up the refrain. Timothy Hopkins looked over at Leslie with an expression of distain, as if to say, "What kind of game is this?" He was rewarded with the sight of Leslie mimicking the dancers by swaying back and forth with the beat. Leslie hummed along. Hopkins no longer pretended to enjoy his company.

In the meantime, Griswold had also entered into the act and ran with the ball as if he were sneaking up on an unsuspecting Whittemore. Just before the twosome arrived at third, he touched Whittemore on the shoulder with the ball. Thoburn, who played his part to the hilt, made a grand sweeping gesture with his right hand, thumb extended, and said, "You're out." Whittemore took the touched ball as if Griswold were cutting in, and continued the waltz toward home base, but now with Dr. Griswold as his partner.

Dr. Jordan thanked Whittemore for the dance and returned to first base, using a somewhat feminine, swishy walk to get there. All the students were laughing to the point of tears, but some of the more sober guests—such as the Lathrops, Fesler, and Hopkins—decided that without the excitement of competition, they could spend their time better elsewhere.

Leslie heard Timothy Hopkins mutter, "I have better things to do," as he got up and walked toward his waiting carriage. The Lathrop brothers left, without a word to Leslie. At least Bert Fesler, following in their footsteps, said his good-byes.

Leslie was left sitting alone in the only five chairs set up for the game. He looked over at Fletcher Martin and motioned for him and Fred Behn to come and sit with him. It looked as if Fred could use a place to sit. They immediately joined him, with Fletcher on one side and Fred on the other. It was as though a cloud had lifted from Leslie's shoulders. With Fletcher and Fred on either side, he felt he could really enjoy the game.

The faculty still needed one more out to end the inning, and Frank Dennis more than obliged them. Howard, the faculty pitcher, resumed trying to get a ball over the plate. He did not have to try too hard because Dennis had decided to try to hit and miss any ball pitched to him, no matter where it was. Three balls were pitched and three times Dennis took terrific swipes at hitting them, but missed them so badly that he ended up on the third occasion purposely sprawled in the dirt. More laughter. Even Reverend Thoburn had to smile. He was beginning to enjoy himself.

The top of the fifth inning finally ended. The score was still seniors five, faculty three. And it was the faculty's turn at bat.

During the break between innings, Leslie again thanked Fred Behn for his kindness when they first met. "I'm sorry Ellen and I haven't been by to see you," he said.

Fred said, "My saloon ain't the kind establishment people like you and your wife frequent. There'll be other times when you and the missus can stop by and see Widow Malgren and me at the farm. In fact, with Thanksgiving coming up, why don't you and the missus drop by and join us for some vittles? Fletcher, here, said he'd drop by because Irene is going to visit friends."

Leslie thought, why not. He said, "I should be able to make it, but Ellen will have to cook for Bolton."

Fred insisted, "Bring them both along. Two more mouths will be nothing for us to feed on a day like Thanksgiving."

Fletcher interrupted. "Knowing Bolton, I doubt if he would fit in, Leslie. I'm sure you would enjoy yourself, but I don't think Bolton would, and I need someone like you to make sure I don't drink too much. The next day, I'm going up to Lick Observatory with Dr. Whitman, my roommate, and some of his friends."

How could he say no? With conviction, Leslie said, "I'll be there with Fletcher."

Fred's face lit up with anticipation "Wonderful. Wonderful. The whole town of Mayfield will be looking forward to meeting you."

Leslie hadn't thought about it that way, but it would be the first meeting of the Stanford administration with the Mayfield folks. He would have to discuss it beforehand with Dr. Jordan. Slightly less enthusiastically, he said, "Yes, I'll be there."

Their conversation ended as the bottom of the fifth inning began. Dr. Miller was up. Previously he had struck out. Whittemore was pitching the ball, slowly, directly over the plate. It looked as if he were trying to give the faulty a good ball to hit. Miller stuck out his bat and Jack threw a ball at it. The ball dribbled across second base into center field. Miller headed for first. Dennis, on second base, turned around to track it down. Brown from his center field position also approached the ball. Miller headed for second base. Both Dennis and Brown pounced on the ball. From the crowd's perspective, it appeared as if they were wrestling one another to see who would throw the ball to third. Miller touched third and was heading home. By the time Dennis had triumphed and thrown the ball to catcher Chadsey, Miller was being congratulated by his teammates for the ill-gotten homer. Everyone noted how Miller had made a wide circuit around the wounded Chadsey, just to make certain there was no reoccurrence of the ill-fated accident. The faculty had gained a run, and the score was five to four. The seniors still prevailed.

With the travesty of the Whittemore and Jordan infield waltz and Dennis in the dirt and now Miller's fluke home run behind them, the seniors decided to settle down and play a normal, fun baseball game. Whittemore resumed his normal pitching prowess and struck out Griswold, Warner, and Bryant, in order.

The sixth inning proved to be quite boring after all the previous excitement. No one from either side scored or even reached base. For one more inning, Howard's arm was holding out. He struck out Trebgloan. Cooley hit a fly ball to Swain, and Stephens stuck out. The faculty was also not successful. Swain hit a high fly ball to Wallingford, which he caught. Both Jordan and Howard struck out. At the end of the sixth it was still five to four, for the seniors.

By now, it was four-thirty, and the light of a dull fall day was dimming. The game had been going on for two and a half hours, and even the most stalwart of the fans were beginning to fade away and wend their way home. Carriages with wives and children were the first to go, then most of the Roble girls, with their light blue blankets. About ten senior girls remained, along with most of the Encina males. A few of the Encina daredevils sitting on their narrow windowsills remained to watch the rest of the game in the glow of an autumn sunset.

On the sidelines, Leslie heard Dr. Jordan counsel his team to do the best they could, but to move the game along because it would be difficult to play in the dark. From Dr. Jordan's huffing and puffing, Leslie could tell he was fatigued.

Because of the darkness and the game's duration, balls became strikes, and those players who might have been safe were out. No one argued the calls. The umpire was also tired.

The next three innings were played quickly and without incident, except that in each of the innings the seniors scored three runs. They hit home runs and hits to the infield and outfield that were difficult to see, so were dropped. The faculty could not see the pitches too well, so missed them with their bats, or were too tired to run quickly enough to beat out an infield hit and were called out. At the bottom of the ninth inning, it was a runaway win for the seniors, now leading fourteen to four.

By now it was almost dark. Only Leslie, the senior ladies, and faculty members remained on the sidelines, along with Jasper Paulsen and his bus. Jasper was still waiting to see if he would be hired for the evening. Everyone else had gone home or was in the dining hall getting ready to have supper.

The ninth inning was the faculty's last chance to win. Dr. Jordan rallied his troops around him. They were a bedraggled-looking group. Most of their faces were caked with a mixture of dirt and sweat. A few had minor bruises and cuts, and everyone's uniforms were filthy from falling down in the dust and weeds.

Leslie thought that somewhere within Dr. Jordan's middle-aged, tired body, there remained a kernel of competitiveness that caused him to fool heartedly think the faculty still had a chance, and to say, "Now, gentlemen, we have one more inning to beat these young pups, and we can do it. I know there is only a slight chance we can make ten runs in the inning, but there is a chance. All right, let's show them what we can do."

Most of his fellow teammates thought he was crazy, but they still gave a half-hearted cheer—but a cheer in any case. Even in the semi-darkness, Jordan could feel new energy being brewed.

But Jordan's words of encouragement did not improve Dr. Griswold's swing or Dr. Warner's eyesight. Both of them struck out, but with hardy swings that made loud swooshing sounds. Then the fates seemed to favor the faculty, and Dr. Bryant miraculously saw Whittemore's pitch, and with a whack sent the ball down the third base line. He was safe at first. Dr. Swain hit a high fly ball that Brown in center field lost in the darkening sky and dropped. By the time he found it and threw it to the infield, Bryant was on third base and Swain was on second. Miracle of miracles, the star of the team, Dr. Jordan was up.

So far, Jordan had struck out twice and grounded out once, so he was "due." In the dimming light, he focused on the white ball coming out of Whittemore's right hand. He could only guess which part of the plate it would cross, but he swung his bat with all his might at where it might be—and it was. Another whack, but this one looked like it was gone, on its way to no man's land. Dr. Jordan took off running, his tight pants rubbing against his belly, and his tired legs looked as if they were running in quick sand. He was rounding first and heading for second.

Steven Brown, the senior's center fielder, was only half-heartedly looking for the ball Jordan had hit. In many ways, he thought it might be best if he did not find it.

By now, both Bryant and Swain had scored for the faculty. Jordan was slowly making his way to third base and rounding it. It appeared as if he might have sprained an ankle or both ankles, or perhaps his legs were cramping up. Whatever the reason, Leslie thought he could have walked faster than Jordan was running.

Brown found a ball—it might have been Jordan's ball or another ball hit previously and lost—but a ball it was, and Brown instinctively picked it up and threw it to the relay man, Stephens, who in turn threw it to Chadsey at home plate.

Leslie watched as Dr. Jordan crossed third base and began his run toward home plate. Halfway there, Jordan could see Chadsey standing there with a broad grin on his face, and in his hand was a ball. For a second, Jordan had the animal urge to attempt to bowl Chadsey over, but the smile was his undoing, and instead he literally fell into Chadsey's arms. His stamina had finally given out. His weary legs would not allow him to move another inch. Chadsey gently touched him with the ball, and Thoburn with pity in his voice said, "You're out."

The two men, Chadsey and Jordan, hung together as if they were Siamese twins, as the two teams surrounded them, cheering, laughing, and crying. The first LSJU faculty versus seniors baseball game had ended with the seniors victorious, fourteen to six.

Leslie had to help Dr. Jordan to his rig. He could not walk without assistance. Leslie drove him to Escondite Cottage, and Dr. Jordan continued to lean on him as he made his way from the rig to the cottage's front door. He had not said a word to Leslie.

Miss Jessie must have heard them coming up the steps, and was there to greet them in the doorway. Leslie managed to move Jordan's large frame between them so Jordan would have continual support. In the doorway, with his arm firmly grasping his wife's petite shoulders, Dr. Jordan stopped for a second and looked back at Leslie and uttered his first words since the final out: "It was a good game, wasn't it, Leslie. I think it was a memorable game, right?"

"It was truly memorable. See you on Monday, Dr. Jordan."

As the heavy door shut, Leslie could faintly hear the good doctor say, "See you on Monday, Leslie."

He unhitched Jordan's horse, led him to the small stable, undid the horse's harness, rubbed him down, and fed him. When he was finished, he made certain the stable door was shut. Then he proceeded to walk toward his home on Alvarado Row. Now in the dark, with only dim moonlight to guide him, he thought, "It was quite a day. There is much to tell Ellen. I'm sure she will think men are crazy to get up to such antics, but it was fun. Next year, I'll take Louis."

As he passed the playing field, the only remnant of the game was the scoreboards, which were still attached to the ladders standing behind first base. Leslie could not see in the darkness, but he wondered if—as far as the scoreboards were concerned—the game had never ended. At the bottom of the eighth inning, the scorer had given up and gone home. No one noticed. It had become too dark to see.

When the moon came from behind a dark cloud, Leslie saw a brown ladies' jacket in the thick brush. Someone must have either lost or left it behind. He picked it up and took it with him. He would give it to Frank Batchelder on Monday morning to place in the lost and found box. Someone might sorely need that jacket and would be pleased to get it back.

As Leslie continued his way toward the lights of Alvarado Row and home, two unrelated thoughts crossed his mind: the first was how lucky the University was to have David Starr Jordan as their first president. Of course, he had his faults. What man—or woman, for that matter—didn't? But for all his theatrics, procrastinations, and insecurities, he was ideal for this fragile university struggling for its survival. The second thought was more of an observation. Leslie could feel faint traces of rain droplets on his face. By the time he was on Alvarado Row, walking toward the candlelights of his home, the droplets were drops. His coat and the lost jacket, he had slung over his arm, were wet. Was this the beginning of the promised autumn storms he had been warned of by the locals? He could hear his dogs barking and could see Ellen opening the front door in anticipation of his arrival. It had been a long day, and even though he had not played, he felt drained and tired.

CHAPTER 31

▼

"A PERENNIAL PICNIC"

Sunday, November 15, 1891

After the steady drumming of rain on the rooftop awoke Ellen Elliott, she could not get back to sleep. Beside her, Leslie was gently snoring. They always slept apart at first, facing away from one another. As the night progressed, he would turn toward her, and sometimes stretch out his hand and touch her.

It must be close to two o'clock, Ellen thought. She enjoyed these times of wakefulness. It gave her time to think about what was going on around her. During the day, there was no time for contemplation.

Leslie was aware that he snored and tried not to disturb her, but over the years she had grown used to it. In fact, when they were apart, which was seldom, she missed her husband's arrhythmic, monotonous sounds, which only became annoying when he was very tired or had something on his mind. Tonight, because of the arduous prior day, he had hardly moved from where he had fallen into bed, and intermittently he made whimpering sounds, as if someone or something were nudging him.

Ellen knew each day's events, and particularly yesterday's, exhausted poor Leslie. It was mental fatigue, not physical. He worried about Dr. Jordan. He worried about the University. Would it survive? Would anyone be seriously injured at the game—players as well as spectators? From what Harriet Marx had said when she dropped by yesterday evening, his worries were warranted. Harriet asked why men were so competitive and enjoyed beating up on one another. A learned man, such as Dr. Jordan, acted like a young pup when he was playing some fool game. She and Ellen agreed they would never understand.

Harriet had come over after dinner, under her umbrella, though the steady rain, and said her husband had eaten a few morsels, taken a bath, and gone to bed. She said his body was covered with bruises, and both his knees were scraped and bloody from falling on the hard adobe ground. He reminded her of their four-year-old son. Still, David Marx had insisted it was a glorious event, and he fell asleep with a smile on his face. She told Ellen one of the seniors had his cheek severely cut, and Dr. Wood attended to it. She was sure the young man would proudly wear the scar from the mishap for the rest of his life, as if he were a member of a German dueling society. The two women agreed that type of thinking was what led to warfare. It would not be so if women, rather than men, led nations.

After exhausting the topic of the day's events, she and Harriet had discussed the food they might prepare this coming Friday for their open houses. It would be November twentieth, the third Friday in the month, and it was their turn along with the Woods, Richardsons, and Griffins to welcome faculty and students into their homes for light repast and entertainment—a reading perhaps, or a piano recital.

The concept of the open house had followed Dr. Jordan from the University of Indiana. He was always working to bridge the gap between faculty and students. In this isolated environment, there was not much of a choice. With only the saloons and brothels of Mayfield close at hand, it behooved faculty wives to organize some form of alternative entertainment. Going to the city for the weekend was too expensive for most of the faculty and students. Ellen had taken the lead in organizing the Decalogue, the ten Alvarado Row cottages, into two groups. The first five homes—including the Elliott's—closest to water tank and furthest from the Quad were open on the third Friday; the second five on the first Friday. At their first planning meeting, Jessie Jordan had unexpectedly appeared and automatically assumed leadership of the events. Ellen got some credulous looks from her friends, but ignored them. She had learned to cater to Jessie's whims. Leslie had never said anything, but she knew he expected servility in her relationship with the president's wife as part of her wifely duties. For her, being servile was the most difficult task.

She almost chuckled out loud. When they were alone, she referred to Leslie as the mouse. Aptly, in the same circumstances, he called her the lion.

So far, the Elliotts had one open house in October, which was moderately successful. Forty to sixty students visited, and a handful of faculty and their wives. This was to be expected because neighbors saw so much of one another during the day that there was no motivation to see them again in the evening.

Familiarity, in this case, was part of the landscape. Ellen remembered one beautiful, cloudless morning when, after she had prepared Leslie's lunch and seen him off to work, she had gone to her back porch and watched all nine of her neighbors go through the same routines. She had shouted out "good morning" to no less than five of them from her back porch, and only the limitations of her voice precluded greeting the remaining four. No trees, shrubs, fences, or woodsheds shielded them from one another's view.

Ellen knew, or could guess, many things about her neighbors, and she was sure they had the same knowledge about her and Leslie, and even about dear little Louis. No one said anything, but she guessed all the wives knew exactly when their neighbors were making love, usually in the morning on the weekend. She and Leslie did.

But soon all this would change, as she knew from past experience living on the campus at Cornell. Trees and lawns would be planted, and good friends and neighbors would depart for other local housing or another university. Already, last night, Harriet had told her she and David were thinking of buying a lot from Timothy Hopkins and building a home in his new Palo Alto development. Irene Butler and Lucy Fletcher were also considering building their girls' school there. Ellen knew she and Leslie could not afford to build. And even if they could, she doubted Leslie would want to. Sometimes he returned to work after dinner and didn't return home until almost midnight. Last week, after Ellen put her foot down, Leslie explained he and Dr. Anderson were discussing which classes should require extensive knowledge of Latin. Leslie would not leave until Dr. Anderson had moderated his requirement for Latin. Leslie's explanation caused Ellen to appreciate how her diminutive husband stood up to the daunting head of the English Department.

Workers had already begun building two more cottages on Alvarado Row, closer to the Quad. One of them would be for Dr. and Mrs. Branner, who would be arriving after the New Year. He would be the head of the Geology Department. The other was for Dr. Griffin and his family. Dr. Griffin was not satisfied with having a home so similar to his neighbors, and he could afford to be choosy.

Dr. Branner's new cottage would have eleven rooms, including seven bedrooms, making it much larger than the Elliott's and the other nine original homes. Ellen understood these improved accommodations were to be expected since Dr. Jordan considered Dr. Branner, his roommate at Cornell and good friend, to be his heir apparent—the next president of the University. She wondered if Jordan had considered her Leslie for the post. No one knew what was going on at the University better than he, but she knew he would always be the man behind the man. He told her how he preferred that role, but did he really? Even for her it was difficult to know what her husband really thought and felt. He so controlled his feelings.

She wondered if Dr. and Mrs. Branner, coming from Indiana, truly understood what they were getting into. She remembered the glorified picture Dr. Jordan had painted for Leslie. The Branners would have to adjust to the University's dust, ants, and problems with the help. Dust from the dried hay and manure combined with adobe dirt to get into everything, everywhere. Ellen considered herself not a fastidious housekeeper, but better than average, and she had learned to leave dust where it fell until she could write in it.

Ants were another matter. Now, with the rainy season upon them, what was once just a bother would become a calamity. Cooling cupboards had been built on the north sides of the homes, and it was there that ants particularly liked to gather. Rather than being a deterrent, insect powder bought off the cart from Mr. La Piere was an enticement. The ants thrived on it. Leslie had repeated to her Frank Batchelder's story that when he boarded in Mayfield, his food was regularly served with ants, as if they were part of the garnishment. He concluded the people in Mayfield ignored them. Ants had bitten the Elliotts during the night, and the following morning they found them crawling about in their bed sheets. Ellen found them scurrying about in Louis' hair.

At Cornell, she had always managed to have industrious live-ins to help with the cleaning and cooking, but in the West such help was a rarity. Jessie Jordan had already run through three—or was it four—cooks, and Ellen had lost her live-ins to better accommodations or changes in plans. Ellen and Leslie were always on the lookout for someone to help with Louis, but up to now no one had appeared they could trust. Hopefully, Louise, Ellen's sister, and her parents would soon be joining them to lend a hand. Bolton was more of a hindrance than help. He and Leslie were like vinegar and oil, but she had a hunch Bolton would soon be moving out, God be willing, to marry Lucy Fletcher.

On the positive side, the Branners would find excellent fruits and vegetables were easy to come by. Chinese gardeners made their daily rounds with whatever was in season. And Mr. La Piere was always on time with his grocery cart. But once La Piere was gone, he was gone. Any forgotten item would have to be borrowed from a neighbor. It was strange, but some of the ladies were always the borrowers and others were always the lenders. She wondered which Mrs. Branner would be.

Dr. Branner would also have his share of pioneer and picnic duties. One of the wives had said to Ellen—it might have been Mrs. Miller—that their living style was similar to being on a perennial picnic. Ellen thought it such a good analogy that she repeated it several times to others. Obtaining water for drinking and cooking was part of that picnic analogy, but it was not the fun part.

She knew she was being critical when she regularly reminded Leslie that Senator Stanford had obviously not done his homework when he plunked more than five hundred men, women, and children into a region incapable of satisfying its need for water. Leslie would reply that such a happenstance was not new for Californians. Water in California was always in short supply.

Running water from the tap was available for the cottages, the dormitories, and the Quad buildings. But that water was from the Searsville Reservoir, and it not only had a disgusting broth-like look, it also smelled disgusting, particularly when it was raining, as it was now. Silt from the reservoir's banks slipped into the water.

Leslie stirring in his sleep interrupted Ellen's thoughts. In one movement, he turned toward her and threw his right hand in her direction. When his fingers found her side, he withdrew them, and in a second returned to a deep sleep. Ellen was able to return to her thoughts.

Dr. Branner, from the photos she had seen, appeared to be a very distinguished man, with his neatly clipped beard and refined features. She wondered how he would take to joining his colleagues, each suppertime, as they wended their way with pails in hand to the water tank to obtain precious artesian spring water to be used for cooking and drinking. Unfortunately, Dr. Branner would find living close to the Quad did have its drawbacks. Each and every evening, he would have further to go than the others.

Leslie had told her there were plans afoot to run a pipe from the distant tank directly to the midst of Alvarado Row, where a hydrant would be installed that would lessen the walk for some. But eventually the well would dry up, and what would happen then? When Ellen brought up this problem to Leslie, he reassured her several of the professors, including their friend and neighbor, David Marx, were working on a permanent solution to the water problem. For the time being, they would have to put up with the look and smells of Searsville water for bathing and external uses. Knowing professors as she had most of her life, Ellen knew the solution to a problem, particularly a practical one, might be a long time coming.

As Ellen listened to the rain still drumming on the roof, another thought struck her: from rain came mud—yellow-brown, adobe mud. Immediately after the ten cottages had been built, a boardwalk had been installed along Alvarado Row, and boards had been placed linking the walks to each home. It had been a happy sight to see Louis with the other children in their red wheelbarrows, and clattering trains of wooden cars running up and down the new walkway. Certainly she and the other mothers felt more confident their little ones were safe. But those boards ended where Alvarado Row ended, and the well-trodden dirt paths that led to the safety of the Quad's asphalt-covered patio would now become quagmires. Students living in the halls were lucky. A paved walkway linked their halls to the Quad, but there were no boardwalks or paved walkways linking the faculty homes. With all the rain, members of the faculty and their families would find their shoes, hems, and cuffs caked with adobe mud, weighing them down as if they were attached to the earth with glue. Attempting to clean those shoes or garments with Searsville water would be next to impossible.

Ah, the joys of their perennial picnic. Surprisingly, with that humbling thought in mind, Ellen drifted into dreams of soft, green hills and the coiffured lawns surrounding Cornell University—a civilized way of life.

The shower's patter slowed its cadence and eventually ceased. Silence allowed Ellen's soft breathing, joined by her husband's snoring, to become the dominant sounds within the cottage's walls.

CHAPTER 32

▼

"LOOK FOR SUSPICIOUS CHARACTERS"

Monday, November 16, 1891

Leslie, as usual, was the first one at the office. As expected, Dr. Jordan was late. He merely nodded his morning greetings, looking as if every bone in his body ached when he moved. As quickly as he could, he disappeared down the hallway to his office.

After nine o'clock, a bevy of visitors appeared at the counter. There were so many that Leslie had to help Miss Stillings. The male students, faculty members, and even assorted Menlo and Mayfair residents had one common complaint: either their pockets had been picked at the game on Saturday or their personal belongings had been stolen from their rooms at Encina Hall. Watches, purses, wallets, jewelry, and money had been purloined.

One poor soul had all the money he expected to live on for the rest of the semester stolen. Leslie asked him to come back tomorrow after he had a chance to discuss the fellow's plight with Dr. Jordan. Somehow, they would work out a temporary loan for him, even if Leslie had to take it out of his own pocket.

At one point in the morning, Dr. Jordan made an appearance to find out the cause for the hullabaloo. When he found out what the problem was, he beat a hasty retreat back to his office.

He was not able to ignore the happenstance for long because Timothy Hopkins appeared, dressed impeccably in morning coat and top hat. He looked as if he were going to visit the Queen of England. Without a word, he only paused at the counter, then swept around its left side. With long, manful strides he walked down the hall to Dr. Jordan's office, opened the door, and walked in, shutting the door resoundingly behind him. No one, including Leslie, had moved to deter him.

After Mr. Hopkins left, Burt Fesler, the master at Encina, came in and asked to see Dr. Jordan, and huddled with him in his office for a considerable period of time.

By the lunch hour, at which point only a few stragglers were coming in, Leslie heard Dr. Jordan shout, "Leslie, come in here and bring your lunch."

Leslie dutifully obeyed. After he sat down, he waited for Dr. Jordan to decide which path their conversation might take.

"As if an assassin were not enough, we have thieves amongst us." Dr. Jordan uttered the phrase as if it were a line from a Shakespearean play. "And would you believe it, they managed to relieve Mr. Hopkins of his gold watch at the game."

Leslie's concern had been building all morning, magnified by his encounter with the poor lad who lost all his monies. With deep emotion, he said, "This is awful, Dr. Jordan. The authorities must be notified at once. I believe we are in the jurisdiction of the San Jose police. This is not a prank. It's a monstrous crime."

Dr. Jordan was not surprised to see Leslie upset. His registrar had strong convictions about what was right and wrong. But unfortunately he had little understanding about some of the realities of life. Dr. Jordan said, "I'm afraid not, Leslie. We'll have to handle this matter ourselves. You forget that our founders do want to face the possibility of their friends knowing that attendees at their university are thieves."

Leslie was not to be deterred from contacting the police. "Their concerns are crazy: first, an attempted assassination; now, this. And how do you know how they feel? How could they already know what has happened when they are in Washington?"

"I was informed about their feelings by Burt Fesler, who conveyed the thoughts of their brother-in-law, Ariel Lathrop."

Leslie looked distraught. "So what are we to do? Act as if nothing has happened?"

"No, we will act. As you know, Burt Fesler was here, and he said it was as if someone carefully scouted out the rooms before the game and determined which were unlocked. Most of the victims were the types who do not believe there are any thieves about, so they did not think of locking their doors. Fesler surmised that during the two to three hours of the game, almost all the unlocked rooms were looted, with the exception of those on the corner facing the diamond. The thieves knew enough about the hall's viewing area that they purposely stayed away from that corner."

"Interesting, interesting. Whoever controlled this evil operation was not only dastardly but also ingeniously evil."

"Burt also informed me that Mr. Lathrop has taken the matter into his own hands. He has already penned a lengthy diatribe to the senator informing him of the general lawlessness of the rabble we have accumulated."

"It must have made Ariel's day. He and his brother have a loathing for whatever our students do, good or bad. I can only think it is some kind of jealousy because of the life they never had."

"I wish I could tell both of them to go to hell in a chariot, but I'm afraid their relationship to our founders will never allow me. It is something I must learn to live with, Leslie. But between you and me and the lamppost, I do hate both of them."

Leslie knew it was time for a new subject. There were certain words he did not want to hear anyone say about another person, and hate was one of them. "And what will we do to rid ourselves of these bad seeds? And I mean the thieves, of course, not the Lathrop brothers."

"On Ariel's side, he has asked Burt to hire several deputies to patrol both halls, night and day, to make certain the thieves do not strike again."

"But since no one has seen the thieves, for whom will these deputies be looking?"

"Suspicious characters."

"Ah, hah, yes, of course, suspicious characters. And whom may I ask will Mr. Fesler or Mr. Lathrop hire as deputies to judge, purely on sight, who are or are not suspicious characters?"

"Several stalwart citizens of Mayfield."

Leslie had a quizzical look on his face. "Mayfield, yes, the very hub of righteousness."

"Yes, Mayfield. I can see from the look on your face, Leslie, you find this ridiculous, and I agree, but it is no laughing matter. Ariel is going into Mayfield this afternoon and will seek Constable Coulter's recommendations."

Leslie tried to contain his incredulity. He said, "I'm sorry, dear Doctor, if there were to be any suspicious characters about the campus, it would be assuredly those same Mayfield citizens."

Jordan's mouth twisted itself into a sardonic smile. "It is what Ariel wants to do, and I am not about to attempt to stop him. I know the senator is a reasonable man, but I don't want to waste the few opportunities I might have to change business office policy, on this matter. I do plan to initiate my own investigation. Do you remember the chap who helped us find out who masterminded the flat-car incident?"

"Yes, the fellow who came into your office and volunteered the mastermind's name—Pudge, wasn't it? And the informer's name was Sam; yes, Sam Cutter. Forgive me, but I have no faith in informers, and I would trust young Sam Cutter about as far as I could throw him."

"You are probably right, Leslie. But the fellow did come forward, and thank God for that. And he seems to have knowledge of the goings on within Encina, so I plan to contact him and see if he can be of service regarding this matter."

"Do you want me to contact him for you?"

"Yes, would you please send him a note regarding some trumped-up record issue, and when he appears, turn him over to me."

Leslie said, "I wish you had some kind of privacy. Frank and the rest are good workers, but I do question whether they will keep their tongues tied if they see you and Sam together."

"My thought exactly. I'll excuse myself and wander over to the chapel area, and you can bring Mr. Cutter to me so we can have some privacy."

"Will you discuss the matter of the attempted assassination?"

"No, not unless he brings it up. I do understand most of the campus is aware of what has happened."

Leslie responded with "apparently," and let the matter drop. He could see in Dr. Jordan's eyes that he felt badly about leaking the information to his wife, but what was done, was done.

Leslie was not happy with either Dr. Jordan's or Mr. Lathrop's solutions. In his heart, he felt going to the police was the only right thing to do. After all this, he had no appetite for lunch. He excused himself and returned to his desk. As he left, he saw that Dr. Jordan was devouring a thick beef sandwich with great relish.

CHAPTER 33

▼

A KILLING MACHINE

That Same Day

Just before French class began, Sosh greeted Sally with a subdued "good morning" when she sat next to him. She, in turn, barely acknowledged his greeting. Judging by her activity, she was very busy fussing with this and that, but she did manage to drop a small envelope into Sosh's lap, which he retrieved and stuffed into his trouser pocket.

Not a word passed between them until class was over and she was ready to depart. "See you tomorrow," she said cheerfully.

Sosh responded with his own, "See you tomorrow," and she disappeared out the door. The suspense of finding out what was in the envelope was unbearable. Had she found a place where they might meet?

Since the game on Saturday and their kiss, Sosh could not get Sally out of his mind. One part of him wanted to eliminate her from his life. He could move to another seat in the class. If she spoke to him, he could pretend not to hear. He could wipe the slate clean. She was trouble, no doubt about it. But another part wanted to run around Encina Hall, shouting, "Sally kissed me. Sally kissed me!" Any thought of ending the relationship was overruled by the taste of that kiss, which, he imagined, still lingered on his lips. Some fire within him had been ignited, and try as he might, he could not put it out.

As soon as he could, he ducked behind one of the arcades and pulled the envelope from his trouser pocket. In flamboyant, rounded script Sally had written, *Dearest Sosh, meet me at Roble Bridge at five o'clock tonight. Please do not tell any-*

one. You may be followed, so take a roundabout route. See you tonight. Your friend,
Sally

Sosh reread the intimate salutation several times. No one, not even his mother, had referred to him as dearest. He could feel his heart racing. But her words cautioning him about being followed gave him reason to pause. The churning feeling in his stomach revived, and those same misgivings reappeared in his mind. Who might follow him? And why? Was Sally paranoid or was he?

Later that afternoon, he told Will Greer he was going to the library and not to expect him for dinner. He walked ostensibly toward the Quad and made a quick turn south toward the site of the camp's buildings. There he pretended to be looking for someone, and took off in the direction of the senator's stock farm, which also happened to lead to Roble Bridge. The wooden bridge was ancient, spanning the usually dry San Francisquito Creek. It moaned and groaned whenever any weight passed over it.

Every fifty yards or so, Sosh stopped abruptly and slowly turned around, as if admiring the landscape, and continued on. Even though he saw no one, the thought of unknown parties following him was enough to make him feel queasy.

Roble Bridge came into view. No Sally. Sosh remembered Professor Richardson and his family lived in Cedro Cottage, on the other side of the bridge, but there was no sign of them, either. He decided, as a precaution, to step behind a clump of bushes and wait. In the distance, towards the stock farm, he could hear the senator's horses nickering, and occasionally the raised voices of a rider or trainer, but otherwise there were only the hooting of distant owls and the silence of early evening in the countryside.

Sally's whispered "It's me, Sosh; I'm behind you" startled him. He turned around, and she was about ten feet from where he stood.

In the early twilight of the autumn evening, she was more beautiful than before. Her blonde hair was pulled back and tucked under a cotton bonnet. Her face, usually pale, was flushed either with excitement or from a hurried walk from Roble Hall. She stepped forward and grabbed his left hand and began to pull him further into the brush. He gave way, more than willingly, and felt as if she could lead him wherever she wished. He used his other hand to ward off stray branches that brushed into his face.

For some time the couple proceeded, and Sosh began to wonder where they were going. Suddenly, the foliage gave way to a clearing about fifteen to twenty feet in diameter. In the midst of the clearing was an improvised, rustic love seat, made from interlacing boughs and branches, where two people might sit, side by side. The seat appeared to be the handiwork of someone expert in working with the materials nature provided. Luckily it had not rained recently, so the area and seat were dry.

Sally stopped and carefully inspected where they planned to sit. "Sometimes birds or animals do their waste here," she explained. *So she has been here before,* Sosh thought.

The two young people sat facing each other. Sally draped her arm so her hand gently touched Sosh's shoulder. Up to now, Sosh had not said a word. For the first time, he sat back, took a deep breath, and viewed his surroundings. "What a beautiful spot. Who could have made this wonderful seat?" he asked.

"I've been here before when I wanted to get away from all the ruckus at Roble. I've no idea whose handiwork the seat is, but so far, I've never seen anyone else here. I'm sure it will be discovered by others like us." Her hand on his shoulder gripped his coat. "Sosh, we don't have much time. It'll be really dark soon, and I didn't bring a lantern, and I noticed you didn't either, so I'd like to tell you about the revolver and explain why I had it at the opening ceremonies."

Sosh sat with his two hands clasped in front him. He could still see Sally's features in the dim light. He said, "You're right. I'll try to keep quiet."

Slowly, quietly, and unemotionally Sally told him her story.

"I was six years old when my daddy, Henry Brewer, was shot to death by gunmen hired by the railroads. He was a rancher who, with several of his friends, was working several thousand acres of leased land. They intended to buy the land from the Southern Pacific Railway. It was called Mussel Slough and was located near Hanford, California. When my daddy began working the land, the sale prices quoted to him and his neighbors were from two dollars and fifty cents to five dollars per acre. He and his friends pooled their financial resources, accumulated from years of working in the gold mines. They excavated an irrigation ditch to bring water from the King River. With water and hard work, the land bloomed with acres and acres of barley, wheat, and fruit trees.

"About thirteen years ago, they approached the railroad agents to buy the leased land, and found the price had risen to between seventeen and forty dollars per acre. They were told to either buy the land at the high prices or quit it without compensation.

"During the next two years, the railroad and my daddy and his friends spent lots of time in courtrooms and legislative chambers trying to gain control of the properties. But it seemed the law was always on the railroad's side because of all the money they gave to legislators and judges. Another problem was that, during that time, Leland Stanford was governor of California and wielded horrendous power."

Sosh nodded his head. He was beginning to understand.

"As the day approached when eviction papers would be formerly served, my daddy and his friends decided to take the law into their own hands and show the rest of the country how unfair the judicial system was. They thought public outcry would be their judge and jury, even though their own destinies might be death.

"On the night of May tenth, eleven years ago, I still remember hearing my daddy and other men talking in low voices in our family dining room. My mama, brother, and I were in the kitchen. There must have been a lot of men at the big table. Usually twelve could sit there, and extra chairs had to be brought from the kitchen. Every so often, my daddy stuck his head into the kitchen, asked for more coffee, and gave my mama a big black coffee pot to fill. I remember following her into the dining room, holding onto the hem of her dress. Through the cloud of cigar and pipe smoke, I watched as she put a fresh pot on the table. I saw my daddy at the head of the table."

Sally's face lit up with the memory.

"When I walked by him, he leaned over and ruffled my hair and gave me a smile, but even as a child, I felt it was not a happy smile. The men were talking and whispering at the same time, as if they had a secret they didn't want to share. I saw rifles and shotguns everywhere, leaning against the wall, chairs, table. I'd never seen so many guns in our house. Daddy kept his in the barn.

"Next day, as usual, my younger brother and I went to school. Just after noon, the principal came and got us and took us to his office. Uncle Bill, daddy's brother, was there. I could tell he'd been crying and I knew something was wrong. I knew it was about my daddy.

"As we stood before my uncle, waiting for him to say something, anything, he broke into tears. He turned away from us, and when he turned around he was able to speak. He said, 'Your daddy's been shot and killed, and I've come to take you home to your mama.'

"We just stood there, not knowing what to do.

"My brother asked our uncle, 'When is daddy coming back?'

"Uncle Bill wasn't expecting the question. He tried to be as gentle as he could. 'No, honey, he's gone, gone to heaven.'

"I was mad, not at my uncle, but at my daddy for leaving me. We had always been close. Some neighbors and relatives said too close. My thought was, how could he leave me like this? I must have said, 'Gone, gone to heaven. He couldn't leave me. No, no, he wouldn't leave me. I want to go with him.'"

Even in the retelling, Sosh noticed Sally's voice trembled.

"My uncle told me I couldn't go where his brother had gone and I would have to stay with my mama and help her.

"Without knowing what I was doing, I ran to my uncle and began to hit him with my fists, screaming and shouting, 'No, no, he wouldn't leave me. I want to go with him.' I kept saying it over and over until the screams became sobs, and my throat raw. I could no longer speak. I must have fainted because that's all I can remember."

Sosh understood how emotional retelling those events was for Sally, and started to say something, but Sally gently put her fingers over his lips and continued to speak.

"When I got older, I heard Walter J. Crow killed my daddy along with five other ranchers at a shoot-out. The railroads had brought in Crow and another hired gun by the name of Mills D. Hart, in case there was any shooting when the eviction notices were served.

"On the morning of May eleventh, the two gunmen drove onto our ranch in a buggy driven by the U.S. Marshall. In the marshal's pocket were the eviction orders, signed and sealed. Crow and Hart were acting as the railroad representatives. Along side the buggy were more than a dozen mounted, armed deputies.

"The ranchers were waiting for them. They rode up on their horses and surrounded the buggy and deputies.

"I was told the marshal got down and started walking toward my daddy with the eviction papers in his hand. When shots started ringing out, he was struck to the ground by a bucking horse. It saved his life.

"No one could say who fired first, but the educated guess was it was Walter J. Crow. He certainly did most of the shooting and killing. Everyone said he was a killing machine. While still seated in the buggy, he shot my daddy twice in the heart. He must have known exactly who the leader was and picked him off first. He jumped to the ground, shotgun to his shoulder, and blew two ranchers off their horses. Reloading, he killed three more. While this was happening, the ranchers shot the other gunman, still sitting in the buggy. The marshal and deputies managed to stay out of the line of fire, and with all the commotion going on, didn't fire a shot. None of them were killed, wounded, or even grazed.

"Crow fled into a nearby cornfield. They thought he got clean away because they couldn't find his body. But next day they did. Someone followed a trail of blood into the cornfield and found it some distance from the shoot-out. There was blood everywhere. He must have been shot in the back and died a slow death, attempting to find his way through the tall cornstalks. It was like a maze, and he was going in circles. The slower, the better was what the folks in Hanford hoped happened.

Sally hesitated, and Sosh thought she was finished. He started to say something, but Sally put her fingers to his lips again and said, "I'm almost finished. I want to bring my story up to date."

She continued, "Two year's later, my mama married a man named Mr. Forrest. Her new family moved to Anaheim, near Los Angeles, and I became Sally Forrest. My mama had two more children by Mr. Forrest and never mentioned my daddy's name again. I never forgot it. I've a picture of him with us that I always carry. I'd show it to you, but it's too dark to see it now. But one day I want to show it to you. In some ways, I think you and he are a lot alike. Not in looks, but the gentle way you talk and the way you look at me and let me say what's on my mind."

By now it was so dark, Sosh could just make out the outline of Sally's face, about three feet from his. He waited to make certain she was finished. He still had some questions. "I understand how you feel, but killing an old man who is about to die of old age won't bring your father back."

Sally moved closer to Sosh, as if in the chill of the night, she might gain some of his warmth. "I understand that now. But as I grew up in Anaheim, my only thought was to avenge my father's death. I taught myself how to shoot in our orange groves and convinced my stepfather I should have a revolver to protect my virtue when I came up here to college. When I saw they were giving examinations in Los Angeles for free tuition to LSJU, I thought it was right and proper the Stanfords should pay for my college education. In the back of my mind, I must have always thought one day I would try to assassinate the senator."

"What happened at the opening ceremony?" Sosh asked.

"I was next to a wooden stand photographers had put up in the oval in front of the podium. I used its timbers to steady my aim. When the sun came out from behind a cloud, Mrs. Stanford got up with her umbrella to shade her husband and stood right in my line of fire. To my way of thinking, there was no reason she should die for what her husband and his cohorts did. I couldn't pull the trigger."

Sosh said, "There's a rumor going around that someone tried to shoot the senator three days ago. Was that you?"

"Yes. I hid in the brush beside the road, where I knew he would pass, and when he was in my sights, I pulled the trigger."

Except for the moonlight, the two of them were sitting in complete darkness. Sosh could feel Sally's warmth and could hear her breathing. He had never felt so close to a person in his life. Then he heard a rustling sound in the bushes, which startled him. "What was that?" he whispered.

Sally didn't appear to be concerned. She was used to sitting in the dark and hearing strange sounds. "Might be a squirrel or some creature who makes its home here. I hear them all the time. I'm sure no one knows about us coming here."

How could she be so sure? Sosh thought. His heart was still beating fast, but he tried to be calm like Sally. He asked, "So what happened?"

Sally was quiet, as if she were carefully choosing her words. "I'm not sure. I missed, but I don't know why. I had the man square in my sights and I'm very good at hitting targets. But when it came to killing a man, it was different. Or maybe it was my daddy trying to tell me killing the senator was not the way to avenge his death. I started thinking my purpose in life had to be more than just being hung for murdering an old man. What that purpose is I have no idea."

Sosh was happy to hear what she was saying, but he had to ask, "Do you still have the gun?"

"Yes."

"Do you still plan on killing anyone with it?"

"No, when I can, I'll throw it away." She had another thought. "I take that back. There is one person I might shoot, and that's Sam Cutter for pestering me and trying to hurt you."

Again, they heard a rustling in the bushes. This time it was fainter, but persistent, as if whatever it was might be going in another direction. For the first time, Sosh sensed Sally's fear.

She said, "Let's leave."

They immediately got up. Sally took his hand. "Just follow me. I know a quick way out."

When they got to the cement path leading to Roble Hall, and from there to Encina, Sally quickly embraced Sosh and told him, "I'll see you tomorrow at class."

Sosh asked, "Do you think it was Sam Cutter?"

"I hope not," Sally said, and hurriedly made her way toward the safety of Roble Hall. Some distance behind, a disconsolate Sosh followed. It had to be Sam, he thought.

CHAPTER 34

▼

"FOUR GLORIOUS DAYS
OF FREEDOM"

Thursday, November 19, 1891

On that Thursday, dark clouds hovered over the campus. Not only were there clouds that brought rain, but also clouds of work and worries about preparing for midterm tests and researching and writing papers soon due, and beyond that, final examinations to be taken toward the end of January of next year. And then—too soon for most—the second semester would begin on Tuesday, February second, and the academic cycle would begin all over again.

Tempering these worries were thoughts about what to do during the Thanksgiving holidays. Classes would shut down on Thursday, November twenty-sixth, and take back up again on Monday the thirtieth. Students and faculty would have four glorious days of freedom to do or go wherever they fancied or could afford.

For those students who lived any distance from the campus, the decision to go home was out of hand. Even for those who lived a day's journey, and that included most, it was hardly worth the effort of enduring hard travel for half their time off. For those who lived in the immediate area—the Peninsula, San Jose, San Francisco, or Sacramento and its environs—it was an opportunity to invite student friends to visit for Thanksgiving dinner with family, relatives, and friends. The problem was which student friend or friends to expose to their family, or the other way around.

Those students who remained on campus—and they were in the majority—were considering whether, if the weather held, to trek over the Black Mountains to Pescadero, La Honda, Big Basin, or Santa Cruz. The new Lick Observatory to the east of San Jose was another tantalizing destination. As conveyances, most would use their feet. Some would use a horse and buggy, and the more daring would use newly acquired safety bicycles.

Sitting and studying in his room in the afternoon, Fletcher Martin thought about his holiday plans only a week away. The last of Irene and Lucy's students had vacated Adelante Villa. Edith Jordan had returned to Escondite Cottage to help take care of the new baby, Barbara, and to wait for Irene and Lucy to relocate their school. The two women had decided to spend their Thanksgiving with friends from Harvard Annex, now living in Berkeley. Irene invited Fletcher to go with them, but he balked at the thought of spending time with four young ladies who were old college acquaintances. Irene agreed he would feel out of place.

On Thanksgiving Day, Fletcher would go to Fred Behn's farm, east of Mayfield, and join Fred's friends for a Thanksgiving feast. Dr. Elliott had been invited, but was not able to come because of family obligations. He told Fletcher Ellen would have liked to go, but her brother, Bolton, presented a problem. He did not want to be bothered with Mayfield riffraff.

Fletcher was looking forward to meeting Mayfield citizens who were already familiar to him because of Fred's and his barber Frank's descriptions.

Then he would join Dr. Whitman, his roommate and faculty adviser, and three of his friends as they ascended Mt. Hamilton and visited Lick Observatory. It would take them most of the three remaining days, but it might be just the thing to set Fletcher's mind into new flights as he made changes to the proposed master's thesis he would submit for Dr. Whitman's review at the end of the semester.

Fletcher felt the trip up the mountain would give him time to discuss his premise in detail with Dr. Whitman to make certain it would be substantial enough to withstand the rigorous tests established for a master's thesis.

On that same day, in another wing of Encina Hall, Bump Cooper unlocked the door to the room he shared with Milt Grosh, co-captain of the newly formed football team. Bump always locked his door. He had done the right thing because Mr. Fesler held a meeting on Monday night and told everyone to lock their doors because there were thieves around. Bump looked down and checked the floor to see if an envelope from the registrar had been pushed under their door. Even though both he and Milt were doing fairly well with passes on most of their papers and tests, there was always the possibility of being sent over the edge of the earth. Bump personally knew of eight students who had been sent home. His first roommate, Freck, had been one of them. There was no envelope, just bare carpet that was already beginning to show the wear and tear of active young men's heavy soles. Bump breathed a sigh of relief.

As expected, the room was empty. Milt was working with other team members on the new football field next to the new men's gym. They were putting up goal posts at each end of the field. Dr. Marx had helped with calculations to be used when hoisting the heavy iron piping into position.

Bump should have been there, but he had to some work on his term paper, entitled "Description of a Roman Banquet." The paper was due to be handed in to Dr. Barnes for his class "Greece and Rome," before the Thanksgiving weekend. Bump was still doing the research and hadn't begun the writing. Suddenly, he found himself doing what he had promised not to: waiting until the last minute. This would be his first college term paper. He had worked on shorter papers for his English classes at Riverside High School, and always gotten good grades, but it was totally different at LSJU. Bump couldn't get over how different some of his fellow students were from those he knew in high school. There was one fellow—who must have been all of twenty-six years of age—in Dr. Barnes class, and he had actually visited Greece and Rome. He had been a sailor on a ship for almost three years and traveled all over the world. He even had his own typing machine, like the one Frank Batchelder used in the administrative office.

Bump had accumulated several books from both the small library in the Quad and Dr. Barnes' personal library. He also heard that Dr. Whitman, Fletcher Martin's roommate, had some excellent books about the Romans and Greeks, but they were in Latin, and although Bump's Latin was improving, he still did not feel comfortable translating text into English.

He grabbed a deep red delicious apple from a plate of fruit on the study table, which he had taken from the dining hall, and took a mighty bite out of it. It tasted sweet and tart. He sat at the table, with research cards strewn around him and a blank piece of paper and pencil in front of him, and crunched his apple as he looked at everything around him. His mind couldn't help but wander to the new gym that was just about completed down the road from Encina.

He had heard it would have seven of the latest overhead and side showers. He had never had a shower, unless you called a shower having a bucket of cold water doused on you. He wondered what the experience would be like, standing there with no clothes on, and all the other boys looking at each other. Thank goodness he had some body hair. He had seen boys who had no body hair at all, and everyone said they looked like girls. Bump had never seen a naked girl, so he really couldn't say. He had seen his younger sister, but that didn't count because it was when she was five or six years old. Later, he wouldn't look at her if she didn't have her clothes on. After all, she was his sister.

At the new gym, there would be lockers for all the students to stow their athletic gear. Milton had told him the gym would have special pulleys with weights and hydraulic rowing machines the football team could use. Japanese curled hair mattresses would be available to work out on, as well as dumb bells and Indian clubs. Imagine having all that equipment available to use!

Milton had told him that he and Jack Whittemore were working out what the football team would do to get into shape. The team would start practicing each afternoon at four-thirty after the Thanksgiving break. And Jack was lining up some teams to play after the first of the year, including the state university across the bay. Dr. Sampson would be joining the faculty next term and he would be their coach. He had all kinds of football experience.

But that was football, and Bump was supposed to be reading the books and notes before him and writing his report about Roman banquets. Who cared about their banquets? The only reason he had chosen the subject from a list Dr. Barnes had prepared was that he thought it would be an easy subject about which to write.

Bump heard some one was gently knocking on the door. No one usually knocked that way. He got up and opened the door. It was Walter Fong, standing there and smiling broadly. Walter always looked the same, with sparkling clean clothes, unwrinkled and new looking, and dark hair crisply cut in the latest fashion. Bump couldn't imagine him looking dirty or mussed up, mad, or even downcast. Rumor had it Walter took a bath every other day. And unlike everyone else, Walt wouldn't consider barging in without being asked. Now, he stood in the doorway, just standing there, even though Bump was holding the door wide open for him.

Walt's smile became broader, showing even more of his perfect white teeth. Bump's teeth were all right, but some of the other students, including the girls, already had missing or cracked front teeth.

"Hi, Bump, do you have a minute?" Walter finally asked. "Is it all right if I come in? I hope I'm not disturbing you."

"Of course not, Walt. Come on in. I was just digging a little, but I haven't even cracked a book yet."

Walter was surprised Bump was already using the Stanford slang term 'digging' for studying.

They moved to the study desk, and Bump pulled out a chair for Walter. "Sit down. Take a load off."

"I've just been to see Sosh and Woody."

"How's Woody doing? Last night he was complaining of a cold."

"Fine, fine. He had no complaints. He's digging just like you are. I think we all are. I was wondering what you and Milt were planning to do for Thanksgiving?"

"Absolutely nothing. As you know, Milt and I are from Southern California, and getting home would take at least two days, so it isn't worth it. Since the dining hall will be closed, we'll probably go to the camp for dinner. Would you like to come with us?" Bump knew Walter did not have many friends. There were no Chinese in Southern California, so it was hard for Bump to understand why so many people resented them.

Walter said, "My father wanted me to invite you, Milt, Sosh, and Woody to visit San Francisco and Chinatown. Sosh accepted, but Woody said he couldn't come because his parents will be coming up to see him, and they're going to visit Congress Springs. What do you say, Bump? I'm sure you'd have a good time. My father will pay for everything. He wants to meet you all and thank you for your friendship."

Bump didn't hesitate. He and Milt had already talked about one day visiting San Francisco's Chinatown, which was like a foreign country, but on the train was only an hour away.

Bump said, "Of course we would. That's really nice of you, Walt. Milt and I already talked about visiting Chinatown. You know, we haven't even been to San Francisco yet. He'll be all for it, and what a big experience for us going to a big city like San Francisco. I'm afraid our little village, Los Angeles, can't hold a candle to it."

"Great. Do you have recitations next Wednesday afternoon?"

"Yes, but I think they'll be cancelled because of the holidays."

"Then we can catch the train at Menlo together in the afternoon. Then, from the station take a hansom to the Palace Hotel."

"The Palace Hotel! We're going to the Palace Hotel? My parents will never believe it." Bump got up from his seat and was jumping up and down like an excited dog about to be fed. "Wow. We're going to San Francisco. We're going to Chinatown." He ran over to where Walt was sitting and gave him a big hug.

Walt grimaced. He still was not used to the way his fellow students smelled. But he tried to look pleased when he saw Bump so happy.

"I've been to the Palace several times with my father. It is an exciting place. I'm sure we'll have fun there."

After Walt left, Bump returned to his studies; the books on his pile were waiting to be opened. He picked up one of them and looked in the back for the index. "Banquets, Roman, 114–115." But his mind was racing with thoughts about San Francisco, Chinatown, and the Palace Hotel: how exciting and what an adventure! He couldn't wait to write to his family in Riverside. He was so lucky to be a student at LSJU!

CHAPTER 35

▼

"IN THE PRIVACY OF A STALL"

Tuesday, November 24, 1891

Since their last meeting, Sally had completely ignored Sosh. She came and went from their French class, hardly speaking a word to him. Thanksgiving Holidays were only two days away, and Sosh was waiting for her arrival. He looked toward the door at the back of the class, and instead saw Sam Cutter glaring back at him. Sam was so jealous of his relationship with Sally. Sosh was dying to know whether it was Sam who had followed them, and if he had heard Sally confess to attempting to assassinate Senator Stanford. If so, that could be a real dilemma. He wanted to ask Sally about it, but decided to wait until she made the first move to resume their friendship.

At least Sosh didn't have to worry about what to do during the Thanksgiving holidays. With some misgivings, he had accepted Walt's invitation to visit San Francisco and Chinatown. He knew the situation there was far from peaceful. Tongs fighting one another and hatchet men's antics were described daily in Hearst's San Francisco paper. It was so bad Sosh decided not to tell his mother about his trip because she would worry about him. When Bump excitedly told him how much he and Milton wanted to go, Sosh knew the two of them were completely ignorant about what was going on. They did not read the papers and had no idea how dangerous it was. Sosh was relieved when he heard Woody would be with his parents.

Just before class began, Sally swished in, apparently in a dither. After spending a considerable amount of time arranging and rearranging her skirt and petticoats, she sat down next to Sosh. After her usual "good morning," she turned so her back was toward the back of the room and hastily dropped another envelope into Sosh's lap. With the same kind of discretion, Sosh secretively retrieved the envelope and stuffed it into his deep trouser pocket. This one was considerably fatter than the last. She must have written more this time.

After class was over, without saying good-bye to Sally, he ran to the underground men's room, as if it was matter of urgency. There, in the privacy of a stall, he read what she had written to him.

Dearest Sosh,

I am sorry I have treated you like a stranger these past few days. After you read this, I hope you will understand.

Yes, it was Sam Cutter in the bushes, not a rabbit or squirrel. Somehow he followed us to the special place I thought was so secret. And worst of all, he heard every word I said about my attempts to kill Senator Stanford. Now, what I did appears so hopelessly childlike and stupid. I am certain if my father could have counseled me from his grave, he would have convinced me of my stupidity, but it is too late for that now. It looks like what I did will follow me to my grave, and I certainly deserve it. Somehow I will make amends for my misdeeds.

Sam is a very crafty young man. I do not think there is any limit to what he might do to get what he wants. And from what he says, one thing he wants is I—as his girl and, eventually, his wife.

If I do not go along with his desires, he said he will turn me into the authorities, and I might be hanged for my felonies. Under these terms, there isn't much I can do for now except appear to go along with what he wants. Later, I may be given the opportunity to elude him.

I have convinced him that you and I are merely friends. I have also had him swear he will do you no harm. If he does harm you in any way, I told him, I would confess my guilt.

For the time being, there is no formal tie between us. "I am his girl," as he would say. And since he holds me on a pedestal, I am certain he will do all in his power to guarantee my virginity until we become married, including holding in check his own sexual appetites.

I think you are wise enough to understand what I am doing. Even though we have known one another for only a brief period, I do love you, Sosh. Given time, I know we will be together. How that will happen, I have no idea. But be patient, my love. Sally

Sosh carefully put the letter back into its envelope and returned it to his pocket. He sat there, mystified at how his life had taken such a turn. To have such a woman love him was beyond his comprehension. But his feelings for Sally were mixed. After all, he hardly knew the girl. And at nineteen years of age, he was not about to swear his love to an almost stranger. He took a deep breath and exhaled, got up from the stool, opened the stall door, washed his hands, and climbed the cement steps to ground level, where it was a cloudy but rainless day.

He began to walk back toward Encina Hall. Suddenly, his steps quickened. It was as if a stone had been lifted from his shoulders. He felt relieved. He knew Sally would continue to be a friend. And if she said they eventually would get together; they would.

All he could think of was that he was a young man going to college, and this was a special time to live life to its fullest. Nothing like this would ever happen to him again in his lifetime. And, at least for now, he didn't have to fear Sam. For the first time, he began to look forward to his outing to San Francisco and Chinatown.

CHAPTER 36

▼

"THE BUGLE TOOTED AWAY"

Wednesday, November 25, 1891

At almost four o'clock, Bump Cooper, Milt Grosh, Sosh Weinberg, and Walt Fong were among the forty to fifty students waiting at the Mayfield Station for a train to San Francisco. The journey of thirty miles would take approximately one hour, traveling through the northern peninsula towns of Menlo, Redwood, San Mateo, and San Pedro and terminating at San Francisco's Third and Townsend Terminal, in the middle of the city.

The one-way fare from Mayfield was ninety-five cents, a vast sum for struggling students, and for that matter, for other less well-to-do citizens. As they lined up at the ticket office facing Mayfield's Third Street, the boys started to dig deep into their pockets for fare money. Walt Fong saw them doing this and softly said, "Please don't worry about the fare. My father gave me money for all our expenses when he saw me this afternoon. He said it is a small repayment for the friendship you have given me." Walt proceeded to pay for all of them.

His guests' reactions were, "Oh, gosh, you shouldn't do this" and "We really appreciate it." But all three boys breathed a collective sigh of relief. They had hoped this would happen, but had brought along enough money to cover basic expenses just in case.

After they boarded the train, Walt led them to seats where they would be facing each other. Walt and Sosh faced Milt and Bump.

A high-pitched steam whistle blasted in their ears as the train got under way. It was the same sound heard regularly on campus. Gradually, the locomotive and its passenger cars picked up speed to about twenty-five miles per hour.

Because of the screeching sound of steel wheels against steel rails, and the continuous creaking and moaning of the passenger cars as they swayed from side to side on the slightest curve, passengers found it impossible to carry on a normal conversation. But soon the louder sound of back and forth shouts between Stanford students drowned out all the rest.

"Do you know Billy Williams, he's from Sacramento? Don't you think he's cute?"

"My goodness, I thought you were staying at Encina. Are you pledging Sigma Nu?"

"My Daddy's meeting us in San Francisco and driving home to Woodland. Do you need a ride?"

"What do you have in that sack?"

"Jelly sandwiches and chicken salad crackers."

"May I have some?"

"Have you seen my *Uncle Tom's Cabin*? I've got to read it before Monday and write a darn book report."

At first Walt Fong sat quietly. He was trying to get used to the odors gathered around him. His sensitive nostrils picked up the stale smell of cigars and cigarillos, and the pungent aroma of spilled beer and whiskey. He could smell his companions' sweat and the heavy perfume of an older women sitting across the aisle. When he first arrived at LSJU, the distasteful smell of young men's sweat had made him nauseous. One time, when he was waiting to get into the dining room, with all their sweating bodies surrounding him, he had to rush outside so he would not vomit on himself—or worse, on others. Even now the memory of what might have happened repulsed him. Out of necessity, he had gotten used to the sweat, but the intense perfumes were still noxious.

After the conductor came by and punched their tickets, Walt's face took on a serious expression. He lowered his head and motioned to his friends that they should draw closer. He had something to say to all of them, for their ears only. With their heads bowed, and with Walt in their midst, the young men huddled as if their coach were conjuring up a play for a football game.

Bump spoke first. "Thanks, Walt. And thank your father, too, for paying for the tickets. None of us expected to be treated like that."

"Yes, you're a peach to do that," agreed Sosh.

Walt said, "You're very welcome, all of you. But my father wanted me talk to you before we arrived in San Francisco. He made a special trip here this afternoon to tell me some bad news. He didn't want to use the telephone or telegraph. Last night, a tong's member was killed, and the tong leaders are blaming my father for his death. This morning they sent him a message threatening his life and mine."

Bump reacted with an "Oh, my goodness." Sosh and Milt were quiet but looked pensive.

"My father wanted me to tell you this because right now it's not a good idea for me to visit Chinatown. But if you still want to go, he and his bodyguards will go with you, and he will guarantee your safety. But he will not let me accompany you."

All of the boys looked disappointed. They were looking forward to being with Walt in his neighborhood. Milt said, "That's too bad. I wrote my parents and told them about the trip, and they wrote back that it was sort of dangerous, but if I wanted to go it was all right with them. To me, it's a real adventure, and I just can't imagine not doing it. I still want to go."

Sosh nodded when he heard Milt's words. Life was too short to miss an opportunity like this, he thought. "I'm with Milt," is what he said.

Everyone looked at Bump to see what his reaction was. He looked rather sheepish as he said, "Gosh, this is a little bit much for me. People getting killed and notes being sent threatening Walt. Things like this just don't happen in Riverside, but I guess that's one reason I'm here." He looked over at Walt. "I'm sorry you won't be with us when we visit your hometown, but I'm with the rest. If hatchet men don't frighten them, they sure as heck don't frighten me."

Walt wasn't surprised by how his friends felt. He knew they were an adventuresome lot. He wasn't sure what his father would say, but he knew he would keep his word about being with them and guaranteeing their safety.

The three boys beamed at one another and cuffed each other's shoulders. They'd show those hatchet men.

Once they quieted down, Sosh had a question. "I know a little bit about Chinatown, but I'm afraid it's from people who don't like Chinamen because they think they've taken jobs away from them. I believe your people are victims just like we Jews, and also the Irish, Negroes, Italians, farmers, and laborers."

Walt agreed with Sosh. "You're right, we have much in common. My father wants me to be part of the Anglo-Saxon community, but it is difficult. You and I know how they pick on us." Milt started to say something. Walt quickly said, "Please, no offense, Bump and Milt. I know you two are different, and it is people like you two and Sosh and I who may change the way things are. That is why my father wants to meet you. You will visit Chinatown and meet my father. Unfortunately, you will not meet my mother. She's very shy and can't speak English, but she sends you her best wishes. When you are in Chinatown, she'll visit me at the Palace Hotel."

Milt said, "Well, that's too bad. I'd like to meet your mom."

"We all would," Sosh said.

"As I said, she is very shy, and unlike my father, has never learned the English language. I am her only son, so she—as you say it—spoils me."

Bump could already see that Chinatown was very different from Riverside. He hoped one day he could introduce Walt and his new friends to his mom and dad.

Walt continued speaking. "As you'll see, my father is a very important man in San Francisco. He's the president of the Sam Yup Company, the most powerful of the Six Companies that rule Chinatown."

Bump looked doubtful. "Six Companies?" he said. "I thought when you were in the United States, you were ruled by the president and other people in Washington, DC."

"That's true, Bump," Walt answered. "Except when you are Chinese living in Chinatown, you are ruled by Six Companies and the consul general of the Chinese consulate in San Francisco. I have no idea how this arrangement came about, but I wager Senator Stanford and his friends had a hand in it."

Sosh added, "The railroads didn't want United States laws interfering with their taking advantage of Chinese laborers."

Walt thought Sosh might not realize he had just made a derogatory statement against his father. But in his heart he knew it was true: the Six Companies did take advantage of Chinese laborers on behalf of the railroads. He hoped Sosh did not say anything like that in front of his father, but he could not tell him not to because it might hurt Sosh's feelings. Instead, he partially agreed with him. "In some ways you're right, Sosh, but the Six Companies do some good things for the Chinese workers, and the arrangement did work out for them. The Companies settled legal disputes when the Chinese had no rights in the United States courts. They issued exit visas and did all kinds of charity work, such as taking care of workers who were injured on the job or became ill. My father told me they sent a thousand dollars to the victims of the Johnstown Flood." Walt felt better after telling Sosh the Six Companies and his father weren't all that bad.

Sosh was still inquisitive. "So, why is there bad blood between the tongs and your father's Six Companies?"

Before Walt could answer, a young man in a battered top hat jostled the group. He had a silver flask in one hand and was taking sips of what smelled like whiskey. The aroma that hung around him made Walt feel queasy again. The young man's speech was already slurred. "So what're you fellows up to? Are you anarchists plotting to blow up something? Come on an' join the fun. It's holiday time." He gave them a broad grin and continued his drunken stagger down the aisle, grasping onto the tops of upholstered seats or passengers' shoulders to keep from falling, as the car swayed from side to side.

The train came to an abrupt stop as the conductor cried out, "Redwood, Redwood, everybody out for Redwood."

The young man was not prepared for the train's stop, and he toppled over and lost his top hat under an empty seat. Walt and Bump jumped into the aisle, and after a great deal of bumping and struggling, helped the young man to his feet. Sosh went down on all fours, got his hat for him, and plopped it back on his head. The young man gulped out a "Thank you," gave them all a broad grin, took another swig from his silver flask, and returned to his original route weaving toward the back of the train.

A few minutes later the conductor shouted, "All aboard. All aboard."

While this was going on, Walt and his companions watched the jostling as people got off the train and others got on, including more Stanford students. And there were more greetings, back and forth, from people who knew one another. Bump didn't recognize any of the new shining faces.

Once the train started up, the boys resumed their huddle, and Walt continued what he was saying. "Sosh asked me why the tongs and Six Companies weren't getting along. About ten years ago, Congress passed a law banning immigration from China. It was a very unfair law." He lowered his voice, and his face, usually so complacent, took on a frown. "Chinese workers who had returned to China to visit relatives were not allowed to come back to the states. Senator Stanford and other senators told my father the law was temporary and would be declared unconstitutional, but that never happened. And now it is about to be extended another ten years. As I'm sure you understand, the people of Chinatown are very, very upset."

Sosh asked, "Upset with our government or upset with the Six Companies?"

Walt answered, "Both, but the Six Companies, with my father as its most outspoken leader, has always supported the United States, and now the people of Chinatown no longer trust him or the Six Companies. Now they look to the tongs, who are just a bunch of thugs, to protect their interests. We call them 'highbinders.' Have you have heard of that name?"

The three young men shook their heads; even Sosh had never heard the term.

Walter was not surprised. The happenings in Chinatown were seldom correctly reported to the outside world. "My father told me the tongs' leaders do not like that I'm going to LSJU with Senator Stanford's support. They say my father thinks he's too good to educate his son in Chinese ways and so he wants me to get only an Anglo-Saxon education. I know my father wants me to be educated both ways so I can understand both worlds and help bring them together."

Milt said, "I can certainly see why it wouldn't be good for you to traipse around with us in your neighborhood with all this going on."

Bump and Sosh nodded in agreement.

"Thanks, Milt. I told my father you'd understand. He'll come to the hotel and talk to you. My mother unfortunately won't be able to, as I have explained. Unless something comes up, you'll visit Chinatown, and my father will arrange for you to see the sights there, have a wonderful dinner, and go to a Chinese theater." Walt stopped talking. He was looking up the aisle. The young man with the top hat was on his way back to the other end of the train. Behind him, a long line of Stanford students, along with some of the passengers' children, were singing, shouting, and dancing. One of the students had an old army bugle and was blowing it energetically, not attempting to make any tune.

The top-hatted young man put both of his arms around the four huddled boys. Over the sound of the blaring bugle, he shouted, "Come on, you Stanford fellows. Don't be so darn serious. Follow us." In a friendly manner, he pulled a somewhat reluctant Walt up from his seat. That did the job. Without further coaxing, the other young men joined the dancing line. Walt had a big smile on his face. The cares of his father and Chinatown were forgotten. The young man with the top hat yelled, "Have fun! Finals will be here soon enough." The bugle tooted away, its notes making no sense at all

As the line of students wound down the aisle, they chanted, "LSJU, LSJU, LSJU, rah, rah, rah!" Most of the other passengers smiled at what was happening, but a few had disgusted looks on their faces, as if they wished they had taken another train.

Sosh, who was dancing and singing with all the rest, thought this was a special kind of fun, something he had never experienced before—Stanford students, men and women, together, laughing and shouting, as if all the cares of the world had nothing to do with them. As if they were different from all the rest of the world. It will end soon enough, he thought. Pangs of economic woe were already in the air. But for now, he was going to enjoy every second. He leaped on top of an empty seat and led another vigorous Stanford cheer. Even those passengers who were not students couldn't help themselves; they joined in.

"LSJU, LSJU, LSJU, rah, rah, rah," they shouted again and again.

CHAPTER 37

▼

"IMPERVIOUS TO HER PRECARIOUS POSITION"

That Same Evening

At very nearly six o'clock, the train filled with celebrating LSJU students arrived at the Third and Townsend Station. Grabbing their light valises, the four friends made their way through the crowded station. With the holiday weekend approaching, it was one of the busiest times of the year. Some of the students were coming home to San Francisco and had someone there to meet them. Several Stanford families with children also were spending the holidays in the city with their relatives. Conductors' voices calling out departures, names shouted back and forth in greeting, the chug-chugging of departing trains, shrill whistles blowing, and babies and young children crying at the tops of their lungs all mingled together, creating a cornucopia of sound. The foursome stayed in a tight group as Walt led the way through the throng, toward the entrance at the northeast side of the station.

Outside, it was more evening than dusk. Yellow haze from lit gaslights combined with the final orange and yellow rays of a late autumn sunset to create a setting of burnished gold.

From where they stood, the boys could see six- to eight-story buildings to their left, lining Market Street, the main street that ran diagonally southwest, cutting the city in half. To their right were the glistening waters of the bay, with lights floating by on tall-masted sailing vessels, and in the distance, the scattered lights of the East Bay villages. To their left, overlooking the city, a hill was dotted with homes, their windows reflecting the sun's last rays.

While his friends were taking in all the sights, Walt hired a hansom to take them to their hotel. The boys climbed aboard with their bags. The driver, seated above them in the back, shouted down, "Where would you like to go, young gentlemen?"

Walt answered, as if it were an every day occurrence, "To the Palace Hotel, please."

The driver guessed he had students from Stanford's new university on board. They would be his first customers from there. "To the Palace it is," he said. After looking down in front of him to make certain all were safely seated, he snapped his whip over the heads of his matched gray geldings, while making a clucking sound deep in his throat. Bump, Milt, and even Sosh were speechless with awe as the hansom jerked into motion and they were on their way, heading northwest on Third Street.

If it had been busy at the station, it was more so on the streets in the heart of the West's largest city. Everyone was hurrying home or performing last minute errands in preparation for tomorrow's Thanksgiving dinner. The street itself was filled with horses, singles and in teams, pulling all kinds of conveyances: carriages, drays, and red and white buses. The broad dirt thoroughfare was gutted from the tracks of countless wheel rims. Sosh was dismayed as he watched fast- and slow-moving vehicles crisscrossing in front of one another, narrowly missing colliding. The air was filled with dust and more dust, smells of horse manure, and the falling veil of an early evening mist.

Looking on both sides of Third Street, Sosh saw that the paved sidewalks were filled with a wide assortment of local inhabitants: businessmen, miners, cowboys, and clerks, as well as women dressed in the latest fashion, with tall hats adorned with flowers or fruit. He guessed some of the women were prostitutes. He had seen a few of these ladies of the street in Omaha. He doubted Bump or Milt had any idea about what their duties were. Adding more confusion to all this human traffic were lamplighters carrying their cumbersome ladders, and Chinamen with loads of fruit and vegetables teetering on poles balanced on their shoulders. The one thing they all had in common, Sosh thought, was that everyone was moving hurriedly and going in different directions, and at times, cutting without warning across the street in front of their hansom, causing the driver to pull back on his reins and curse the errant pedestrian, who had already disappeared back into the mass of humanity.

The group went five city blocks northwest on Third Street and turned northeast on Market Street. Now there were too many people and too many sounds to differentiate one from the other. "Overwhelming" was what Milt was thinking. Overwhelming.

In front of them, the boys could see the red night lamps of other hansoms making their way up Market Street. At the juncture where four streets intersected, there was some kind of statue, but the boys' attention was diverted to an accident involving a dray and a carriage in the middle of Market Street. As their hansom swung around it, they could see that one of the huge horses pulling the dray was lying flat on its side, unable to get up. It must have stumbled and slipped on something. It looked as though the carriage had collided with the fallen horse. One of its wheels had come off and was lying next to the curb. They could see that the occupants of the carriage, now standing outside on the busy street, were waiting for someone, anyone, from a livery stable to come to their rescue and replace the wheel. The dray's driver was standing over the horse, apparently contemplating how he could get it back on its feet. The accident must have just happened, and already traffic was backing up on Market Street.

Bump heard a raucous "honk, honk, honk," and looked around to see what appeared to be an open coach, with some kind of engine pulling it instead of horses. The driver had goggles on and a long canvas coat, and he looked as if he were getting exasperated at the long wait caused by the accident. "Honk, honk, honk." He did it again, with no reaction, except people giving him looks of distain and wondering what he expected them to do.

The boys' driver shrewdly maneuvered around the happening and the jam it had caused—plus the accumulated gawkers—and continued on his way. In a short time, with a triumphant sound in his voice, he yelled down to them and pointed to the building they were passing on their right, "There it is, boys—The Palace, finest hotel in the West."

It looked it. Seven stories high, the yellow brick structure stretched a full block along Market Street.

Milt had aspirations to be an architect, so he carefully observed the building from top to bottom. Looking up at the Palace Hotel's roofline, he guessed the decorative cornices at the roof's edge were rococo in origin. He saw that all the windows were bay windows. He knew that sort of window was considered to be an aspect of San Franciscan architecture—windows that allowed the maximum amount of light because of the city's foggy days. He wondered if the concept of the bay window originated from San Francisco Bay. He would have to ask Professor Brown, who was interested in architecture, too. At the building's corners, he could see what looked like gold disks protruding from the corners and running up and down the building. Were those ornaments or part of the internal structure? Another question for Professor Brown.

The hansom turned right on New Montgomery Street and got into line with others waiting at the side to drop off guests. Except for Walt, they all stood up to get out. They thought they would have to walk the rest of the way.

The cab driver shouted down to them, "Hold on, young gentlemen. I'll get you there. You just have to be a little patient while we wait our turn to make the grand entrance."

As the waiting hansoms moved closer to the entrance, Sosh realized the line of gigs and hansoms was turning directly into the hotel. Palace Hotel guests did not have to trouble themselves to walk through the entrance to the reception area. They were driven.

After a wait of twenty minutes or so, their cab entered a grand courtyard, and the cab driver proudly announced, "Gentlemen, Palm Court." Walt had been there before, so he knew how overwhelmed his companions must be. Sosh, Milt and Bump stood up in the hansom and took in the grand view that surrounded them. Walt heard them exclaim, "Oh, my goodness," and "This is unbelievable," and "Gosh, this is something else." He could understand how they must feel. The inner courtyard was truly something else.

They had entered the hotel's confines on a driveway easily wide enough for two carriages to maneuver. It was paved with alternating white and black blocks of marble. Surrounding the court on three sides were white colonnaded balconies, seven stories high. Guests, some obviously inebriated, were leaning dangerously far over the railing, watching the arrival of new guests and shouting down words of greeting to them. Most of their words were unintelligible. Whatever they were shouting, plus the sound of horses' hooves click-click-clicking, echoed on the marble surface, giving arrivals the impression of being in an extremely large, hollow chamber. Above the entire enclosed area, a glass roof cast an orange gray hue, from the evening sky, over the entire area and its occupants. All of this created a spectacular and eerie way to be greeted.

Several Chinese dressed in pink kimonos lined both sides of the road. Their purpose was to remove horse manure, a nominal byproduct of the convenience of alighting within the hotel. The boys watched as the Chinamen scurried in and out between oncoming hansoms and carriages, as they performed their duties.

The young men's hansom made its way to the end of the huge court, enclosed by a jungle of potted trees, and made a u-turn, stopping to let its occupants out.

The tallest majordomo Sosh had ever seen was there to greet them. He was a Negro, dressed in formal attire: black tails, top hat, and sparkling white gloves. He opened the hansom door and graciously helped them alight. "Welcome to the Palace Hotel, the grandest hotel in the world," he said in a deep, melodious voice.

Walt reached up to the driver and paid him his fare. From the man's expression, it must have been generous. Once everyone and the baggage were safely out of the cab, the cabbie tipped his hat in farewell to the boys, snapped his whip, and he and his hansom began its trip out of the courtyard, back into the ongoing stream—now more of a river—of traffic on New Montgomery Street.

They did not have to bother with checking in. The majordomo recognized Walt by sight and said, "Mr. Fong, your room number is 456. The staff of the Palace Hotel will do everything in their power for you and your friends to have a grand time." And with those words, he flicked his fingers and a band of Chinese bellhops descended on them to take their few bags to their rooms. Again, Walt must have rewarded the majordomo handsomely because his face broke into a broad smile, showing gold-studded teeth, as he said, "The son of Wu Sing Fong and his guests are always welcome."

Sosh thought that anywhere else besides San Francisco or a city in China, Walt's reception would be entirely different. Most Omaha hotels would decline his or his father's patronage, just as they did Sosh's family. Jews were accepted as guests at only a few hotels in New York and Chicago, and those were far from the best. It would be worse for the Chinese.

"Before we go to our rooms, there's a lot I want to show you." Walt motioned to Sosh, Milt, and Bump to follow him. After seeing the reception area they were prepared for anything.

They passed through more greenery: pots of orange, lime, lemon, and palm trees planted in huge green and yellow Italian earthenware pots. Gigantic bronze braziers filled with glowing coals, used to heat the reception area, stood like sentinels posted to guard it. "I want to show you where we will have dinner," Walt said, turning into a wide doorway that led out of Palm Court.

After a brief walk, they came to the Palace Hotel's colossal dining room. It was in another of the courtyards between the hotel's wings, and had another breathtaking view. It was as wide, long, and high as the reception area. Four-story walls were painted the shade of pink peach blossoms and covered with flowing French rococo designs. Huge, shimmering chandeliers hung from the glass-covered ceilings. Chairs, upholstered to match the pink peach walls, surrounded heavy oak tables, which were covered with pink peach china settings and heavy silverware, all on pink linen tablecloths. Everything was pink peach! Similar to their own

Stanford Quad, the entire area was interspersed with ovals of greenery, consisting of delicate ferns and young palm trees.

Because it was only seven o'clock, the dining room was empty. "Fashionable people eat at nine," Walt announced. Bump knew he wasn't fashionable. His stomach told him that. He was used to eating at six or so with the rest of the Encina mob.

"Before we go up in the elevator, I want to show you one more thing."

"Oh, my goodness, we get to ride in an elevator," Bump blurted out. He couldn't help himself. The elevators at Encina fascinated him, but they were still not working, and he had never ridden in one. Except for Walt none of the boys had.

They followed Walt as he led them to the right, down another sumptuous hallway, which was paneled with dark oak wood. Hanging on the walls were countless framed photos and paintings of the forty-niner times. Pictures of rivers clogged with dusty, dirty miners panning for gold, and more photos of wooden shacks and saloons: this was the beginning of the infant port of San Francisco. In the bay, with Angel Island in the background, hundreds of abandoned sailing ships could be seen; their sailors had deserted the ships to become miners.

What a dynamic city, Sosh thought. Only fifty years ago, and what a change! He could feel his heart beating with the pure excitement of being in such a fabulous place.

The hall ended at the secondary entrance to the hotel, opening onto Market Street. Walt turned to his left and went through two swinging doors leading to the drinking parlor. It had numerous round tables, surrounded by luxurious red leather-upholstered chairs. To the right as they entered was a long marble bar, ornately embellished with brass female figurines at its corners, and a polished brass footrest running the length of the bar. Beside the figurines were four-foot high lights with large glass globes, supported by brass fittings. Overhead, a curved ceiling with stained glass windows let in the evening's last light.

Three bartenders, complete with red garters on their sleeves, white shirts, and handlebar moustaches, stood behind the bar. Behind them hung plate glass mirrors that reflected the opulent setting, the bartenders' backs, the faces of the young men who had just entered the room, and a large painting—almost ten feet tall and eight feet wide—of a beautiful girl standing atop a mountain peak. Walt and his friends turned to face the painting. Milt immediately was struck with the vivid blue of the sky surrounding the girl.

Walt Fong beamed as they looked at the painting. "This is what I wanted to show you."

One of the bartenders asked, "Gentlemen, what can I get you?"

Sosh appreciated that he didn't call them boys or young men. They ordered four sarsaparillas. They stood with their backs to the bar, facing the picture. Bump was certain he had never seen a woman as beautiful in his life. He asked Walt, "Who is she, Walt? Is there really such a person?"

Walt didn't respond immediately. Apparently, his thoughts were on other matters. He said, "She's Maude Adams, and yes, she's a real person, a famous Broadway actress. She visited San Francisco a few years ago, and I saw her in a play at the Golden Gate Theater, a melodrama called 'Men and Women.' The play was marvelous, I thought, and when she was on the stage, every eye, including mine, watched her." From the tone in his voice, it was obvious Walt was smitten with Miss Adams. This surprised Sosh. He had never heard Walt talk about any woman before.

Bump was thinking how Maude Adams resembled Delores, Sally's friend and the girl of his dreams.

Milt was interested in knowing more about the painting; he asked, "Who's the painter? I've never seen such bright colors, particularly the blues."

Walt said, "I'm not sure. I think he's a local artist." He looked over at the bartender and asked, "Excuse me, do you know who painted the Miss Adams' picture?"

The bartender gazed at the painting as if he were mesmerized by it the same way his customers were, then he said, "Maxfield Parrish. He comes in here every so often and stares at it just like you and me. The painting paid off some of his bar tab. I've heard say he was in love with the lady. When she was in town, she dropped by with him to see her portrait, and I can tell you for a fact she is just as beautiful as in the painting, even more so. We sell lots of drinks because of her. I've seen men look at her and drink all evening, without saying a word."

Milt looked at the painting carefully and noted every detail It pictured a young woman facing the sun, descending in the west. The ivory skin of her face, neck, and arms glowed in its last rays. Behind her was a vivid blue sky, filled with billowing white clouds. Thoughtful breezes had caused her thin dress to cling to her full breasts and thighs. Where the dress ended, at her knees, the flesh of healthy calves, ankles, and bare feet could be seen. This was a beautiful, dark-haired, robust, mature woman, with her naked feet planted firmly astride a mountain peak. Milt noted that the look of serenity on her face showed she was apparently impervious to her precarious position.

The four young men spent a long time finishing their sarsaparillas, silently gazing at Maude Adams, without sharing their thoughts. Eventually, they finished their drinks and left the bar to go to the suite of rooms they shared.

CHAPTER 38

▼

"A NEMESIS NOT
A SAVIOR"

Thursday, November 26, 1891

Next day, Thanksgiving Day, it was close to eleven o'clock when Fletcher Martin began walking from Encina Hall to Mayfield. From there, he turned north on Page Mill Road toward the San Francisco Bay. His friend, Fred Behn, had invited him to come to Thanksgiving dinner at the farm he and Widow Malgren owned, about four miles north of the county road.

Fletcher was not looking forward to the dinner. He would know only a few of the guests, and he never felt comfortable in the presence of strangers—or for that matter, in any gathering of more than four people. Fletcher thought Dr. Elliott would go with him, but Leslie told him he felt obligated to spend the day with his wife and son, in spite of the presence of Bolton. "Tell, Fred, there will be another time," he said. If it hadn't been for Fred's friendship, Fletcher would have begged off, too, and insisted he had studying and researching to do. But with Fred—and of course, his brother, Jorgen—there, perhaps it might work out. Irene had said it would be good for him to be on his own for the holiday. Tomorrow he would be off with his roommate, Dr. Whitman, and some of his friends on a hike to Mt. Hamilton and the Lick Observatory. It would be a full weekend, the first in a while not devoted to his studies and Irene. He already missed her.

The weather was still holding. There were some gray clouds in an otherwise blue sky, but they did not appear to be rain bearing. With so many Stanford students either traveling or hiking or biking, Fletcher hoped it did not storm. He had never seen such an adventuresome lot in his life. He could imagine plenty of broken arms and legs after the weekend on those rutted roads and steep paths. If it stormed, things would be worse.

Most of the farmhouses he passed had rigs and wagons, with tethered horses scattered around them. People must be inside celebrating and thanking the Lord for the bounty received during '91. Fletcher had heard that '90 had been very wet, with record rainfall and floods throughout the Bay Area. Crops had been wiped out by the flooding caused by the storms. For local farmers, thankfully, the weather in '91 had been drier. Two wet years in a row would have been disastrous for most of them.

Fletcher thought to himself that he, too, had much for which to be thankful: for starters, Irene had changed his life. He had found inner peace and academic challenge at Stanford, as well as Fred Behn and other new friends.

At the third farm on the right side of Page Mill Road, Fletcher spotted a mail-box beside the road with "Malgren" painted in large black letters.

As Fletcher walked up a still-muddied path marked with the footmarks of large boots and dainty shoes, he saw Fred's broad figure on the farmhouse's piazza. He was waiting outside for Fletcher's arrival so he could greet him. What a friend!

Fletcher couldn't help but marvel at the way Fred climbed down the steps, keeping himself upright as he dragged his wooden leg from one step to the next. In a second, he was grasping Fletcher around the shoulders and giving him a bear hug that almost crushed his ribs. Fred always greeted him like that. Fletcher started wincing when he saw him coming. He was the only man Fletcher knew who showed such physical affection for another man. Fletcher returned the hug, but not with quite the same ardor. It must be the Danish blood, he thought.

After the bear hug, Fred stood back and looked Fletcher over from head to foot. It had been two weeks since they had last seen each other. "Well, I swear, I think my soldier friend has put a little weight on his skinny bones. Suits you. Must be Irene's tender love," he said and smiled knowingly. "I used to be able to look right through that thin body of yours. Sorry she can't be with you today, but I bet she's having a high time with her college chums." He looked behind Fletcher, as if there might be someone else there. "I notice Dr. Elliott didn't make it," he said.

Fletcher could see Fred was disappointed. It would have been the first meeting of the administration with the people of Mayfield. "Sorry, Fred. He felt obligated to stay with his wife and child. You know how that is."

Fred smiled. "I can understand that. No matter. Come on in, and I'll introduce you to the cream of Mayfield's society."

With an actor's flourish, Fred took Fletcher's arm, led him up the stairs, flung open the front door, and said in a dramatic voice loud enough that everyone in the room stopped whatever they were doing: "Hey you sots, stop your drinkin' m' free booze for a second so you can meet m' friend, Fletcher Martin. He might look long in the tooth, but he's one of those cussed Stanford students that're turning up everywhere in our gardens, either sleepin' or drinkin' or pissin' or doin' all three at the same time."

Every face turned in Fletcher's direction. They all shouted something that sounded blasphemous, dealing with the shortcomings of Stanford University. He couldn't make out the exact nature of what they said, but he could tell by the expressions on their honest faces that they were still glad to see him, regardless of his pedigree.

The assemblage was totally male, and every one of them had a large glass in his hand, filled with either beer or wine or the hard stuff. Fred made sure Fletcher's hand was also filled with a glass frothing with beer. No teetotalers here. The ladies must have been back in the kitchen doing some last minute preparations, he thought, with their children as tasters or stirrers.

Fletcher wasn't sure, but he thought Fred's male guests were waiting for his arrival, just as Fred had been. Wordlessly, they formed a scraggly reception line, and Fred started introducing Fletcher to each of them.

By now, Fletcher knew his face must be flushed, for he could feel himself getting flustered with all this attention. There was no way in the world he could remember all the names and what Fred said about each of the men. Later, he thought, he would try to seek them out and refresh his memory.

The first two faces were familiar. Jorgen, Fred's younger and even bigger brother, pumped his right hand as if he were churning butter, which caused the beer in Fletcher's left hand to drip on the floor. In the process, Jorgen gave him a sly wink, as if they were fellow thieves. When Fletcher looked down at the coarse brown rug on which he was standing, he could see remnants of countless other beer stains. One more would not matter.

The next face, already shining from too much wine, was his barber, Frank Schmidt. Fred knew that Fletcher had been to Frank's shop several times, so he didn't bother with a formal introduction. He saved that for the next man in line.

"Now, here is a man all of your Stanford ladies know like the backs of their lily white hands, but I doubt whether you've even heard of him. This is George

La Piere, your friendly grocery man who delivers the groceries every day in his cart to the fair wives on Alvarado Row. But not today, right, George?"

Mr. La Piere was a short man, who if he looked straight ahead would see the top button of Fletcher's coat. He was going bald, and the hair over his ears was slicked back with a thick, shiny hair goop of some kind. His eyes looked as if they were always wide open, and he had a quirky smile that never left his face. Fletcher couldn't tell whether one could trust that face or not.

Mr. La Piere answered Fred's question. "Not today, Fred. I made sure to tell the ladies yesterday I'd be eatin' turkey just like them. Otherwise, they'd be standing out there even in the rain, waiting for something they forgot. I had one chase my cart a quarter of a mile for shortening she needed for a cake. She was breathing so hard, I thought she was going to pass out before she'd done her baking." He smiled broadly. "But I'm not complaining. Enjoy every minute of it. T'was pretty dull around here until they arrived."

Fred pulled Fletcher along as he moved on to the next man. "This is David Coulter, our elected constable. A man you only want to meet here, Fletcher, not when you're traipsing around town, getting into no good." When Fred said this, he was no more that three inches from Fletcher's face, so a fine spray of Fred's spittle, enhanced with the aroma of stale liquor and cigars, rained on Fletcher's senses. "And be careful where you piss. If he catches you with your dong out, he's liable to march you, fly still open, into our world-famous jail. Famous because last month four culprits escaped from there."

The throng, who were listening intently, whooped it up with gleeful laughter at this remark. One of them accidentally slipped on the floor and fell flat on his back. He stayed where he was, rollicking with laughter. Fletcher thought it was more because of the free liquor being served than the words.

All during Fred's introduction, Constable Coulter was shaking Fletcher's hand. He appeared to be a man of the law—not because of the stern look on his square face, but more precisely because of the silver badge stuck to his chest, and even in the safety of Fred's parlor, a pearl-handled six-shooter on his hip. Otherwise, he was a pretty ordinary looking young man, with thinning brown hair and eyebrows that grew in one line under a furrow less, low brow. And, as if his silence were further intimidation that Fletcher would pass on to his lawless student friends, not a word of greeting passed his thin-pursed lips; until Fred mentioned the fellows who escaped from the jail, and he put up his hands in protest and hollered out in an almost childlike manner, "Not true, not true."

His bellowed reaction caused more raucous laughter and the slapping of knees and of other fellows' backs.

The next fellow in line almost pushed Coulter out of the way in his eagerness to grab Fletcher's hand. This prepared Fletcher for the man's grip, which was like a vice closing on his hand. Under the coat and shirt the man was wearing, Fletcher could see a Roman gladiator's physique. "I don't think I have to tell you that this is our village smithy, Dick Donahue. If you've got blacksmithing that needs doing, this is the man who can do it. Careful, Dick, don't take poor Fletchers arm out of its socket," Fred said.

Dick's face turned to one of concern. The man must be a gentle giant, Fletcher thought.

In a high-pitched voice that did not resemble its gargantuan bearer, he said, "I'm sorry. I didn't hurt you, did I? Fred's been telling us about you, and I wanted to tell you how much I appreciate your coming. I've never met a Stanford stoodent before." Dick took a second look at Fletcher and said, "I'm sure other folks have told you that you bear a remarkable resemblance to …"

Fletcher was inclined to interrupt the smithy, but decided it would not be courteous. He had heard the comment so many times.

"… our beloved president, Abraham Lincoln."

Everyone within hearing distance agreed. "Yes, he sure does," someone said, and "Remarkable likeness," said another.

Fletcher smiled and said, "A few others have said that, and I appreciate the comparison."

Until Dick moved on, his large frame blocked Fletcher's view of the next man, who stood patiently waiting his turn. He was of average height, with the beginnings of a full beard on his kindly, intelligent face. Fletcher could have mistaken him for one of the older professors on campus.

Fred spoke to the older gentleman. "Here he is, Bernard. The man I was telling you about. I met him four month's ago—after he tells me a dog just pissed on his face."

Fletcher had never forgotten about his first encounter with Fred, when he had slept outside his saloon all night and Fred made him welcome the next morning.

"Fletcher," Fred continued, "Bernard Mayer's our druggist and postmaster, and as I understand it, lender for already a few of your student friends who've been asking him for small advances on what their parents might be sending them."

This was another gentle man. Fletcher could tell by the way he shook his hand and looked him squarely in the eyes. Mr. Mayer smiled at Fred's remark and said, "It ain't much, Fred. The poor kids need somethin', and I put it on the books for them. They're a good bunch, and I feel proud that some of them consider me their friend. The door to my pharmacy is always open for them. Some of them are strugglin' so, they don't even have ends to try to make meet."

Fletcher, whose first beer was finally taking effect, got into the spirit and said, "Well, if I need money for a beer, I'll know who to come to."

Bernard was also beginning to feel the alcohol. "Well, I do have certain standards, and I'm afraid that if you're a friend of Fred's, you don't meet them." He said this without a trace of a smile on his face.

The room was silent, as if someone had just farted. But Bernard smiled, and his witty remark made everyone bend over with gales of laughter. As far as Fletcher could see, at this point, anything remotely funny was considered to be knee-slapping, rib-punching hilarious. The atmosphere of laughter and camaraderie was contagious.

The scraggly line had become a scragglier circle, and everyone was moving to get closer to Fred and Fletcher and whomever he was meeting, so they could hear what was being said and add their comments, which hopefully would be equally hilarious. Even Constable Coulter had dropped his lawman demeanor and was slapping backs and making fun of what was going on, but they all quieted down when the next man who stood waiting to grab Fletcher's hand was introduced. When Fred Behn cleared his throat, they all knew this was going to be a good one.

"Ahem, well, we have a real horn tooter here—a horn tooter extraordinaire, if I may quote the French. He's the leader of our University Band that the good senator called on to be part of the opening ceremonies. But this tooter is a little different; he also manages to be the principal of our school, Mr. Albert Dornberger. Where's your brother, Al?"

Mr. Dornberger had gray hair and a thick gray mustache that completely covered his mouth and jaw. He reminded Fletcher of a shorter, thinner Dr. Jordan. His steely blue eyes never left Fletcher's, not even when he was talking to Fred.

"Home, sick with a bad cold, Fred. Sends his best to you and the widow. Most glad to meet you, Mr. Martin. Fred here told me about your experiences in the Indian Wars. We're certainly glad to have you amongst us. I'm sure we'll have lots to chat about after dinner."

The tip of Fred's nose showed that he had been dipping it into another glass of beer. Each introduction had gotten more and more expansive. This time he lowered his eyes, as if praying. "Now, dear friends, a moment of silence as we greet our very own representative of the Almighty, who has graced us with his presence." A small, dark-haired man in a black suit and a collar turned backwards stepped into view. "Our beloved priest, who will one of these days look down on us and utter some words that only he and Fletcher understand, and then throw some dirt on our faces—Father O'Riordan."

As the priest stepped up to Fletcher and vigorously pumped his hand, Fletcher whispered into his ear, "*Damnant quod non intelligent.*"

The priest smiled as he said, "*Rem acu tetigisti.*" Father O'Riordan looked over at Fred and spoke for all to hear. "And I thought we Irish had all the blarney. I'm beginning to think you Danes have a special brand of your very own."

Everyone hooted at the remark. During the uproar, Father O'Riordan managed to whisper into Fletcher's ear, while gripping his hand in his and gently squeezing it, "He thinks the world of you, and if you are his friend, you are ours."

Those words warmed Fletcher's heart. Through misting eyes, he looked around the room and saw faces—even Constable Coulter's—filled with friendship.

Abruptly, Widow Malgren came through the kitchen's swinging door. It was as if she were waiting for a cue to make her entrance. She was exactly right for Fred—a large woman who looked as if she could hold her own with any man in the room. She went right up to Fletcher and gave him a welcoming hug, drawing him up to her ample bosoms. "Good to see you, Fletcher." He could smell good cooking odors in her graying hair. Turning to the room of bleary-eyed males, she said, "Now, if you men can stop jawin' and drinkin', you can help us set the tables. We've got lots of good food, and it's ready for eatin'."

Wives and children poured out of the kitchen and into the parlor, creating a real hubbub in preparation for the feast that would now be the center of everyone's attention.

Fletcher had never seen so much food in his life. The huge dining table, extended and extended again, was piled with plates of turkey and ham and bowls of mixed vegetables, yams, mashed and broiled potatoes, coleslaw in a mint sauce, and all kinds of bean and green salads.

The children had their hands slapped when they started to serve themselves, but everyone shushed so that Father O'Riordan could deliver the shortest Thanksgiving Prayer, Fletcher had heard in his life.

"Thank you, dear Lord, for all this and for each other." Everyone said a quick "Amen" and started eating.

Fletcher thought he was a good eater, but he saw some—including Donahue, the blacksmith, and Coulter, the constable—take five, even six, helpings. When a plate or bowl even started to look empty, one of the wives would get up and take it into the kitchen and come back with a new bowl, hot and filled to the brim.

Quickly the bowl would be passed from hand to hand, and soon it would again be empty.

During the meal, members of both sexes disappeared for a few minutes through the side doors into the backyard. Two outhouses were available about fifty feet from the doorway, but most of the men and children, and a few of the ladies, used the bushes for privacy.

The only lull in eating was before desert and coffee were served. Bowls, as well as the dirty plates and cutlery, were whisked away by female hands and brought into the kitchen for washing. Only white linen stained with drippings from careless hands, mouths, and bottles remained on the table. By then, Fletcher felt he absolutely could eat no more, but more plates and bowls appeared. This time they were filled with fruit, strawberries, peaches, and apricots; chocolate- and vanilla-frosted cakes; and apple and apricot pies. Everything looked so good; he thought he should try just a sliver of this and that. After he had helped himself, he looked down at his plate and saw it was crammed with goodies, all of which had to be eaten. Fletcher felt as if he had doubled in size. For four hours, they had been eating.

Then, miraculously, the ladies and children disappeared, returning to the kitchen and leaving the men alone. The men's tongues were loosened in the friendly surroundings—helped by Fred, who returned to his liquor cabinet and brought out bottles of old brandy and whiskey he had saved over the years, some dating back to Civil War days. Fletcher, who usually didn't touch the hard stuff, couldn't constrain himself. Just a taste, he thought.

The conversation at the table commenced with a series of jokes and stories about dumb cowboys or miners that had been told over and over again, but were still funny when enough alcohol had been imbibed. Fletcher thought the most hilarious was the one told by Father O'Riordan, in his broadest, most Irish brogue, about the Irishman with three daughters. Each daughter had a beau with a different faith: Protestant, Hebrew, and of course, Catholic. It was a forgone conclusion: the Catholic suitor would prevail.

When the supply of jokes ran out, the discussion turned to more serious, local issues. Fletcher found himself the center of a storm brewing over the relationships between Senator Stanford, Mayfield, and the person most of the townspeople considered to be a scalawag, Tim Hopkins.

Bernard Mayer, the druggist, began the diatribe. "He had no right, no right at all, to ask us to close our saloons."

Fred Behn, who remained on Fletcher's right and acted as his interpreter and guide for the proceedings, whispered, "He is talking about your Senator Stanford."

Bernard heard what Fred said. "You're damn right I'm talking about your senator, the pride of California, who thinks he is king over all he sees. Most of the time, I see that man as a nemesis, not a savior."

Albert Dornberger, principal of the school and leader of the band, quickly interrupted him, and said, "Now, go easy, Bernie. He and his wife have done much for the community and the elementary school, and have even gotten uniforms for the band."

Mayer was not finished. "Yes, Al, like any king. If he or his queen sees something they like, they will throw some money at it, but it all comes at a cost. And when the king and queen want their subjects to do something, such as give up our drink, they expect the whole lot of us to jump at their bidding."

Father O'Riordan could not contain himself. He looked directly at Fletcher, whom apparently everyone considered the University's spokesman, as he said, "Fletcher, you must understand what really sticks in our craw is that the senator is producing and making money from the very beverages he wants us to outlaw in our community."

As if to confirm what had just been said, Fletcher could hear everyone at the table grunt, or say or shout, "Yes," or "You're right" or "Tell it to him, Father." Or other words to that effect.

The priest continued, "The senator forgets that most of us who live in Mayfield work hard. We're the ones who built that university of his from the ground up," and he pointed in the direction of LSJU. "We plowed the hayfields, dug the hard ground for foundations and cellars, cut the stone, and hung the doors. And now we suffer from the dust from those stones in our lungs. Some of us fell from scaffolding and roofs and died—like Widow O'Grady's poor husband, with every bone in his body broken. And none of us can see the harm, after a man has worked hard all week, of going to a place where his friends are and lifting a pint or two to his lips. No harm at all."

Men in the crowd repeated what the priest said and added their own comments. "No harm at all. No harm at all."

"We work hard all week, what's wrong with a drink or two?"

"So what gives him the right to tell us what to do?"

Fred stood at the side, with a slight smile on his face. He knew his friend would have to respond and he wondered what he would say.

Fletcher didn't have a choice in the matter. Every face turned in his direction, including that of a four-year old boy who just happened to be carrying a dirty plate back into the kitchen. Fletcher wasn't used to all this attention, and when he started talking, his voice sounded wobbly with all the wine and beer he had drunk.

"You will never hear me deny that right," he said.

Everyone cheered, including the little boy.

That cheer gave him more courage. He had more to say. "But I think you know Mayfield offers young men more than just drink."

Fred Behn knew what he was about to say and spoke up. "And we all know who is behind the pleasure houses offering women, dope, and cards. On the outside, it looks like the Chinaman, Quong Wo, but really it's the senator's young friend, Tim Hopkins."

Fletcher looked askance at his friend. "Do you have proof of that?"

"No, just lots of rumors from people who've seen Hopkins and Quong Wo with their devious heads together. Thick as thieves, they were. I'm sure you don't know that Quong worked for Hopkins, and Hopkins considers Quong's mother more of a mother than his own. The two of them are like brothers. Remember how Hopkins nearly ran you over last time you visited me? I found out he was on his way to Quong's laundry—and not to have his shirts done, either. He went there to get his share of the pleasure house's profits."

Everyone guffawed at this. In the small town of Mayfield, everyone knew what was going on. Fred decided they'd had enough serious talk. He could see his friend was taken aback at what he had just said, so he started to tell the group a story he had just heard. It was about a farmer who had a daughter, and a traveling salesman stopped by one evening and asked if he could spend the night.

Fletcher was blindsided and dumfounded by Fred's revelations. There was no way in the world he would challenge the truth of his friend's words. He decided to ask him later if he had any solid proof to back up his charges. But then he thought, even if there were proof, who would be willing to arrest and prosecute a man like Tim Hopkins? On second thought, he decided it would be better to wait for an opportunity when he could do something about how the Stanford male students were being fleeced. The only person he could think of who might help him was Dr. Elliott. But for the time being, the best thing he could do was to get drunk.

From then on, Fletcher concentrated on sipping brandy that tasted so smooth he hardly knew it was trickling down his throat. Along with the rest, he laughed heartily as the jokes unfolded. He could only listen because he had never told a joke—dirty or otherwise—to anyone in his life.

It was dark by the time Fred packed Fletcher in the back of his wagon and made his way to Encina Hall. Luckily, he knew which room was Fletcher's. He helped his friend stagger up the stairs, and with the assistance of his roommate, Dr. Whitman, laid him out on his bed and covered him, fully clothed, with a blanket. He was fast asleep before Fred had made it out the door and into the hallway.

CHAPTER 39

▼

"LIKE FIREFLIES
IN DAYLIGHT"

Friday, November 27, 1891

When Bump woke up, he looked up at the tall, pink-painted, frescoed ceiling and had no idea where he was. On the walls were paintings of California scenery, and strewn everywhere was men's clothing. Then he remembered: he was staying at the Palace Hotel—beyond a doubt, the most palatial place he had ever seen in his life. On the other side of the room, Sosh and Milt were still sleeping in a huge double bed. Bump looked over at the other side of his bed and saw bare sheets. Walt, his sleeping partner, must be in the bathroom. Thinking about Walt jogged his memory. Bump slung his legs over the side of the bed. They were tired from all the walking and running up and down stairs and hallways. He called over to the sleeping twosome, "Hey, fellows, rise and shine. Mr. Fong will be here at ten, and we have to get ready for our trip to Chinatown."

Suddenly, the room became a beehive of activity.

Promptly at ten, Mr. Fong knocked, and his son let him in. Sosh, Bump, and Milt were nervous about meeting such a distinguished person. They were totally surprised by his appearance. Walt had said his father was Western in his ways as well as Chinese, but no one expected Mr. Fong to be sporting a closely clipped beard and hair, and to be attired in the latest men's fashion. His outfit looked as if it had come directly from London, complete with top hat and red velvet vest. Sosh thought he looked as though he had stepped out of the latest edition of *London's Menswear*.

Mr. Fong must have noticed the surprised looks on his guests' faces because his first words were, "You all thought I would be wearing a queue and kimono?" But the words that followed set them all at ease: "Welcome to San Francisco and soon welcome to Chinatown."

His son introduced his friends, and everyone shook hands. Mr. Fong shook each hand firmly and repeated each name spoken to him, as he looked over its bearer from head to foot. He did chuckle over Bump's name and the reason he had been given it—a reaction that was fully expected. But he did not ask Sosh about his. It looked as though Mr. Fong were in a hurry and anxious to depart. But his voice remained calm, deep, and sonorous, similar to that of his son, as he said, "Now, gentlemen, may I have your attention? I have arranged my schedule so I will be with you most of the day. I understand Walter has already told you there is a great deal of unrest in our city, so please follow my instructions. There will be places where you can speak and others where you cannot. I will let you know which is which. My bodyguards will be with us, and we must all stay close together. Whatever happens around us, do not tarry. Always stay with the group. Are there any questions?"

All of their tongues were tied. Even Sosh did not feel it was the right time to ask questions or express his feelings. If it is so dangerous, he wondered, why not wait and go later?

Mr. Fong hesitated, looked around at the group, and said, "No questions. So let's get started. We have a great deal of ground to cover."

He turned to his son and embraced him before walking out the door, and said in Cantonese, "I'm sorry, Walter, you'll not be able to go with us. Trust me that it is best you stay here with your mother. There will be other times when it is more peaceful."

Walt nodded his understanding and waved to all of them as they walked out of the hotel suite.

Sosh hesitated in the doorway. If it was so unsafe for his son that he could not go with them, how could it be safe for them, strangers?

As if he could read Sosh's thoughts, Mr. Fong said, "Please do not be concerned, Sosh, I promise you will be safe, and you will see sights you will remember all your life. For all we know, this turmoil may or may not last a long time. It is not the best time for you to be with us, but who knows what the future holds?"

Mr. Fong's carriage was waiting for them in the Palace Hotel's courtyard. Up front was a liveried driver, and next to him sat two large Chinamen in dark kimonos, Mr. Fong's bodyguards. The three young men sat with Mr. Fong in the carriage. In the outside seats, at the rear, were two more, large, kimonoed Chinese men—more bodyguards. All four Chinamen had queues down to the small of their backs.

The three young men had not been out of the Palace since their arrival two days before, and it surprised them how cold the weather had turned. Looking up at the surrounding hills, Sosh could see fingers of thick fog, like tentacles, inching toward the city. Luckily, they had brought their heavy jackets with them.

Their carriage became part of the busy traffic making its way back up New Montgomery Street to Market Street, and weaving across the busy intersection to where Montgomery Street made its entrance, and from there, four blocks north to California Street. The carriage with its matching gray horses made a quick left turn on California Street, and at the intersection of California and Dupont it pulled over and stopped. Mr. Fong motioned that they should get out. From there, they would walk.

The group of three students and five Chinamen now stood looking north down Dupont. Just by looking down Dupont Street, they could tell it was the entrance to a different world. There were immediate architectural differences. Most of the buildings on the streets surrounding Chinatown were two- to four-story gothic-style buildings. The Wells Fargo Bank standing on the corner of California and Dupont was a typical example. The buildings on Dupont were totally different.

Before walking across California Street, Mr. Fong asked the young men to gather around him. "From now on, please stay close together. There are thirty thousand people living in these twelve city blocks." He pointed across the street. "So it will be easy for you to get lost. I do not want that to happen. Two of my bodyguards will lead the way. I will follow them, and you three follow me. The other two guards will be at the rear. I have told them to insist you stay with us. I will give you signals where to turn and when we can stop. Some people may come up and try to speak to you. Do not speak to them or to one another until I say it is all right. All right, gentlemen, let's go."

The procession crossed the street and started walking up Dupont Street.

Bump, for one, was starting to think it might have been wiser to stay with Walt and his mother in the safety of the hotel. Milt was already beginning to crane his neck so he could see the architecture around them. Sosh couldn't help himself: he was excited about the prospect of seeing a new world, a world about which he had only read.

Mr. Fong looked up at what was going on above their heads. To an untrained eye, it would appear to be an almost imperceptible flickering of light. Mr. Fong knew the lights that were looking down on them as they entered Chinatown came from small mirrors guided by unknown hands and eyes. He did not want to alarm his young friends, but from the reflections he could see from windows three and four stories above, the tongs were announcing their arrival. In Cantonese, Mr. Fong spoke softly to his bodyguards, "Be alert. They know we are here."

Mr. Fong's wife, Walter's mother, had counseled him to tell the tongs of his intentions to bring the students on a tour of Chinatown. He could not bring himself, the highest authority of the Six Companies, to seek out protection from these outlaw groups. Out of deference to his son and his guarantee of safety for his friends, perhaps he should have followed his wife's advice. Now he was putting these poor innocents into the mouth of jeopardy. They were only a half a block up Dupont; he could still have the group turn around and tell them their tour was cancelled. But not a bone in his body would allow him to do this.

The procession moved ahead on Dupont Street, deeper into Chinatown. Above, like fireflies in daylight, bright reflections of small mirrors followed them.

CHAPTER 40

▼

"THE GOING GOT ROUGHER."

That Same Day

Dr. Whitman shook Fletcher to awake him. Today they would be hiking up Mount Hamilton to see Lick Observatory. "Fletcher, Fletcher, you have to wake up. It's seven o'clock, and we have to catch the half-past-eight train from Mayfield to San Jose if we are going to make it to Lick during daylight."

Fletcher woke up with the first shake and looked at Whitman with glazed eyes. "What? Yes ... train ... Where is Fred? How did I get home?"

Dr. Whitman smiled. "He brought you and tucked you into bed. You were out like a light."

Fletcher, fully clothed, threw one leg over the cot's edge and then the other, and tried to focus on where he was and what he had to do. He stood up and felt a wave of nausea run through his body. His gangly frame teetered and wavered like a tall tree about to blow over, but he managed to regain his balance, and said, "Yes, I have to get washed and dressed." And without saying another word, he slowly made his way into the hall toward the lavatories. He had to go to the water closet very, very badly.

Whitman watched Fletcher's quick exit with a smile on his face. He had never seen Fletcher in this condition. His other friends would meet them outside the hall at half past seven, and it would take at least thirty minutes to walk to the Mayfield station, so that did not give them much time. When Fletcher came back into the room, Whitman told him to dress rough and tumble. No telling where they would sleep that night because there were no sleeping accommodations on top of Mt. Hamilton or at the observatory.

Within thirty minutes, Fletcher managed to wash hastily, put on some old soldiering duds he still had, and pack a few articles of clothing and some toiletry items in his kit bag, which he could throw over his shoulder. He walked gingerly down the stairwell with Professor Whitman. There was a dull drumming in his brain. He still did not feel well. He understood that what he felt was called a hangover.

Outside, in the early, sunlit day, it was surprising how many other students were up and getting ready to go to the surrounding areas. Whitman told Fletcher a gathering of more than twenty safety bicyclists would be following them up Mt. Hamilton on Saturday.

Whitman's friends were waiting, and he quickly introduced them to Fletcher. Gregory Peters and Stuart Wilhelm were renting rooms in Menlo and were graduate students like Fletcher, but in the Math and Physics Departments; another friend, William Lucent, was a graduate student at the university in Berkeley. Fletcher had seen the young gentlemen around the Quad and several times before with Professor Whitman, but had never met them. All of them were dressed in slouch hats and baggy hiking shirts and pants, with colorful string ties tied in the latest fashion. Fletcher thought they all looked like brothers with their even, masculine features and thin mustaches. Stuart had a thin goatee along with the mustache.

He could tell from their pallid complexions, and because they were wearing boots that were shiny and not cuffed and worn like his own, that the three young men were not used to the outdoors. He began to have some misgivings about the whole enterprise. He made sure to fill his canteen with plenty of drinking water.

Everyone was in good spirits as they strode toward Mayfield Station.

"Wonderful day," said Stuart, giving Fletcher a broad smile. He had bright shiny teeth, and his fingernails were clean.

It took them longer than the usual thirty minutes to get to Mayfield. William Lucent had a difficult time keeping up. He looked as if he were more into sauntering than briskly walking. Fletcher found that if he did not watch himself, he would be several yards ahead of the pack. Because he walked so much on his own and with Irene, and had not had this problem with her, it was difficult for him to understand how these gentlemen, Whitman included, could not keep up with him.

The train to San Jose "Garden City" was late, but only by five minutes. On board were other students who were either going to visit relatives in San Jose or continuing on to Salinas or to Los Gatos and transferring to the narrow gage railway that traveled over the Black Mountains to Santa Cruz and the Pacific Ocean.

At ten o'clock, Fletcher and his companions disembarked at the San Jose station and started their trek toward the distant mountaintop east of San Jose, where the Lick Observatory was located. Fletcher had heard and read about the observatory. A great telescope was housed there that showed any object on the moon larger than a barn, and also revealed glittering moon craters and superb glimpses of Saturn and its rings. For the first time in his life, Fletcher would see the sights of the universe. He was looking forward to it.

Leland Stanford Junior University, for all its isolation from East Coast intellectual centers, was blessed with geographical challenges on both sides. To the west was the Pacific Ocean, highway to Asia and the South Seas; to the east, the Coast Range, barren and treeless, stretching north and south, with its two most prominent landmarks—Mt. Diablo at the northern end and Mt. Hamilton at the southern—acting as portals to the greater San Francisco Bay Area.

Sighting Mt. Diablo was the best way to know which direction was north from the University because every road and building seemed to be built without knowledge of a compass. But it was Mt. Hamilton, at 4,440 feet, hovering above the city of San Jose that could be seen most clearly. Further east, beyond Mt. Hamilton, the great snow-capped peaks of the Sierra Mountains, some rising to more than 13,000 feet, could be discerned on a clear, wintry day.

For young, healthy eyes, if it could be seen, it should be visited, climbed, conquered.

What made Mt. Hamilton particularly inviting was the world-famous observatory founded by James Lick, on its uppermost reaches. Lick, another of the multitudinous Californian millionaires who had made his money from gold in the Sierras and a booming real estate market, at first wanted to immortalize himself by erecting a monstrous statue in Golden Gate Park. George Davidson, who at the time was president of the California Academy of Science, urged him to finance an enduring scientific undertaking. Fortunately, Lick took Davidson's advice. Completed in 1887, two years later, Lick Observatory was turned over to the University of California for operation.

Visitors to the observatory found that once beyond the San Jose environs, the going got tough. The slopes of the mountain were rocky and covered with thickets of chamisal. Sparse chaparral and dwarf Spanish oaks were the only vegetation softening its hillsides. One dirt road, principally one-way, and treacherous with numerous hairpin turns, ascended the peak. Carts and carriages going up this road had to be prepared to back down if they met traffic going the other way.

The increasing numbers of safety bicycles being pushed half way up and ridden back down added more hazards. If a cart going up met a bicycle going down, broken bones, or worse, resulted.

For the experienced hiker, the trip up the mountain was relatively easy and safe. There was only one way to go, and that was along the side of the fairly well defined roadway. Unfortunately, that road rose within twenty-four miles from four hundred feet above sea level to four thousand feet. For the inexperience hiker, this rate of incline was arduous. Three of Fletcher Martin's companions found this to be the case; only Dr. Whitman appeared fit for the journey.

It took the five men two hours to get to the base of Mt. Hamilton. It was noon when they arrived at a fork in the road, with left leading to Alum Rock Park, and right to Lick Observatory. Fletcher calculated that at the rate they were hiking, it would be almost five o'clock before they arrived, well beyond the half-past-three appointment Dr. Whitman had made with Professor Sawyer, the Berkeley man in charge of the observatory. Fletcher hoped their tardiness did not mean they would be unable to see the giant telescope in action.

For Fletcher, if not a vigorous hike, it was certainly an interesting one. Early on, he gave up any hope of setting some kind of pace for his companions. For the first two hours, from noon to about two o'clock, he learned they were more interested in fauna or in geological or botanical delights and discoveries than arriving on time at their destination.

All five men—Fletched decided it was best to join them—stopped at the least provocation and discussed at length a bird in flight or a plant that to Fletcher's eyes resembled a weed, or a small snake's flattened remains in the middle of the roadway. Fletcher was never certain whether it was the peculiarities of the object they looked at and discussed so seriously that accounted for the delay, or whether in actuality they were catching their collective breaths and resting. Whatever the purpose, he did not mind. Life was too beautiful to mind anything.

Besides the fact that his companions could not be described as rogues of the great outdoors, Fletcher discerned that they, along with Dr. Whitman, were homosexuals. As his roommate, Fletcher had quickly surmised that Dr. Whitman was not interested in women. It was never discussed; in fact, except for discussions about labor unrest in the United States, Fletcher and he only talked about academic matters related to the Greek or Latin language or Greek or Roman historical happenings.

Fletcher could not recount a specific time or incident that caused him to have these thoughts about his mentor and roommate. They were based instead on Fletcher's insights gained by being around men almost continually for a decade, in extremely close quarters, under all kinds of emotional situations at West Point and in the army. Not that Whitman's sexual orientation mattered to Fletcher in the least one—way or the other. This was not the case for others. Fletcher knew of men who married and had children and never revealed their true preference. If they had, he was sure they would have been immediately discharged.

Security in his personal sexual orientation did not cause this indifference. This was far from the case. If the truth were known, he had been a virgin until the last few months, and it was only with Irene's guidance that he had learned the joys of sex with a woman. Many times during his army days, he had wondered why he had not followed the same path as his perennially boasting fellow officers. Then he would think of his handicapped sister and the leering faces of his so-called school chums when he caught them in the act of attempting to rape her, and additionally his deep-set respect for his mother and other ladies like her. He knew he could not face himself if he in any way forced his sexual appetite on any women, regardless of her station in life. If it were to be a life of masturbation, so be it. He would not deny to anyone that the thought remained that if he had met a gentle, caring man, perhaps his sexual preference might have been different. Professor Whitman might have been a prospect at one time, but Fletcher's love for Irene had eliminated that possibility.

So, trudging up the road, the intrigue between the two male couples was both fascinating and diverting for Fletcher. It was obvious he was not supposed to know what was going on. Whitman would probably tell him later. In fact, now that he thought of it, that was probably the reason he had been invited to come along in the first place. Fletcher had felt recently that Professor Whitman had something on his mind, something he wanted to tell him. He would soon find out if he had guessed right.

Something else kept nagging at Fletcher's thoughts; namely, what Fred had told him about Timothy Hopkins controlling the vices offered by Mayfair to Stanford's male students. Fred would not lie to him. He had to tell Dr. Elliott about this, but what could Dr. Elliott do?

When the going got rougher, Fletcher noticed Gregory Peters and Stuart Wilhelm had a hard time keeping their hands off one another. As Fletcher would have done for Irene, the two men wanted to protect each other from potential falls or any kind of mishap. If Gregory stumbled on an errant rock, Stuart rushed over and steadied him. If the roles were reversed and Stuart fell to the ground, Gregory knelt over and gently pulled his friend to his feet and helped him regain his footing. In passing, there might be a supportive hug and pat, and a fleeting look of concern between the two.

When this happened, Fletcher deeply felt the concern and love the two had for one another. In his own heart, tinges remained of the loneliness he once felt when he witnessed such tender exchanges between two people, irrespective of their genders. No more the case, thank God, he thought, with the existence of Irene in his life.

William Lucent, Dr. Whitman's apparent chum, was the most poorly prepared of the lot and was experiencing both exhaustion and physical pain. The closer they got to the peak, the worse he became.

Convenient signs had been placed along the roadside, marking the distance to the observatory. At long last, a sign came into view that said, "Two miles to Lick Observatory."

Lucent strode up to the sign, turned his back to it, and using it as support, slowly slumped to the ground, ending with his face held in both hands, staring at the rocky earth. "I can go no further," he murmured in a voice just barely audible. It was obvious to his companions that the words truly described his circumstances.

Whitman rushed to his side. "William, it's only two more miles. Thirty to forty more minutes and we will be there." He glanced over at Fletcher. "Fletcher, can William have some of your water? We've run out."

"Certainly, here. Take what you need. I can replenish later."

They were all standing around Lucent, looking down at him. After he had satisfied his thirst, he resumed his face-to-the-earth, head-in-hands position. Whitman knelt beside him on one knee, with a protective arm around his shoulder. He said something that Fletcher could not hear. Whatever it was, William's reaction was to say rather testily, "No, Henry, I simply can't keep going. You fellows go on and I will catch up. If you wait for me, there's a good chance the observatory may close and the journey will be for naught."

There was another whispered admonishment from Dr. Whitman, which Fletcher could only guess were words to the effect that he would not consider leaving his beloved. Lucent's reaction was to raise his head from the ground with, surprisingly, a wide grin on his face. It was then that Fletcher understood why Whitman loved him. He looked around at his friends and said, "Well, gentlemen, I am afraid I have given out. Let me regain my wind and I will soon be with you." His positive demeanor made everyone feel better.

Dr. Whitman slowly rose to his feet. He seemed reconciled to the fact that they would have to go on without William. "Shall we proceed?" he said to the other three men in a voice tinged with regret.

The water canteen was left with William. They told him they would make the peak and arrange to see the observatory in thirty minutes. If William did not arrive by that time, Fletcher, Gregory, and Stuart would tour the observatory and Dr. Whitman would come back for William. Everyone agreed this was the best arrangement that could be made.

William assured them he just needed some time to catch his breath and he would be following shortly behind them.

As calculated, the now four men arrived at the mountain's crest at close to five o'clock. The sun was beginning to lower in the west; in another half hour there would be darkness.

A child's high-pitched voice rang out from near by: "You are it. You can't catch me. You can't catch me." It was the group's first sign that the observatory must be close by.

Coming around a curve in the road, they encountered five two-story homes constructed of yellowed brick. Fletcher reasoned they were homes for scientific personnel and their families. The twenty-six-mile-one-way trip would be too difficult for a daily commute. The terraced homes were clustered together, forming a windbreak of sorts for a shared, interior court, from which the high-shrilled sounds of children at play could be heard.

Outside the compound, laundry blew in the breeze. Men's red underwear and white sheets were hanging on lines drawn between two posts. A six-foot ladder leaned against the side of one of the homes. Other than that, there were no visible signs of human habitation. Fletcher got the feeling of an isolated Army outpost, similar to ones he and his family had occupied. As the group passed the houses, he felt unseen eyes watching them from behind lace-curtained windows.

From the almost-level roadway next to the homes, the road began a steep climb to the top of the mountain and the site of the observatory. Here, the rate of ascent sharpened to a thirty-degree slope. This final stretch was most formidable. Half way up, everyone needed to take a breather. All of them stopped and faced north to take in the full breadth of the valley's terrain, stretching below them.

From their four-thousand-foot perch, they could see the Bay Area as if they were eagles. A magnificent sunset was taking place before their eyes. As for the peninsula they called their home—several spires atop buildings, particularly in downtown San Jose; some towers; church steeples; and several lonely water towers and windmills occupied this strange land, where billowing clouds of dense fog substituted for grass and fields and orchards. As their eyes moved west, clusters of these landmarks poking out of the fog bank marked townships such as Santa Clara, Campbell, and Los Gatos. To the north, up the peninsula, stood the premier city of the west. And south of that city a single chimney stood above the clouds. It was LSJU's chimney. For Fletcher, it was like seeing a friendly face in a room full of strangers.

The group turned their backs on the panoramic view before them and resumed their hike, another twenty yards up the steep road. They could look up and see the observatory administration buildings and the giant observatory. From an opening in its dome, a canon-like telescope jutted out. Professor Sawyer must have prepared it for their arrival. The buildings and observatory were constructed from the same yellow bricks as the homes. Fletcher reasoned there must be a quarry of yellow adobe near by.

A sign directed visitors to the front door of the administration building. Above its roof, the stars and stripes flew, and "James Lick Observatory" had been cut in the cornice over the portico. Next to this building was the object of their journey: the round observatory building, with its immense convex roof. It was huge. Fletcher guessed the housing for the telescope was about eighty feet high and eighty feet in circumference. It had only been in operation for the past three years, and when Fletcher observed isolated wheelbarrows and signs of workmen still completing projects, he saw many similarities to the still unfinished university he was attending.

Professor Whitman was about to knock on the front door when a familiar voice rang out from about ten yards back.

"Hold up, wait for me." It was William's tired but pleased voice. He had just managed the challenge of the last incline and was making his way to where they stood. As promised, he had recovered his breath and caught up with the group. Professor Whitman smiled. He was visibly relieved. Everyone was. Now, as a group, they were ready to meet Professor Sawyer and look upon the universe's wonders.

After Professor Sawyer had opened the door for them and they were walking into the main building, Professor Whitman passed near Fletcher and said quietly, so that only Fletcher could hear, "You know."

Fletcher responded with a nod, a silent yes.

Seeing this, the professor mouthed a single word for Fletcher's eyes only: "Good."

CHAPTER 41

▼

"SOCIALISTIC TENDENCIES"

That Same Day

Milton, looking up at the buildings lining Dupont Street, could see that many of the residents had decorative overhanging balconies filled with potted yellow and orange flowers. Filling voids of space were Chinese lanterns decorated with red or black symbols or with stripes of every color imaginable.

Bump kept his incredulous eyes on the sights passing before him. Crossing California Street to Dupont was like entering a different world. It was an experience he had never felt before. He realized he was truly a country bumpkin. He deserved his nickname.

Chinese people of all shapes, ages, and both sexes were standing still, walking, talking, or looking at the strange procession passing by them. Some of the girls were giggling at the sight of the three young men. With two bodyguards moving ahead and making way for them, and two bodyguards behind them making sure they did not tarry, Bump, Milt, and Sosh had only fleeting glances at the waves of humanity surrounding them.

Bump tried to concentrate on particular people so he might describe them to his mother later, in his Sunday letters. Coolie-capped Chinese men, with their long queues, dressed in glazed black robes, passed by them. On one of the corners, a woman stood holding the hand of her two- or three-year-old daughter. Both were dressed in colorful short jackets, with long pants, and white stockings and black slippers. Men with slender hands and fingers wore dress-like kimonos. Women wore pants; men wore dresses. Bump found it confusing.

A swiftly moving, muscular man carrying two enormous baskets of vegetables caught up with and passed them. A stout bamboo pole slung across his drooping shoulders supported the heavy baskets. He wore blue denim trousers and jacket, and a coolie straw hat. Bump saw most of the other men wore the same blue denim and hat. Their bare feet were tucked into straw-topped slippers.

A cobbler sat on the sidewalk by his store; before him was a simple wooden box used as his workbench. In his hands were his tools and a leather boot he was repairing. He looked at Bump with inquisitive eyes. His face was wrinkled like an overripe crab apple, and when he smiled at Bump, he revealed a single lower row of yellow teeth. Bump could not tell whether his smile was friendly or not.

Sosh viewed the surroundings with different eyes. As they went past alleyways leading off the main street, he looked down them and glimpsed tangles of sheds and doorways to he-knew-not-what: opium dens, brothels, and gambling dens? He saw tall, heavyset men dressed in black jackets and trousers, with pork pie hats. Were these men the highbinders, or hatchet men, about whom Walt had spoken? Was this where the "yellow peril" thrived? Surprisingly, it reminded him of the back streets of Omaha.

A simple wooden sign, for some reason in English, which read "Fish Alley", identified one alleyway. The procession slowed and stopped, so Sosh looked down the alley and saw counters filled with live shrimp squirming on wicker trays and strange exotic fish piled precariously on top of one another. Seller and buyers were shouting in Chinese, haggling over prices. The street's stench was a horror to Sosh's nose. He wondered how anyone could buy fish in such a place, with such an aroma in the air.

The group began to move again, but at a much slower pace due to the denser human traffic.

Sosh determined much of the exchange of money and services was performed outside the shops, on the sidewalks. He saw two Chinamen seated in close proximity. The one man was peering into the other's ear and using some kind of narrow instrument to adroitly dig wax out of it. The man to whom the ear belonged had shut his eyes and had a look on his face of pure delight.

Sosh saw a banker or accountant who was working out sums on his counting machine, while his customer waited for the results. A chemist was grinding up a concoction of what appeared to be tiny dried seahorses for a waiting client. Sosh thought was this mixture an aphrodisiac?

As they moved along, each of the boys wanted to point out something new to his companions, but looking back at the stern expressions of the guards striding in their wake, realized it might be better to wait until they got back to the hotel to discuss what they saw.

A sight came into view that caught all of their eyes. Coming toward them was the wife of what must have been a wealthy man. She was tottering on hideously tiny feet, supported on either side by companions, probably her maids. It was impossible for her to support herself. In her right hand, she held a half-opened sandalwood fan; in her left, a white silk embroidered kerchief. She was dressed in a pale blue silk jacket embroidered with brilliant yellow chrysanthemums.

Sosh realized that to his Western eyes, she was too gaudily dressed. He shuttered at the sight of her deformed feet. But to Chinese eyes, she was an object of beauty, her miniature feet the sign of her husband's wealth. Who needed normal feet when servants were there for support? He thought how this trip was an extraordinary occasion. Here he had insights he could have gained only here in Chinatown or in China, itself. It was a thought he would have to share with others later.

The group of Stanford students and their guardians came to a halt because a young Chinese boy, no more than six years old, had rushed up to Mr. Fong, handed him a note, turned around, and dashed back into the crowd. The boy's appearance took Mr. Fong's bodyguards by surprise, and they looked at Mr. Fong to see if they should give chase.

"For what purpose?" Mr. Fong said to them. "There is no one to chase." He shook his head. He unfolded the note and read its contents:

Honorable Wu Sing Fong,

Safe passage for your Western friends has not been granted.
Your party should turn around and go no further. Otherwise, your young men face dire consequences.

Wang Fat Tong

Mr. Fong put the note and its hideous contents into the pocket of his Western style coat. What an affront, he thought. Someone would pay for this, but for now vigilance was his first priority.

He motioned with his hand for everyone to resume making their way up Dupont Street toward the Man Far Lo Restaurant, where they would eat before attending a nearby Chinese Theater.

In silence, the procession proceeded.

Bump noticed they were passing several four-story houses, elaborately decorated with fretwork and festooned with lanterns. They turned into the second house and walked directly through two swinging doors, held open by their bodyguards, into a central lobby. From his nose and eyes, he realized it was a restaurant.

At the end of the lobby, Bump could see a staircase leading up to other floors. Most of the doors to adjoining rooms were closed, but some were partially opened. As they passed, he saw the first floor was used for storage and offices, and he figured that since the smell of cooking was particularly intense and pungent, it must be the kitchen's location. The smell was not unpleasant, but familiar—reminding him of when his mother overcooked, and sometimes burned, vegetables.

Down the hall and up the stairs they tramped. The bodyguards' heavy footsteps in front of them and behind them sounded as if they might go through the timbers of the staircase. As they passed doorways on the second floor, Milton looked in and saw coolies dressed in blue denim, with dark pork pie hats, sitting on benches at simple wooden tables, with large tin dishes filled with copious portions of rice and odd-looking concoctions. The dining hall had walls with no ornamentation. Only men were in attendance, and in their broad fingers were thin sticks of wood, which they were using as eating utensils. Milton could not imagine eating amidst such surroundings. He felt relieved when they moved past the open doors to the next stairwell.

There were stairs to climb to the third floor, and their fat attendants' footsteps resounded in the stairwell. In the middle of it, the procession suddenly came to a halt. For some reason, the boys found themselves unable to move either way. They heard a commotion at the top of the steps—hurried footsteps and the thud of what could have been body blows. Then they heard the same footsteps at the bottom of the stairwell, but this time high-pitched voices screamed out words that could be taken either for expressions of pain or obscenities. Because they were stuck in the middle, neither Sosh, Bump, nor Milt could tell what was going on. Sosh was about to shout something to Mr. Fong, but Mr. Fong's deep, reassuring voice said, "It's all right boys, just some overzealous admirers. Our guards sent them on their way."

The group continued up the stairs.

Sosh decided not to question his host. Their safety depended upon his good will. He noticed the accommodations on the third floor were more commodious. Their bodyguards hesitated at the open doorway, as if this were where they were supposed to eat. But Mr. Fong said some words in Chinese, and the entire procession continued down the hallway.

Through the open doors, Bump noticed that again there were only male patrons. They were dressed like the merchants he had seen on the streets below, wearing dark silk pants and jackets. They sat at black teak tables, on carved square stools, also made of black teak. On the walls, Bump saw painted lanterns and carved wooden hangings. Scrollwork screens divided the room. He could hear loud, unpleasant sounds as the diners spoke to one another in Cantonese. More and more, Bump was not looking forward to his meal. He noticed Mr. Fong appeared to be agitated, almost angry.

As the group approached the fourth and final floor, Sosh, who had also viewed the scenes below, realized the social hierarchy of Chinatown had unfolded before their eyes. The first eating floor was for coolies, the second for merchants of moderate means, and he was certain the floor to which they were ascending was for the haughty aristocracy. That was where they and their host, Mr. Fong, would eat. He was right.

Sosh saw a man waiting for them at the head of the stairs, undoubtedly the owner of the establishment. He was dressed in an elaborate kimono made of blue and yellow silk with red, fire-belching dragons embroidered in its fabric. He was an impressive sight. Even though not a word was understood, Sosh could tell the owner was deeply apologetic for some reason. Was it for what had happened in the stairwell? What had happened? Had the group been attacked by the Tongs? The owner and Mr. Fong spoke in subdued but intense tones as he led them through the entranceway into a rectangular dining area, to a table situated against the far wall. Waiters dressed in green silk kimonos bowed almost to the floor as they seated the eight men in high-back chairs facing the room and the other diners.

This dining room was drastically different from the ones they had seen below. Milton looked around and calculated the room measured thirty by sixty feet, extending the full width and length of the building. Its walls were adorned with full-length scrolls, gold tapestries, and beautiful paintings of Chinese landscapes: forests, trees, and valleys peopled with finely detailed residents. Suspended from the ceiling at regular intervals were elaborate, cut-glass chandeliers, each with six gaslights supported from a central four-sided metal frame painted in Mandarin red, and decorated with gold Chinese characters. The gaslights were dimmed so the room was brightest at its far end, where sunlight streamed in from a large windows opening upon balconies looking down on Dupont Street. Except for sunlight at the far end of room, the diners ate in the semidarkness of the dimmed gaslights.

In the background, Sosh heard young women singing in high-pitched, sing-song voices. The notes they sang were to a key unfamiliar to Sosh's Western ears.

After he sat down, and his eyes adjusted to the dim light, Sosh saw the other diners were sitting on square teak stools, not high-back chairs—another subtle indication of the high position their host, Mr. Fong, must hold in the Chinese community. White linen tablecloths covered all the tables. And Sosh saw that white linen napkins and silver eating utensils—knives, forks, and spoons—were placed before him, Bump, and Milt.

The other patrons were either old or very old men, all stout and placid looking, deeply engrossed in either eating or talking. No one looked at the new arrivals; except from time to time, one of the diners would catch Mr. Fong's eye, and silently nod a greeting.

Sosh sat next to Mr. Fong; then Milt and Bump. The four bodyguards did not enter the dining room. They remained outside in the hallway. So far, Mr. Fong had not spoken to them, except for the reassurance on the stairs. Sosh assumed this might be a Chinese custom, but then Mr. Fong said in an extremely friendly voice, "I hope you enjoy your luncheon. It may consist of dishes you are not accustomed to. If you do not like what you see, please do not eat. We will understand."

Everyone assured him they would try all of the dishes and would certainly enjoy them.

Here in the restaurant's confines, Mr. Fong was relaxed and he attempted to make conversation with his guests. He asked each of them about where they lived, what their parents did for a living, what they were studying at school, and what occupation they might follow. In a way, it was an interrogation, but a pleasant one. Everyone listened to what the others had to say because it was interesting to hear about their classmates. They were not the kind of questions they asked of one another. Sosh was absorbed at first in what was being said, but soon he realized what was going on at the other tables was too unique not to be observed.

He finally traced the source of the young female voices—they were coming from another table, twenty to thirty feet away, surrounded by young Chinese girls. In the semidarkness, Sosh could barely make out their faces, but he could see they were unlike any girl's face he had seen before. Over their eyes, instead of eyebrows, were arches that looked as if they had been drawn in charcoal. Their faces were snow white, as if dusted with heavy flour. The whiteness accentuated the charcoal arches and their lips, painted a grotesquely bright vermilion. They sang in monotonous, lilting voices, without expression or pauses. Equally expressionless were their faces.

Sosh had read about young Chinese girls being torn from their families and sold into slavery. He wondered if he were listening to the voices of slave girls.

Bump was at the end of the table closest to the singers. He, also, was entranced with them, but for another reason. One of them was motioning to him, as if she were trying to catch his eye. In spite of her disturbing make-up, the girl reminded him of his sister.

Small portions of food were served to them upon minute china dishes by countless waiters, all dressed in the same green silk kimonos. Sosh could only vaguely make out whether it was fish or fowl or of some other unknown derivation. He tried all the dishes and found the fish dishes to be quite tasty. The rest were bland, similar to the Jewish concoctions his mother had served. As soon as he put down his fork, the dish was whisked away and another, totally different preparation was put in its place.

Between courses, Sosh saw something at the very end of the room, in the dimmest part that caught his eye. It was a man lying on a couch. Abruptly, he heard Mr. Fong asking him a question.

"Now, Sosh, tell me about yourself. Where are you from?"

Unwillingly taking his eyes off the reclining man, Sosh responded, "Mr. Fong, my family lives in Omaha, Nebraska."

Mr. Fong said, "I'm interested in all parts of the United States. I want to find out more about each of them. One of these days, I am going to take my family on a train trip across the country so they can realize what a great country they live in. Omaha is a big city in the middle of the United States. As I remember, many railroads go through it. Is that correct?"

"Yes, sir, because it is in the middle of the United States, Omaha has become the meat processing capital of the country. One whole area of the city is devoted to slaughterhouses."

Mr. Fong was thoughtful. Animals were slaughtered on the premises of eating establishments in Chinatown, or butchers did the job for their patrons. There was no need for slaughterhouses, as such, in the area. Any restaurant or shop—or home, for that matter—could dress meat. "Sosh, have you ever been to a slaughterhouse?"

"Yes, sir, unfortunately. The father of one of my friends managed one and he invited me to come and look around."

"And what did you think?"

Sosh knew he was getting into dangerous ground. His thoughts might be too socialistic for his questioner's ears. Throwing caution to the wind, he answered honestly. "I didn't like it. I wished I had never seen the place because it was difficult for me to accept what happened there."

"To the animals?"

"Yes, to the animals, but also to the men who worked there."

Sosh's reply reminded Mr. Fong that his son had explained to him why Sosh had gotten his nickname: because of his socialistic tendencies. Thinking about some of the work places around Chinatown, he decided to change the subject. "And what does your father do?"

"My father died three years ago. He was an artist, a painter."

"A painter, that's interesting. Is he well known?"

"No, but my mother recently wrote to me that some local art dealers are interested in his works now that he is dead, and wanted to buy some of them. At our house, his paintings are everywhere: under the beds, filling the closets, in the barns. When he was alive, I remember he said no one wanted to buy his paintings. Now that he's dead, it's all different. If the dealers want to buy, we have plenty to sell."

Everyone was listening to what Sosh had to say. He had not discussed his family matters, particularly about his father.

"And what are you planning to do, Sosh? What will be your field of interest or what profession do you plan to follow?

Sosh was expecting Mr. Fong might ask such a question. Older people usually did when they were attempting to make conversation. He was worried how he might answer, but he had to be honest.

"I wish I were like Bump here, who wants to be a doctor, or Milt, who wants to be an architect. I really don't know what I want to do. I have always been interested in laboring men and women, improving their work conditions, so perhaps I may become a union organizer." When Sosh said that, he could see a quick look of apprehension in his host's eyes.

Mr. Fong laughed to himself at the thought of his son befriending a potential union organizer. Perhaps the tong was right, and it was dangerous to expose Walter to such thoughts. But no, that was his son's decision. "Well, Sosh, as you probably know, you would not be too popular around here. There are no unions in Chinatown," was what he said.

Sosh looked Mr. Fong straight in the eyes and said, "I know, Mr. Fong. I know."

From that look, Mr. Fong decided to move on to Bump and question him about his background and future.

As Sosh pretended to listen to the others answer Mr. Fong's questions—Bump mentioned that caring for animals on his family's ranch led him into medicine—Sosh's eyes returned to the spectacle of the man lying on the couch in the darkest part of the dining room.

The man was blissfully smoking what must have been a bamboo opium pipe. Beside him was a small oil lamp, its flame uncovered, and a jar of thick black paste that looked like tar, but Sosh assumed, had to be opium. Occasionally, the man refilled his pipe. The act entranced Sosh. He would dip a wire into the opium paste and twirl it in the flame of the lamp, and transfer it, bubbling and sizzling, into the bowl of his pipe. If he had dropped any of the red-hot opium, he would have severely burned himself. After this ritual was accomplished, he sank back on his wooden pillow, in complete bliss, and drew the gray-white smoke into his lungs. He was in a dream world of his own making, Sosh thought; in some kind of Chinese heaven.

Out of the corner of his eye, Mr. Fong could see Sosh watching Wang Fu smoke opium. By now, Mr. Fong had decided this excursion had not been a good idea. When he entered the dining room, he saw with Western eyes what was happening there. He was proud of the dining room's decorative appearance, which could be compared with any in the city, including the palatial Palace Hotel. Then, when he saw and heard the singing girls, whom he had previously found so entertaining, he realized his young companions might take a dim view of the lives these girls were forced to lead as slaves. His guests did not realize that if these girls had remained in China, they would be dead by now, either killed by disease or famine or by their parents at birth. Lower-level female infants were prized for one thing: their eventual sale as slaves. Here in Chinatown, these girls were well fed, well dressed, and still alive.

Wang Fu's taste for opium was also difficult to explain to outsiders. Mr. Fong had never succumbed to the exquisite happiness offered by the opium pipe; still, he could understand how others might be enticed. If Wang Fu wanted to smoke opium, that was his concern. Under its influence, he lived a life of blissful serenity and hurt no one. On the other hand, Mr. Fong could understand how Sosh might be repulsed by what he was seeing as another sign of Chinese decadence.

The thought kept running through Mr. Fong's mind that he, too, had become somewhat ambivalent about life in Chinatown. Some of this was caused by his son's attitudes and presence at LSJU. Walter also asked questions about slavery and the use of opium, and Fong answered them as well as he could. Mr. Fong's ambivalence forced him to think that perhaps he was no longer suited to be a leader of the community, but who else could act as a bridge to their Western neighbors? If he gave up, who else would help retain the Chinese traditional life?

Deep in his own thoughts, Mr. Fong forgot about his duties as a host. He looked around the table and saw that his guests had completed their meals and were now drinking weak green tea. He motioned with his hand for the attention of the owner and signaled for him to bring the check.

He smiled warily at the boys, got up from his chair, and said, "I hope you have enjoyed your meals. Now we should be on our way to the theater. I know you will enjoy the performance." What he thought was, if you think the surroundings at dinner were unusual, wait until you see what happens at the theater.

As Sosh followed the group out of the dining room, he looked for a last time at the opium-smoking fellow. By now, his pipe had fallen to the table at his side, and he appeared to be in the nethermost depths of what must be "opium paradise." Sosh noticed that neither Bump nor Milton glanced in the direction of the opium user. He wondered if they were even aware of his presence.

As the group passed the table surrounded by the singing girls, Bump looked for the young girl who had reminded him of his sister. He felt a small hand force a note into his coat pocket, and saw her innocent face smiling up at him. Mr. Fong had not noticed what had happened.

CHAPTER 42

▼

"A STEAM ENGINE GOING THROUGH A SILK TENT"

That Same Day

The Chinese theater was on Jackson Street, only a block away from the restaurant. Mr. Fong, the three young men, and their guards walked into a simple doorway and up two flights of stairs to the middle of a U-shaped hallway. A distinguished gentleman dressed in an elaborate crimson silk kimono was there to greet them—again, probably the owner. He led them past doors, some of which were partially open, so the boys knew they were at the balcony level, looking down at the theater's stage. Continuing to walk down the right side of the U-shape, they stopped when the owner opened a door with black Chinese symbols painted on it. Mr. Fong and his guests filed into a small box with four seats, two in front, two in the rear. Before them was the stage. Mr. Fong carefully allowed Milt and Bump the two front seats, and he and Sosh sat behind them. The bodyguards remained outside in the hallway.

A play was in progress. Three actors were on stage. Milton soon realized that the "woman" lying full length on the stage floor—obviously in some sort of pain because she was moaning and groaning—was actually a man. All of the actors were men. He had seen only a few plays, and none of them had men acting as women.

Sosh had seen numerous plays in Omaha. This theater was totally different. The stage had no flies, shifting scenery, or curtain. It was an elevated platform, about thirty feet across, with doors at the left and right side, through which actors made their entrances and exits. In the center of the stage, toward the back, were stacked odd chairs and tables piled haphazardly on top of one another: props not in use? There was no attempt to create any sense of reality. Chinamen must accept that a play was really "a play," thought Sosh.

On stage, another "woman," holding a cup of tea, stood beside the writhing actor on the floor. A third actor, apparently a doctor, was prancing around the reclining woman, bending down and looking at her anxiously and grasping her hand, while his patient appeared to be in the throes of death. If he were a doctor, Sosh reasoned, the "lady" with the tea must be a nurse. Suddenly, the patient gave a violent shudder. Her whole body heaved, and she shuddered once again.

In the background, Sosh heard strange, out-of-tune music, similar to what he had heard in the restaurant. Musicians located in a small balcony directly over the center of the stage were playing instruments unlike any he had ever seen: long-handled guitars with odd-shaped bodies; wind instruments held in a vertical position, but sounding like flutes; hollow sounding drums; and of course, gongs of all shapes and sizes that were beat when there was a need for dramatic effect, which seemed to be constantly. Sosh was reminded of the drum rolls in vaudeville shows he had seen at the Orpheum Theater in downtown Omaha.

The action on the stage—the writhing patient, the concerned doctor—called for a crescendo of gongs and drum beats. The doctor darted forward, dropped to his knees, put his hands under the skirts of his patient, and without ceremony pulled out a baby doll.

Everyone in the box, except for Mr. Fong, was completely surprised by this turn of events. Sosh found himself letting out a high pitch yelp of surprise. He hoped the others didn't hear him.

Adding to the hysterical event, the doctor pressed a button, causing the doll to squawk like a seagull being pushed off its perch. It was yet another surprise for the boys, and they found themselves hunching over in laughter. While the doctor triumphantly waved the doll in the air for all to see, and the doll squawked, the nurse leaned over and administered tea to the rapidly recovering mother.

The simulated birthing elicited a subdued chuckle from the audience seated on bare benches in the auditorium below. Sosh could tell they had seen this scene dozens of times before. Some of them were more interested in looking up to their right, toward the box, where their young Western guests' raucous laughter was more humorous to them than what was happening on stage.

As Sosh expected, the audience were all men, dressed in the same blue denim and soft pork pie hats that never seemed to part from their heads. From his vantage point at extreme stage right, Sosh could see the audience's faces, as well as the actors. It was hard to know whether the audience were enjoying themselves because, except for the sounds of slightly perceptible guttural chuckles, their faces were immobile and expressionless.

While this was going on, Bump managed to pull the note the young girl had given him from his pocket and read it, without being observed. In a young, girlish hand was written:

Help! Help!

I am prisoner. Save me. When play over, pretend go WC. I will meet you. Do not tell Mr. Fong. He will tell my master. He beat me. Mei Lee

What should he do? She was a young girl calling for help. What if his sister had called for help, and he had not done anything about it?

Bump looked back at the stage to see the doctor exit stage left with great bravado, still waving the doll in midair, as if it were the national flag of China. As he exited, looking up at his Western fans, he created a final crescendo of loud squawks for their ears only. As expected, all this clamor caused an outbreak of high-pitched laughter from the Western guests. Now completely recovered, the new mother got up and sauntered off stage in very manful strides, without any attempt at femininity. She left through the right-side door, followed by her nurse, who totally lacked sympathy for her once near-death patient.

The music from above the stage came to a finale with rapid beats of the drum and crashing sounds of the gongs. As if controlled by a master switch, the audience abruptly got up all at once and started to mill around, breaking into groups of three and four. Immediately, the volume of loud Chinese voices intensified. It was intermission.

"The performances go on all day and all night," Mr. Fong leaned over and explained to them. "The audience changes every two hours or so. As you saw, all the performers are men. The plots of the play are fairly simple. This play was luckily a comedy, so I am sure they appreciated your laughter. The wife complains of not feeling well and her husband brings in a doctor, who claims she has all kinds of maladies. We saw the final scene, where it turns out she was pregnant. In a few minutes, they will start a new play with the same actors playing different parts."

Bump had made his decision. He said anxiously, "Mr. Fong, I have to go to the WC. Where is it?"

"At the end of the hallway, Bump. I'll have my guards go with you."

He shouted out something in Cantonese, and a guard stuck his head into the box. Pointing at Bump, he told the guard about his needs, and the guard motioned for Bump to follow him. Looking down the hall and seeing it was empty, the guard pointed toward a doorway painted bright green, about half way down the hallway, and said, "That WC. Come right back."

Walking alone for the first time since he had arrived in Chinatown, with his heart beating like a drum, not sure what he was getting himself into, Bump moved rapidly toward the green doorway. Before he got there, the young girl's face, arm, and hand appeared from another doorway, just beyond his destination. Her vermilion lips silently mouthed the word "help." And her small hand made urgent gestures, beckoning him to come quickly. Bump started running to the doorway. The door was open, but the young girl had disappeared. He burst into a small, unfurnished room, which looked as if it were used for janitorial supplies and storage.

In the room, Bump saw a monstrous Chinaman, dressed in a black kimono, holding the girl captive. He had a hood over his face and must have weighed more than three hundred pounds. The girl was trying unsuccessfully to break out of his grip. Then Bump heard other men entering the room behind him, through the same door he had just entered. The sound of the door being bolted shut resounded in his ears. He looked around and three more men, similar in attire and size to the man holding the girl, had entered the room and were moving aggressively toward him. One of them was dragging a large burlap bag, large enough for a subdued man to be stuffed into: Bump. He felt the hairs on the back of his neck rising. Unwittingly, he had fallen into a trap, just like the animals he used to hunt.

Bump's thoughts returned to saving the girl. He turned back to her, but she was no longer in the monster's grasp. She was moving toward him like the rest of his captors. Her helpless expression had changed to loathing and hatred. She was one of them. Like the country bumpkin he was, Bump had been duped. The girl was the bait.

He felt hands reaching for him. The young girl had fallen to the floor and was attempting to grab his legs to make him lose his balance.

Bump was getting rankled. He didn't like being duped and he didn't like the thought of a Stanford footballer being taken down by four hatchet men and a singer. He guessed his assailants didn't know he was a footballer, and as far as he was concerned, surrounded by a team trying to tackle him. But to get through the opposing team, he needed a good head of steam. He surprised the approaching kidnappers by pulling free of the girl's hands and running toward the back of the small room. Now he felt ready to make his moves. He doubled back toward the entrance and ran headlong into the midst of the group—his head down, and his legs churning as if he were struggling to go over the goal line for a touchdown.

The Chinamen, never having played football, were ill prepared for Bump's headlong run. It was like a steam engine going through a silk tent. One of the hatchet men fell backward, the wind knocked out of his oversized belly. Bump ran over his body as if it were a good size bump in the road. The young girl who was grabbing for his legs felt flailing boots coming down and smashing her fingers. She pulled her injured hands away, grimacing in pain.

Once he had broken through the human melee, only the bolted door remained in his path. He lowered his head, protected by long hair specially grown for the football season, and became a human battering ram. Giving way to his momentum, the doorframe splintered and screws from the hinges flew like bees from a disturbed hive. The sturdy door fell backward with a loud, resounding bang into the hallway. Bump ran out of the room. He was free.

Not hearing anyone giving chase, he slowed from a run to a canter, which turned into a swagger when he saw Mr. Fong's bodyguards moving toward him, concerned about the time he was taking. He looked back at the splintered doorway and the door now lying flat in the hallway. He dusted some of the remnants of the wooden splinters off his clothes and decided not to mention anything about the adventure he had just experienced. For one thing, he was ashamed of his gullibility, and he knew Mr. Fong would be extremely unhappy about the way his guards had been derelict in their duties. Why should they pay for his stupidity?

One of the guards, choosing to ignore what he could see at the end of the hallway, asked hopefully, "You all right?"

Bump, acting as normal as possible, took a deep breath and said, "I'm fine. Sorry I took so long. Problems." He made a wry face anyone with toilet problems would understand.

The guard smiled, then his face changed to one of concern. "You have big bump on head."

Bump felt his forehead. Yes, he had a welt the size of a golden eagle, and it was beginning to throb. It must have been the door. "Oh, that. I bumped my head on something or other. Nothing, nothing at all." So now there was another reason to call him Bump, he thought.

His smile reassured the guard. "Good," he said.

Through an international system of sign language, the guards beseeched Bump not to mention whatever had happened to Mr. Fong.

Bump nodded. He would not say anything.

After Bump had gone to the WC, a vender stuck his head into the box. He was selling two-foot long sticks of sugarcane.

Mr. Fong asked, "Would you like to have some to munch on? It has a pleasing taste."

Sosh and Milt nodded. What else could they do? Neither of them had ever eaten cane in such a state. Each piece was wrapped in waxy paper. Sosh took his and inserted the formidable object into his mouth and started to nibble away. The cane was hard, but with perseverance he was able to bite off some of its sticky mass, and found that it had a saccharin, sweet taste.

Milton took one bite of the stuff and didn't like it. He continued to hold the stick in his hand, not knowing what to do with it.

Sosh nibbled away and took in all the sights surrounding him

On the other side of the theater, in boxes similar to theirs, were obviously rich Chinese men with long silk tunics. A woman dressed in a colorful gown sat behind each man, her hands constantly attending to his wants. She would light his cigarette or feed him something from a small dish or give him tea to drink. It looked like he did not speak to her. It was as if she anticipated all his needs by reading his mind.

Sosh saw that the galleries above the boxes were filled with more women, probably prostitutes, in all their splendor and glory. He could see they wore costly brocades and dangling jewels. Coal black, greased hair stood like towers above their white powdered faces, with their arched eyebrows, painted eyes, and lips. They fluttered large, painted paper fans, and on occasion, whispered to one another or made a laughing face without uttering a sound.

Sosh watched as Milton looked over at the ladies. He could only assume Milton had no idea how these ladies made their living. He would have to explain later, when they returned to their hotel room. In many ways, Sosh was glad he had been raised in Omaha. Even though it was not like Chicago or New York City, it had certainly given him a background he would not have had if he were raised in a small California town, like Bump and Milton. Both of them would learn many things in their years at LSJU—some good, some bad. Sosh already had some of that education.

Sosh began to worry about Bump. Where was he? He could see Mr. Fong's face; he was also worried. Mr. Fong stood up and was about to go into the hallway, when Bump casually strode in. He had a broad smile on his face, as if he had taken a long walk in the park.

"Where were you?" Sosh asked.

Bump innocently responded, "The water closet, where do you think?"

Sosh was not convinced. "What took you so long?"

Mr. Fong wanted to ask the same questions, but decided to let Sosh be the interrogator.

Bump raised two fingers.

Sosh said, "Oh, sorry." Looking again at Bump, he saw the welt on his forehead and was about to ask him how that had happened, when Bump gave him a hard look that communicated the words, "Don't say another word." He mouthed the single word, "Later."

Sosh bit his tongue.

Bump couldn't get over how perceptible Sosh was. Later, he would tell him the story, but not now, with Mr. Fong listening.

Bump settled back into his seat, gave a quick sigh of relief, and looked around the theater, as his confederates were doing.

From the way some of the women in the galleries across from them were looking at him, Bump decided they knew what had just happened and blamed him for whatever might befall the young girl who had tried to kidnap him. He could swear one of the women, who looked older than the others, was looking at him with an intensity he had never experienced before. Also, one of the old gentlemen was looking at him with incredulous eyes. Someone must have told him about his escape through the bolted door. He was obviously not happy about something, and Bump had to think it was his thwarting of the attempted abduction. The man must be part of the tong. The look on the old man's face made Bump feel good. Next time, the tongs would think twice about trying to kidnap a Stanford footballer. He wished he could tell someone the whole incredible story, but his lips were sealed.

In fact, taking into account what had just happened, the whole trip to Chinatown made him feel queasy and uneasy. It had certainly been interesting, and there would be plenty to write about to his folks back home. All this had certainly taught him a lesson. His gullibility had almost been his downfall.

Bump thought he would be very happy and relieved when they left the theater and retraced their path down Dupont Street and crossed California Street, back into the life with which he was familiar. He wondered how Milton felt about all this. He was certain by the expression on Sosh's face that he had enjoyed every minute.

Looking over at Mr. Fong, who appeared to be deep in thought, Bump felt Mr. Fong would also be happy when he and his charges left Chinatown.

CHAPTER 43

▼

"A DIGGER OF THE TRENCHES"

That Same Night

Night had fallen on the heights of Mt. Hamilton, and with darkness came cold breezes that penetrated heavy clothing to the skin. A half moon gave some semblance of light, and a campfire, painstakingly built by five men under the duress of darkness, was the only source of warmth. All five men were sitting or reclining around its crackling flames. Care was taken to protect themselves from red-hot embers that might alight on clothing or exposed skin.

Professor Powell had been a gracious host at the observatory. He not only showed them incredible sights through the giant apparatus, such as one of Jupiter's satellites passing before the distant planet, he also accompanied them back to his residence among the cluster of homes they had passed. There, his wife and children had served the group a simple repast of beef stew in large tin tureens and cups of black coffee to fortify them for their out-of-doors slumber. Afterwards, he directed them to a nearby barn where they could spend the night, and suggested they make use of a campsite and well near the barn, for building a fire and filling their canteens. From his and his family's demeanor, Fletcher had felt this was not the first nor last time they would give succor to late arrivals.

Fed and relatively warm, the five men now gazed into the flames of the campfire. At first no one spoke. Fletcher could tell Professor Whitman had told the others about his knowledge of their sexual preferences. It made life much simpler for all. Their sexual preference set them apart from most others. It was like

Fletcher's understanding of their feeling set them free. Now Gregory Peters held Stuart Wilhelm in his arms, and although Fletcher did not see them kiss on the lips, kisses were being freely exchanged. Professor Whitman was somewhat more circumspect in his relationship with William Lucent, who sat in front of the professor, using Whitman's knees to support his back. Fletcher could tell by their looks and freedom of manner that they all considered him to be a friend. Perhaps now he would learn why he had been invited to accompany them.

"You know I am leaving at the end of this school year," Whitman began. He was looking at Fletcher.

"Yes, you already told me."

"And now you know why I am leaving. At first I was only considering leaving because of the university's isolation, then someone told Jordan about my predilection." There was no rancor associated with his words. They were matter of fact.

Fletcher did not know quite what to say. He was truly surprised Dr. Jordan would make such a judgment. "I didn't know sexual preference was part of academic qualifications," were the words he used. The other three men intently followed what was being said.

Gregory Peters joined in. "Stuart and I will be joining Henry at the University of California. We think the atmosphere for intellectual growth will be far better, there. Although, I am sure there will be the same prejudices."

Professor Whitman held up his hand, as if to halt Gregory from speaking further. "Gregory, let me speak first to Fletcher. I prefer that he hears of my plans from my lips."

Gregory slumped back without a further word, accepting Whitman's approach.

"What Gregory said is true. I have accepted a professorship at California, beginning the next academic year. I will be an associate professor and will be next in line to be a full professor and potentially head of their Classical Literature Department. The current head, Professor Teeters, has already told me he plans on retiring in the next five years."

"Congratulations, Henry. You must be very pleased." Fletcher leaned forward and shook the professor hand.

"I am. I am," said a smiling Whitman, "And I am particularly pleased my qualification are appreciated at the Berkeley University. They do not know my inclinations and I plan to be much more circumspect in the future."

"So why the difference between California and Stanford?" Fletcher was sincerely baffled.

Whitman was slow in responding. He was considering his older but less-worldly-wise friend's position in the matter. He would remain at LSJU when Whitman moved on. "Stanford is a new university, while California has already established its academic status. A husband and wife fund Stanford, while the people of the state fund California. Dr. Jordan is newly appointed to be Stanford's president, while Dr. Kellogg has been president for more than ten years." Whitman leaned back and let Fletcher absorb the meaning of his words.

Fletcher understood. "So you are saying Dr. Jordan dismissed you because of Senator and Mrs. Stanford's influence."

"In so many words, yes. When William and I met in Menlo, someone must have seen us having an innocent glass of wine together. Unfortunately, that someone put two and two together and it came up as a homosexual relationship, which as it turned out was true. Shortly afterwards, Dr. Jordan met with me and very discreetly asked if I were homosexual. And when I answered in the affirmative, he graciously told me that since I had already told him I was considering moving on, he would like to consider that I would resign at the end of the school year."

"Dr. Elliott mentioned this to me and asked me why you wanted to leave. I told him I knew nothing about your plans. I waited for you to say something, but you didn't, so I thought you had changed your mind. So why do you tell me now?"

"I will recommend that you take my place and I believe Dr. Jordan will agree. I also wanted you to know I will be at a nearby university where I might be able to help your career."

"Are you suggesting I should follow you like the others?" Here Fletcher made a gesture with his hands including the other three men.

Gregory moved his body so he was in an upright position, and like a student in class, dutifully raised his hand. "May I speak, Henry?"

"Certainly, Gregory. I'm sorry to have put you off."

Gregory looked directly at Fletcher. "Collectively we have come to the view that the environment at Stanford will not be conducive to academic freedom, principally because of Dr. Jordan's inability to stand up to the founders' conservative opinions. These thoughts are not merely based on Henry being asked to resign."

"Have there been other incidents like this?" Fletcher couldn't help himself: his voice was becoming emotional. This was the second time in a few days he'd had to defend his university and his loyalty to Dr. Jordan. He was looking at Gregory for an answer, but it was Dr. Whitman who responded.

"Yes, unfortunately." Whitman knew Fletcher would want details. "You know I did my graduate work at Johns Hopkins."

"Yes, I remember you told me, and your framed diploma reminds me of it daily." Fletcher was trying to relieve himself of some tension.

Dr. Whitman smiled and said, "I am very proud to have been associated with that institution." The smile disappeared as he asked, "Have you heard of Charles Pierce?"

"No, I'm sorry, I haven't."

"Brilliant man. Brilliant. Some say he is the most intelligent man in the United States. He may turn out to be America's greatest philosopher. For five years he taught philosophy at Hopkins, including a yearlong course in logic. All this ended seven years ago, in 1884, when he was dismissed. So you see, he was at Hopkins before my time. Still, faculty members who were lucky enough to have heard him lecture told me he possessed the most original and powerful intellect they had ever witnessed. I have read some of his papers, and even though philosophy is not my field, I would tend to agree with them."

"Was he released because of his inclinations?" asked Fletcher.

"Yes." The smile returned to Whitman's face. "But in a totally different direction: he was and is a ferocious womanizer. And, unfortunately, he was married to a woman with absolutely no sympathy for adulterers. I believe Zina is her name, and I heard she believed punishment for adultery should be either life imprisonment or death, or if it were possible, both."

The group laughed at the thought, and Gregory said, "Poor old Charlie certainly picked the wrong one if he were going to be promiscuous."

Dr. Whitman continued, "I'm afraid poor old Charlie suffered from other calamities, as well. He and Zina divorced, and shortly afterwards he married a woman he had met years before, who was twenty years younger than he. Her name is Juliette. And their marriage, too, has not been without misadventures. Word has it Pierce can be violent and erratic at times. The cocaine he regularly uses to relieve a severe case of neuralgia may cause this. Cocaine is a common remedy, as you know, but addiction is one of its drawbacks. So you can see, his personal behavior does leave much to be desired. But unlike homosexuality, adultery and addiction are somewhat accepted in our society."

Fletcher felt Whitman was getting caught up in the intrigue of his story and had forgotten the reason for bringing up Pierce in the first place. He gently tried to nudge him back on track. "So, what did Pierce do after '84?" he asked.

"His father, Benjamin Pierce, also a brilliant man, was superintendent of the United States Coast Survey for many years, and employed Charles. At one time, he held positions at both Hopkins and the Coast Survey. But after he left Hopkins, Charles depended on the government job for sustenance. Then his father died, and I understand he now believes his job at Coast Survey is in jeopardy—enough so that he has begun searching for another position."

Now Fletcher could see where this lengthy preamble was leading. "Did he apply at Stanford?"

"Yes."

"And?"

"We understand Dr. Jordan turned him away."

"With some justification I would say, considering his erratic disposition."

"Here we part company, Fletcher. Look around at the cadre Jordan has assembled—mostly young and unproven academics like myself. None are from Ivy League's vaunted halls. He made offers to many of those, but none accepted. I was tantalized by thoughts of the West, rather than by his promises of unparalleled resources, which has not held up. Note our inadequate library. None of us has Pierce's brilliance, not even close. In spite of his misdeeds, his presence at LSJU would have been like a beacon. Everyone would have gained from its brightness—students and faculty alike.

"LSJU's status in the academic community is in its early stages of enhancement. Developing a reputation for conservatism and for being more concerned about personal traits than about creativity and scholarship will certainly not improve its prospects for attracting outstanding faculty or students."

"The world of academia is like a small pond. One ripple births a wave," said Gregory, with a knowing look on his face.

Fletcher decided it was time to express his feelings. He would not beat about the bush. "I am not as sure as all of you appear to be. What you say is certainly logical. My thoughts are based on feeling—my feelings. What I have seen of Dr. Jordan causes me to admire him greatly. He seems ideally suited for a young university. He himself is young and enthusiastic, perhaps too enthusiastic at times. It is understandable that he wants to satisfy the founders, his employers, particularly at these early stages. If he judges this is not the right time to absorb the talents of a rather unstable genius, I would trust his judgment.

"As for the senator and his wife, I am certain they are extremely conservative and want no bad word to be uttered regarding their institution since, in their eyes, it personifies their son. I can forgive them for much of this, especially because they are not requiring tuition. Their generosity has given many of us an opportunity we would not otherwise have had.

"As for my place in all of this, please don't forget I consider myself to be a yeoman among the intelligentsia, a soldier in the trenches—or a digger of the trenches, for that matter. All of Mr. Pierce's brilliance would go straight over my head." At this, he swiped his hand over his head, like a diving blackbird. "Unlike you, I crave only to do my research, and with the opportunity you might present me, to teach others of my love for the classics and its history. With my future in the hands of my beloved Irene and her close ties to the University, I doubt very much I would venture to the other side of the bay."

William Lucent spoke. "You may not have a choice, Fletcher. To get ahead in your beloved field, you must have a doctorate, and no such degree is offered at Stanford. You will probably have to attend classes at Berkeley for instruction at that level, and Dr. Whitman will probably be your adviser." And here he smiled slyly. "So be careful what you say."

Fletcher knew William was absolutely correct. The thought that he would always remain an instructor with his present degree had already crossed his mind.

Professor Whitman leaned toward Fletcher and manfully clapped him on his back, a sign of true feelings. "I don't think Fletcher has a worry in the world. I will always be there if he needs me."

Stuart Wilhelm had enough of this serious talk. He was falling asleep in his partner's arms. In fact, he had just dozed off and awakened with a jolt. "Enough, enough of this academic gossip. I'm falling asleep, and I assume we will have to get up in the very early hours to make our way back to Mayfield. I suggest we douse the fire and get ourselves to our lavish accommodations."

Everyone arose, chuckling at his description of the barn they would soon inhabit.

Using moonlight for illumination, they put out the fire with pails of water from the well and made their way to the barn. Inside, there was some degree of warmth, plus two horses that gave notice of their presence by snorting their reluctance at being disturbed. The place reeked of their smells.

After entering, the five men parted company. Fletcher climbed a narrow wooden ladder to the loft. He was used to such surroundings and soon made a comfortable nest in the hay for sleeping. William Lucent and Professor Whitman went to one end of the barn, Gregory Peters and Stuart Wilhelm to the other. From the sneezes and coughs, Fletcher could tell that the hay adversely affected William's hay fever.

In spite of all this, Fletcher slept soundly. He dreamed of Irene's warm presence.

CHAPTER 44

▼

"IT WAS AN EAGLE."

Saturday, November 28, 1891

Immediately behind the barn where Fletcher was sleeping was a hen house. A rooster's crowing, announcing his dominance and availability, awoke Fletcher from a sound slumber. He heard his companions stirring below. Eventually Professor Whitman called out to him, "Are you awake up there, Fletcher? We're going outside to use the outhouse."

"Join you in a second, Henry. I have a need, but it's not urgent and I can wait." Fletcher thought it was wise to let the other four men have some time to get themselves ready.

After ten minutes or so, he got up, descended the steep ladder, and opened the large double doors to the outside world.

It was still very early in the morning. In the semi-darkness, fog hung in the air. Everything in sight was covered with dew, almost as if it had rained. Fletcher could just barely make out the time on his vest watch: six o'clock. It would be another hour before the sun's dim rays lit the day and began to dry up the mist. About forty or more yards in the distance, he could see the vague shapes of three men standing near a solitary outhouse, waiting.

When he reached them, he saw they were a dismal lot. All of them were disheveled looking, with clothes covered with hay, and dusty and grimy faces—a far cry from their dapper appearance the day before. Looking down at his own apparel, Fletcher saw his appearance was no better. Even hobos would have steered clear of them. They would have to wait until they got back to Stanford to have a good wash. Gregory was picking straw off Stuart's jacket. Fletcher thought the two men were like friendly monkeys grooming each other.

Professor Whitman was inside the outhouse, doing his toilet, while William was still recovering from a siege of hay fever he had endured all night. He looked as if he still needed eight hours of sleep instead of eight hours of trekking—though fortunately it would be all downhill.

A young girl of ten or eleven years shouted to the group from the direction of the staff residences: "Mom wondered if you'd like hot coffee and porridge."

In a chorus, the four men responded, "Yes, please." Fletcher thought he heard Professor Whitman join in the response from his solitary position within the outhouse.

When it was finally Fletcher's turn to relieve himself, he was not surprised at the accommodations. A single hole had been dug into the rocky soil. It was about five feet deep. Over the hole, a crude stool had been built, just solid enough to support the weight of a person. Beside the stool was a sheath of newspapers and catalogs. Fletcher had at one time preferred squatting, Indian style, but once he got back to civilized water closets, he had drifted back into sitting while he waited for nature to take its natural course.

When he rejoined his comrades, two girls had just arrived, accompanied by their mother, carrying trays of tin cups filled with boiling hot coffee and tin dishes filled with porridge, also boiling hot. The four men had completed their daily ablutions, including washing their faces and hands as clean as they could with the cold well water. If they were not awake before, they were certainly awake after dashing cold water on themselves. Fletcher thought now we appear presentable.

Fortification from drink and porridge was just what they needed to get off to a rousing start on their journey back to Stanford. They thanked the ladies with all their hearts. Professor Whitman offered them a dollar coin as payment for their efforts, but they would not think of accepting it. He did manage to slip the coin into one girl's pocket, where he assumed she would find it after they had departed.

Their sojourn completed, they began their trip back down the peak. Fletcher immediately noticed the mood among the hikers descending, as opposed to ascending, was as different as night from day. Everyone was in high spirits and cracking jokes; even he was the butt of some humor about a new vice of which he was unaware.

Professor Whitman began it all. "So, dear Fletcher, we heard some rumbling sounds like canons booming from the upper reaches of our domain last night."

Fletcher at first had no idea what he was talking about, and in a serious voice responded, "No, I didn't hear a thing. I must say I slept soundly."

William picked up the joke. "Well, Fletcher, if you did not hear those canons booming, could it be that you might have been the source of those raucous sounds?"

Now he understood. Others, including Irene, had told him of his nighttime shortcoming. "You mean you heard me snoring?"

It was Gregory's turn. "Snoring, no. Blasting, yes."

"You mean I also farted?" This was new information for Fletcher. Under the circumstances, any or all of this might have happened. He decided to join the merriment. As they talked, they were almost running down the peak. Certainly the pace had quickened. "Are you sure it wasn't the horses?"

Stuart added sarcastically, "Yes, it was the horses. They made their way up the stairs to the loft, and there they decided to serenade us with a series of explosions that almost knocked the barn over. I thought the locals were attacking us for trespassing. It is strange you heard none of this."

By now they were all smiling and waiting for their turn to add to the fun. Giving up on Fletcher, they turned to their next victim: William Lucent and his problem with hay fever.

Before they knew it, they had passed a sign indicating "Smith's Creek," almost half way down the peak. It was just nine o'clock. Time and distance were going by at an incredible pace. At this rate, they would arrive home in the early afternoon.

Continuing their descent of Mt. Hamilton, the five men met a group of about twenty Stanford wheelers just beyond Smith's Creek, pushing their bikes before them, up the mountain. Fletcher knew them only by sight. Gasping for breath, the wheelers used the encounter for a brief rest.

"Good morning, gentlemen. Fancy meeting you here," William said to them in too cheery a manner, considering their fatigued condition.

The apparent leader of the pack said, between deep gulps for air, "We may have bit off too much. But we'll have at it. Much easier to coast down."

Gregory was incredulous. "My God, you plan to coast down this mountain on your wheels?" He looked around at the group and said, "Are you all insane?"

Fletcher thought his remark was insensitive. It upset a wheeler who asked rudely, "How else? On our bellies?" The rest, who were within hearing distance, laughed at his quick response. He continued, "Why do you think we'd bother pushing our wheels all the way up here if we didn't plan on a fun ride down?"

Professor Whitman decided it was time to introduce people. "My name is Professor Whitman, and these are my friends: Fletcher Martin, William Lucent, Gregory Peters, and Stuart Wilhelm. We're also from Stanford."

The leader was conciliatory. "Sorry, professor, that Frank was rude with your friend. We're all bushed from the climb. My name's Harold Kessler, class of '92. There are twenty-two of us, so I'm sure you won't mind if I don't introduce everyone. I do want to advise you we have only another two hundred yards or so to go and we'll be turning about and beginning our coast. It would be wise to get to the side when you hear us shouting."

More chuckling from the crowd, and someone added, "Wise, indeed."

Fletcher could not contain himself. Even though they were halfway down the hill, there were still many hairpin turns, which were dangerous for horse and cart, and even more so for freewheeling men and bicycles. "Harold, I hope you and your companions know what you are doing. There are many sharp curves on this road, such as the one you just passed and the one just ahead." He looked forward twenty yards and could see the road took a serious turn, with mountainside on the left and a steep drop on the right.

"We appreciate your concern, professor." Because of Fletcher's age, Kessler assumed he, too, was a professor. "We're all experienced wheelmen and have coasted on similar terrain in the Black Mountains, on the way to La Honda. We'll be cheering all the way down, so if there is any traffic, they should hear us coming."

He clearly wanted to hear no more of Fletcher's misgivings, and turned to his companions and shouted, as if her were leading a cavalry charge, "Come on, wheelmen, let's get going!" With that, he motioned with his hand for his colleagues to continue their push up the hill.

When the wheelmen were out of sight, Professor Whitman stopped in his tracks. The other men followed suit, and he said, "We're lucky to have met them going up the road, rather than down." Everyone nodded in agreement. Fletcher thought about the impetuousness of youth, Lord protect them.

Dr. Whitman continued, "In any case, I do not want to predict doom for their endeavor, but I don't want any of us to be part of it, if they self-destruct."

William put a protective hand on Whitman's shoulder and said, "Now, dear Henry, don't get all lathered. They're big boys, and I'm certain they can take care of themselves."

Fletcher wished that were true, but doubted it. From what he had seen at Encina, young men had an uncanny belief in their invincibility and immortality. One day of fighting the Sioux would have taught them otherwise.

"So it is very obvious what we will do when hear them coming," said Henry.

"Get the hell off the road. That's what. And wait until every last one of them has passed," was William's reply, at which everyone concurred.

"All right, William, let's continue, but with great caution," said Professor Whitman, still looking worried.

"With great caution it is," William said, almost jauntily, trying to humor his loved one into better spirits.

The five men continued their descent, but Fletcher noticed they were no longer as carefree as they were before their encounter with the wheelmen. All of them, including him, were constantly diverting their glances to look over their shoulders at what might be coming from behind.

Finally, after just rounding another hairpin turn, with an equally deep embankment yawning beside it, they heard distant voices shouting, "Stanford, yeah! Stanford, yeah!"

Professor Whitman cried out, "They're coming!"

Fletcher had never seen five men, himself included, move so fast in his life. They scrambled to the safety of the hillside by the road—luckily a straightaway—fifteen yards from another hairpin turn. From their protected position, Professor Whitman whispered, "If they go out of control, we should be safe."

The shouting Stanford wheelmen were getting closer. Fletcher reasoned it was not the first ones in the pack who concerned him. Those daredevils would make it through unscathed. It was the ones at the end of the line who might go sailing off the road due to fatigue or timidity. He was not a religious man, but he found himself praying for everyone's safety.

By now the first onslaught had made the turn and was on the straightaway. The leader of the group, Kessler, was among them. As he whizzed by the older men hiding in the brush, he touched his cap and shouted, "Yeah, Stanford!" More wheelmen followed, cheering, "Stanford, Stanford, yeah, Stanford!" But Fletcher noticed their exuberance was diminished, compared with the frontrunners. Their shouting was more from rote than brashness. By now, he reckoned, half of the riders had passed. They were still coming, but singly, no longer in packs.

A lone rider narrowly missed going off the road, and Fletcher saw fear in his eyes as his wheels slipped toward the edge. But he regained control, righted himself, and assumed the jaunty look of one who had won a victory over adversity.

Now there were longer intervals between bikes, and Fletcher could barely hear another wheelmen approaching, shouting out his Stanford cheer. This should be the last, he thought.

With wonderment, Fletcher saw Gregory and Stuart getting up from their safe positions. They must think all the wheelmen have gone by, he thought. Fletcher and Professor Whitman simultaneously shouted at them, "Get back, get back! There's one more."

The two men froze, as if in a tableau. Finally, the meaning of the shouted words dawned on them, and they ran back to the side. But it was too late. The late arriving wheelman was in view and had taken his eyes off the road for a second while making his turn to see what the two men were doing. His curiosity was catastrophic because he was a few seconds too late applying his brakes. His wheels slid out from under him, he went out of control, and in an instant he and his bicycle disappeared over the mountain's edge, down the embankment.

All five men ran to where the wheelman had disappeared; Fletcher was first. His heart was pounding. He knew he was assuming the physical state of being in battle, as if he were still fighting Indians.

"Are you all right?" he shouted down the hillside to nothing but bushes and undergrowth. To his right, he saw a fractured bicycle dangling on some low lying branches, its wheels still spinning, but no rider. "Where are you? Where are you?" he shouted.

His companions shouted with him, making quite a clamor. But when their crying ceased, the only response was bleak silence, broken by distant birds chirping and the wind whistling.

"I have to go down there and get him," said Fletcher.

Professor Whitman looked at him in disbelief. "No, Fletcher, I won't let you. We'll get help, and then rescue him."

Fletcher was already moving toward the edge. "If we wait, he may die. I won't let that happen."

Whitman could see from the look in Fletcher's eyes there was no way to dissuade him. "What should we do?" he asked. Whitman knew Fletcher was battle seasoned, accustomed to making life and death decisions. Looking over at Gregory and Stuart, he saw they were anxious to help but guilt ridden. Why, Fletcher wondered, had they been so careless?

"Go back up the hill and get some help from the people at Lick. We'll need a cart to get that poor boy to a hospital. Also, we need ropes to haul him up, and hopefully a stretcher. It was as though Fletcher were giving orders to subordinates.

Dr. Whitman said, "I'll go." And without another word, he began to run, retracing their tracks back up the hill toward the observatory.

The other three companions stood there, wanting to help. William forlornly asked, "What can we do?"

"I don't know yet. If he's fairly close, we'll make a human chain to get him the rest of the way up. I'll let you know. Just listen to what I say when I find him."

With that, Fletcher dropped to the ground, maneuvered himself over the edge, and started to work his way slowly down the mountainside, from bush to bush and tree to tree.

It was precarious going. He felt his boots slipping on the rocky ground and steep incline. Easily he could lose his balance and tumble downward. It was pure good fortune a scraggly tree or prickly bush allowed him some foothold or something onto which to grab. Even though the weather was cool, he began to sweat profusely, causing his eyes to smart from the salt, temporarily blinding him. At this rate, he wasn't too sure how long he could continue. His clothes were tattered and torn, and his hands were bleeding from grabbing sharp brambles and thorns. Lord knows what the rest of his body looked like under the heavy clothing he was wearing.

He shouted, "Where are you? I'm coming. It'll be all right. Where are you? Stanford wheelman, where are you?"

Perhaps it was saying "wheelman" or "Stanford," but something caused a weak voice to call out, "I'm here, over here. I'm here, to your right."

Fletcher looked to his right, and there was the forlorn figure of a young man in a crumbled, horizontal position, saved from further tumbling by the protective stump of a withered tree.

Fletcher got to the young man by a circuitous route, using whatever he could to hold onto as he went. He fell to his knees, beside the young man.

The poor fellow's face was blackened with dirt and streaked with blood. He looked up at Fletcher and smiled feebly. "Thanks for coming. Wasn't sure I'd ever get out of this. Never prayed before, but I did now. I heard you hollering for me. Thanks."

Fletcher took his hand in his and held it tenderly. "You're all right now. I'm Fletcher Martin."

"Michael Newberg. I can't get up on my own. It's the right foot, hurts bad, probably broken. Where are my wheels?"

"Back up the hill. We've got to see to you. What do you think? Can you stand? Here, let me get a footing and see if we can get you to your feet."

Fletcher stood up and tried to gain a footing on the incline where he would be able to give Michael some support. Once he steadied himself, he reached down and put his arm under Michael's arm, and together they got him back on his feet.

When Michael was standing, he winced as he attempted to put weight on his right foot. "I'm not sure. I thought it was broken, but maybe it's just sprained. I broke my arm two years ago, and the pain was excruciating. This hurts, but not like that."

Fletcher said, "Thank goodness. Put your arm around me, and we'll see how far we can get."

The two men slowly and painstakingly ascended the mountainside. Several times Michael fell to the ground, and Fletcher had to pull him back to his feet. Fletcher felt more sweat dripping from his brow. Minutes had gone by, and they had gone only twenty yards from where he had found Michael. He looked up the cliff. They had at least another forty yards to go, an impossible task. Fletcher didn't think he had the stamina to get them both back to the road. He would need help. Between breaths he said, "Just a second, Michael. Let me call to my friends. Maybe they can help us."

He called out in as loud a voice as he could muster, "William, Gregory, Stuart, I've got him! I've got Michael. We need help. We need help!"

This became their routine: for five or ten feet they would struggle up the hill, then for a few minutes they would rest, and Fletcher would call out to his friends. After doing this several times, Fletcher heard William replying in the distance, "Fletcher, Fletcher, we can hear you. You're off track. Move to your left and you'll see us."

Fletcher, in his desperation, had gone in the wrong direction. At this rate, it would take another four or five attempts to get within sight of his friends. Looking straight above him, he saw William's face leaning over the side of a slight outcropping. Fletcher had no idea how he had ever gotten down that slope, but he was there.

"We see you, Fletcher. Henry's up top with a stretcher and cart. We've got more help from the observatory. You two will be all right now." William's reassuring words were music to poor Fletcher's ears.

Fletcher saw two men he did not know, bound with ropes to one another, making their way toward them. How long had it been? One, two hours? Time had no meaning. Fletcher was finished; he had no stamina left. He could not move. He had a death grip on Michael's waist so he would not fall again. There was no way in the world he could lift him back up now because Michael was unconscious. Fletcher whispered to the man in his arms, "Michael, I can go no further. They're coming down to get us. We'll be all right."

Their rescuers were only ten feet away. And then they were there, prying Fletcher's protective arms, hands, and fingers from around Michael. The two men held Michael between them and started back up the hill.

Professor Whitman was there as well. He said, "It's all right, Fletcher we'll get back up the hill together."

Henry put out his hand toward Fletcher, who attempted to grab it. But Fletcher put too much strain on the branch of a small tree, and it broke loose. Henry could only watch as his friend slid away from him and disappeared back down the mountain slope.

His body seemed to be airborne. Fletcher shut his eyes, put his hands up to his face, and assumed a fetal position as he bounced like a punctured ball down the rocky hillside. An excruciating pain ran through his left arm. He opened his eyes and saw through protective fingers a nearby bird in flight. It was an eagle. Would this be his last earthly vision? Strange thoughts came over him, as if he might join the eagle. His eyes closed. Darkness closed in around him, like a protective shroud, and there were no more sights, sounds, or feelings.

CHAPTER 45

▼

"STANFORD'S FIRST HERO"

Monday, November 30, 1891

Students returning on Sunday from their Thanksgiving visits noticed differences in the air. Occasional showers and crispness at nightfall had been the custom during the fall. Now, the sunset came earlier, and a sudden strength leaped into the winds. On Sunday night, heavy rain fell for extensive periods. With daylight, a different panorama had been created, with deep puddles and slimy adobe mud that stuck to young ladies' shoes and hems, and to young men's boots and cuffs, like glue. At a time when the need for washing with clean water was greatest, the tap water from Searsville Lake ran murky and rank.

Monday was always a busy time for Leslie Elliott. It did not help matters on that particular very early Monday morning that Ellen had discovered their new cellar was flooded from the rain. For two hours the two of them bailed water. Leslie cursed the Business Office and Ariel Lathrop for the shoddy material and workmanship. It was just like them to cut corners to save a few dollars.

So when he arrived at the office, Leslie was already worn out. Then there was the mail for him to pick up from Menlo, and to be sorted by Frank. Because of the long weekend, four bags were waiting. Frank groaned when Leslie asked him to help him bring the bags in from the cart he had parked at the west end of the Quad, near the chapel. Their boots were soaked from walking through puddles.

Most of the correspondence was new applications and inquiries for the fall '92 term, sent from high school graduates located mostly in the Western and Midwestern states; some dealt with entering the second semester, beginning in February of '92.

One fellow by the name of Beverly Johnson, from Sacramento, had been persistent and sent a third letter for his son, Ernest. Mr. Johnson still maintained Mrs. Stanford would sponsor and recommend his son for admittance.

When he had received the second letter, Leslie had questioned Dr. Jordan about a reply to Mr. Johnson. Dr. Jordan had told him he surmised Mr. Johnson was a Negro, and they should ignore the matter. When Leslie questioned him about Mrs. Stanford's involvement, Dr. Jordan shushed him-such a thing was preposterous. Mrs. Stanford seldom involved herself, and certainly not for a Negro. Dr. Jordan reiterated what Leslie already knew: no Negro would be accepted at LSJU. The matter was closed. Leslie thought Mr. Johnson would have to find another college for his son to attend, though none came to mind. Now, with this third letter, Leslie wondered whether he should bring it up again, but decided the matter was hopeless. He put it at the bottom of his pile of things to do.

The long holiday weekend itself had issues with which Leslie needed to deal. The minute he walked into his office next to Dr. Jordan's, he heard his name called out.

"Leslie, Leslie, come here, please."

Leslie could tell by Dr. Jordan's tone of voice that this morning would be more intense than usual. Lucky man, Dr. Jordan did not mention any flooding in his Escondite Cottage home, which had been built by a Frenchman, not by the Lathrops.

"I think there is a war going on, and it's between our students and the gods of misfortune," Dr. Jordan moaned. He was sitting at his desk, with his head in his hands, staring down at piece of paper upon which he had hastily drawn a list. "Here, look at this." He raised his head and held the list out to Leslie to read.

In dark, bold script, Dr. Jordan's flamboyant but readable handwriting read as follows:

Thanksgiving Casualties

1. *Fletcher Martin, multiple abrasions, broken left arm—at Villa*

2. *Michael Newburg, wheelman, broken right leg—at San Jose Hospital*

3. *Chauncey Phillips, wheelman, broken left leg—at San Jose Hospital*

4. *Frank Cushman, wheelman, badly sprained ankle, at Santa Cruz Hospital*

5. *Archie Rice, poison oak, Encina*

6. *Miss Francis Shranck, poison oak, Roble*

7. *Miss Edwina Keiser, poison oak, Roble*

8. *Joe Cook, poison oak, Encina*

9. *Herbert Davenport, poison oak, Encina*

Leslie looked up at Dr. Jordan with a surprised look on his face. "The wheelmen's broken bones were to be expected, knowing what that mad lot gets up to, and poison oak is part of our landscape—Bolton, my brother-in-law, can attest to that. But broken bones, particularly when Mr. Martin is involved, surprises me. He seems quite a reserved person to get himself in such a predicament. Was he wheeling with the rest?"

Jordan got up from his seat and strode around the office. Leslie was still surprised at how imposing a figure he made, in spite of his girth, with his height and thick, broad shoulders. "Whitman, his roomie, came by the cottage last night and told me what had happened. Apparently we have a hero in our midst. Poor Fletcher was accompanying Dr. Whitman and his friends"—and here he made a leering face, which Leslie thought was uncalled for—"in a jaunt up to the observatory. On the way down, they got in the way of our thrill-seeking wheelmen, who decided it would be fun to coast down the mountain."

"*Coast*? You must be pulling my chain. One can hardly coast on those contraptions, so inaptly named 'safety bicycles.'"

"Yes, coasting on the safety bicycles that are proliferating around our campus like minnows. They are everywhere, and I guess you and I will soon be riding one to get back and forth from our domiciles. Anyway, I was distracted. One of the wheelmen, Michael Newburg, misjudged a turn and went over the edge. Luckily, Whitman and his group were in the area, and Fletcher voluntarily went to his rescue."

A bell sounded in Leslie's head. "Fletcher is also Irene's good friend."

"The very one, Leslie. I think we will find it is more than a mere friendship. I like the fellow, as you know. I wanted him to assist Captain Harkins, but the good captain found Fletcher's army discharge was too much to swallow. Whitman has already mentioned him as his replacement. With acts like this it is apparent he is of the very caliber we would like to have on our faculty. A real man, I would say."

"Unlike Dr. Whitman." Leslie would never agree with the reason Whitman had been asked to leave.

"Unlike Dr. Whitman." Dr. Jordan knew how Leslie felt, so there was no reason to discuss the matter further. "Newburg paid for his act with a broken leg, and another of his compatriots went out of control further down the hill and also suffered a break. Mr. Martin, a bystander, involved himself by going to Newburg's rescue, and nearly got killed in the process. From all accounts, I would say we have a full-fledged hero, which would be Stanford's first."

Elliott held out the causality list and asked, "So, what would you have me do with this?" He already knew what the answer would be. They knew each other so well that conversation was for verification, not revelation.

"Check on the status of each of our poor fledglings, with their broken or itchy wings, and tell me if I should personally visit them to help in the recuperation process."

Leslie started to back out the door. "I'll give you a report this afternoon. You might start to make plans to visit Mr. Martin this afternoon. I am certain the students will also think of him as a hero, and some of them may have heard why Whitman will no longer be with us. It would be well to make your plans known as soon as possible for hiring Martin as Whitman's replacement. Knowing Irene's feeling for him, it would make them both happy."

Jordan pretended to be miffed. "Confound you, Leslie, always beating me to my own thoughts. I'll leave early this afternoon and stop by the Villa to see them both. Also, it will give me a chance to see how those two young ladies are proceeding with their plans for a new school. I want to get Edith out from underfoot. Miss Jessie is turning her into a surrogate mother for our two young ones."

Leslie was outside the doorway when he thought about the new letter from Mr. Johnson. He stuck his head back in and said, "And what about Mr. Johnson? Another letter came in the post today. We should contact him, one way or the other."

Dr. Jordan made a motion with his hand as if to say he had more important matters to deal with at the moment.

Leslie considered his gesture an act of dismissal and said, "I'll make a point of talking to you before three o'clock about how the students are doing."

Leslie rushed down the hallway toward Frank's desk. He would need his help. Leslie had guessed right about the Johnson matter. The father's letter belonged where he had put it.

CHAPTER 46

▼

"LINCHPIN FOR A NEVER-ENDING WHEEL"

That Same Day

When asked about what he remembered of his fall and eventual rescue, Fletcher had responded tersely, "Very little"—which, at the time, was the truth of it.

It had been more than forty-eight hours since the accident happened. Slowly, as he lay in bed in the Villa's extra bedchamber, he was able to dredge up bits of memories from his brain's many repositories. The morphine shots he had been given did not help matters. Cobwebs still remained, and some memories were cloudy, but somehow glimpses of treetops, branches, bushes, gray skies, brown dirt, rocks, and excruciating pain were beginning to make sense.

A recurring dream of being with his mother had come to him over the past two days, but in it his mother had a dual personality that embodied both herself and Irene. Dressed in a white frilly dress, with an elegant blue and white hat sitting primly on her reddish brown hair, she held out her arms to him. He tried to run to her, but his feet were mired in quicksand. Fighting his way free, he could feel the softness of her body as he clung to her, but the softness vanished, and instead his left arm felt a new and intense pain. He reasoned this was when his body careened into a boulder, ending his journey down the hill and also breaking his arm.

He remembered opening his eyes after the accident and seeing the sky clouding over in anticipation of rain. Amid the clouds, an eagle soared. Could that have been the same eagle he glimpsed when his catastrophe began? It swooped and hovered directly above him, as if waiting.

But he was alive. He remembered running his tongue over his parched lips and tasting sand and dirt. He smelled the pungent scent of his body and the accumulation of smells from dead leaves and earthy matter. He looked at his left arm, which was causing him so much pain. It was at an odd angle and he saw crimson blood seeping though his dirty coat sleeve where the radius bone must have partially broken through his skin. Mercifully, this sight and the continuing pain caused him to loose consciousness.

In a dream, he was walking through the doorway of his parent's home and his mother and Donna, his handicapped sister, were there to greet him.

Donna said, "Fletcher, you're safe now. Mother and I will take care of you." And they both embraced him.

Fletcher was so happy, he was crying. Donna had been born without speech. He said, "Donna, you can talk. I've waited so long to hear you speak."

Donna said, "It's all right, dear brother. It's all right." She looked beautiful and there were no signs of the malignancies that had tainted her life.

Fletcher again spoke. "Donna, it's so wonderful to hear your voice."

Donna's image blurred and another familiar voice responded; it was Henry Whitman's. "Fletcher, it's not Donna. I'm sorry. I know how much you loved her. But you're going to be all right. We have you now. And we have a doctor here who'll take care of you."

Fletcher did not want his long awaited conversation with his sister to end. With his good arm he flailed at his rescuers. "Go away. Go away," he cried, until he had no strength left.

Fletcher had found himself looking up into a new face that must have been the doctor's. The man said, "This will make you feel better."

He had felt a sharp pain in his exposed shoulder, and afterwards the soft sounds and sensations of an oblivion that made absolutely no sense at all.

He surmised that now it must be either Sunday or Monday. He was not sure which. Irene had drifted into his room several times to feed and bathe him. It made Fletcher feel ridiculous to be so helpless and dependent.

He was on his right side, looking directly at a mirror sitting on the bureau at the other end of the room. He could not move, so the mirror gave him a view of what was going on behind him, but it also gave him a frontal view of what he looked like to others. It was not a pleasant sight.

His left arm was flung up into the air in a semi-cocked position, held firm by thick coatings of plaster of paris. The break had occurred in the lower part of his arm, so the cast included most of his hand and part of his shoulder. He could see the tips of his fingers, but he felt spasms of pain when he tried to move them. Irene told him the doctor had said it would be weeks before the pain would go away, and one or two months before they could cut off the cast. Breaking a bone was a serious affair. If the radius grew back malformed, Fletcher might be partially disabled or permanently unable to use his left arm. Tears had come into her eyes when she said, "You could have been killed."

In the mirror, he could see his gaunt features enveloped by three or four days' growth of dark stubble. Irene had said she'd already sent Bert Hoover to Encina to gather Fletcher's clothing and books and his razor, brush, and strop. She told Fletcher she had never shaved a man before, but soon would have to do so.

After Irene left, he had drifted in and out of a healing sleep.

A soft knock on the door, and the sound of a man scuffing his boots while he waited, woke Fletcher. It was Irene, and someone was with her. "Fletcher," she whispered, and in the mirror, he saw the door slowly open. "You have a visitor."

It was Dr. Jordan, his soft sombrero in his hand. Because he had ridden Winter from Escondite Cottage, he was still huffing and puffing. His lower pants and boots were mud spattered, and his eyes and moustache drooped even more when he saw Fletcher's circumstances. He went to Fletcher's bedside and took his right hand in his.

Fletcher spoke through swollen lips, "Dr. Jordan, good to see you." Somehow, he managed a grim smile.

A smile of a hero, Dr. Jordan thought. As they had made their way up the stairs, Irene had told him the San Jose doctor had to use more than sixty sutures to stitch up Fletcher's wounds. Coming down that hill, his body must have been knocked about like a rag doll. Jordan could not help himself: what he saw and what he had heard from Irene brought tears to his eyes.

"Fletcher, Fletcher," he moaned, as if there was a turnip in his throat. It was one of only a few times in his life that he could not speak. He would not let Fletcher's hand go, and eventually Fletcher had to pull his hand from Dr. Jordan's grasp.

"How is Michael?" Fletcher asked. His speech was slurred, but understandable.

"Michael?" Jordan looked askance at Irene for assistance.

"Michael was the wheeler Fletcher rescued," Irene answered in an icy voice.

Now comprehending, Jordan responded, "Fine, fine. A bone was cracked in his right leg, not broken as had been reported, but he won't be doing any coasting for at least six months. But back to you, Fletcher, I wanted you to know

you're Stanford's first hero. Everyone on the campus is talking about your bravery. If we had a medal, I'd pin it on you right now."

For almost twenty-four hours, Irene had contained her feelings: on Saturday,
when she had been having tea with Lucy and her friends from Harvard Annex;
she felt something was wrong, very wrong. She could not say if this feeling had
come over her at the exact time Fletcher was tumbling down the hill, but it was
close.

When the doctors had told her Fletcher was almost killed, it had been as
though a scene in a play were being replayed. If something happened to him, it
would have been the second time she lost the man she loved. It was too much to
bear. Fletcher had told her how he attempted to save an Indian boy, and put his
own life in jeopardy. And she knew of the harm he had caused to himself by disobeying an order to kill Indian women and children at Wounded Creek. She
knew how altruistic he was when another person was in danger-it was the greatest
menace to his own well being.

Hearing Dr.Jordan extolling Fletcher's act, Irene's hands went to her face and
her whole body was racked with sobs as she cried out, "Hero? He almost killed
himself for that stupid boy. His arm's broken. There's not an inch of his body
that isn't sutured, scabbed, black and blue. Hero is not a word I want to hear."

Dr. Jordan, not knowing Fletcher's history, could not understand how his
praise warranted Irene's outburst, but gentleman that he was, he turned to Irene,
put his long arms around her, and gently embraced her. She fell into his arms,
sobbing. It was as if a gallant tree had succumbed to an axe's final blows.

"It's all right, Irene. He'll be fine," he murmured. He continued to hold her in
this fatherly embrace while she gained control of herself. Eventually, she gave him
a little nudge indicating it was time to free her, and she pulled out an embroidered kerchief from a pocket in her frock and blew her nose vigorously, twice.
She would have to take care of her man. She had to be strong for both of them.
She had the strength to do it. The tree stood tall again.

Jordan stood back, surveying the scene of Fletcher, with his left arm slung
above him, silently watching his beloved blowing her nose, and thought if there
were ever a time for good news, this would be it. He placed himself equal distance
between the two lovers and dramatically announced, "In spite of the unfortunate
circumstances, I have good news for both of you."

Both Irene and Fletcher held their breaths, wondering if what the good doctor
was about to say was what both of them had discussed and prayed might happen.

Jordan moved closer to Fletcher. He could feel the drama of anticipation in
the air and relished it. "Fletcher, I have the honor of offering you a position in

our Classical Department as an instructor in Latin and Greek language and history at the stipend of $1,750 per annum."

As Dr. Jordan spoke, Irene's face transformed from woebegone to radiant with happiness. Perhaps, she thought, misery does begat happiness.

Fletcher said, "I accept with gratitude."

Jordan again grasped his right hand, and was about to vigorously shake it, when he thought better of it. "Good, you are instantly part of the staff. I am certain Dr. Whitman will have duties for you to perform when you are able."

Fletcher had something else on his mind. He said, "Doctor, I have more to say."

Both Irene and Jordan stopped, as if their movements had been caught in a photograph. Irene's eyes were glistening with anticipation. Jordan appeared as if he had no idea what was going to happen.

"Irene, come around where I can see you," Fletcher said.

"Yes, Fletcher."

"Dearest Irene, one more time I've learned life is too precious not to take advantage of every minute, and I want to share those minutes with you, the woman I love. Would you be my bride?"

One lost love and one almost lost had cured Irene of any pretense of being a reluctant bride. "Yes, yes," she said and leaned over and gently kissed Fletcher on the lips. It appeared they would not separate, even with the presence of Dr. Jordan.

Eventually Irene stood upright, straightened herself, and she and Fletcher looked over at Dr. Jordan, as if his being there lent an air of officialdom.

"You're the witness, Dr. Jordan, we're engaged." Fletcher said, and they waited for him to say something profound.

Dr. Jordan stood there enjoying every second, realizing he was witnessing another chapter of the ongoing saga of life: first strangers, then friends, and eventually partners in marriage. He had gone through the sequence himself twice. Now he was part of someone else's. He said, "I'm so grateful to be part of such a momentous occasion. Later, when we're back to normal, Jessie and I will have you over to share some of the senator's fine champagne, which he gave me, and which we've been saving for such an occasion."

In spite of her emotional outpouring, Irene was glowing. Dr. Jordan could not believe the transformation his words had wrought. "We shall never forget your kindness in coming here and bringing us this wonderful news," was what she said.

"You two have created your own good news for all of us," was Jordan's response.

Dr. Jordan had a second sense of when it was best to exit, and this was the time. Whatever might be said or done next would only be a let down. After one last touch of Fletcher's hand and a gentle hug for Irene, he made his way through the doorway, saying, "I can see myself out."

Fletcher and Irene said their farewells and nodded their heads almost in unison, acknowledging Jordan's departure. She was holding Fletcher's hand. They were lost in each other's gazes, wordlessly relishing their happiness.

In his rush to depart, Jordan almost tripped on one of the steps in the stairwell. He thought it would have been a fine kettle of fish if he'd joined Fletcher with a broken leg or something. And he realized he had forgotten to ask Irene about her plans for their school. He had wanted to tell her about his idea for a new name for the school, Castilleja. Oh, well, he reasoned, he would do it next time. Jessie would be pleased with the news. It would be Stanford's first marriage. They would have to make a do of it.

Outside the Villa, he mounted his horse, and while riding back to the Administrative Office, continued his contemplation about how it was impossible not to intertwine one's life with those around. Yes, there would be a marriage, and children, and perhaps a child would eventually attend Stanford. It was like a never-ending wheel, and he served as the linchpin holding it all together. What a wonderful life!

CHAPTER 47

▼

"It Was My Error"

Friday, December 4, 1891

Dr. Jordan again asked Dr. Elliott to join him in his office. Neither man sat. What Dr. Jordan had to say could be said standing. He held a letter in his hand. From the pink color and small size stationary, Leslie suspected it was from Mrs. Stanford.

Dr. Jordan kept the letter in his hand and said, "Mrs. Stanford wrote to me from Washington. It's about Ernest Johnson's application. She wonders why I have not contacted him about admission. And in so many words, advises me to do so."

Leslie's face filled with deep concern. This was totally unexpected.

Dr. Jordan's tone of voice became artificially anxious as he said, "Leslie, Leslie, I asked you weeks ago to reply to this young man. You must have forgotten. Would you please get a letter of acceptance, with an apology for our tardiness, off to him immediately, accepting him for next semester, and a letter of explanation to Mrs. Stanford telling her about your forgetfulness."

Fully understanding his superior's intent, Leslie said, "Yes, Dr. Jordan." And he added to the fabrication, "That one must have slipped by me. I'll explain to all concerned that it was my error, not yours. I am sorry if it caused you any embarrassment."

"None at all, Leslie. I understand no one is perfect-not you, not I." Almost as an afterthought, he added, "And when Mr. Johnson arrives, probably with his father, please make sure he is warmly welcomed."

When Leslie walked out of the office, he became aware of the enormity of his new assignment. From now on, it would be his responsibility to make certain Mrs. Stanford heard only good reports from the Johnsons.

CHAPTER 48

▼

"A PAIN IN HIS HEART"

Friday, December 18, 1891

It was the last day of French class, before the Christmas Holidays began. Sosh was thinking that he would not see Sally until the next year. Even though they did not speak and Sally, because of Sam, had moved her seat, she still gave Sosh regular, reassuring glances of her continuing love. A pain in his heart told him that he would miss her. As she approached, he began to smell her fragrances. He breathed in deeply. Then he felt the reassuring grip of her hand on his shoulder. He looked up, and she was smiling at him. He looked back at where Sam usually sat, and his seat was vacant. He was late for class. He watched as she continued to her seat. There were no words between them, but he knew their bond was still strong, if anything stronger. Why the pain in his heart? Was it the thought of not seeing her for a few weeks or was he falling in love?

CHAPTER 49

▼

"HOLIDAY IN NAME ONLY"

Monday, December 21, 1891

By now most of the faculty and students had left the campus for their homes. Because the vacation would be two weeks long, almost all the students, except for those living in the Midwest and East, had departed.

Because final tests would be held during the last week of January, and a multitude of term papers would be due then, the holiday was in name only. Much work remained to be done, and there was really no let up for the students, on-campus or off, who had to spend long hours studying, researching, and writing.

Members of the Alpha Phi fraternity were surprised that their president, Winko Winters, had invited Sam Cutter to his parent's opulent home in San Francisco. It was not a secret that bad blood was brewing between them. Of the two, Winko was the one who attempted to work out compromises with those students who were not members of fraternities or sororities, known as barbarians. The leader of this group was Sosh Weinberg, and he and Winko were most respectful of one another. Sam, on the other hand, did not pretend any understanding. As far as he was concerned, the barbarians were just that. There was no reason their voices should be heard.

Winko confided to close friends that he hoped, during the holidays, to win Sam over to his side. This was important because Winko would graduate in two years, and it looked as if Sam were positioning himself to be the next president of

Alpha Phi. Members heard Sam and Winko discussing how they planned to spend the holiday season doing decadent activities, mostly drinking.

Delores, Sally, Betsy, Bump, and Milt had returned to Southern California aboard the good ship *Santa Rosa*. Sally, Betsy, and Delores were to get together later in the week in Los Angeles. His mother, who would accompany him by train to San Diego, picked up Woody at Encina.

Sosh was not looking forward to his holiday. His mother had asked that he visit distant cousins living in San Francisco. They were orthodox Jews, and Sosh had grown used to Christmas traditions. He wished Sally were with him. He remembered that last day in class, and her touching his shoulder. He knew he would count each day until he saw her again.

With Irene's assistance, Fletcher continued to recuperate at the Villa. Weather permitting; he was now walking to the Quad. Plans were afoot for him to return to Encina Hall in the New Year.

CHAPTER 50

▼

"RUMORS ARE NOT ENOUGH"

Thursday, December 24, 1891

On Christmas Eve day, Fletcher Martin visited Leslie. He came in the afternoon, when activity in the Administrative Office was minimal due to the advent of the holiday.

Leslie was pleased to see Fletcher and surprised how well he looked. His arm was still in a sling, but his complexion was healthy looking, and most of the bruises on his face had healed.

Leslie's office was half the size of Dr. Jordan's. His office furniture was limited to the essentials, a desk and two chairs—but a multitude of bookshelves lined the walls, already filled with binders containing information about prospective students, test scores, and preparatory schools.

When Fletcher sat down, it was apparent he was still in pain. He took some time before he spoke. He had carefully thought about what he was about to say. "I wanted to tell you about the Thanksgiving dinner at Fred's. Fred told me something about Timothy Hopkins I thought you should know. He said that Hopkins and his Chinese friend, Quong Wo, control the gambling, sale of opium, and prostitution going on in Mayfield."

Leslie was surprised. He had never liked Hopkins, but never thought a friend of the Stanfords would do something illegal. "Does Fred have any proof?" He asked.

Fletcher said, "I had the same question. No, he doesn't. It appears to be only rumors, but Hopkins has been seen visiting Quong Wo, on the sly. I think I told you that he and his horse nearly ran me over on one of those visits. I don't think Fred would tell me such a thing, if he didn't think it was true."

Leslie looked thoughtful. "Rumors are not enough." Is what he said.

"I know, but I still wanted you to know. I have no idea what we can do about it. Hopkins is such a favorite of the Stanfords." Fletcher took a deep breath of resignation.

Leslie knew Fletcher expected him to do something. All he could say was, "For the time being, we'll have to wait and see. Hopkins may overstep and show his hand, and then I can tell Dr. Jordan, but not for now.

CHAPTER 51

▼

"1892" CHASING "1891"

Monday, December 28, 1891

During the holidays, of the total campus population numbering more than five hundred and fifty, about twenty-five women had remained at Roble Hall, and almost seventy-five men were at Encina Hall.

Shortly after the main body of students had left for the holidays, three Encina stalwarts had personally delivered a large envelope to Mrs. Richardson, mistress at Roble Hall. In their presence, she opened the envelope and withdrew a hand-engraved invitation, complete with illustrated lettering and a scene of a baby in diapers representing "1892" chasing a withered old man, "1891." She had read the following message, aloud,

Dear Mrs. Richardson and the Young Ladies of Roble Hall,

Join us as we turn out '91 and welcome '92.

Your attendance is respectfully requested at an Entertainment to be held at Encina Hall on Thursday evening, December 31, 1891, at 7 o'clock to be followed by Refreshments in the Dining Room. Please convey your hoped for acceptance to the undersigned.

Mr. Hubert Fesler for the LSJU Men at Encina Hall

Mrs. Richardson had graciously told the messengers a response would be forthcoming.

She was a woman of her word, and two days later a positive response had been delivered: *The Roble ladies would be happy to accept.*

Now, after the initial roars of approval, the consequences set in. It would be Encina Hall's first social event. Much must be done during the intervening few days: a play had to be cast and staged, and lines learned; words to songs practiced; and bright, witty speeches and limericks written and rehearsed. It was vitally important that everything be in readiness for their first feminine guests.

CHAPTER 52

▼

"LANGUISHING IN AN AUSTRALIAN HOSPITAL"

Tuesday, December 29, 1891

Irene received the following note from Bruce Hornsby's sister. Hornsby had been Irene's fiancé, the fellow lost at sea.

December 5, 1891

Dear Irene,

Wonderful news! We just received a letter from the American consulate in Honolulu informing us that poor Bruce is alive! A passing schooner rescued him. He suffered from amnesia and has been languishing in an Australian hospital all these months. He recovered his memory a month ago and will be returning to the United States shortly. We know you are as happy about this as we are, and I promise to keep you informed of Bruce's arrival home.

Your loving sister-in-law to be, Penelope

The note dropped from Irene's hand. Unlike her friend, Lucy Fletcher, she was not one to swoon, but if there were a time when swooning was appropriate, this would be it.

CHAPTER 53

▼

"STANFORD IS READY TO PLAY FOOTBALL."

Thursday, December 31, 1891

It was New Years' Eve, and a young man was running up Encina's stairs, shouting, "They're coming. They're coming. It's raining cats and dogs outside, and they're still coming to our party. I looked out the window and I could see them coming and they're carrying green boughs and umbrellas."

Shortly afterwards, Encina's entrance doors swung open, and in swished Mrs. Richardson, followed by twenty-five wet and bedraggled young ladies. Raincoats and hats were removed and hastily given to attentive young men, who tagged them and whisked them to upstairs rooms, where they would be kept under lock and key. Brown and black dresses, adorned with sashes and ribbons of bright red, orange, and various shades of blue, were unveiled, immediately enlivening the lobby with the colors of the rainbow. The boughs they brought with them were taken to the dining room and added to the greenery already in place. Everyone felt excitement in the air.

Each lady was seated and given a program of the events that were about to unfold. Before them was the broad landing on whose "pesky step" some of them had previously tripped. The landing had been turned into a temporary stage upon which, the program informed them, O. D. Howell's amusing little farce would soon be performed.

Before the stage was a drawn, makeshift fire curtain, made up of sew together, grayish bed sheets, upon which was emblazoned in cardinal fabric the words "Encina Opera."

After everyone was seated, the lobby's electric lights were turned off, and for a few seconds all of its occupants were enveloped in complete darkness. This lapse caused the young ladies and Mrs. Richardson to wonder what they had got themselves into. When the darkness continued beyond a reasonable time, one young lady had to stifle a gasp of alarm. From the activity behind the curtain, the problem was apparent: they could not draw the curtain. To everyone's relief, the fire curtain finally arose, revealing the bright interior of a sleeping car, with accommodations for two, one above the other.

The players made their entrance from the right staircase. The first was a black-faced porter, burdened with far too many traveling bags and Gladstones, which he constantly banged about and dropped, accompanied by a continuous babble of mumbled excuses. Following him were two young ladies—or better said, seemingly young ladies, because two gladiators of the budding football team, Carl Clemans and Wesley Anderson, played the roles. Their arrival in full feminine dress and make up—including bustles; petticoats; powdered skin; rouged cheeks; eyes that were heavily lashed and darkened; arched eyebrows; and red, red, cupid lips—brought the house down. For several minutes, all action stopped while members of the audience chortled their amusement and disbelief at what they were seeing.

After the audience returned to some semblance of normalcy, the two "women" dismissed the porter with a tip that, from his look of undisguised displeasure, was not even close to his expectations. He exited stage right, mumbling more incomprehensible words of annoyance.

The "ladies" were left to discuss small matters of daily life, such as the idiosyncrasies of some of their relatives—the manner in which an uncle snored, the way a cousin ate, and how an aunt married numerous times, usually younger men.

Some of their remarks were quite caustic and funny, but it really made no difference because if a comment failed to cause amusement, one of the "ladies" managed to find something to do, such as pulling up her stockings or pulling down her bustle or putting on slightly smeared lipstick—all automatically causing side-splitting laughter.

Suddenly, two more actors made an abrupt and unexpected appearance, almost falling down the stairs. It was one lady's husband and brother. The husband went to the other lady—played by Clemans—and swiped the wig off the top of his head. Horrors! The young lady was in truth a man. The inhabitants of

Roble were watching the enfolding of what could have become a sordid tale. Thank goodness, the villain, Clemans, had been exposed as the basest of woman-izers-one who pretended to be another woman.

Happily, all turned out well. Anderson, the other "lady," realizing the wrong-ness of her ways, miraculously discovered how her husband was truly wonderful, and that "she" in fact loved him dearly. Her brother had the villain in a headlock, proving once again that those who do wrongly get their just deserts; in this case, incarceration for stealing affection. The two newly recreated lovebirds hugged, and with much relish, faked an extremely, passionate kiss. Brother and porter, who for some mysterious reason reappeared, looked on approvingly. Clemons, his head enfolded by the brother's arms, watched with abject failure written all over his face. The curtain went down to thunderous applause.

Due to the continuous ovation, the play's company were given three curtain calls. From appearances, the players, too, were thoroughly enjoying their own performances. Each time the curtain went up, they were caught entertaining themselves in a new tableau. The final tableau revealed Clemons now holding the brother in a headlock; the porter, brother, and "lady," still in full dress, were poised to pounce on the two of them. After the curtain fell for a final time, more thumping and bumping could be heard behind it, culminating with a final crash-ing sound, apparently caused by the sleeping car set being crushed and destroyed as the cast larked about. From the sounds of it, many of Encina's young men had to suppress an intense desire to rush behind the curtain and join the melee.

Once some degree of normalcy returned, a rather circumspect Professor Dou-glas Campbell made his entrance stage left, and took up a position before the cur-tain, with his mandolin in hand. A short, chubby man, he announced, "I will sing two melodies by Stephen Foster: 'Silver Threads among the Gold' and 'I'll Take You Home Again, Kathleen.'"

During this brief intermission, whispered words were passed from one Encina fellow to the other: "Right after the songs, get in line to go on stage."

Professor Campbell was deeply engrossed in his rendition of Foster's songs. The professor was a tenor; what he lacked in vocal prowess, which was a little off-key, he made up for in earnest, dramatic phrasing. A few of the Roble ladies found themselves brushing aside a tear or two as the professor melodically recalled his fondness for his aging mother. The next song was equally somber. Listeners got the impression that although the professor wanted to take Kathleen home, she was neither interested nor available. The song ended on a sustained note, almost on key, that caused the professor's face to turn rosy red—so red, the audience was concerned for his health.

They graciously gave Professor Campbell a rousing cheer and more applause. Professor Campbell accepted their ovation with a wave of his pudgy hand.

In the meantime, Carl Clemans, having doffed his female attire, returned to center stage and announced, "Gentle ladies, as you see from your program, our little entertainment has ended. We hope you have enjoyed it." Appreciative sounds and gentle clapping of slender hands could be heard. "You will note on your program that our banquet is about to begin, but to make the task of determining which of our gentlemen would escort our guests to the dining room, we have concocted a little test, which will both assess your knowledge of the science of podiatry and reward you with three entertaining companions."

On cue, Encina men rose from their seats, and with a noisy scuffling of soles, started to move toward the improvised stage. In single file, they walked behind the fire curtain, until there was no more space. The remaining men were held back for the second viewing. The fire curtain began its slow ascent, stopping when the men's shoes and legs were revealed up to their knees. Either because of shyness or because of lack of information, two of the feet were facing the wrong direction. With whispered prompting, this slight mishap was corrected. Eventually, all the shoes pointed correctly toward the audience.

Most of the shoes were black and well polished. Some were heavy-duty plough and "hard knock" shoes. A few were the fashionable oxfords with the new, narrow tips. All were clean, with trouser cuffs that came reasonably close to their owners' shoe tops.

Clemans chose, at random, a young lady. She passed in front of the line of male extremities and made her selection of three pairs. The owners made their way around the curtain and appeared as full-sized young men. After a few words of introduction, they stood quietly by their selector's side as another lady strolled by the stage filled with feet. The process moved along fairly quickly, and soon the entire first group had been chosen. Those waiting at the side of the stage moved in as their replacements.

The curtain remained in its semi-open position, and the audience giggled as they watched dismembered appendages troop on, appear in disarray, and turn to face the onlookers. One young fellow's extremities did not fail to catch everyone's eyes because of his scuffed and muddied work shoes, red socks, and near bicep-hugging cuffs. One of the less mannered Encina fellows laughed out loud. For a second, the red socks appeared ready to make a hasty retreat, then righted themselves and faced the audience squarely, and resolutely.

Edith Wilcox was the first young lady chosen to select her dinner companions from the second group. She was a senior who had transferred from the University of the Pacific, and the only single lady in the Class of '92. Without hesitation, she chose the red socks as her first selection and two pairs of worn but clean plough shoes as her second and third. When the three fellows appeared in front of the curtain, Bert Hoover was the one wearing the red socks. He looked chagrined.

After all the Roble ladies had been fully equipped with escorts, four fellows were left over. Miss Wilcox asked her escorts if they would mind if she added one more to their ranks. No one demurred, and three additional ladies ended up with the pleasure of four escorts instead of three.

That done, the doors to the dining room were flung open. Mr. Clemans, in good cheer, shouted out, "Everyone's invited to partake of our offerings on this grand New Year's Eve of 1892!"

Taking care not to rush in, as they usually did, Encina men purposely stood back and graciously allowed the young ladies to enter the hall before them. Looking on, Burt Fesler, Encina's master, who was acting as chaperon, almost rubbed his eyes in disbelief. The ruffians were taking on the semblance of gentlemen. It was hard to believe.

Once everyone was seated at the five long dining tables, Japanese waiters began serving trays of ices, fruits, cakes, nuts, and lemonade. Conversation, at first subdued, soon became so loud it was difficult to hear a nearby person unless he or she spoke up.

Seated across from her escorts at the end of one of the tables, Miss Wilcox engaged in questioning the young men, mostly about from where they came. Bert Hoover found himself talking at length about the wonders of being raised in Salem, Oregon. By carefully asking another of her escorts a few questions, Miss Wilcox was able to end Hoover's lengthy dissertation and allow the others to speak.

At about half past eight, the eating of delicacies had slowed down—enough so that Mr. Fesler decided it was time to begin the final part of the entertainment. He gently tapped his glass with his spoon three times to gain attention. Almost immediately, everyone stopped talking and gave him their full attention. For Fesler, it was another time for disbelief.

"Welcome, Mrs. Richardson and young ladies, again, to Encina Hall. We hope you've enjoyed your evening as much as we have. Now we have a series of short speeches about familiar subjects, from both residents of your hall and ours." He introduced Miss Shirley Baker, who gave some insightful remarks about "The University versus Social Life." Immediately following her, Charles Field gave the audience some humorous insights into "Life in Encina"; Miss Hatte Estes did the same for "Life at Roble"; and Mrs. Ellen Elliott, who was also one of the chaperons, told them revealing tales about the "The Decalogue"; finally, Will Greer gave them his impressions of arriving at the Palo Alto Farm during those first days before the opening ceremonies.

Their remarks made both Encina and Roble residents think back to all that had happened to them during these past few months. When the flatcar prank, the painting of the '95 Oak and water tank, the first Roble reception, the faculty/senior baseball game, the opening ceremonies, the appearances of Senator and Jane Stanford, the Searsville water, and the trudging through rain and adobe mud were mentioned; class members-regardless of gender-couldn't help but be impressed by the frequency of their shared experiences.

Breaking in on these thoughts, Burt Fesler spoke to the gathering. "Now I would like to introduce the president of your student body, Jack Whittemore."

Whittemore, tall and handsome, had been sitting with some of the football players toward the back of the dining room. He stood up and told them, "I want to let you know that just before we broke up for Christmas vacation, your student council selected cardinal as our school color."

Cardinal was the favorite, so everyone shouted their approval of the selection.

"And we have an official school yell now, and I want you to join me as we do our yell for the first time in public. Here is how it goes: 'Rah, rah, rah, pause, rah, rah, rah, pause, rah, rah, Stanford! Stanford! Stanford!' All right, now everyone up on your feet and let's raise the roof so that even our friends across the Bay can hear us."

There was the rumble of chairs legs against wooden floors as they all got to their feet, and Whittemore vigorously led them as they shouted out, "Rah, rah, rah, rah, rah, rah, rah, rah, Stanford, Stanford, Stanford!"

The yell was loud, but apparently not loud enough because Whittemore exhorted the group, "Hey we can do better than that. One more time, and this time let's raise the rafters."

"Rah, rah, rah, rah, rah, rah, rah, rah, *STANFORD! STANFORD! STAN-FORD!*"

This time chandeliers rattled, drinking glasses shattered, and some thought they heard dining room windows cracking. Dr. Jordan and his family heard the "Stanford" part of the yell at a small New Year Eve's dinner they were having at Escondite Cottage, about half a mile away.

Jack Whittemore showed his appreciation by applauding their efforts, and said, "Now I have one more surprise for you. We have a new professor in attendance that will be joining the faculty next semester. He has many years of football experience, and just tonight he agreed to act as advisory coach for our team. I have the pleasure of introducing Professor Martin Wright Sampson."

Professor Sampson arose from the table he had been sharing with Whittemore and the players, his friend Professor Miller, and some of the chaperons. He was a good-looking, beardless young man, taller and more muscular looking than most of his fellow professors.

Speaking in a deep, sonorous voice that projected self-confidence, he said, "I want to tell you how excited I am to be here at Leland Stanford Junior University. My old friend, Dr. William Miller here, told me about all the wonderful things happening at this campus. I understand from your football co-captains, John,"—he pointed to the seated Whittemore—"and Milt Grosh, that many of you chaps are already getting into condition doing running drills and calisthenics for next year's games. Let me tell you this: we may not be the biggest team around, but we will certainly win our share of games."

Robust cheers from the group broke into his speech. Sampson stood there appreciating the enthusiasm.

He continued, "And when we don't win, we will give our opponents a good run for their money."

Cheers from all corners of the room again interrupted him. Even the Japanese waiters applauded and stood and listened with looks of awe and admiration on their faces.

Then he added one more phrase that brought the house down: "Particularly the State University at Berkeley."

When the cheers had died down, he said, "We need to line up teams to play, and I already have some ideas about games to play in January and February. Who knows, if all goes well, we may even play our State University friends in a few months. They have already challenged us."

More cheers. This time some of the young men, forgetting their newfound social skills, were so enthusiastic they started standing on their chairs. The young ladies were laughing and shouting, and one of them joined her male rooters and climbed up on her chair. From appearances, the desire to win football games would be another shared experience in '92.

Professor Sampson had more to say. "As I see it, no particular qualifications are necessary to be a good football player—just a good heart and not minding a bump or two. So if any of you gentlemen"—he looked around at the male students—"would like to join us at practice, just come out to the field. Sorry, ladies, as yet they haven't come up with a feminine version, but all of you are certainly welcome to come and watch us practice. See you in '92 and have a wonderful Happy New Year."

Professor Sampson resumed his seat and found that everyone was grabbing for his hand and shaking it. Perfect strangers were clapping him on the back. He was being treated like a hero, and the team had not yet won or even played a game. Yes, he thought, William was right. Stanford is ready to play football.

CHAPTER 54

▼

"WASHED OUT TO SEA"

That Same Night

After half past ten that evening, most of the attendees at Encina's first social event were sound asleep. They would not greet 1892 until the following morning. A few of the more energetic Encina fellows slipped out of their rooms and made their way by the light of the moon to one of Mayfield's many saloons, which would remain open all through the night.

Small faculty dinners, similar to the one Dr. Jordan had, ended around eleven o'clock. By midnight, the time at which upstart '92 vanquished old Father Time from his stay on earth, Leslie and Ellen Elliott were sound asleep, only to be awakened by the sound of firecrackers bought in Chinatown and set off in Mayfield. Leslie raised himself on one elbow and kissed his wife on her forehead, saying, "Happy New Year, dear Ellen."

Ellen returned the kiss and whispered, "Happy New Year, Leslie." Her husband rolled over and returned to a sleep of the innocent.

In those minutes before following her husband back to sleep, Ellen had two troubling thoughts. She had seen Irene that day, and Irene appeared to have the weight of the world on her shoulders. Could this be a sign of trouble brewing between her and Fletcher? Would the June wedding take place? And Leslie had relayed to her what Fletcher had told him about Timothy Hopkins? Was it possible the rumors were true, and Hopkins was behind all the gambling and opium being offered in Mayfield? And what could Leslie do about it? Ellen worried that her righteous husband would think it his duty to do something. Hopkins was the

Stanfords' prince, no one could stand up to him-not Leslie, not Dr. Jordan; no one. Her only concern was to keep her husband from involving himself.

Before drifting off to sleep, her last thought was that it had been an eventful year. What would '92 bring?

Sam Cutter stood at the edge of Pier 54 on San Francisco's Embarcadero. He had just watched Winko's head disappear under the murky waters of the Bay. It was just a matter of fate, Sam thought, that the two fraternity brothers had ended up at the edge of the pier after drinking too much at a local tavern in celebration of the New Year. Winko had accidentally slipped and fallen headfirst into the water. When his head bobbed up, he was about twenty feet away. It was obvious he could not swim; he called out for help. From the look on his face, he fully anticipated his friend would jump in and save him. Sam stood there, immobile.

The second time he came up, Winko looked as if he knew what fate had planned for him. His cry for help was feeble, and his arms flailed in a vain attempt to keep his head above water.

The third time, he was unconscious, his head lolled to one side. The peace of death had prevailed.

Sam waited several minutes and then threw himself fully clothed into the water. He was a good swimmer. There was no need for others to know that. He made a quick circuit of the area, returned to the dock, and pulled himself to safety.

"Help, help!" he cried out. "My friend has drowned!"

A policeman passing by at the end of the street heard his cries and ran to help.

Officer Kevin O'Rieley later reported there was nothing he could do for the drenched and distraught young man who had valiantly tried to save the life of his drowned friend. They were not able to recover the body.

With prevailing tides, it may have been washed out to sea.

978-0-595-43794-8
0-595-43794-X

Printed in the United States
86387LV00004B/1-18/A

9 780595 437948